The River Calls Us Home

Betty McInnes

The People's Friend
CLASSICS COLLECTION

Published in Great Britain by DC Thomson & Co. Ltd,
Dundee, Glasgow and London.
© DC Thomson & Co. Ltd., 2019
www.dcthomson.co.uk

Since 1869, fiction has been at the heart of every single issue of "The People's Friend" magazine. Now, through "The People's Friend" Classics Collection, modern readers can rediscover and enjoy the best-loved and most popular serials from the magazine's story-telling past, many of which have never before been published in book form.

"The River Calls Us Home" by Betty McInnes was first published in 1991. Written specially to commemorate the city of Dundee's 800th anniversary, it was an instant hit with readers of the "Friend" and proved so popular that, uniquely in the magazine's history, it was republished in its entirety in 2009 for the magazine's 140th birthday celebrations.

Chapter 1

CHRISTINA KENNEDY was born in April 1890, as the clamour of the bells summoned the jute workers of Dundee to another day in the mills. She was treated with scant ceremony. Bessie McCutcheon wiped the baby's nose and mouth, wrapped her in a blanket and popped her hastily into the carved wooden crib that had rocked Christina's three brothers before her. Then Bessie and Dr Alexander concentrated all their efforts on the middle-aged woman in the bed.

Presently the doctor shook his head.

"William Kennedy will be a sad man, I fear, when his ship docks and he finds himself the father of the lassie he hoped for – and a widower, forbye!"

* * * *

Four years later, the baby had grown into a pretty little girl who had captivated her brothers and gone a long way towards mending William Kennedy's grieving heart.

It was a fair spring morning, the sky hazy blue and the Tay estuary shining silver, on Christina's fourth birthday.

The little girl stood with her father at the window of the fine big house her grandfather had built close by the river. Once, the Kennedy family had owned a fleet of whalers, but the cruel Arctic ice had crushed so many of the brave ships.

Poor yields of whale oil, and a scarcity of whalebone for the corsets of fashionable ladies, had put paid to the rest.

William had pinned all his hopes on one last venture. He tugged nervously at his beard, his gaze, like Christina's, fastened eagerly westwards. He fished out a watch on the end of a gold albert and frowned at it.

She was late! What could be hindering her? Some mischance in the dock? He should have been there himself, instead of leaving the arrangements to his two older sons . . .

"Papa! She's coming!"

Christina flattened her nose against the glass. Then she became quite still, mouth open, scarcely breathing with excitement.

The ship came slowly and majestically from the yard that built her. She was graceful, yet sturdy, with tall masts, and furled creamy sails square rigged on the mizzen-mast. A drift of smoke from the tall funnel was dark against the sky.

"Oh, Papa! There's my ship!"

William laid a hand on her golden head.

Now he knew why he'd chosen to stay at home. He'd wanted to watch the pleasure on his daughter's face, as the ship named after her sailed from the Tay.

The *Christina K.*

"Aye, my wee lass," William said gruffly. "It's your very own ship."

Christina had been still for at least three minutes, which was a record for her. Now she whirled on her toes, eyes dancing.

"Ernest, Ernest! Come and see the *Christina K*. You're missing it all!"

Her brother Ernest had drifted back to his books, wearied with waiting. Good-naturedly, he rose from the desk in answer to the imperious summons.

Ernest seemed immensely tall and grown up to Christina, but he was barely fourteen, too young to join his brothers, George and Arthur, on the bridge of the *Christina K*. Secretly, he was thankful, for he was an uneasy sailor and he had no love of the sea.

But his eyes widened as he saw the ship.

"Papa, she's beautiful!"

"She's my big, bonnie ship!" Christina sang blithely.

The older man laughed tolerantly at her antics. Fishing in his pocket, he drew out a red leather box.

"Aye, and this is yours, too, Chrissie. A keepsake to mind you of the birthday of your ship."

Christina fumbled with the little box, its catch defeating her small fingers. Ernest stooped to help her and her mouth dropped open in wonder.

* * * *

"A brooch, Bessie?" Martha, the cook, said.

Bessie McCutcheon took a thick wad of flannel to lift the smoothing iron from the range. She held the iron a short distance from her red cheek, gauging its heat.

"Aye, a bonnie brooch, special-made in silver. Fancy giving a four-year-old a thing like thon!" Bessie declared.

"Some people have more siller than sense!" Bessie

smoothed Christina's lace-trimmed petticoat with loving fingers, then applied the iron energetically.

"Mind you, Martha, she's a bonnie wee lass. But what a brooch! Did you ever hear the like? The bairn will lose it, she's so flighty!"

"Aye, she can twist her pa round her wee finger. And she knows it. She's a spoiled wee madam!" Martha nodded grimly.

* * * *

Chrissie skipped along the stony beach in front of the Kennedy house. Her father and two older brothers were all in Antarctica, on board the *Christina K*, and she'd been left in Bessie McCutcheon's indulgent care.

Bessie had her own theories on the benefit of fresh air and allowed Chrissie out in all weathers. She loved to stand on the shore imagining the *Christina K* sailing home across the bar.

But today was warm and the ship wasn't due for some months. Chrissie was clad in a sparkling white starched pinafore over a pale blue linen dress, intricately smocked.

Bessie had polished her buttoned boots vigorously that morning, but she needn't have bothered. They already had a white line of salt and sand along the uppers because Chrissie had been jumping on the wet seaweed to make it pop.

The girl was sitting so still, huddled in the shadow of a rock, that Chrissie almost jumped on her instead of the seaweed.

She stopped just in time, and smiled.

"I'm so sorry. I didn't see you. Nobody comes here usually – the Broughty Ferry fisherfolk keep their boats further along the beach. Are you one of them?" Chrissie asked curiously.

"Naw. I'm a half-timer at the mill, learning the spinning," the girl admitted grudgingly.

There was an awkward silence. Chrissie examined her new acquaintance frankly.

She felt sorry for her. They were about the same age, but the girl's lank hair was scraped back and tied so fiercely on top of her head with twine it looked as if she would have trouble smiling. She clutched a black shawl covered in wisps of golden strands, and wore a nondescript blouse and skirt. Her feet were wrapped clumsily in jute cloth, like small sacks.

"Is it pleasant, working at the mill?" Chrissie enquired politely.

"Pleasant!" She gaped incredulously for a moment, then to Chrissie's distress, fat tears welled up and rolled down her cheeks,

"I canna keep my ends up! I tried an' tried, but the mills run so fast. The foreman came roaring at me again, so I ran away. And I'll no' go back!"

The mill girl's words made no sense to Chrissie, but her sympathetic heart ached.

"Oh, dear. Where will you go?"

The mill lass wiped her eyes on her shawl and stood up.

"I've an auntie that's a fishwifie in the Ferry. She'll maybe let me do the gutting for her. I'd rather gut fish than go back to the mill."

Chrissie longed to help. She suddenly remembered the two farthings she had in her pinafore pocket, all that was left of her Saturday penny.

"Here, this is for you. Take it."

The mill lass stood still, staring at the two farthings. Then her expression darkened until her eyes looked angrily black. She lifted a fist and struck Chrissie's hand away. The farthings went flying, to be lost for ever amongst the shingle.

"Keep your money!" the girl shouted in Chrissie's face, then ran off clumsily in her shapeless footwear.

* * * *

Chrissie was still weeping indignantly when she arrived home.

"She was horrid, Bessie! Horrid manners and horrid clothes! She wouldn't even take my farthings!"

"No, she wouldn't. That was charity, Chrissie. The lassie had her pride – if nothing else." Bessie made no further comment, but her mouth tightened grimly.

It was pitch dark next morning when Chrissie was wakened rudely. There was a popping hiss as Bessie lit the gaslight.

"Come, lassie. Up you get!" she ordered in a tone that brooked no argument.

"But – but –" Chrissie rubbed her eyes. It was raining and windy outside, as well as being dark. It must still be the middle of the night.

"What time is it?" She yawned as Bessie helped her dress.

"Half-past four. Come – eat your brose."

Chrissie was too sleepy and confused to argue. Besides, Bessie wore a grim look that subdued her.

"Fetch your cape, Chrissie. We're going out," Bessie said.

Hood pulled well over her head, Chrissie could hardly believe it when Bessie took her hand firmly, and they set off into the teeth of a westerly wind and driving rain, along the Dundee Road. It was like a bad dream.

"Where are we going, Bessie?"

"You'll see."

Early though it was, there were plenty of people about. Fishwives with creels of fresh fish walked from Broughty Ferry towards the town. Vegetable and milk carts from the farms loomed out of the dark, their drivers huddled beneath pieces of sacking.

Bessie climbed the hill when they reached the first mass of tenements at Blacks Croft. Chrissie trotted along valiantly at her side, too cold, wet and miserable to complain.

They stopped on the cobbles outside a large, arched gateway. The ground seemed to shake under Chrissie's feet.

"Where are we?" she whispered.

"Outside the mill."

Bessie's face looked stern in the dawn light. Chrissie wiped her nose on the back of her hand and decided to keep her questions till later.

Suddenly there was a raucous din that made her cling to Bessie and whimper with terror. Bessie laughed softly and touched her face.

"Wheesht, lamb. It's only the hooters for the beginning of the shift."

When the noise ceased, even the thunder of the mill seemed quiet. Chrissie found that she was holding her breath, waiting.

"Look!" Bessie ordered, pointing.

In the grey light, Chrissie could see that doors were opening all up and down the street. She could hear the clatter of hundreds of pairs of boots on the tenement platforms and stairs, and the soft, swishing sound of jute as many jute-clad feet shuffled along. Down the street from all sides poured a vast army of men and women.

Most were cheery, despite the wind and rain and the early hour; the street echoed to shouts and laughter. Bessie appeared to be well-known.

"Aye, Bessie! Lost your soft job?" someone cried.

Some of the younger men greeted Bessie with a wink and a squeeze of the waist, which made Chrissie stare. She'd always thought of Bessie as old, but now saw that her nurse was buxom and bonnie, with clear, unlined skin.

Surrounded by this endless mass of people, Chrissie's head was spinning. The brose had long since ceased to warm her, and she was ready to cry. Only stubborn pride stopped her.

There were only a few stragglers now, hurrying into the factory. Bessie bent down and spoke quietly.

"This is what your mill lassie was running from. Do you blame her? Never judge people too hastily, my lass."

Chrissie nodded solemnly, not really understanding. She was to remember Bessie's words in years to come, and wish she'd acted on them . . .

Bessie smiled more cheerfully and put an arm round Chrissie's shoulders.

"Come away, my wee lamb. My sister Biddy lives over there. She's just had another bairn, so she'll be in."

They clambered up the outside stair on to the stone platform that ran along the outside doors of the tenement.

Biddy gave a squeal of delight when she saw Bessie. Tucking the tiny baby she'd been feeding into the open drawer of the dresser, she hugged her sister fondly.

Then she turned to Chrissie.

"Ah, the wee motherless hen! And her so bonnie!" Biddy wiped her tears from her eyes, then bellowed so fiercely it made Chrissie jump. "Get away ben, you lot!"

The three small, curious faces in the doorway of an adjoining room disappeared hastily. Another boy, older and taller than Chrissie, stood his ground.

Biddy bent down to Chrissie.

"Would you like a piece, dear?"

"A piece of what?" Chrissie was baffled.

"Ma, she's a gowk!" The boy doubled up, laughing noisily.

"You mind your manners, Danny Murphy. Miss Christina's a lady. She's no' in the habit of dining off bread and dripping like the rest of us – nor a jelly piece, neither."

"She'll take a jelly piece, Biddy," Bessie intervened. "If you have a scrape o' jam to spare."

While her sister hastened to do the honours, Bessie cooed to the baby.

"Not at the mill, today, Danny?" She smiled at the lad.

"I've had the mill-hoast. I've been bad with it, but I'm not coughing so much now. Ma says I'll be back the morn."

Biddy dealt out bread and jam to all the children, then settled down by the grate for a blether with Bessie.

Chrissie and the boy bit into thick slabs of bread and eyed one another cautiously. He was a well-built lad with sturdy legs. His thick, curly hair was very black, and his eyes the deepest blue Chrissie had ever seen. There was a dimpled cleft in his square chin which hinted at mischief.

"What do you do in the mill?"

"I'm a shifter. I shift the empty bobbins."

Chrissie was none the wiser. He took another bite of bread and munched, studying her.

"Are you the whaler's lassie?"

"My papa owns three whaling ships. One of them's named after me," Chrissie told him proudly.

"We use the whale oil in the mill, for softening the jute. It smells awful."

Chrissie was hurt and insulted, but couldn't think of a suitably cutting reply. Then he smiled. It warmed his merry blue eyes, and made her feel breathless.

"But you smell sweet, wee lassie. You smell like flowers."

That was Chrissie's first meeting with Danny Murphy, whose tongue had a cutting edge, and whose sweet words could warm a lass's heart . . .

Chapter 2

CHRISSIE'S eldest brother, George, had married in 1897, the year of Queen Victoria's diamond jubilee. The marriage had been very quiet and simple, in the midst of the lavish jubilee celebrations. Jean brought nothing to George except her own cheery, loving self.

Without a word being said, Chrissie knew that George's choice of wife was a sore disappointment to their father. She wasn't sure why, but she grew to love Jean dearly and looked forward to her visits with the baby Georgina, a delightful little bundle of joy.

After every trip to the Antarctic, William Kennedy seemed to grow more and more tight-lipped. Only Chrissie was able to make him smile.

Ernest, who worked in the office of the Kennedy Whaling Company, explained that Papa was disappointed because Jean brought no dowry, and times were hard in the whaling industry. There were no whalers being launched from the Dundee Shipbuilders' yard, but in 1901 a ship called the *Discovery* was built to explore the Antarctic.

As if her own Papa hadn't explored most of that fearsome place already! Chrissie was scornful as she watched the new ship set off on her trials. A fine ship, but in Chrissie's opinion, not half as fine as the *Christina K*, berthed in King William IV dock!

William Kennedy had higher hopes of his second son. Arthur had his eye on Miss Elizabeth Bowers, a jute merchant's daughter. More importantly, Lizzie Bowers had her eye set firmly upon Arthur.

The Bowers family were a little less pleased, but Lizzie was a determined young woman. The wedding ceremony was arranged for June, the reception to be held afterwards in the Bowers's newly built mansion in the West End.

"You are to be bridesmaid, Christina, with my sister, Harriet. You will wear pale pink," Lizzie decided.

"I hate pale pink!" Chrissie stuck out her lower lip mutinously.

"Why not a deep rose-pink for the attendants, my love? The colour will set off your bonnie white gown much more emphatically," Arthur suggested diplomatically.

Lizzie agreed graciously, while Arthur winked at Chrissie behind his beloved's ramrod-straight back. Chrissie suspected her quiet brother had the measure of Miss Lizzie and would handle her with good-natured dexterity. Suddenly, she felt happier about the match.

* * * *

Harriet Bowers thought Chrissie was the most beautiful girl she had ever seen.

Harriet's admiration was completely untainted by envy, because she had no illusions about herself. Although she and Christina were both newly turned fifteen, Harriet was already a head taller, skinny and gawky, with a thin, clever face and dark, flyaway hair that was always untidy.

The two girls smiled shyly when they first met for the fittings of the rose-pink gowns. They both liked what they saw.

"Which school do you go to?" Harriet asked Chrissie when she got the chance.

"Mrs Brough, the minister's wife, teaches reading, writing and arithmetic, but my papa says I'm to go to Miss Black's school next term. Your papa recommends it for finishing off young ladies," Chrissie answered without enthusiasm.

"Why, that's where I go!" Harriet was excited. "We can be friends, if you like. I don't have a best friend," she offered hopefully.

"Oh, I'd like that!" Chrissie grinned.

Harriet was dazzled by the smile, but thoughts of Miss Black's Establishment for Young Ladies brought her down to earth. She sighed.

"I'd rather go to the Public Seminary, but my parents won't hear of it. I want to study science, algebra and geometry, like the boys do," she confided.

"Ooh! You must be clever!" Chrissie's eyes were wide.

"How can I be – if I don't get the chance?" Harriet said sadly.

The dressmaker turned her attention to Chrissie, leaving Harriet to her thoughts.

If I marry Charles Rankine, as Papa hopes, then I'll study anything I please, Harriet told herself. Charles is a darling, and will let me do it, I know. She closed her eyes tight, and prayed fervently.

Please, God, let me marry Charles Rankine one day. I do love him so. And please make him love me, too. For ever and ever, Amen . . .

The weather was kind the day Arthur Kennedy married Lizzie Bowers. It was a stylish assembly that congregated afterwards on the close-cut lawn of the Bowers's stately mansion.

The bride's two attendants stuck closely together.

The deep, rose-pink colour of the gown suited Chrissie well, and she was well aware of many speculative glances. On the bodice of her dress, much to the bride's chagrin, Chrissie defiantly wore the emblem of her father's trade — the silver brooch of the *Christina K.*

Chrissie felt strangely detached, as if she were a spectator watching a play. It was an odd sensation, but she felt so muddled these days, she wasn't unduly surprised. As she grew up, she became aware that her settled life was changing. And she didn't know why.

Only the other day, Biddy Murphy, whose crowded tenement had become Chrissie's second home, had cradled the young girl's face in her rough, red hands. She'd stared long and hard with an oddly sorrowful expression.

"Ah, lassie! Such a bonnie face. You'll break a poor laddie's heart without even knowing it!"

The remark had shaken Chrissie badly, but despite all her pleading, Biddy refused to explain.

So Chrissie stood with Harriet beside the laburnum tree, sipping iced lemonade, and hoping anxiously that she wouldn't break any hearts today . . .

Charles Rankine was also standing a little apart, observing the guests quietly. At twenty-five, he looked a solemn young man, tall but not very robust after childhood rheumatic fever.

He viewed the blushing bride with unfeigned relief. Lizzie Bowers had been suggested as a suitable wife for him at one time. Fortunately, Lizzie had other ideas.

"The bride and bridegroom!" the toast rang out.

Charles lifted his champagne glass towards Arthur Kennedy. He looked a strong, capable man, well fitted to cope with Mistress Lizzie. The best of luck to you, old chap!

Charles's parents had not been deterred, though. Their interest was now concentrated on Lizzie's sister, Harriet. She was younger and infinitely more amenable – and Charles had to agree that a union with the Bowers family was certainly desirable from a business point of view.

He turned his attention idly to young Harriet. Rose-pink did little for her. It even seemed to diminish her remarkable eyes, which he liked for their clear, frank intelligence.

A nice lass, caring and thoughtful. He could do worse, Charles thought, and he could afford to wait.

He'd enjoyed studying at St Andrews University, and was now ready to learn all he could about the running of Rankine Mills. There was plenty of time for Harriet – and matrimony.

The other bridesmaid came suddenly into view, stepping from the shadow into full sunlight. She stood for a moment with her face turned up to the sun. Charles caught his breath.

He had noticed the lass in church. What man wouldn't pay

attention to such a bonnie face and figure? But now, as she lifted her head and smiled at the blue sky with such youthful abandonment, he felt a tug at his heartstrings. Almost without realising it, he was drawn towards her.

Charles stopped in front of the two young girls.

"Harriet, you – you performed your duties well." It sounded pompous, but he could think of nothing else.

Harriet had watched Charles walk purposefully towards them, and her heart had begun to sing. She was almost afraid to look at him, because her eyes might reveal too much. In confusion, she turned to Chrissie.

"Charles, have you met Arthur's sister, Christina Kennedy?"

"Not yet," he said quietly. Chrissie held out a hand shyly. He took it and held it in both of his, looking deep into her eyes.

"Christina, I'm pleased to meet you," he said formally.

Harriet watched their meeting with sick foreboding. There was a light in Charles's eyes that seemed to illuminate his grave, serious features, making Harriet long for him desperately, and despair of ever having him.

Chrissie was not impressed by Charles Rankine. A long dreep o' misery, Bessie would have called him.

Still, Chrissie was prepared to be friendly, because Harriet had confided in her how much she cared for him.

When she felt him press her hand and looked up into his eyes, she was astonished to see the dawning light of admiration there.

She wanted nothing to do with him! He belonged to Harriet, and she wouldn't hurt her friend for anything! Chrissie pulled her hand away hastily and stepped back.

"If you will excuse me, Mr Rankine, I must go to my papa now."

She turned and ran, but not to the mansion house and her father, who was in conversation. Chrissie hurried blindly down a path where dark laurels hid her confusion.

She let out a little scream of alarm when a man stepped out of the bushes in front of her. Then she recognised him.

"Och, Danny! It's only you!"

"Aye, it's only me," Danny Murphy said grimly.

Chrissie smiled at him. She felt better, safer, with Danny around. Since that first meeting, they'd played together, talked together, had heated arguments together and laughed and joked together. He'd been like a brother to her.

No, Chrissie thought suddenly, that's not quite right. More than a brother . . .

"What're you doing here, you gowk? If they catch you, you'll be out on your ear," she warned.

"I was outside the kirk. I wanted to see how the gentry got wed. I've been watching the carry-on in the garden," he growled, his black brows frowning.

He stared at her so intently it frightened her. Yet, in a strange way, she rejoiced, as if she'd been waiting all along for Danny to look at her like this . . .

He must have moved closer; perhaps she had moved forward, too. She could smell the oily jute on his clothes, pleasantly familiar.

At eighteen Danny was well-built and powerful, his black hair thick and curling. Chrissie caught her breath. She hadn't noticed how fine and handsome he'd grown. It was as if she had wakened, and met a handsome stranger.

A stranger, but for the merry blue eyes. She'd always loved his eyes . . . Loved? Chrissie's thoughts paused, startled, then leaped forward. Yes, loved!

"Chrissie –" His hands rested on her shoulders, his face close to hers. "I'll make something o' myself, one of these days. I'll work and read and learn, and be somebody. As good as any of these folk." He jerked his head towards the garden angrily.

"I know you will, Danny." She touched his face gently.

His arms went round her and he kissed her lips softly for the first, sweet time.

"Chrissie, will you wait? Will you promise?"

Nestled in his arms, she nodded.

* * * *

With all the family at Arthur's wedding reception, Bessie McCutcheon took the chance to visit her sister. It was easier these days, with a horse-drawn tram running from Broughty Ferry to Dundee. What luxury!

Child-bearing and millwork had taken its toll on Biddy, and with her bad legs she couldn't manage the tenement stairs now. She didn't complain. Biddy's great joy was to lean her elbows on the window-sill and watch all that went on below.

They were chatting over a cup of tea when Danny came in.

"Where have you been, son? You missed your dinner," Biddy remarked.

He gave a tight grin.

"I've been to the wedding, to see Chrissie in her finery."

"Oh, aye?" Biddy studied him warily. Her smile had faded.

"I hid in the bushes and watched her. She was like a rose, Ma. All the young men were after her, but it was me she chose!"

"What blethers!" His mother snorted scornfully. "Why should she look at the likes of you?"

He lifted his chin.

"Because I'm the one for her. I'll be better than them all one day."

Biddy lifted her eyes to heaven.

"Will you listen to the lad havering. Besides, she's little more than a bairn yet, and bairns are fickle."

"Chris knows her mind," he argued stubbornly. "She gave me her promise!"

Groaning, Biddy shook her head.

"Aw, Danny son! It's just no' possible."

He came close, his blue eyes blazing.

"I'll make it possible! Chrissie Kennedy is the only wife I'll ever take!"

He turned on his heels and stormed out.

Bessie McCutcheon had turned pale with distress.

"Oh, Biddy! What have I done? I should never have brought that lassie to your house!"

Chapter 3

CHRISSIE enjoyed her two years at Miss Black's school. Miss Black taught little else but the perfecting of an elegant copperplate hand, enough arithmetic for a lady to keep a check on the household budget, knitting and embroidery, and above all, ladylike manners and deportment. She'd had grave reservations about accepting the daughter of a whaling skipper, but the Bowers family had spoken up in Chrissie's favour. Miss Black had been pleasantly surprised to find the girl well-disciplined and accomplished.

She wished she could say as much for Harriet Bowers!

Harriet's behaviour puzzled Chrissie. Her shy, easy-going manner had changed since her sister's wedding.

She and Chrissie were still best of friends, but now there was a subdued restlessness in Harriet. She had no patience – her writing was like a hen scraping on a midden, Bessie said. And her embroidery was an impatient disgrace.

On the other hand, she flew accurately through arithmetic problems and swiftly totted up long columns of figures, while others laboured. Then she sat staring idly out of the window . . .

The eruption came one day when Harriet was struggling to master crochet. She flung the grubby cotton on the classroom floor and stood up.

"Miss Black, I want to study biology."

Miss Black turned pale.

"My dear, that's an indelicate subject for young persons."

"Oh, no, it isn't! I want to find out how my body works. If you're not prepared to teach me, then I shall leave!"

And leave she did, that very day, striding out with her head held high, never to return.

Mr and Mrs Bowers discovered to their consternation that they had another stubbornly determined daughter on their hands. They gave in with stunned resignation, and allowed Harriet to attend the Public Seminary.

Chrissie, a few days after her seventeenth birthday, told Danny about Harriet's latest examination success.

They sat in mild sunshine at the top of the Law, with the river estuary and the Fife coast beyond spread out before them. It was a wild, high place, dominating the town, with only a rough track to the top. You could see all the factory chimneys from it, belching out black smoke. They came here whenever Chrissie could get away, to talk and be alone.

"She had top marks in most subjects, Danny!"

He lay on his back, chewing a blade of grass.

"Och, I canna stand clever women!"

"Thanks very much!" Chrissie cried indignantly.

"You're different." He pulled her down into his arms. "You're clever in other ways, and beautiful."

She stroked his hair. He was so handsome, she felt as if she melted inside when she looked at him . . .

"Chrissie, I've joined the Volunteers."

"You mean the soldiers?" She felt a sudden chill.

"Aye. It's one way to get ahead. The sergeant says if I keep on, I'll get a stripe by Christmas."

"Oh, Danny!" She felt tearful, afraid, even though the Volunteers did little more than drilling and marching on the Magdalen Green.

"Don't cry, sweetheart," Danny begged.

He couldn't bear to see her cry. He kissed her. And kissed her again . . .

With a supreme effort of will, Danny pushed her away.

"Chrissie, we must get married soon, or – or else –"

Chrissie was flushed, breathing fast, her eyes shining.

"Yes, Danny, yes. I'm seventeen now — but you must bide in patience for a little while longer. My papa believes I'm still a bairn, and I must persuade him otherwise!" She laughed confidently.

William Kennedy was, in fact, very much aware that his little girl had grown into a very marriageable young woman.

He watched Chrissie alight from the electric tram and hurry along the garden path. Oh, but she was bonnie! And so happy today . . .

Well, he could make her happier still, with the news he had for her. Happy, and secure for life! That's what he wanted for his lassie.

When he heard her in the hallway, he opened the study door.

"Chrissie, will you come in?"

"What is it, Papa?" Chrissie looked up at him, her happiness fading a little. It must be something serious; his face was set in solemn lines.

He sat down, and she sat opposite, wondering.

"Chrissie, you must know how bad trade is. Our stocks of oil are dwindling, and we lost a good order last month because folk complain the smell of whale oil taints the bacon wrapped in sackcloth. If I had more capital to spend, to refit the ships, I could mechanise. That's the way ahead, using engines."

William paused, smiling at her puzzled face. He'd been carried away. He couldn't expect a young lass to understand his worries.

"Aye, well, that's by the by. I've worked the *Christina K* hard, Chrissie, and she's badly needing an overhaul. We must have more capital if we're to keep our heads above water. Today I was given the chance to have all the money we need!"

Chrissie touched the brooch at her neck, and her eyes shone.

"Oh, Papa! That's good news!"

He shifted uncomfortably in his chair.

"Aye, well. The fact of the matter is that young Charles Rankine has formally asked my permission to court you.

"He hinted that if the outcome is – er – favourable, his firm will put up the money we need. What d'you say to that?" He leaned forward eagerly.

Chrissie couldn't hide her shock and dismay. She'd met Charles Rankine from time to time since Arthur's wedding, but he'd always been formally correct. There had been no hint of this!

"But – but he's such a long dreep o' misery, Papa!"

William Kennedy laughed indulgently.

"Och, don't judge the man too harshly! I'll grant you he's no oil painting, but they say he's a couthie man, and kindly. He's had the running of the mill since his father's illness and the workers like him well – and trust him, which is more than you can say for most!"

He looked at his daughter thoughtfully.

"I think Charles Rankine has had his eye on you for a while, Chrissie. He's just been waiting till you were a grown woman. That says a lot for him!

"You know I'll not force you if you're dead set against him, but think on it, lassie. You could save us all. Oh, Chrissie, what do you say?"

She turned her head away. Her thoughts seemed wee and frightened, scurrying round and round in terror in her head.

Danny! Oh, Danny! What am I going to do?

Chapter 4

WILLIAM KENNEDY studied his daughter. She was obviously dismayed. But wasn't that natural in a young and innocent lass? Perhaps he'd broached the subject of Charles Rankine's courtship rather clumsily.

He leaned forward and took Chrissie's hands.

"My dear, you're old enough to understand the situation. I'm at my wits' end – the whales just aren't there any more. If this season's no better . . ."

He gave a twisted smile.

"I haven't even told your brothers how desperately short of money we are. Mind you – I suspect Ernest has more than a suspicion. He's studied the ledgers.

"Chrissie, I've never owed anyone a penny. If we get into debt, I'll have to sell the *Christina K.*"

"Oh, Papa, no! Not my bonnie ship!"

He nodded heavily.

"It could come to that – without Charles Rankine's help."

Chrissie stormed out into the street. The driver of the electric tram clanged his bell and slowed down invitingly, but she shook her head and kept walking.

Along the Ferry Road, and into the town, then up the steep brae that brought her up by Dudhope Castle to the slopes of the Law. Mounting the track she'd walked with Danny only that morning, she stood at last on the summit, the wind tugging at her skirts.

How happy they'd been for those short, stolen moments. Now everything had changed.

Chrissie longed for Danny and, looking down on the long roof of the mill where he worked, she imagined she could see him. Bonnet pulled well down over his black curling hair, he was admiring the new engine that ran the main shaft. A hundred and fifty belt-driven machines in the spinning flat depended upon it . . .

Then on the breath of a wind, Chrissie heard the whisper of a little mill lass, weeping plaintively . . .

"The mills run so fast I canna keep my ends up!"

Chrissie found herself shivering. The mills would run faster than ever now, with the bigger, better engines they were making.

Her gaze wandered to the east, to another spread of blue slate roof, another tall, red-brick chimney. Rankine's Mill.

She felt the beat of panic in her throat. Surely she wouldn't have to marry the man? How could she, when she was promised to Danny?

Her vision blurred with tears, she looked beyond the Old Steeple to the harbour where the *Christina K* lay idle. Chrissie's fingers closed protectively over the brooch on her bodice. She knew she would have to fight to save her ship!

She turned away and scrambled recklessly down the path. This time she headed west towards the road to Perth, and the newly built mansions of the well-to-do.

Harriet Bowers was surprised and delighted when the maid

showed Chrissie into the study. She jumped up from her desk, and the two friends hugged one another affectionately.

Their friendship was as strong as ever. Harriet knew all about Chrissie's love for Danny, and if she doubted the wisdom of it, she kept her thoughts to herself.

"Chrissie, how grand! I haven't seen you for ages!"

Harriet was studying her friend intently, and what she saw troubled her. Chris was pale, her hands like ice, her eyes dark with unhappiness.

Harriet led her to the warmth of the fire, blethering away.

"My fault, of course. I've had my nose in my books all winter. I take the exams for the Higher Grade Leaving Certificate soon."

She poked the coal into a cheerier glow. It flared up, and she was glad to see the warmth bring colour to Chrissie's cheeks. Harriet went on chattering. She knew her friend would tell her what was troubling her in her own good time.

"I've joined the suffragette movement!"

"You haven't!" Chrissie's eyes grew round.

Word of the women's campaign for the vote had reached Dundee recently, and her father's reaction had been scathing. Women making a right nuisance of themselves, even defying the police!

"We're organising a grand march through Dundee on the first of October," Harriet went on excitedly. "I'm to carry a banner with *Votes For Women* on it, and Daisy Marchmont will walk in front, banging a big drum. You'll march with us, won't you?"

"Oh, Harriet, I don't know what will have happened by then!" Chrissie cried miserably.

Bit by bit, the story came tumbling out. Harriet listened quietly, a bright hope fading.

Charles Rankine wanted Chrissie as his wife. Which meant he had no intention of marrying Harriet . . .

He had continued to visit the Bowers's house since Lizzie's marriage to Arthur Kennedy, and Harriet's feelings had grown and matured. She'd hoped he came to see her. Now she realised how often Chrissie had been there, too.

But Charles had shown no more than polite interest in her. It was Harriet that could make him laugh, who could shake him out of his natural reserve with her frank observations.

Others thought Charles Rankine a sobersides, but Harriet knew better. He was her darling, the only man she could ever love. And he wanted Chrissie!

Harriet bent to poke the fire.

"Will you marry Charles?"

Chrissie knew how Harriet felt about Charles Rankine – her friend would make him a perfect wife. Oh, why must the daft man be so blind to Harriet's excellent qualities?

"I may have to – to save Papa from ruin. Oh, Harriet – I'm sorry," she cried in anguish.

Harriet lifted her chin.

"Don't you worry about me!" She stood up abruptly, tall and slender, hair as untidy as ever, her remarkable eyes alight with determination.

"I'm going to be a doctor. It'll take years of hard work. I'll have no time to think about Charles Rankine, I assure you!"

As soon as Charles Rankine received William Kennedy's permission to court his daughter, he invited himself to afternoon tea. Poor Bessie was thrown into a frantic tizzy of preparation.

He arrived by hansom cab, and was greeted most warmly by William. The house gleamed with polish, and the air was filled with the smell of baking, but Charles scarcely noticed.

William Kennedy opened the parlour door with a flourish.

"Chrissie, here's Mr Rankine to see you, my dear!"

Their eyes met across the room, and Charles felt breathless. Chrissie's hair shone like smooth gold and was pinned high on her head. Her blue gown enhanced her figure becomingly.

Bessie had even daringly brushed Chrissie's cheeks with a hare's foot dipped in a little rouge, then applied the same to her lips.

"Not a word of this to your pa, mind," Bessie had warned. "Or I'll get my head in my hands and my lugs to play wi'!"

Chrissie was glad of the rouge, for she was sure she had gone as white as milk. Charles seemed taller than ever standing in the doorway. And so solemn, not a single smile on his lips!

Hastily recalling her manners, Chrissie smiled and shyly held out a hand.

"How do you do, Mr Rankine?"

"I'm very well, thank you, Miss Kennedy." He took her hand, just the tips of her fingers.

'Sit down yourself down, man!" William invited heartily. He plumped himself into the only armchair, leaving Charles no option but to sit on the sofa beside Chrissie.

William had scarcely embarked upon an outline of the whaling industry when Bessie wheeled in the tea trolley. It was laden with dainty sandwiches, scones, pancakes and a sponge cake oozing with fresh cream and strawberry jam. The best china was out, and the silver tea service gleamed in the firelight.

Bessie was dressed like a parlourmaid for the occasion. She gave Chrissie a broad wink as she withdrew.

Chrissie giggled, but hastily smothered her mirth with her hand. Stealing a quick glance at Charles, she found he was watching, amused.

She quickly poured out tea and handed him a cup.

"One lump or two, Mr Rankine?"

"Three, please, Christina."

He was teasing her! Or had an awfully sweet tooth!

He accepted a genteel sandwich, which vanished in one bite. Silently, Chrissie pushed the plate towards him. He looked as if he needed a good feed.

"Aye, September and October is the best time for big whales out by Greenland, if they're to be had," William was saying. "I sailed with the Antarctic expedition in 1893, when Chrissie was only a baby, but Dundee ships are underpowered for the Antarctic, Charles. There's where the future lies – in bigger, faster ships."

He paused, sighing.

"I doubt I'll see it! Aye, well, I'll take the *Christina K* to the Baffin Sea with Arthur. George will sail on the *Windward*, and we'll see what the future holds for us."

Charles met William's eyes. He guessed, accurately, that he was being given a free hand to woo and win Chrissie.

"Harriet's going to be a doctor," Chrissie announced.

Charles turned sharply.

"Is she really?"

"Yes. She's joined the suffragettes, too. She wants me to be in the procession in Dundee," Chrissie went on recklessly.

Her father fixed her with a warning glance.

"No daughter of mine would want to be seen dead with those rowdy besoms! If you want my opinion, Mr and Mrs Bowers don't have their sorrows to seek wi' Miss Harriet and her daft notions!"

He delicately wiped cream off his mouth and folded the lace-trimmed napkin with an air of finality.

"Chrissie, when you've finished your tea, take Mr Rankine into the garden and show him the daffodils. There's a grand show," he said artlessly.

Chrissie rose dutifully and led the way outside.

Charles followed. The garden ran wild and untended down the slope towards the railway line, with the wide river and the hills of Fife beyond. It was ablaze with golden daffodils, but he had eyes only for Chrissie.

She had paused on the path, lifting her head and looking out over the estuary with the rapt look he had first loved in her. She spoke dreamily, forgetting he was there.

"I stand here when my ship goes to sea. I watch her until she's a wee speck on the horizon. I feel as if part of me has gone with her; there's a hollow space that only fills up when she comes home again . . ."

Chrissie's voice trailed to a halt. Danny hated her to mention the *Christina K*. It was a painful reminder of her station in life – so far above him. So she'd never talked about the emotions the ship aroused in her before.

Glancing up, she found Charles Rankine regarding her gravely. She met his eyes frankly for the first time, and found herself suddenly liking him.

"You understand, don't you, Charles?" It was a statement of her wonder, not really a question.

Greatly daring, he took her hand and held it as they watched the ships on the river and the yellow daffodils swaying in the breeze.

* * * *

There was a new baby in the bottom drawer of Biddy Murphy's dresser.

Biddy's older daughters were in the mill, and she had become their bairnminder. Her working days were over, and the pennies were welcome.

She was sitting by the grate knitting when Danny stormed in.

"Wheesht, you'll wake the wean!"

"I don't give a damn!"

Biddy rested the knitting on her lap.

36

"What's up, Danny? Your face is as long as a wet week."

"It's her – Chrissie!" he said through his teeth. "She's taken a fancy man. I saw them in Kennedy's garden in the Stannergate, holding hands."

Biddy's heart missed a beat.

"What took you to the Stannergate on a working day?"

Danny wrenched off his cap.

"The axle broke on the docker's cart and the bales spilled off, giving the horse an awful fright. The carter stayed to calm the poor beastie, and I was sent to Stannergate on the tram to fetch the blacksmith."

He ran his fingers through his hair distractedly.

"I was fair pleased thinking I might see Chrissie. Och, I saw her all right – and I wish I hadn't."

Biddy studied her son's furious face.

"It's young Mr Rankine, from Rankine's Mill. A fine man. One of her own kind, Danny. I warned ye, mind!"

He pushed his face close, so close she could feel the heat of him, and was almost afraid.

"And I warned you, Ma! I'll be better than him one day!"

She flapped a hand impatiently.

"Och, Dan, have sense! You and your books. Buying books is like throwing money down the Scouring Burn!"

"It's the way to get on and make money. Chrissie's mine, Ma. No other man will have her!"

* * * *

The sermon that Sunday morning seemed endless, and William Kennedy frowned at Chrissie's fidgets. She picked

37

at Sunday lunch like a bird, and left the house as soon as her father had settled down for his afternoon nap.

She had to be careful. She didn't want to be seen by any of her family. Ernest was walking out with a grocer's daughter from Hilltown, and George and Jeannie and their family lived not far from the infirmary. The real danger, though, was Chrissie's brother, Arthur – or rather his wife, Lizzie, Harriet's sister.

Lizzie had had several miscarriages, and was expecting again. This time she was taking great care, and hardly walked anywhere. Arthur drove his wife around gently in a sprung carriage behind a placid pony, and there was no knowing where they would turn up.

Chrissie didn't feel safe until she reached the rough track, and then her feet flew to keep her Sunday tryst with Danny on the Law.

He was standing staring broodingly at the factory roofs, his back to her. She stole up behind him and put her hands over his eyes, kissing the back of his neck beneath the strong, curling black hair.

"Guess who, Dan." Chrissie laughed. "And it's not yer ma!"

He reached up and gripped her wrists, then turned. She flinched at the look on his face.

"Chrissie, how long have you been daffing wi' that dreep Rankine?"

Danny glared at her; he had no words to express his misery. Chrissie looked at him, colour draining from her.

"Oh, Danny! I was going to tell you, but I didn't know how!"

Hesitantly, she tried to explain. She made a poor job of it, stammering and pausing to wipe away her tears. He heard her to the end, grim-faced, then his blue eyes flashed.

"And you're forced to take up with Rankine, because he's rich and has a fancy for a bonnie face! And I'm of no account because I'm just an orraworker making my way! I'll no' stand for it, Chrissie!"

He looked so handsome and brave, her heart melted. She laid her head on his chest and they clung together.

"Danny, what can we do? How can I fight when it's my father and brothers that'll suffer?"

He kissed her tenderly.

"Just you mind that you love me – and that I love you – when Rankine comes to call. We're promised, honourably and truly. And dinna you forget it!"

Danny pulled her into the lee of their favourite rock, a secluded sheltered spot they'd made their own. They sat down on the grass, and Chrissie put her head on his shoulder. For a little while she was happy and contented, his arm warm around her.

"I'll be a better man than Rankine one day, Chris. Folk will look up to me for what I've done." Danny grinned. "Maybe they'll put a statue to me on the Law, where I kissed and cuddled with my Chrissie!"

Chapter 5

WILLIAM KENNEDY and his sons sailed from the Tay at the beginning of June. Arthur was reluctant to leave, for Lizzie had lost the bairn she was expecting.

George sailed on the *Windward*, his bonnie Jeannie waving him goodbye from the quay. Georgina and wee Hughie fluttered white handkerchiefs long after the depleted whaling fleet had passed Broughty Castle.

Chrissie was once more left in Bessie's care.

"I want no breath o' scandal to touch her, mind, Bessie!" William had warned. "Mr Rankine's a grand catch, and there's plenty mothers in Dundee green-eyed because he's settled on Chrissie. They'll be on the look-out for scandal. I trust you to look after my lass."

"Aye, Mr Kennedy," Bessie replied awkwardly. Knowing what she did about Chris and Danny Murphy, she couldn't look the poor man in the face.

On the twentieth of August, a hurried memo was delivered to Charles Rankine in his mahogany-panelled office.

He called his carriage immediately and set off to find Chrissie. She received him in the parlour with the door left wide, so that Bessie could chaperone.

"Christina, how would you like to meet the Queen?" His eyes shone with suppressed excitement.

Chrissie clasped her hands, eyes shining.

"Queen Alexandra? I'd love it! But she never comes to Dundee, Charles."

"Well, she's coming now. The Royal yacht – the *Victoria and Albert* – will berth in Dundee harbour, and the Queen will travel from Aberdeen by train on the twenty-third and go on board. She's sailing to Denmark to visit relatives.

"I've been asked to join the people being presented to Her Majesty on the platform. And I can take a partner, Christina," Charles explained triumphantly.

His courtship had been progressing slowly, and he was impatient to be seen in public with Chrissie. The royal visit presented a perfect opportunity.

Chrissie hesitated. Her presence by his side would cause the spate of speculation she was trying hard to avoid. Oh, she longed to meet the Queen – but the price was so high!

"I don' t know, Charles . . ." He reached for her hands.

"Please say yes! It – it would honour me to have you with me," he said sincerely.

The plea went straight to Chrissie's heart. She would never love him as she loved Danny, but she liked him well enough. He'd never been anything but courteous and kind. How could she say no?

"I'd be delighted. Have I got time to trim my best hat and practise my curtsey, Charles?"

"Oh, Chrissie, my darling!"

He was exultant, catching her in his arms. For a breathless moment something flared between them, a warmth that startled Chrissie. She was not as innocent as he believed her to be, and so she recognised the glowing light of passion in his eyes.

She held her breath, then he released her quickly and stepped back.

Danny would never have hesitated to kiss me, Chrissie thought. But Danny's not a gentleman! She immediately felt ashamed.

The Royal yacht had a stormy passage as she steamed into the Tay, escorted by the Royal Navy cruiser *Argyll*. Fortunately, the rain ceased and the wind moderated next day as an array of pretty hats assembled around Tay Bridge station. At three precisely, the royal train pulled in.

The Lord Provost welcomed Queen Alexandra and her daughter, the Princess Victoria, when they stepped from the train.

There were gifts of fruit, and bouquets of roses, then Chrissie was dazzled to find herself curtseying to the Queen and Princess and exchanging a few words with a regal and gracious Alexandra.

Her moment of glory lasted only a few seconds before the royal party swept out of the station to face cheering crowds, but Chrissie knew she'd never forget the meeting. Deeply moved, she held fast to Charles Rankine's arm, not caring what interpretation people put on their closeness.

They lingered behind the others in their party, knowing it would be impossible to reach their carriage in the crush around the station.

"Oh, Charles, thank you so much. It was wonderful!"

Chrissie sighed.

He smiled down at her fondly.

"I hope it's the first of many delightful outings."

"No, it's no'! It's the last!" Danny stepped out of a doorway and stood with legs braced, glaring at Charles.

"Danny! Aw, Dan, please!" Chrissie's eyes begged him not to make a scene.

Charles was startled by the appearance of the hot-eyed young man. He looked down at Chrissie.

"You know this man?"

"Aye, she does!" Danny broke in. "I'm Daniel Murphy, and Chris is promised to me, Mr Rankine. We were to wed – until her father sold her to you to save himself!"

Charles stared hard at Danny. He looked beyond the orraworker's clothing and saw a handsome young man with angry, honest and intelligent eyes.

"There was no question of selling Christina. I simply asked her father's permission to court her," Charles countered.

"I may have mentioned that our union might be profitable to both our families, but the decision to marry me, or not, is Chrissie's. She's free to make up her own mind."

"Free?" Danny snorted. "With her father's business in ruins if she says no?"

Charles considered Danny's words. There was a hard edge of truth to them. He turned to Chrissie.

"Is it true? Have you told Mr Murphy that you'll marry him?"

He saw the answer in her eyes.

"Oh, Chrissie, have you thought about it properly? Do you know what your life would be like with him?"

Danny took an indignant step forward.

"Aye, she knows, Mr Rankine, and she's still willing. I'll not be an orraworker all my days. I may be poor the now, but I'm a better man than you'll ever be!"

Looking down at him, Charles found himself envying his rival's health and his look, particularly the broad-shouldered frame that spoke of power and strength. Daniel Murphy was right. He was the better man of the two.

Charles bowed his head.

"Chrissie, I can't take you on your father's terms. You must come to me willingly – or not at all. And you must give me your decision now."

Oompah! Oompah! The brass band at the Craig pier seemed unnaturally loud. Chrissie could hear loud bursts of enthusiastic cheering as Queen Alexandra and the Princess were driven off to the reception the town council had prepared for them. Dundee hadn't seen such a sight for many a year, with flags and bunting flapping in the windy spatters of rain.

She heard and saw it all as if in a dream. She looked from her handsome, beloved Danny to the grave, kindly man she had grown to like and respect. She knew what her decision had to be.

"I'm sorry, Charles. I told Danny I'd marry him because I love him. I want to be his wife."

August 23, 1907, was an historic day for Dundee, and a day Chrissie Kennedy would never forget. She'd had a taste of the life of luxury and excitement she would have led with Charles Rankine. And she'd turned her back on it and and settled for the hardships of a juteworker's wife.

* * * *

Chrissie was on her knees, wrestling with some weeds in the overgrown garden, when the jingle of a harness brought her to her feet.

"How nice to see you, Lizzie!" Chrissie greeted her sister-in-law with a dutiful peck on the cheek.

Lizzie tethered the pony and trap to the porch rail and slipped a nosebag over the placid little animal's head. She looked grim.

"Could we go inside, please, Christina?"

Christina's heart sank, but she smiled brightly.

"Yes, of course."

She led the way, pausing by the kitchen door.

"Here's Lizzie come to visit, Bessie. May we have tea and a piece of your shortbread, perhaps?"

The two young women were no sooner in the parlour, with the door closed, than Lizzie rounded on Chrissie.

"What's this I hear about you turning down Charles for a juteworker?"

Chrissie lifted her chin mutinously.

"It's true. I don't love Charles Rankine, and I'll not marry him. I'm pledged to someone else."

Two angry spots of colour appeared on Lizzie's cheeks.

"You're daft, Christina! Charles will be one of the richest men in Dundee one day, and you've humiliated him. Taking up with a juteworker, indeed! Who is this man?"

"His name is Daniel Murphy and he works in the High Mill," Chrissie answered defiantly. "His father's a road-sweeper, and his mother's one of the kindest women I know. They live in a tenement in Lochee."

"His father's a – a scavenger?" Lizzie's voice rose to an outraged squeak.

Chrissie was angry. Tutored by Danny, she was fluent in Dundee's distinctive dialect, and she slipped into it now.

"Aye, Lizzie, Mr Patrick Murphy's a scaffie, and he's kept busy. There's plenty work for scaffies in this toon."

Lizzie all but wrung her hands.

"The Kennedys will never live this down. I can only imagine you've been led astray by an unscrupulous rogue, Christina."

"Danny is hard working and honest and I'll ask you not to insult him. Otherwise, I shall ask you to leave."

Lizzie plumped herself on the couch, glowering.

"I'll not leave until I've made you see sense! I feel responsible in your father's absence, Christina. He'd be horrified if he knew how that woman – Bessie – has been letting you consort with rude, common folk!"

There was a muffled snort of indignation from the door. Lizzie was on her feet and had it wrenched open in an instant. Bessie was caught in the act, her ear at the keyhole.

"So! I'm glad you heard that, Bessie McCutcheon, because

when Captain Kennedy returns I shall insist that you are dismissed."

"Lizzie, no!" Chrissie cried in horror.

Bessie rose with as much dignity as she could muster.

"That's for the master to decide, Mistress Lizzie! I did what I believed right. I wanted Miss Christina to see how other folk live. I'd no idea she and my nephew . . . To tell you the truth I'm as heartsick as you are! I wish it hadn't happened."

"Aha! The man's your nephew. Now I understand! You hope to advance your family!" Lizzie exclaimed grimly.

"Stop it!" Chrissie cried in dismay.

Bessie's dander was up. She glared at Lizzie.

"I'll tell you one thing for sure, Mistress Lizzie!"

"And what's that?"

"You're no' getting a single bite of my good shortbread!" And with a sniff, she headed for the kitchen, slamming the door.

Lizzie stared after her angrily.

"Well, really! What a cheek! Your father will hear of this, Christina. That woman must go!"

Chrissie had never been so angry. To hear Lizzie threatening dear, loyal Bessie was more than she could bear. She held the door wide open.

"Please leave, Lizzie! It's none of your business how I live my life."

Lizzie gathered up her gloves with dignity.

"There's gratitude for you. I only wanted to help. I needn't

47

have bothered!" And with that she swept outside.

Chrissie's anger evaporated quickly and now she was sorry she'd been so unkind to Arthur's wife. She followed her outside.

Lizzie was busy with the pony. Stony-faced, she untethered the beast and climbed aboard the trap. Chrissie touched her arm hesitantly.

"Lizzie – I'm so sorry about the baby . . ."

For a moment Lizzie Kennedy was caught unawares, and Chrissie had a startling glimpse of the depth of her sorrow and suffering. Then she nodded quickly and gathered up the reins, urging her little pony on to the Dundee Road.

* * * *

Harriet Bowers didn't know what to think when she heard that Chrissie had turned Charles down. She admired Chrissie's devotion to Danny, and pitied Charles because he'd been rejected. She couldn't stop hoping he might turn to her for comfort, but . . .

She was still determined to be a doctor. She loved Charles, but she didn't want to be married – yet.

Someday . . . maybe . . . she thought as she strolled among the roses.

"Penny for them, Harriet?" Charles was leaning against the summerhouse in the sunshine. Smiling, he held out a penny, which she took gravely.

"I was thinking about you and Chrissie," she admitted.

"Oh! That's something I try not to think about! I work harder than usual, smoke and drink more than I ought, but I still find myself –" He broke off.

Harriet remained silent, studying his tall, spare frame, the quirky curve to his lips and the kindness of his steady, intelligent eyes. He returned her stare.

"Chrissie tells me that you want to be a doctor."

"Yes, I've been accepted on the strength of my exam results. Are you shocked, Charles? Mama had to be revived with smelling salts when I told her!"

"No, I'm not shocked." He grinned. "A liberal dose of common sense is just what the medical profession needs."

"You're just teasing me!"

"No, I'm not!"

Charles looked down into Harriet's wide eyes. He was very fond of her and they got on well. He knew he must marry one day, and if he couldn't have the woman he loved, perhaps . . .

"What about marriage – and children?" he asked curiously. "Would you have to give up your career?"

Harriet's heart gave a wild leap, but she paused gravely to consider the question.

"I think it would be a great wrench," she answered honestly. "But if I truly loved the man, I would do it for him."

Chapter 6

THE mild, misty spell of September weather broke at last, and the suffragettes marched along the high street on October 1 in chilly rain. Chrissie was with them, persuaded against her better judgement by Harriet's infectious enthusiasm.

"Don't you want the vote, Chrissie?" Harriet had challenged her.

"Well, yes, I suppose so, but –" Chrissie wasn't sure what she'd do with a vote if she had it. Surely her small mark upon a ballot paper wouldn't change anything? She said as much to Harriet.

"Of course it would! Imagine if a whole army of women had the power to vote. We could change the world! There would be women in parliament keeping an eye on the men. A woman Prime Minister, even!" Harriet's eyes glowed with fervour.

"The Prime Minister a woman? Och, Harriet, what nonsense!" Chrissie giggled.

"Well, maybe that's going a wee bit far," her friend agreed with a grin. "But you must come, Chrissie, to help me hold my banner. It's huge, and I can't manage it on my own!"

So Chrissie marched, holding one end of a rain-soaked banner which proclaimed in red paint *Votes For Women . . . Now!* They marched to the vigorous beat of Daisy

Marchmont's big drum, shepherded dourly by most of Dundee's impressively tall policemen.

Chrissie felt horribly conspicuous and embarrassed. She spotted a disapproving group waiting for a tram outside the Town House pillars, and recognised some of the ladies who'd been her sternest critics. Her feet began to drag reluctantly.

Suddenly the interested crowd began to swell. The shifts had changed at the mills. There was Danny with a group of millworkers, all cheering loudly!

He caught her eye and waved furiously, blowing her a kiss.

"Look, lads. There's Chrissie, my bonnie lass. Votes for women, say I!" Danny waved his cap, and all the millworkers cheered themselves hoarse.

Chrissie felt a lump in her throat. With Danny she wouldn't sit aimlessly at home with an embroidery frame. She would be his companion and helpmeet, working shoulder to shoulder with him to make a living. It would be hard, she knew, but she would be the equal of any man. She would earn her right to vote.

Chrissie hoisted the banner higher, giving it a defiant shake as the procession wound past the scandalised group by the Town House.

"Votes for women, now!" Chrissie and Harriet shouted in unison.

* * * *

When the whaling fleet was spotted beyond the Abertay sands, Danny went with Chrissie down to the quay.

51

They stood hand in hand, waiting for the *Christina K* to dock. They didn't speak much, and waited a good bit apart from the others.

Chrissie was sorrowful and anxious. Word had got around that the *Windward* – her brother George's ship – had been lost at sea.

She could see his wife, Jeannie, standing motionless, facing into the keen wind from the east, her hands clutching her two bairns as if she'd never let them go.

Wee seven-year-old Hughie wriggled and broke away. He raced over to Chrissie.

"Auntie Chris, my ma's greetin'! Is my daddy dead?" he whispered, wide-eyed.

She hugged him.

"We hope not, lovie. Some of the *Windward*'s crew were saved. Maybe your daddy's among them." It was all the comfort she could give the lad. Nobody knew for sure.

Danny gave the boy a gentle push.

"Away back to yer ma, Hughie. Gie her a hug. She needs all your love the now."

"Aye, Danny." Hughie nodded solemnly. He had great respect for Danny, who was a dab hand at bools.

Lizzie Kennedy sat in the pony trap, straight-backed, not looking at anyone, least of all the young man standing by Chrissie's side. Yet, if asked, she could have given an accurate description of him. Very handsome, in a bold sort of way!

The pony stirred restlessly in the cold wind. From the

corner of her eye Lizzie could see George's wife, with their two lovely children and felt a familiar stab of jealousy and longing. When would she have a bairn of her own to hold?

The *Scotia*, captained by Captain Roberts, berthed first. There was the nervous laughter of relief from some of the group. She had done well, taking two black whales. Most of the other whalers were "clean", they said. It had been a disastrous trip . . .

Chrissie felt her heart swell with pride when the *Christina K* sailed in.

"Oh, Dan, isn't she beautiful?"

He frowned. He'd no love of the sea. Apart from the occasional trip up the Tay to Newburgh, Danny preferred to keep his feet on dry land.

"It could do wi' a lick o' paint," he observed truthfully.

Fortunately the remark was drowned by the bustle of the ship's arrival. Chrissie's fingers tightened anxiously on Danny's sleeve as William Kennedy appeared on deck to supervise the ropes.

When all was secure and the gangplank lowered, he was first down, making for Jeannie, who stood white-faced and motionless on the quay. He took her cold hands.

"Your man's safe, my dear."

"Oh, thank God!" She seemed to come back to life, leaning against her father-in-law, sobbing.

"Aye, well – " William cleared his throat. "George was in the water, dear. Not too long," he added hastily, "but he's still very weak. I doubt he'll go to sea again."

She looked up quickly, her joy fading.

"Where is he?" she asked quietly.

"In the sick bay. You'd best go to him, Jeannie."

He watched Jeannie climb the gangplank with the two children, then heaved a sigh and turned away. When he saw Chrissie his face lit up. He held out his arms.

"Chrissie, my lass!"

She hugged him. He smelled of tarry rope, the sea and pipesmoke – a comfortable, remembered blend that had no comfort for her now.

He held her at arm's length.

"Let's look at you. You're a sight for sore eyes, Chrissie. You must be in love!" He laughed. Tears sprang bright to her eyes. "Oh, Papa –"

He frowned, then glanced around sharply.

"Where's Charles? I thought – I expected him to be with you."

Danny stepped forward.

"I escorted Chrissie to the dock, Captain Kennedy. The foreman gave me leave."

"Who the devil are you?" William Kennedy demanded in bewilderment.

"I'm Daniel Murphy, and Chrissie and I – well, we've been courting for years. I've come to ask your permission to marry her, sir." Danny came straight to the point as usual.

William Kennedy turned back to his daughter.

"Chrissie, tell me he's blethering! I thought you and Charles Rankine would have reached an understanding by now." This was even worse than Chrissie had expected. She wished Danny had brought up the subject of their marriage more gently – but that wasn't Danny's way.

"Papa, Charles and I did reach an understanding. I told him I couldn't marry him because I love Danny. Papa, we want to get married – with your blessing, of course," she explained nervously.

William Kennedy had been sustained throughout the long, gruelling journey by the thought that his daughter's future was secure. Now she was telling him she wanted to marry this – he took in Danny's working clothes in a quick, outraged glance – this labourer!

"Chrissie, how long has this madness been going on?" William Kennedy turned beetroot red.

Her hand dropped from her father's arm and she moved closer to Danny.

"It's not madness, Papa. I've known Dan since I was a child. I love him very much."

"Love!" her father snorted. "You're only seventeen. What d'you know about love?"

That roused Danny's indignation.

"She kens more about true love than you do, Captain Kennedy. You were willing to sell her to Charles Rankine to save your trade! You took no heed o' Chrissie's feelings in the matter."

"Why, you impudent –" William blustered, all the angrier because he knew there was truth in what the young man said.

Chrissie was dismayed. She stepped between the two men she loved.

"Papa, you mustn't fight with Danny. I'm going to marry him – and nothing will change my mind!"

"I'll not allow it, Chrissie. I'll not give my permission," William Kennedy growled furiously.

Chrissie stood very straight, suddenly feeling older than her seventeen years.

"Then I'll leave your house, Papa. I'll go to Danny, married or not."

"Chrissie!" Her father was shocked. The determined woman before him seemed like a stranger, not his sweet, biddable Chrissie.

There was a long silence, broken only by the screech of gulls and the welcoming cries of women on the quay. Then he bowed his head and spoke in a different tone.

"If you're intent on ruining your life, I can't stop you. But if you do go to this man, you'll go as a married woman. I'll see to that!"

"Oh, Papa!" Tears sprang to Chrissie's eyes and she would have hugged him, but he pushed her aside.

William Kennedy climbed the gangplank of his ship slowly. He went to the stern and stood gripping the rail, staring blindly across the estuary like a man surveying the wreckage of his dreams.

Chapter 7

"I JUST hope you ken what you're doing, Danny Murphy!"
his mother said wearily.

Biddy Murphy was sorely troubled. Her son had won the
whaler's lass, but at what cost?

Captain Kennedy was a broken man they said, close to
ruin, and his son, George, sick with a congestion of the
lungs. And her sister Bessie would lose her job if Mistress
Kennedy had her way!

And what of Chrissie herself? The poor lass wasn't fitted
for life in the one-roomed tenement flat Danny had rented.
He couldn't see it, of course.

"Och, dinna fash yersel', Ma!" Danny smiled.

He was always grinning these days. As well he might,
Biddy thought grimly. He'd fought hard for his lass, and
won her by sheer brass neck.

"I'm thinking of Chrissie in yon wee mousehole, and her
used to the comforts o' the big house," she grumbled.

"It's a start," he retorted calmly. "We'll no bide there long.
I'm on the climb, Ma.

"The foreman's got his eye on me for promotion at the
mill, because I've been learning mathematics and I'm quick
at figuring. And I've been given my stripe in the Volunteers.
I'm lance-corporal now!"

"Marching and drilling and capers on the Magdalen Green.

57

Much good that'll do ye!" His mother snorted.

"It's a way to get on. If I stick at it, I could be a sergeant one day."

"What, you – a sergeant?" Biddy laughed.

"Aye, me! Why not?"

But she shook her head and wouldn't answer. Biddy was gripped by a sudden queasy fear she couldn't explain.

Chrissie should have been blissfully happy, but she wasn't. Her father was resigned to the marriage, but he and Danny couldn't get on. They were too much alike.

William generously offered to give Chrissie a handsome dowry he could ill afford. Danny proudly refused.

"Thank you, Captain Kennedy, but I'll support my wife without any help from you!"

William turned on his heel without a word and stalked out of the room.

"Och, Danny, my father meant it kindly!" Chrissie protested in distress.

Danny looked contrite.

"Aye, I know he did and I'm sorry. But he made it sound like charity, an' that I'll never accept."

She had no answer to that. She was remembering a poor little mill-lass on the beach, and two precious farthings amongst the shingle . . .

George's health improved, but his cough remained troublesome. Chrissie visited him and Jeannie often because she felt relaxed and easy with them. Those two kindly souls had accepted her decision to marry Danny.

On the other hand, Lizzie had not mellowed, so Chrissie saw little of Arthur.

Ernest, who had rooms at the Seagate, close to the office, tried to be sympathetic, but the grocer's daughter had broken off their engagement. Poor Ernest was broken-hearted and not very cheerful company.

Chrissie popped in to see George. He was in bed, and the two women could hear his painful coughing as they talked together quietly in the kitchen.

"We're leaving Dundee, Chrissie," Jeannie told her.

"Oh, no! Where are you going?"

"To a hill farm in Isla. The doctor says mountain air might help George's cough. There's an old farmer in the glen who'd be glad of help."

"But you know nothing about farming!" Chrissie objected.

"We'll learn," Jeannie answered.

She stood up abruptly and went to the window, looking out at the silver ribbon of the river below.

"I hate the sea. Look what it's done to my man. I don't care if I never see the river again!" she said bitterly.

"Nor do I, Auntie Chris!" ten-year-old Georgina added staunchly. "My daddy says we'll have dogs and kittens at the farm. I'm to have a dog of my own to help Daddy herd the sheep." The little girl's eyes shone like stars.

Jeannie smiled, laying a gentle hand on her daughter's dark head.

"Ina's daft about animals, Chrissie. She's been nagging me for years to let her have a dog. Well, she'll have one now!"

There was a whimper of protest from wee Hughie.

"Mam, I don't want to go to the farm. I want to stay in Dundee. I like it here, and I'm to be on the football team. Why can't I stay?"

"It's for your daddy's health." Jeannie sighed. "You're going whether you like it or not – so you must make the best of it!"

* * * *

The wedding was arranged for November 22, 1907. It was to be a quiet, simple affair because Danny refused to allow Chrissie's father to pay for anything ostentatious. It was only a short step from the kirk to the house, and Bessie, who had so far weathered the storm of Lizzie Kennedy's disapproval, had agreed to provide a wedding breakfast.

The day before the wedding, Chrissie was too restless and excited to settle to anything. Bessie shooed her out for a walk in the cold, frosty air.

"Enjoy your leisure, lass. There'll be little enough of it where you're going!" Bessie said darkly.

Nothing could dampen Chrissie's spirits, though. The sharp air brought colour to her cheeks as she walked briskly, watching the trawlers and sprat boats, and another jute steamer heading for the docks where the *Christina K* lay idle for the time being.

Chrissie sighed, her gloved hand going to the brooch pinned to her lapel. The ship needed refitting, but there was no money to do it now she'd turned down Charles Rankine. But she refused to be sad the day before she became

Danny's wife!

Walking on, Chrissie became aware of a new mechanical sound behind her. A new-fangled motor car drew alongside and stopped. Colour flooded her cheeks as she recognised the man who'd been in her thoughts.

"Charles! How – how are you?" She hoped her voice didn't betray her feelings. He was the very last person she wanted to see!

"I'm well, thank you, Chrissie." He smiled at her. "This is fortunate. I hoped to see you before your wedding. I want to wish you well." He spoke gently and sincerely.

"Thank you, Charles." How kind he was. She would always think of him with warmth . . .

"I have a wedding gift for you, Chrissie."

She put up her hand in protest.

"Oh, no! You mustn't!"

It would be too painful to look at something and remember him. Besides, Danny surely wouldn't have it in the house!

Reading her thoughts accurately, Charles smiled.

"Don't worry. It's nothing tangible. I've persuaded my board of directors to agree a contract with your father for batching oil. It means I can offer him an advance to refit his ships."

Her heart leaped, and tears shone in her eyes. Impulsively, she reached for his hand and held it for a moment.

"Charles, I don't know what to say!" she whispered brokenly.

"Just be happy, my dear. That's all I ask."

Charles lifted his cap, then good naturedly shooed away the crowd of little boys who had gathered round his car — a rare sight on Dundee streets. He was glad the complexities of driving occupied his mind, because his vision was misted with tears.

* * * *

Bessie had organised everything perfectly, down to the spray of small white chrysanthemums pinned to Chrissie's blue suit. It had to be blue, Bessie insisted.

"Married in blue . . . Your love will be true!" she said firmly, and that was that.

Bessie stood back and surveyed the bride critically. She clasped her hands and her eyes shone with proud tears.

"Oh, my lassie! You're so bonnie!"

Chrissie hugged her.

"Thank you, Bessie, dear. Thanks for everything you've done for me. But most of all, thank you for giving me Danny!"

Chrissie walked to the kirk on her father's arm, with Bessie following. It felt strange, like a Sunday, yet it was a working day. Danny had been given the whole day off for the wedding.

Entering the kirk, Chrissie saw that Danny's side was packed with well-wishers. Her own turn-out was sparse, with only her brothers and their wives, and wee Hughie and Georgina.

And Harriet was there, of course. Her friend turned and smiled her wide, friendly, joyful smile at Chrissie as her father brought her down the aisle. Chrissie's heart soared with gratitude.

Then she saw Danny waiting for her before the altar, looking strange and solemn in his best clothes. Their eyes met, and his expression lit up with such joy and love it took her breath away.

She went forward, serene and confident, and the minister began the simple service quietly. Danny Murphy and Christina Kennedy became man and wife, for richer or poorer, for better or for worse.

* * * *

"Man, but it was a lovely service! Did ye no' think so, Mistress Kennedy?"

Bessie had mischievously positioned Patrick Murphy at the table next to Lizzie. Lizzie eyed Patrick warily.

"Yes, indeed. Very moving."

"Aye. Minds me o' the day me an' Biddy got spliced. The lads from the cleansing department made an arch o' brushes for us to walk under. That was a moving moment, I'm tellin' ye!" Patrick said mistily.

"Most – most unusual, Mr Murphy," Lizzie agreed.

"My pa and your snobby sister-in-law are getting along like a house on fire!" Danny whispered to Chrissie with a wicked grin.

Chrissie giggled. Patrick had now launched into the finer points of keeping Dundee's hilly streets clean with so much horse traffic going up and down to the mills. Poor, fastidious Lizzie seemed to have lost her appetite.

The wedding breakfast over, there was no excuse to linger. Danny's relatives prepared to leave with the bride and bridegroom on the tram.

Now the moment of parting had arrived, William Kennedy was overcome with emotion. He hugged his daughter, then turned to Danny.

"You take care of her, now!"

"I will that, Captain Kennedy." The two men shook hands solemnly, in total agreement for once.

Harriet planted herself in front of Chrissie, and the two friends hugged fondly. Chrissie had never seen Harriet cry because her friend was not the weepy kind, but there were tears on her cheeks today.

"You be happy, Chris! And if ever you need me, I'll come – no matter what. Remember that!" Harriet whispered fiercely.

"I'll remember." Chris held her close for a moment, then she was swept away, hanging on to Danny's arm, urged out of the house by the boisterous crowd of Murphys.

Looking over her shoulder, Chrissie saw her father standing alone, outlined against a calm sea. The others stood apart in a group, waving, and she waved back, touched by the support they'd given her – even Lizzie! But it was the image of her father that stayed with her. He looked so lonely . . .

The tram arrived, clanking along, and the conductor's jaw dropped.

"Help ma boab, whit's this? The Band o' Hope?"

"Hold your wheesht, man! It's ten pennies an' six ha'pennies for the Tramway Company." Patrick Murphy counted the lordly sum into the man's hand as his flock scrambled aboard.

Chrissie's spirits lifted, and she laughed happily and enjoyed the riotous journey. They all tumbled off when they reached Lochee. The little village on Balgay Loch had become a sprawl of close-packed tenements around the mills and great towering chimney stack of Cox's Lum.

Biddy hugged her new daughter-in-law.

"Mind now, hen, I'm just a few closes doon the street. You come to me if you need anythin'."

She turned to Danny, and gently ruffled the curly black hair of this, her dearest lad.

"Be good to her, Dan. Be happy, and mind an' carry her over the threshold for luck!"

"I will, Ma." He grinned and kissed his mother.

And so he did. After unlocking the door with a flourish, Danny swept Chrissie up in his arms, and made a play of staggering over the threshold with her slight weight.

When he set her on her feet, they stood hand in hand, looking round the single room that was to be their home.

Danny's spirits dropped to his boots.

"Ach, Chrissie, it's no' near good enough for ye."

Chrissie took him into her arms and kissed him.

"You're good enough for me, my darling, and that's all that matters . . ."

Chapter 8

CHRISSIE wakened with a start on Monday morning. She propped herself sleepily on one elbow and saw that Danny was already up, washed, shaved and dressed in his working clothes.

"Dan, what's that racket?"

"It's the factory. It's time for the first shift."

He came and sat on the edge of the bed. It was built into the wall of their wee room like a cupboard, and had a curtain pulled across for privacy. She stretched out her arms and pulled her husband down to her.

"You really should've wakened me up, Dan!"

"Och, you were sleeping like a bairn." He grinned. "Snoring, too!"

She giggled, kissing his clean-shaven cheek. Danny eased her warm arms gently from his neck and stood up resolutely.

"I'm away now, Chrissie. The fire's lit and the kettle's on the hob. There's fifteen bob saved in the tea caddy. We'll need something for our tea.

"I'll be in for my dinner before the one o'clock gun goes off at Dudhope. A sup o' soup and a bit o' bread'll be enough for me, lass."

Chrissie lay back languorously. She could hear his boots clatter along the stone platform outside and down the stair to join his workmates thronging the street. A man's voice floated up to her, joking.

"You're awfy late the day, Dan! I wonder why you dallied?"

"Ach, the lad's taken a bonnie, gentry wife, lucky deevil!" another added.

She heard Danny reply jauntily, but the words were drowned by the steady tramp of feet heading downhill to the mill. They'd never get the better of Danny!

A gentry wife! Chrissie frowned. Well, she'd show them!

She threw back the covers and climbed out of bed, glad to put her feet on the raggy rug. Her father-in-law, Patrick Murphy, had made it from old rags and given it to them as a wedding gift. At the time she'd thought it an odd jumble of colours, but now she appreciated its cosiness on the bare wooden floor.

She washed and dressed quickly, for even with the fire, the room felt chilly. Danny, bless him, had made enough porridge for two and left a pot of tea on the trivet. There was just enough milk left in the churn to make the strong tea drinkable and wash down the porridge.

Chrissie sat at the table and let out a sigh of pure contentment. She'd keep an ear open for the milk-cart, then go out for the shopping with Danny's fifteen shillings. But first, this place needed a good clean . . .

* * * *

Chrissie was tired, wet and dishevelled by the time she'd scrubbed the floor and washed the window, carrying buckets of water from the tap in the back yard. Even so, she couldn't see much improvement. There were generations of grime ground into the floorboards. If only they could afford a bright, pretty linoleum!

Chrissie refilled the churn at the milk-cart, handing over the last few pennies of her own.

She returned to the room, unnerved. She'd brought only a few serviceable items and dresses with her, but even those seemed out of place. The new neighbours had eyed her and muttered to one another. One had laughed outright!

As a gesture of defiance, she wore the blue suit and flowery hat she'd been married in to go shopping. Lochee folk stopped and stared, and the butcher's jaw dropped when she walked into his shop.

He hastily stubbed out a cigarette.

"What can I do for ye, missus – er, madam?"

"A pound and a half of mince and a marrow bone, if you please."

Mince was easy, Chrissie decided. Bessie had made mouthwatering mince, served with fluffy mashed potatoes. Bessie also made beautiful broth with a marrow bone . . .

Bowed out of the butcher's, she headed for the grocer's.

There was so much her small store-cupboard lacked, Chrissie went quite mad, selecting items at random from the well-stocked shelves.

Beaming, the proprietor stood with pencil poised, ready to tot up her purchases.

"Anything else today, madam?"

"Oh, yes. A stone of potatoes, please." She spoke

triumphantly, with mince and tatties still in mind.

There wasn't much change from the fifteen shillings and Chrissie eyed the heap of groceries with dismay. She'd never carry that!

"I'll send the laddie round with it, madam," the grocer offered. He coughed delicately. "I'm afraid there's a threepenny delivery charge."

Chrissie accepted with relief and handed over a silver threepenny bit. The grocer blinked when she told him the address, but she walked out with her head held high, leaving him staring after her, open-mouthed.

Back home, she found the fire had burned low, so she cheerfully banked it up with coal from the bunker. It began smouldering sulkily, giving off yellow sulphurous smoke that made her cough.

Chrissie sang gaily as she sliced onions and vegetables for the soup. She emptied the whole lot into an iron pot with the marrow bone and a few handfuls of barley. Then she filled it up with water from the jug and swung it over the flames.

Only there weren't any flames. She hovered anxiously over the fire, poking it now and then, but it had still refused to respond when the grocer's little laddie came puffing up the stairs, staggering under the weight of the basket. Chrissie was so worried and abstracted and sorry for him that she sent him away, beaming, with another threepenny bit from Danny's sadly diminished store.

When Danny took the steps two at a time and charged in at dinnertime, he found his wife smeared black with coal dust and reduced to tears.

"Oh, Dan! The broth!"

He lifted the lid of the broth pot, surveyed the watery, greasy, uncooked contents and hastily clamped the lid on again. He turned and took his woebegone wife in his arms.

"Never mind, my dearie, we'll have bread and butter."

"And cheese," Chrissie remembered, brightening up. "I went shopping this morning, Dan. I bought ever such a lot with the fifteen bob." She pointed proudly to a few pennies.

Danny turned pale.

"We were meant to pay the rent and buy coal out of that. The factor'll be here the morn, seeking his siller."

"Oh, Danny, I didn't know! I'm sorry!" She burst into tears.

He kissed and comforted her, and to her amazement, began to chuckle.

"Oh, Chrissie, two days married, and you'd have me skint! Lucky I've got another ten bob hidden under the mattress!"

Danny worked his magic on the fire before he left, and it blazed up. In fact, it blazed up so much that it scorched Chrissie's first attempt at mince and tatties. Dan, who could have eaten a horse when he got home from the mill, declared it was the best meal he had ever tasted, and his Chrissie the finest cook in Lochee.

After the humbling experience, Chrissie laid the wedding suit and hat at the bottom drawer of the dresser and gratefully accepted the shawl Biddy had knitted for her. With the expertise of years, her mother-in-law had lined it with cloth from an old overcoat.

Pulled over Chrissie's head and shoulders and reaching down to her knees, it kept her snug and cosy even in the fiercest winter gale.

At first, the strangeness of her new life occupied most of Chrissie's time. Gradually she adapted, her muscles aching with carrying unaccustomed loads of water and washing.

She mourned silently for her smooth white hands. Now the skin was roughened by washing soda and bars of strong yellow soap, her fingers so chapped with chilblains, she hid her hands beneath the shawl.

But she made friends at the steamie, where clothes could be washed with piping hot water for only a few pennies. Scrubbing away at Danny's oil-stained shirts on the washing-board, Chrissie joined in many a joke with the loud-voiced, raucous women.

At first it seemed that all Lochee women spoke at full pitch of their lungs. Then Chrissie realised they were used to shouting above the din of the looms. They had a well-developed sign language, too, which was expressive, but not always polite.

The women were curious about Chrissie's background, and intrigued when she gave details of Bessie McCutcheon's menu in more affluent days.

"Roast beef an' Yorkshire puddin' on the Sabbath? What swank!" Nellie Cafferty roared as she mangled sheets. "My man disnae look for more than a pie an' a pint."

The shirts and sheets washed and mangled, it was home

again carrying the laden basket. Chrissie grudged pennies to the little lads who hung hopefully round the wash-house door with the constant piping cry: "Humph your washin' for ye, wifie?"

She tried so hard to spin out Danny's wages, but sometimes her back ached sorely as she pegged out the clean washing.

The line ran through a pulley outside her window to the massive wooden pole rising on the green behind the tenements.

The greenie pole, bedecked with its lines of fluttering washing, reminded her of the mast of the *Christina K*. Then she would touch the brooch she always wore, and sometimes the secret tears would fall.

"I'll have to get a job, Danny!" Chrissie announced in desperation.

She was tired of struggling to make ends meet on one wage, and more tired still of looking at the bare walls of their one small room. Most of her neighbours worked all day in the mill, their young bairns left with obliging grannies, and it was lonely.

"No, Chrissie!" Danny's square chin set stubbornly.

Chrissie thought he was being unreasonable and it infuriated her. She'd marched with the suffragettes fighting for votes for women. Why shouldn't she work if she wanted to?

"You can't stop me, Danny Murphy!" she flashed at him.

"Oh, can't I? I'm your husband!"

"You're not my master! I've a will of my own, and I'll do what I think fit!"

"I'll not have you working in the mill!" he shouted back angrily. "Never that. Understand?"

"Who said anything about the mill? I wouldn't work in thon place if you paid me pounds!"

"Too posh, are ye?" Danny growled contrarily. "I suppose you'd rather slave in a shop, or behind a bar counter?"

"Aye, I would!"

Danny suddenly dissolved into disarming chuckles.

"Och, Chrissie, love. I can just see you behind a bar! You'd be preaching temperance in no time. All the drunks would be signing the pledge an' wearing the blue ribbon, 'cause they'd fallen in love with your bonnie face. You'd do better than the Salvation Army, and the boss would kick you out."

Chrissie had laughed, and fallen into his arms, forgetting their quarrel. But she got her way in the end, and by the beginning of February 1908, she'd been taken on as a shop assistant by the grocer.

The hours were long and Chrissie was on her feet all day, but she enjoyed the work. She was nimble-fingered, and was soon weighing sugar and dry stuffs, packaging them in blue paper as neatly as the grocer.

Her wages were small, but enough to buy a few comforts. Danny had slippers on his feet instead of jute rovies as he sat poring over his books in the evenings.

While he worked, Chrissie wrote letters to her family. The

73

writing desk had been Harriet's inspired wedding gift. It contained everything a correspondent might need, and Chrissie loved writing in the beautiful copperplate taught at Miss Black's school.

One freezing night in March, the wind whistling and howling along the plettie outside, Chrissie settled down.

My dearest Ina and Hughie,

Little of note has happened since last I wrote you, my dears, except that I believe I have mastered the art of cheese-cutting!

You use this contraption which has two handles and a wire to embrace the mother cheese, then "wheek!" a sharp pull, and there you have a baby cheese weighing more or less the desired amount, to present to your customer . . .

* * * *

Wee Hughie splashed through mud and slush on the farm road, clutching Chrissie's letter. He couldn't wait to read it to Georgina, who was out at the sheep pens.

Och, this awful road, Hughie thought in disgust. In Dundee you could run on stone pavements. You could take off your boots in summer and run barefoot on warm stone. But in this God-forsaken glen . . .

The snow had been grand to start with, white and sparkling, but there was nobody to throw snowballs or toboggan with except Ina, and she was a girl. If only his friends from Dundee were here. What fun they'd have had!

The snow was getting deeper and deeper so he couldn't get out at all. Hours of boredom followed, all about sheep, cattle and grain.

His dad wanted him to learn farming, but Hughie vowed silently that he never would. The moment he was old enough, he was going to sea!

Georgina was leaning on the dyke by the sheep pens, trying to whistle. Girls never could, somehow.

Tam, the shepherd, was with her, and four sheepdogs lay at his feet. One of the dogs growled at Hughie and Tam shushed it. Hughie kept his distance.

"A letter from Aunt Chrissie, Ina! It's a funny one. I haven't seen Mum and Dad laugh so much for a while!"

Ina smothered her annoyance at her young brother's appearance. She spent hours with Tam, a quiet, restful young man with endless patience. She'd just tried to pen some sheep with her boisterous pup. The results had been disastrous, making Tam laugh.

"You've a lot to learn about running dogs, Miss Ina. You've to learn to whistle first, like this –" He put fingers to his lips and let out a shrill, echoing whistle that made the dogs' ears perk alertly.

"Oh, Tam!" Ina's eyes shone with hero-worship.

She'd been trying to imitate Tam's whistle when Hughie arrived and spoiled her concentration. Still, a letter from Auntie Chrissie was something to be savoured. Ina forgot about the shepherd for the moment.

"We'll read the letter in front of the fire and make cinnamon toast at the same time, shall we? Race you back to the house, Hughie! "

Chapter 9

CHRISSIE'S sister-in-law, Lizzie Kennedy, was expecting again. Harriet had come specially to tell Chrissie the news. Danny was at home, too, that spring holiday, but he made himself scarce when she arrived.

Chrissie seated her friend by the fire, proud to play hostess in her own home.

"It's a pity it's not a better day for the Fast."

Harriet agreed, trying hard not to show how shocked she was by the poky little room and lack of so many comforts.

"Are you happy, Chris?" She gave her friend a keen look.

"Yes – very." Chrissie bent to poke the fire into a brisker flame. "Life's hard – but I'm stronger now, because of what I've seen and done, and the folk I've met, good and bad."

Harriet put her hand on her arm.

"It needn't be. Your father's business is doing well, supplying Rankine's with batching oil. He'd be only too glad to help."

Chrissie turned away. Harriet had unwittingly touched on a point of conflict between Danny and her.

"Papa rarely visits us. He and Danny will never get on. Dan refuses to accept Papa's charity."

"But what if there are children?" Harriet gripped her friend's hands.

Chrissie looked at her.

"There will be – in October or November, God willing."

Harriet hugged her delightedly.

"Oh, Chris! A baby! Danny must accept your father's help now!"

Chrissie shook her head.

"Don't tell Lizzie just yet, will you, Harriet?" she begged anxiously.

They looked at one another, and Harriet nodded. She was a medical student, and knew better than most how precarious her sister's condition was.

* * * *

Lizzie carried her baby for seven months, then lost him. She nearly lost her life as well, and the surgeon attending the new maternity wards at the Eastern Hospital decided enough was enough. Lizzie would never have another pregnancy.

When Harriet tiptoed in to see her, Lizzie lay very straight and still, staring at the ceiling.

"How are you, love?" Harriet kissed her cheek.

Her sister didn't speak right away. Then her voice was harsh as she answered with another question.

"Christina's expecting a baby, isn't she?"

"Why, yes, dear, but how did you –?" Harriet was flustered.

"I saw her walking in Lochee. She didn't see me, but I knew right away." Lizzie turned to face her sister.

"She humiliated Charles Rankine and went off and married a juteworker, yet she's to be blessed with a child. Arthur and I will never have the baby we longed for now. It isn't fair!"

Tears stood bright in her eyes and Harriet felt like weeping, too. But what good would that do? It was more important for Lizzie to look ahead.

"Lizzie, dear, there are many little children in need of a loving home. You could maybe try adopting . . . ?"

"A child with unknown vices – a stranger's baby? Never!"

Harriet lifted her shoulders helplessly.

"Then I don't know how to help you, Lizzie."

Lizzie turned her face away.

"I'm strong, Harriet. I'll survive. But I'll not visit Christina."

Charles Rankine met Chrissie by chance. He had deliberately avoided Lochee, only to bump into her in Dundee's Nethergate. The shock took his breath away. Carefully controlled emotions surfaced and he could hardly speak. He still loved her as fiercely as ever.

She stepped back, smiling with surprise and genuine pleasure, and he noted for the first time the thickening of her waistline beneath the concealing shawl. This might have been his child . . . Quickly he smothered his aching sorrow.

"I hope you are well, Chrissie?" he said.

"Very well, Charles." She laughed softly. "Blooming, as they say!"

But she looked so tired . . . and so pale . . . Charles dropped all pretence at formality.

"Chrissie, can I help you? Just tell me if there's anything I can do...and I'll do it!" he offered earnestly.

She studied him gravely.

"Thank you, Charles, but I have a husband. Danny's a hardworking lad – and I have work myself. I've an errand to see to at the Overgate for my employer."

She was obviously amused, her eyes twinkling.

"Charles, it's not an illness, having a bairn. I'll work as long as I'm able. We need the wage more than ever now."

He blinked. This was a very different Chrissie from the girl he'd courted. This woman had pride and independence.

"You've changed, Chrissie. Do you still march with the suffragettes?"

She laughed.

"Och, no! I'm too busy earning my right to vote. I leave the campaigning to Harriet and the other ladies."

"Ladies? They're a militant bunch!" Charles said. "Poor Winston Churchill had a hard time in the by-election. Did you know one rang a muffin bell repeatedly when he tried to speak? Mr Churchill was not amused!"

"It wasn't polite." Chrissie nodded. "Still, he was elected."

"Yes, he seems quite an able man — and as a Liberal, he . . ." He paused, for she was fidgeting to be on her way.

"I won't detain you, Chrissie. It has given me great pleasure to see you again," he said sincerely.

"Goodbye, Charles." Her blue eyes were warm and friendly as she touched his arm lightly, then hurried off.

He watched her until she turned the corner into Thorter's Row. She had scorned his offer, but there were other ways of helping, Charles thought. Devious ways, perhaps, but they would be just as effective.

Chapter 10

BESSIE McCUTCHEON looked at Danny and jerked a thumb towards the door.

"Away to your ma, Danny."

"No. I'll bide!" He folded his arms across his chest.

"Danny, I'll no' have ye in here getting under my feet." Bessie turned beetroot red. "Away to your ma, I said!"

"It's my bairn as much as Chrissie's. I want to be with her," he insisted stubbornly.

Bessie gave him a long, aggravated look, then sighed.

"Well, keep out of my way, mind!" She thrust an empty bucket at him. "Here, make yourself useful. Away to the tap and fill this. We'll need plenty of hot water."

Danny worked obediently all that long, fraught Sunday afternoon, and Bessie had no complaint of him. He held Chrissie's hand when the pains were bad, and kept his suffering to himself.

It was evening, the gas lamp hissing in the small, hot room, when Bessie washed Chrissie's baby and wrapped the tiny mite in flannel and handed the bundle to Danny.

"Hold your little lass, while the doctor sees to Chrissie."

He looked down at a tiny face surmounted by a thatch of black hair like his own. The baby opened blue eyes, and he swore she recognised him and smiled. Danny Murphy bent his head and kissed his daughter, and a tear dropped upon her perfect cheek.

"Alexandra. That's what we'll call her, Chrissie!" Danny declared later.

Now that all the excitement was over, Bessie dozed, exhausted, in the armchair. They examined their new daughter with breathless wonder, as she lay sound asleep in the crook of her mother's arm.

"It's an awful big name for a wee scrap, Danny!" Chrissie laughed.

"D'you mind the day Queen Alexandra came to Dundee, Chris? The day I won you fair and square from Rankine? I watched her step from the train . . . so stately . . . I've never forgotten. I want my daughter to be named for the Queen."

Chrissie lay and looked at him, seeing the tears and the emotion he couldn't hide. She always loved him for his strength, but she loved him then, as never before, for his weakness.

* * * *

Alexandra was barely a month old when Danny came racing home one freezing November night. He burst into the room and grabbed Chrissie by the waist, birling her round.

"Dan, Dan!" she protested, laughing. "What's up?"

"Promotion!" he cried. "We're really on the climb now, Chrissie! All the hard graft has got me noticed at last!

"There's a vacancy in the weaving shed. I'm to be on probation for a while, but if I do well it's permanent! What d'you say to that, Mrs Murphy?" He was bursting with pride.

She put her arms round his neck and kissed him.

"I say it's well deserved, Dan, for the work you've put in. They must've had an eye on you all this time!"

"I was beginning to think studying was a waste of time!" Dan beamed. He couldn't keep still, striding about the room. "I'm to get a grand wage, Chris!

"First thing, we'll get out o' here!" He looked around, curling his nose distastefully. "We can afford better than this. I'll be chapping on the factor's door first thing the morn!"

Chrissie viewed the little room with mixed feelings. She'd hated it at first, but now it was home. They had their ups and downs, but they'd been happy here.

They moved a month later to a tenement flat in Liff Road, approved by Danny because there was a school handy.

It had two rooms and a boxroom with a skylight, which served as Alexandra's nursery. It also had a tiny scullery containing a sink and a tap, and Chrissie no longer had to carry water up the stairs. There was no prouder man in Dundee than Danny Murphy, as he filled the kettle at his own tap and set it on the hob to boil.

William Kennedy paid a visit to view his new granddaughter shortly after the move, accompanied by his two sons, Arthur and Ernest.

"By Jove, she's a wee charmer, Chrissie!" Arthur was boisterously jovial, trying to make up for the absence of his wife. Lizzie had refused to come, despite all Arthur's coaxing.

"She's her father's double!" Ernest remarked, then wished

he hadn't. William Kennedy stared at him stonily.

William had become taciturn since Chrissie's departure. The decline of the whaling industry continued, and although he still sailed with the diminished fleet, it was Arthur, the businessman, who had secured alternative supplies of batching oil to honour the contract with Rankine's.

He'd also branched out into handling more lucrative shipments of Baltic timber. The Kennedys were doing well enough.

William stomped over to the crib and peered in. The baby stared up at him curiously, then smiled and waved her tiny hands. A little spark of joy flared in William's heart.

He fished in his pocket and brought out a gold sovereign. He placed it on the baby's palm, and watched the little fist close tight over it!

William looked up and met Danny's eye.

"That's no' charity, Danny Murphy. It's the bairn's gift, man. You can't refuse that!"

Danny laughed.

"It'll go into the bank for her, Mr Kennedy, and thank ye kindly. I've been thinking of opening an account for the wee lass, and that's a braw start to it!"

* * * *

Danny settled down to the foreman's job. He stood no nonsense from the weavers, yet they liked and respected him for his good humour and sense of fair play. His appointment was made official in due course, and there were strong hints of further promotion.

It seemed to Chrissie anything Danny Murphy turned his hand to must succeed.

A near riot outside the Kinnaird Hall to further the suffragette cause resulted in a strengthening of the Dundee Volunteers, and Danny was made a sergeant. He swelled with pride and happiness, coming home to his toddling daughter, birling her round in his arms while she screamed for joy.

Sometimes, though, Chrissie experienced a pang of jealousy when she watched the two of them together. With their black curly hair and blue eyes, father and daughter were so alike, she felt a bit excluded. And Alexandra worshipped her father, pushing her mother aside to run to him.

Chrissie was delighted to find she was expecting another baby. Chrissie and Danny's second daughter was born on the day of King George V and Queen Mary's coronation in 1911. The streets were a sight to be seen with fluttering royal flags and bunting.

Danny laughed joyfully when he held his second wee lass.

"Chrissie, my darling, this one has to be Mary."

He placed the small bundle in Chrissie's arms and she examined her baby lovingly. Unlike Alexandra, this wee mite had a fuzz of fair hair, and a crumpled pink face just like a little rosebud.

"She's so beautiful . . . Let's call her Mary Rose," Chrissie said.

Chapter 11

THEY were busy, happy years for Chrissie and Danny as their two little lasses grew. Alexandra and Mary Rose were much admired as they played together in the back court, the one so dark-haired, blue eyes sparkling with mischief, the other fair and quiet, with shy, thoughtful, smoky-grey eyes.

Chrissie had little time to spare to glance in the mirror, but she still caused heads to turn when she got dressed up to board the tram for Dundee.

The town itself had changed to accommodate an increase in traffic. The old Cowgate had been widened for the trams that vied with steady streams of horses and carts plying to and fro between the mills and the harbour. Chrissie noted with pleasure that the tramlines aided the horses labouring up Dundee hills, for the cart wheels fitted exactly!

To Chrissie and Danny, the warring Balkans seemed very far away, and the assassination of the heir to the the Austrian throne and his poor wife, while shocking, was far distant from the busy jute mills of Dundee. Then, suddenly, the name of Kaiser Wilhelm of Germany was on everybody's lips.

On August 4, 1914, Mr Asquith, the Liberal Prime Minister, announced to the nation that they were at war with Germany . . .

Chrissie hugged Danny, frightened and worried. There

were posters everywhere with Lord Kitchener's commanding countenance, his finger pointing, ordering young men to join his army.

"Oh, Danny, you won't have to go."

He laughed and kissed her.

"No, my dearie, I'm needed in the mill. The manager says I'll be in a reserved occupation, especially as he's retiring. Jute cloth'll be needed as never before, and we'll be working flat out. Wars are aye profitable for the jute trade!"

He looked regretful.

"Mind you, lass, I'd have liked a crack at Kaiser Bill. The cheek of the man, thinking he can walk into Paris! Our lads will stop him, though!"

Alexandra wormed her way between her two parents to show her father the satchel Chrissie had bought for her first day at Liff Road School. She could hardly wait to get started.

"So you're to be a big schoolgirl! You'll no' need your daddy now, Sandra!" Danny ruffled his daughter's hair fondly.

"I will so need my daddy, even though I'm big! You're not to go fighting Kaiser Bill, Da!" She flung her arms round his knees passionately to keep him trapped.

Mary Rose came through from the scullery to see what all the stushie was about. She watched solemnly, thumb in mouth. Danny picked her up and kissed her rosy cheek.

"Och, it would take a team o' horses to drag me away from my three bonnie lassies!"

Chrissie was reassured. She watched recruiting sergeants visit the town, and admired their smartness and swinging kilts with an easy mind, because they posed no threat.

A patriotic fervour followed the soldiers, and more men volunteered. Dundee folk were singing war songs in the music halls and in the streets, cheery, marching tunes that lingered in your head. It was September, just after the Kaiser's soldiers had been repulsed at the Battle of the Marne, and Chrissie was preparing to write to Harriet. Her friend was a fully fledged doctor now, but her last letter had been rueful, sent from a far-off hamlet in Caithness.

I am an embarrassment to the established medical profession because I am a woman, Chris. They have tried to sweep me under the rug, sending me here, Harriet wrote. *I will prevail, however. Do not fear!*

Chrissie smiled. She had no doubt Harriet would do just that!

She had just put pen to paper when she heard Danny's step on the stair outside. He burst in so wildly she started to her feet.

"Dan, wheesht – the bairns are sleeping!"

Then she saw his face. Her heart almost stopped beating.

"Oh, Danny, what is it?"

"It's Rankine. Charles Rankine. That's what it is!" He gave her such a look she turned icy cold.

"I don't understand, Dan. What has Charles done?"

"Only made me accept his charity. All these years!" He thrust Chrissie aside and began pacing the room.

"I told you the mill manager was retiring. Well, I had a wee dram with him in his buckie last night. More than one, to tell the truth, enough to loosen his tongue. He told me I'd been singled out because Charles Rankine wanted it. He was such a good customer they didn't refuse him!"

"Oh, Dan! Danny!" Chrissie whispered in horror, putting her hands to her cheeks. She knew what a blow this must be to her husband with his fierce pride.

He couldn't keep still, pacing to and fro, clenching a fist as if to strike someone.

"It wasn't all the studying or my skill wi' the engines that earned me promotion – or my quickness at figuring. They never even knew I was there until Mr Rankine pointed me out.

"An' he only did it to keep you in comfort! I can forgive him his fancy for you, but what galls me is that he didn't believe I could support a wife! He wouldn't even give me credit for hard work – he had to interfere with his damned charity!"

Danny crashed his fist angrily on the table. One of the girls roused and wailed sleepily. He paid no attention.

"I'll not stand for it, Chris! I'll not take that man's patronage a day longer. It's the Army for me!"

As he strode to the door, Chrissie came suddenly to life. She raced after him, hanging on his every word, terrified.

"Danny, no! Oh, Danny, let's talk!"

"The time for talking's past, Chris."

His face like stone, he pulled his arm away and gave her a

push that sent her staggering. Then he was out the door and away. She ran after him, screaming, not caring who heard.

"Danny, come back! Please, Danny, listen to me. Come back!"

But she heard his footsteps loud in the close as he hurried off.

Both bairns were awake now and wailing with fright, but Chrissie sank down on the stairs and covered her face with her hands.

* * * *

Eventually Chrissie dried her eyes and went to the frightened children. It took time to settle them. Alexandra kept asking, "When's he coming back?"

"Soon! Go to sleep, Sandra. You'll not be fit for school tomorrow!"

Sandra watched her mother walk away from her. Despite the comforting glow of the nightlight standing in a saucer of water, the little room seemed dark with menace.

She'd never heard her father raise his voice like that before. Even when she'd been naughty she wasn't afraid, but tonight he'd shouted so loudly. She felt chilled and shivered with fear.

Sandra put her arms round her sister, hugging the warm little body close to her. Mary Rose was just three years old, yet she had a calming influence and the icy coldness gradually began to melt.

Clasped in one another's arms, the two sisters drifted off to sleep.

Danny didn't come home that night, although Chrissie sat up waiting until dawn. He returned wearily at dinnertime the next day and slumped in a chair.

"Well, Chris, it's done. The Army took me like a shot. They said I'm just the man they need – a sergeant in the Territorials. They sniggered behind my back, though. The Town Clerk's army, the real soldiers call us. Being a sergeant will count for nothing," he said dully.

"Aw, Danny!" Chrissie hugged him hard. The pride had gone out of her man, and it was Charles Rankine that was responsible! How dare he meddle in their lives!

"I've been to the mill and handed in my notice," Danny went on. "They tried to make me change my mind, but it's too late. I've to report for a medical, then I'll go to the Perth barracks of the Black Watch."

Chrissie couldn't speak. She could only hold him close and comfort him as their happy little world fell apart.

* * * *

More and more men were joining Kitchener's Army. A trainload left with Danny for Perth.

The station had an air of unreality about it that cold day. Chrissie stood on the platform, holding her little girls by the hand, wishing she could waken from this bad dream.

The frosty air reeked of coal smoke from the waiting engine, and steam shrouded everything. Her eyes were bright with unshed tears, but she smiled bravely.

The men were singing, cheerful and excited. It was easier for them, she thought. They had one another to bolster them, but what cheer would there be for the women left behind?

"Don't worry, the war'll soon be over now. The Dundee lads'll give Kaiser Bill a black eye!" one of Danny's companions shouted.

It raised a weak cheer from those standing on the platform and Chrissie glanced anxiously at Sandra. The child had been unusually quiet and withdrawn lately and now her eyes were fixed longingly on Danny. She looked so lost and bewildered that Chrissie forgot her own misery.

"Here, my pet." She lifted Sandra and held her so that Danny could hug his daughter.

"Bye-bye, my wee hen. I'll be home soon, Sandy. You take care o' your mummy for me, mind!" he told her gruffly.

Chrissie then lifted Mary Rose for her father's kiss. The guard was unfurling the little green flag, and Danny and Chrissie looked at one another speechlessly.

The flag waved and the crowd gave a ragged cheer as the train moved off, slowly gathering speed. Danny waved and waved until he could see his wife and bairns no more, then turned away resolutely to face the future.

Chrissie tried to be cheerful for the children's sake. They came out of the station and walked across the road, their feet dragging miserably.

"Do you remember when the King and Queen and Princess Mary came to Dundee, not long ago?" She smiled at them.

Sandra nodded, remembering that warm summer day.

"Daddy had a holiday. We stood in the street and waved flags, and the girls from Keiller's sweetie factory gave

91

Princess Mary caramels."

"Yes. We saw King George and Queen Mary drive past in their carriage, and your daddy said Queen Mary waved specially to Mary Rose."

Chrissie glanced down at her small daughter.

"You're called after Queen Mary, you know, Mary Rose."

"And I'm named for Queen Alexandra!" Sandy put in.

They had reached the corner of the Greenmarket where the old Crown Hotel used to stand. The ancient part of the city called the Vaults was being knocked down to make way for a fine new city hall.

Chrissie pointed to a corner of the wall the stonemasons were working on.

"Look, that's the stone the King and Queen set in place when they visited Dundee."

Mary Rose goggled solemnly and Sandra's jaw dropped.

"They must be awful big an' strong to lift that."

Chrissie laughed.

"No, dear, they pressed a wee button in a jute mill a mile away, and the stone moved into place as if by magic! That's electricity – it's a wonderful thing."

Chrissie recklessly treated them to tea and cream cakes. A justifiable expense, for when they boarded the Lochee tram, the children were smiling and cheerful.

Bairns soon forget, Chrissie thought sadly, as she watched her two little ones laugh and giggle together.

But she was mistaken. Sandra Murphy never forgot the day her father went to war.

Chapter 12

CHRISSIE was forced to go back to work at the grocer's to make ends meet. Biddy Murphy willingly took charge of Mary Rose and Sandra while she worked, and did not refuse the few pennies Chrissie offered her.

"My Patrick's doing fine," Biddy told her daughter-in-law proudly. "He's been put in charge o' the other scaffies in the Dock Street depot. My, but he looks braw these days. He's got an old bowler hat he found on the tip an' a tuppenny Norfolk jacket out o' Raggie Mary's."

"I'm sure he does." Chrissie kept a straight face with effort. "It's very good of you to look after my bairns, Biddy. I don't know what I'd do without you."

Biddy squeezed her arm.

"Och, you'd manage fine, Chris. Besides, it's nice to have bairns to care for, even though I'm nearly run off my legs. My youngest lassie's gone off to be a tram conductress in Glasgow. A man's job for women! Did you ever hear the like?"

Even so, Chrissie didn't like leaving her children. Sandra had more freedom than she considered good for a six-year-old. The child made her own way to Biddy's after school, and Chrissie suspected she did not always go straight to her grandmother's, but ranged around Lochee, exploring its wynds and alleyways.

Sandra, when questioned, buttoned her lip and refused to tell her mother anything. Chrissie secretly despaired and didn't know what to do. Oh, if only Danny were here, she often thought, studying her mutinous daughter anxiously.

The harassed grocer was glad of Chrissie's services as all his young men had volunteered for the Army. He finally recognised she was doing four times the work and paid her another two shillings a week.

* * * *

The letter arrived on Charles Rankine's desk by the afternoon post. He slit open the envelope, then sat staring at its contents. A white feather, the symbol of cowardice.

The sight sickened and angered him. There was no way of fighting back, no way of defending himself. How could he explain to whoever had sent this that the Army had rejected him on medical grounds?

Charles stood up restlessly. If only he had someone who cared for him . . . someone he could talk to . . . this wouldn't hurt so much. He watched the feather flutter from his fingers into the open fire, its pure whiteness shrivelling and turning black, then he strode out of the building, the office staff staring at him in surprise.

There were more cars and lorries on the streets of Dundee now and Charles Rankine's motor caused little interest in Lochee. He parked discreetly in Liff Road, close to the tenement where Chrissie lived, and settled down to wait.

Charles had no clear idea what he would do if he met Chrissie. Perhaps when he saw her he would know . . .

Perhaps just seeing her . . .

He sighed and rubbed his eyes. At least he'd ensured her husband was in a reserved occupation. With Danny safe at home, doing work essential to the war effort, Chrissie and her family would be safe.

It was almost dark when he saw her trailing wearily up the street, holding two bonnie little girls by the hand. His heart lurched and he was out of the car and walking towards her before he realised what he was doing.

Charles stopped in front of Chrissie, blocking her path.

"How are you, Chrissie?" Eagerly, he took in every detail of her appearance. The girlish roundness of her figure and features had fined down, but she was no less beautiful for that. But she was so thin! Didn't she have enough to eat?

She was staring at him, the colour leaving her cheeks. Then her eyes flashed fire and he backed away, startled.

"How dare you come here, Charles!"

He was staggered. What had he done? He gripped her arm.

"I'm sorry – I didn't mean to –"

Indignantly she shook off his hand and pushed past grimly without a word, dragging the children with her. The smaller child looked back over one shoulder curiously.

"Mummy, who's that man? Is he a friend of Daddy's?"

Chrissie's reply floated back to Charles through the chilly darkness.

"No, Mary Rose, he's no friend of ours!"

Chrissie was seething with outrage as she began to cook a meal for herself and the children. The cheek of the man!

What had he hoped to achieve, accosting her? Had he hoped she'd fall into his arms now her man was away at war?

Chrissie dismissed that thought. No, whatever else he might be, Charles Rankine was an honourable man. Watching bacon and eggs in a pan, her temper began to cool.

Perhaps she'd been hasty. Maybe he'd been trying to make amends. He'd obviously been sorely troubled . . .

Chrissie turned the bacon unhappily. Perhaps she should have been kinder. He'd meant his patronage kindly, and kept quiet about it. If it hadn't been for the mill manager blethering, Danny would never have known.

Well, it was too late now. Charles Rankine wouldn't come seeking her company again!

Danny came home on leave, his training finished. He looked very handsome in his uniform, with the dark Black Watch kilt swinging and the red hackle in his bonnet.

Chrissie's heart was bursting with pride. She organised a party for the family, and even Biddy puffed and struggled her way up the stairs, with Patrick heaving from behind.

There were Murphys everywhere, some sitting on the stairhead singing Irish songs soulfully, others spilling out on to the washing green to boot a ball about with the excited bairns. Neighbours joined in, and everyone voted it one of the best homecomings in the history of Lochee.

Lying in bed that night, Chrissie snuggled close to her husband and gave a sigh of pure contentment.

"Oh, Dan, it's so good to have you home!"

He was quiet for a few moments.

"They're sending us to the Front after this, Chris."

"So soon?" Her heart contracted with dread.

He lifted a strand of golden hair lying loosened about her shoulders and put it to his lips.

"They tell me I'm a good soldier. I've been thinking that's maybe the way to get on. How d'you fancy being a regular's wife once this war's over?"

"If that's what you want."

"Aye, it is. I won't go back to the mills, Chris," he said with the familiar determined lift of the chin.

He kissed her, his mouth warm on hers.

"Another thing I want, sweetheart, is a son. Another Danny – only brainier, and not so ready to fly off the handle when his pride's dunted!"

"Och, Dan!" She laughed, her eyes shining brightly. "We could fill the house with lassies looking for a lad!"

He held her close, smiling.

"Why not? We're young, Chris. The war'll soon be over, and then I'll be back. There's years ahead of us!" Danny said confidently.

* * * *

Sandra felt as if she was walking on air. Her daddy was home.

Folk turned in the street to admire him in the kilt, with the proud red hackle in his hat. Ladies smiled at him in the tram, and old men clapped him on the shoulder, and told him to give Kaiser Bill a good punch on the nose.

"Come on, we'll away to Broughty Ferry and visit your

Grandpa Kennedy," Danny announced one Sunday near the end of his leave.

Sandra wasn't keen, but her mother looked even more reluctant.

"Should we, Danny? Papa hasn't been near us since the row over Sandra's schooling."

Sandra pricked up her ears. Her father laughed.

"As if I'd send my lassies to a dame school, and let your father pay for it! They'll learn more about real life from Lochee lads and lassies. It's high time Captain Kennedy came out of the huff!"

William Kennedy was dozing when Bessie came rushing into the parlour in a terrible flap, forgetting even to knock.

"They're coming, Captain Kennedy! They're walking up the path!"

"Who? The Germans?" He sat bolt upright.

Bessie looked disgusted.

"Och, now! I'd no get excited about them! It's Chrissie and Danny and the bairns, Captain."

"No!" Smoothing out his ruffled hair with hand, he hurried into the hallway and opened the door. There she was, his little lass, bonnier than ever.

He held out his arms, and Chrissie ran into them.

When they were all settled in the parlour round the tea-trolley, his two grandchildren sitting on the rug at his feet, William took cautious stock of his son-in-law.

The lad was making Bessie laugh as she poured the tea. He looked very handsome in uniform, William had to admit. He wore the kilt well – he wasn't bandy legged, like some . . .

"Aye, well, Danny, you'll soon be off again?" he asked gruffly.

"Aye," Danny said with a wink at his wife. "They've been holding up the war till I get there. Kaiser Bill won't stand a chance now!"

Chrissie smiled bravely at her husband. William could only admire her loyalty to the man who'd brought her low.

Her clothes were spotlessly clean, but well-worn. The bairns wore new red velvet dresses, white pinnies trimmed with lace and bonnets decked with flowers. Chrissie's self-sacrifice brought a lump to his throat.

He stood up and went to the window, filling his pipe from the tobacco pouch, keeping his back turned to them.

"I've something to tell ye, Chrissie. I should have discussed it with you first, but it was taken out of my hands. I'm just a done old man. It's Arthur that's the boss now."

"How is he – and Lizzie, Papa? I haven't seen her since Mary Rose was born."

"Och, she's fine. Arthur's got a good enough head on his shoulders and Ernest keeps the books, but Lizzie wears the breeks. She's aye poking her nose into the business. It's an awful pity she couldn't –" He paused and sighed.

"Och, well, poor Lizzie," he added more gently. He braced himself and turned round. "The long and the short of it is, Chrissie, they've sold your ship."

"Papa, no!" Her hand shot to the brooch on her blouse.

"I'm afraid so. The *Christina K* is on the Newfoundland

register now. The war's finished the Dundee whaling industry for good, Chrissie. It's fortunate Arthur had the sense to turn to other cargoes years ago."

William sighed and pulled at his pipe. The Kennedy firm was doing quite nicely – but it wasn't like the good old days.

Chrissie's eyes filled with tears. Newfoundland! So far away . . . She'd never see her ship come sailing proudly up the Tay again . . .

Chrissie ducked her head in case Danny noted her sorrow. He'd think she was daft, bubbling over a boat.

William, watching his daughter keenly through a cloud of pipe-smoke, saw her distress and understood.

"I can add an' take away, an' next week we're starting to multiply, Grandpa!" Sandra chimed in.

Her grandfather's expression softened.

"My, but wee lassies are getting awfy brainy these days!"

"It's a grand school, Liff Road. Sandra's very bright, the teacher says." Danny couldn't resist the dig.

"There's more to being a lady than book learning, Danny Murphy!" William scowled darkly.

"A lady? Huh!" Danny said scathingly.

"Can I pour you another cup of tea, Papa? Danny, have one of Bessie's scones, they're scrumptious!" Chrissie intervened hastily, shoving the plate at her husband with a warning glance.

It was no good, she thought. Danny and her father would never get on.

Chapter 13

ANOTHER parting. How could she bear it? Chrissie was growing to hate the station and the huge steaming engine that waited impatiently to carry her man away.

"Have you got your sandwiches, Danny?" she asked as he leaned out of the carriage window after getting on the train. Their farewell embrace had been short but, oh, so sweet . . .

"Aye, lass. They're in my kitbag for later."

"Pack up a sandwich in your old kitbag, an' smile, smile, smile!" Mary Rose trilled suddenly.

They all laughed uproariously, a welcome relief.

Danny looked at Chrissie. He never tired of looking at her. He wasn't much of a hand at writing letters, nor at speaking about his feelings, but, oh, how he loved her!

He hadn't told her so for a good while. He could only look at her and hope that she knew.

She did. Chrissie caught her breath at the love blazing in her husband's eyes. She reached up and held his hands. She wanted to tell him how much she loved him, but there were people watching and listening.

"Mind and wear the warm socks your mother knitted, Dan. And the balaclava and scarf, when it's cold," she said.

"Aye, Chris, I will that." He nodded dutifully.

"Hey wifie, stand clear!" the guard warned, raising the whistle to his lips, his flag poised.

The train jolted, and Danny released her hands. Chrissie could hardly see him through a blur of tears, but she kept smiling. She wanted him to remember her smiling . . .

She smiled and waved until the last carriage disappeared down the track, then covered her face with her hands. Somebody kicked her ankle. She turned to find Sandra glaring at her.

"You didn't let me say goodbye to my daddy! You stood there blethering about his silly socks!"

"Sandra – I'm sorry." Chrissie didn't know what else to say. How could she explain to a child the pain of loving a man? How could she make her understand the emotions hidden behind ordinary words?

Mary Rose looked from one to the other. There were bad feelings between the two people she loved. Her lower lip trembled, great tears welled up and spilled down her cheeks, and she bawled loudly.

Once again, Mary Rose had saved the situation. Sandra turned to her sister with a sympathetic cry and hugged her.

Then their mother bought them each a penny bar of chocolate out of the machine on the platform, and they went home to a silent house.

* * * *

"Drat!" Harriet Bowers had made a blot on her letter to Chrissie. She mopped it up with blotting paper and chewed the end of the pen as she read over what she'd written.

You'll never believe it, Chris, but I'm in Dover. I'm waiting to embark for France with a group of stiff and starchy

*nursing sisters and a giggling gaggle of raw little VADs
– members of the Women's Voluntary Aid Detachment – Red
Cross, to you! I can't tell you where I'm going, of course, but
I'm off to do a worthwhile job at last!*

*The folk of Caithness, bless 'em, are extremely healthy,
and I doubt if I'll be missed. Doctors are badly needed in
France, even women doctors, and when I offered my
services, I was snapped up right away.*

*It's been all hustle and bustle since then, Chrissie, dear,
with no time to visit Dundee and say goodbye. I was given a
short training course in London, then received my orders.*

If you see Charles –

That's where the blot formed, like a tear. No time to say
goodbye to Charles. No time to tell him how she loved him.
War intensified feelings, speeded everything to a frantic
haste, so that vital words were left unspoken for ever.

Harriet dipped the pen in the inkpot.

If you see Charles, give him my warmest regards, she
wrote.

Shortly after receiving Harriet's letter, Chrissie had a
visitor, a stylish young lady with the rosy cheeks of a
country woman. Chrissie opened her arms with a cry of
recognition. They hugged, then Chrissie held her niece away
from her, smiling admiringly.

"Oh, Ina, how bonnie you are— quite the young lady. And
so fashionable. A short dress really shows off pretty ankles!"

"Not really! Ina pouted. Fine feathers don't make good
hens, Auntie Chris! I hate the town."

Chrissie seated Ina by the fire and looked at her with amusement.

"Why come to Dundee, then?"

"It wasn't my idea." Ina grimaced. "Daddy wants me to learn typewriting and Sir Isaac Pitman's squiggles. He says that's the way for women to get on. He's arranged for me to stay with Grandpa Kennedy while I do the course. He says I could earn thirty shillings a week as a secretary."

"That's a fortune!" Chrissie's jaw dropped.

Ina looked glum.

"Maybe, but I don't want to do it, Auntie Chris. I didn't want to hurt Daddy by refusing point blank, but I wish I could convince him that I want to be a farmer! Instead, he's trying to turn poor Hughie into one, and he hates it. He's terrified of cows and hates getting his mud on his boots."

Ina couldn't resist a giggle at that point.

"Poor wee Hughie!" Chrissie smiled.

Ina sighed.

"Hughie would be perfectly happy in Dundee. All he wants is to go to sea. Dad'll not let him, though.

"Since the old farmer died and left the farm to his nephew in Australia, Dad's been in sole charge. He needs somebody to help him, but there's Mum and me and old Eck and – and Tam, of course." Her colour heightened.

"Who's Tam?" Chrissie asked with interest.

"Tam's a wonderful shepherd, Auntie Chris. You should see him with the dogs, out on the hill. He's quiet and thoughtful, and, oh – so caring and nice."

Chrissie was beginning to understand why her brother had sent his daughter to Dundee! George hoped she'd meet more eligible men there, who'd drive all thought of the gentle shepherd out of her head.

Ina had been studying her aunt. Auntie Chris was still lovely, but too thin, and there were dark smudges beneath her eyes.

"How are you, Auntie Chris? You look tired," she ventured.

"Oh, I'm fine!" Chris laughed. "I'm always a bit tired at first when I'm expecting a bairn. It'll pass in time, then I'll be as right as rain."

She tried to make light of the dragging exhaustion and nausea that plagued her this time. The grocer had noticed, and warned her that if she didn't buck up there would soon be someone else after her job.

"Oh, I didn't know about the baby!" Ina hugged her. "Are you hoping for a boy this time, Auntie Chris?"

"Danny's got his heart set on one, but I –" She turned away, weariness overcoming her for a moment. "I don't care one way or the other, so long as the bairn's healthy."

Not long after Ina's visit to Chrissie, Hughie finally decided to do something about his unhappiness.

"Thanks!" Hughie got down from the cart that had brought him from Perth, and generously handed the driver a shilling. The driver grinned and urged the horse on, and Hughie was left standing in Dundee's Nethergate.

Och, it was great to have cobbles beneath your boots

again! He crossed the road, the tackets in his boots making a cheery clatter. He'd done it, he'd got away from the farm.

It was good of the McGregor boys to enter so wholeheartedly into his plan, Hughie thought gratefully as he made his way towards the docks. His father had been pleased when he'd begged to go to Perth market with them.

Poor Dad, Hughie thought contritely. He'd believed his son had come round to farming at last, now that he was fourteen and old enough to leave school. But Hughie knew that he could never be a farmer.

That's why he'd decided to run away to sea. He'd write to his dad and mum as soon as he could and try to explain how the sea kept calling him, and wouldn't let him settle.

Hughie rounded the corner where the Greenmarket was. He had happy memories of fairs there, with roundabouts and sideshows.

He stopped dead. It was all changed! The old houses had gone and a big wall had sprung up, narrowing the open space. He passed the horse trough and went under the Royal Arch built for Queen Victoria years ago.

He put a hand on the stout stonework and grinned up at the towering archway, its crevices liberally streaked with white bird droppings. Pigeon's Palace, they called it! At least they couldn't change this famous landmark! Whistling cheerfully, Hughie headed for the wharf where the ships berthed . . .

* * * *

They said France was a bonnie country, but this part of it certainly wasn't! Danny looked around him at the sea of

106

mud and broken stumps of trees. The trenches weren't one orderly line, as he'd imagined; they were like rabbit warrens zig-zagging here and there.

It was almost dawn and nobody had had much sleep that night because of the furious bombardment the artillery was putting up, softening the German defences.

One of the old soldiers threw a Woodbine stub into the mud beside the catwalk, and grinned at Danny.

"Jerry'll be keeping his head well down. D'you think this is the Big Push at last, Corp?"

Danny had two stripes on his sleeve. The Army had its eye on him, and he was on the climb again. He smiled.

"Aye, it could be. We're going over the top, that's for sure." All round them, men were mustered and ready.

He thought about Chrissie. It was a strange place to be thinking about a woman with her golden hair lying loose around her shoulders and a tender smile on her lips!

"I hope it's the Big Show!" the old soldier was saying. "I'm sick o' filling sandbags day after day. "Are – are you scared, Corporal?" the boy asked tremulously.

"I'd be daft if I wasn't, son!" Danny answered, and the boy smiled at him, comforted.

The bombardment ceased, and the silence was uncanny. There were streaks of light in the sky and a grey concealing mist lying over No Man's Land. Whistles started blowing furiously, all along the line.

Danny grinned at his men.

"This is it, lads. Good luck." With one hand on the ladder

leading out of the trench, he paused and smiled at the white-faced youth.

"Stay behind me, laddie. You'll be all right."

* * * *

As the fighting went on remorselessly in France, Chrissie was ill again.

Yesterday she'd dragged herself to work, but today it was beyond her strength to creep down the stairs. She wrote a note for Sandra to hand in to the grocer's on her way to school, and prayed that the man's patience wouldn't snap.

She was over seven months gone now. If only she could keep working till the baby was born! Food prices kept going up and up, and her pay was docked for every day she missed. With the price of a small loaf risen to fourpence, Chrissie was sometimes at her wits' end to feed her family. She saw the girls off, hand in hand. Sandra would take her sister to their granny's and then go on to school.

She poured another cup of tea, and listened to the utter silence in the house. It seemed more quiet than usual today, with the only noise footsteps coming up the stairs. They stopped outside, and there was a brisk tap on the door.

Chrissie eased herself out of the chair and went to answer the summons. She stared stupidly at the laddie holding the telegram. He held the envelope out to her.

"Are you Mrs Murphy?"

She nodded and took it. She still had a silly smile fixed on her lips as her slow fingers fumbled to open it. The words made no sense at first . . . then they seemed to bore painfully into her head.

Danny had been killed in action.

"No!" She shook her head at the boy. "No. There must be some mistake. Not Danny. He said he would come back!"

Chrissie's voice had risen and the boy stepped back nervously. He hated this job, and it fell to him all too often these days.

Chrissie's neighbours on the stair were alerted by her cries. The kindly women came running and led her gently inside, the telegram still clutched in her hand.

"There, there, hen. You have a nice hot cup o' tea," they advised, ladling in plenty of sugar.

She stared at them, a hand held to her aching back.

"Not Danny. He said he'd come back," she said again. "It can't be Danny, can it?"

The women looked at one another.

"Lassie, come and lie yourself down. We'll send for Bessie McCutcheon to see to ye. We'll bide until she comes," one of them said kindly.

She let them lead her to the bed she'd shared with Danny, and made no protest when they undressed her and made her comfy in her nightie. They sat with her patiently, these kind, busy women who had plenty of work of their own to see to.

Chrissie was hardly aware of their presence. She lay numb and quiet until a sudden sharp pain roused her.

The baby that Danny Murphy would never see would be born that day, in sorrow and much too early. Chrissie buried her face in the pillow and, at last, began to weep . . .

Chapter 14

DANNY'S son was born that cold November night. Afterwards, Chrissie drifted into a stupor of grief and exhaustion. Bessie marvelled as she tended to the baby – she'd never seen one so incredibly tiny . . .

The doctor pursed his lips doubtfully.

"He'll need special care. I doubt his mother's in a fit state to give it. She's undernourished, and with her man gone, life'll not be easy. It might be better if –"

He stopped and glanced uncomfortably at the tiny baby in the crib.

"He's maybe wee, but he'll fight," Bessie said staunchly. "All the Murphys are fighters."

"Aye – well." The doctor lifted Chrissie's thin wrist and took the pulse, frowning.

"She should never have been working these past months."

"The poor lass had no choice." Bessie sighed. "Danny was so proud of this flat, but she couldn't keep it on with the rent rising and only her allowance as a soldier's wife coming in."

The doctor looked sceptical.

"Her father's well off, isn't he?"

Bessie sighed again.

"She has her pride, doctor. Asking her pa for help would have reflected badly on her man – and the captain never wanted her to marry my nephew. Aw, poor Danny!" She dabbed her eyes with a corner of her apron.

The doctor patted her shoulder awkwardly.

"I've given her something to make her sleep. I'll be in again in the morning. In the meantime, try to keep the baby warm."

He glanced into the crib again.

"I've a feeding bottle, glucose and powdered milk in my motor car. Try and get him to feed. If not, then, I'm afraid –" He broke off and shrugged eloquently.

Chrissie drifted gradually back to reality after hours of oblivion. It was a painful reality, but it finally brought acceptance of Danny's death.

The room was hushed, and she turned her head in sudden fear. Bessie was dozing by the fire.

"Where's the baby?"

Bessie was by her side in an instant.

"He's sleeping, Chris. He's smaller than a rabbit, but he's fighting. He sucked at the bottle like a real Murphy!"

Chrissie levered herself up.

"I want to see him."

How weak she was! Bessie had almost to carry her to the crib.

And there he was, Danny's son.

Chrissie thought she had no tears left, but she cried again now. She cried helplessly, afraid she had neither the strength nor the means to give their son the care he needed.

She reached out and touched his soft cheek, her heart filled with a deep and tender love.

"Samuel. That's a good name, isn't it, Bessie?" she said softly. The name had come to her unbidden, but she was certain Danny would have approved.

"It's a grand name, dear. Samuel Murphy has a proud sound." Bessie's face split into a beaming smile.

For days, the baby's life hung in the balance. He lost precious weight, although the doctor assured Chrissie that was to be expected with premature babies.

When Chrissie was on her feet again, she sent Bessie away, despite her protests. Alone, Chrissie concentrated on fighting for her son's life.

Biddy Murphy, bless her, had put aside sorrowing for her son and was caring, day and night, for Danny's two bewildered lasses, leaving Chrissie free to look after the frail baby.

Sammy was a week old and still clinging grimly to life when Chrissie had a visitor. She answered a tap on the door and found her father standing on the doormat.

Once she would have flung herself into his arms. Now, sorrow and adversity had given her dignity. William Kennedy's eyes misted.

"How are you, my dear?"

"I'm well, thank you, Papa." Her lips brushed his cheek, then she stood back, inviting him in.

He accepted awkwardly, looking about him. The tenement flat was spotlessly clean, but it lacked so many comforts . . .

He stood in the middle of the room. It was warm, the fire blazing from coals heaped on it.

"I was much saddened to hear about Danny, my love. One more terrible tragedy," William said gruffly.

"Yes, I'm not the only one mourning today, Papa."

William crossed to the crib and peeped in. He was shocked at the frailness of the tiny baby.

"Chrissie –" He turned to his daughter urgently. "This is no place for an ailing bairn. He needs special care. Come home where you belong – and bring your girls with you. I'd welcome you all gladly."

She stiffened.

"You forget – this is my home, Papa. My husband's home. I prefer to stay here."

William saw he'd offended her. He shouldn't have criticised the place, but he was an old sailor, used to speaking bluntly! He blustered on.

"Don't I have a say in the welfare o' my grandchildren? Och, this is no time for pride, lass!"

Her blue eyes blazed fiercely.

"Oh, yes, it is a time for pride! My man gave his life for his country, but you still think he wasn't good enough for me? You've always despised Danny – and his family. If I'd married Charles Rankine and his money you could have boasted about your fine son-in-law then!"

"Chrissie, please –" William backed away before the onslaught.

She spread her arms.

"This is my home, Papa. Don't you ever forget it!"

William had his pride, too, and his temper was roused. He

glared at his daughter.

"Very well, you've made your choice and I'll abide by it. I'll not come again, Chrissie!"

Chrissie wasn't angry any more. She leaned weakly on the table, filled with remorse yet unable to take back a single word. What she'd said was only too true – and her father knew it.

William went quickly to the doorway, then hesitated for one last, worried look at the crib. Such a wee bairn . . . part of himself. Tears of anguish choked him, hard and painful after the anger. He bowed his head, afraid she might see his suffering.

"Goodbye, Christina."

Chrissie stood motionless. Once, she could have run into his arms and he would have made everything right for her. Not any more. She had changed too much— and so had he.

She noticed for the first time how old her father looked. Careworn . . . the keen light gone from his tired eyes . . . the broad shoulders hunched . . .

With deepening distress, Chrissie realised she couldn't let him go like this, saddened and bitter. Somehow she must make him understand what her home meant to her. Perhaps, then, she would have some comfort.

"Papa, wait!"

He turned at once, his face alight with hope.

"Chrissie – are you coming with me?"

The room blurred as she shook her head. The cheap oilcloth on the table was cold to touch despite its bright colours. Her fingers caressed it.

Danny had laughed when he presented the oilcloth on her birthday.

"I canna afford red roses, Chris, but these roses will never fade."

A wave of desolation washed over her.

"No, Papa, I've not changed my mind. This is my home."

She looked around the room, tears running unashamedly down her cheeks. The photo of Dan in uniform stood proudly on the mantelpiece. He seemed to smile approval. She reached out and lifted it and held it close to her heart.

"Everywhere I look . . . everything I touch, holds a memory of Danny," she said softly. "And memories are all I have left now. So don't ask me to leave, because I can't. My memories are the only comfort I have."

Hope died in William as he listened – and understood at last. He'd loved his wife dearly, and still mourned her in the shabby old house he stubbornly refused to leave.

He summoned up a shaky smile.

"Very well, Chrissie."

This time he didn't hesitate. He went out quickly, closing the door behind him.

Chrissie listened to his footsteps going downstairs, faltering a little at the turn where the gaslight was dim. Then she let out a sigh that sounded more like a groan and crossed to the window.

Outside, she watched her father walk away heavily, like an old man, into the grey, smoky chill of the November twilight. Tears ran down her cheeks. Danny's death, which should have united father and daughter, had driven them further apart.

* * * *

The baby seemed stronger, so Chrissie sent for Sandra and Mary Rose. They came into the room quietly, and stood hand in hand. Chrissie opened her arms.

They ran to her and she hugged them, crying. Mary Rose wept loudly, but Alexandra didn't say a word.

Looking at the child, Chrissie was worried. Bright blue eyes that had once sparkled mischievously were dull and lacklustre, and her springy black curls hung lank. Chrissie's heart went out to the lost and lonely little soul who'd idolised her daddy.

Chrissie tried to draw her daughter into her embrace, but Sandra wriggled free.

"Come and meet your brother Sammy!" Chrissie said brightly, but held a warning finger to her lips. "Shhh, you must tiptoe and be very quiet. I've just got him to sleep."

She led them to the crib, and the two little girls craned over their brother in breathless wonder.

"Oh, Mum, is he real? He's just like a wee dolly!" Mary Rose was awed.

Chrissie smiled.

"Yes, love, he's a real baby, only very small. We must take great care of him."

A few days later, Chrissie was alone in the flat, sitting by the fire sewing, when a tap on the door interrupted her.

Opening it, she was surprised to see her sister-in-law.

Lizzie hadn't come visiting since Mary Rose was born and now she looked ill at ease.

"May I come in?"

Chrissie stood aside, and Lizzie swept past quickly. She stood, taking off her gloves, her eyes going to the crib.

"My dear, I'm so very sorry about Danny . . ."

"There's many in the same situation, Lizzie."

"Indeed. It's a dreadful time."

Lizzie walked over to the crib and stood looking down at the sleeping baby. Her face was impassive; Chrissie couldn't tell what she was thinking.

"He's perfect – but so tiny!" Lizzie said softly, as if to herself.

Before she could reply, Chrissie was overcome by a fit of coughing. Lizzie turned, frowning anxiously.

"You're not well!" Lizzie said in concern.

"It's just a cold."

"Maybe – but if the baby . . ." Lizzie paused and stared at Danny's son. Then she turned to face Chrissie.

"Your father says you've refused help. How will you manage with your two little girls and a sickly baby?"

She stopped for a moment, her eyes shining with a pathetic eagerness. She took a step forward, clutching Chrissie's arm.

"Chrissie, give me the baby! Arthur and I are well off. We can afford to give him all the nursing he needs!"

Chrissie wrenched her arm away, horrified.

"No!"

And yet she had two growing girls to feed and clothe . . .
How could she manage? She couldn't go out to work with a
baby requiring constant attention . . . Desperate, anguished
tears sprang to Chrissie's eyes, and she backed away.

"No, Lizzie!" she repeated. Lizzie followed, pulling at her
arm.

"Oh, my dear, I know it's hard for you, but if I take
Samuel you can see him whenever you wish, I promise!"
She paused. "He'll have a better chance with me . . ."

It was true. Could she deny her son his best chance of life?
Chrissie hid her face in her hands.

"Lizzie, I can't!"

Sammy stirred and whimpered, his weak cry forlorn.
Lizzie went swiftly to the crib and soothed him.

"Hush, my little pet . . . my little darling . . ."

Chrissie watched in wonder. The haughty, abrasive Lizzie
Kennedy had been replaced by a gentle, motherly woman.
Chrissie's heart ached for them all.

"Take him, Lizzie!"

"What?" Lizzie stared. Chrissie turned away, unable to
bear the expression on the poor woman's face.

"Take the baby. Take him away with you this minute –
before I change my mind!"

Lizzie's eyes were bright with tears.

"Oh, Chrissie, thank you. It's for the best, I'm sure."

Chrissie was speechless with misery. She could only nod.

Lizzie stared unhappily at her sister-in-law, wondering
what to do. Then the baby began whimpering in earnest.

Swiftly, Lizzie picked Samuel up and wrapped him cosily in his blanket. Holding him protectively against her shoulder, she hurried to the doorway.

There she hesitated for a moment, looking back. She longed to comfort Chrissie, but she knew better than most that words are of little comfort when you lose a child.

Shielding the baby tenderly from the freezing air, Lizzie ran lightly down the tenement stairs and towards the waiting car. She had always sworn she'd never take a stranger's child into her home, but this wasn't a stranger. She knew the virtues of Samuel's parents, aye, and the vices, too! Joy made her heart beat faster.

Chrissie tried to put on a cheerful face when her daughters returned home.

"Your aunt Lizzie is to look after Sammy in Uncle Arthur's big house in Downfield. Isn't he a lucky wee lad?" She smiled to hide her heartbreak.

The two little girls looked uncertain, staring doubtfully at the empty crib.

"When will Sammy come home again?" Sandra asked wistfully.

"Oh, when he's big and strong," Chrissie answered airily, folding tiny baby clothes that had been drying on the pulley. Her hand rested gently on the small garments for a few moments, before she resolutely opened the dresser drawer and put them away, out of sight.

Chapter 15

BESSIE MCCUTCHEON was furious when she heard what Lizzie had done. She barged into William Kennedy's study with scant ceremony.

"Captain, you canna let that woman take Chrissie's bairn! It's heartless when she's weak and sorrowful with nowhere to turn!"

He looked at her coldly.

"Bessie, you forgot I offered my daughter and her children a home here. She chose to reject me. I consider Lizzie's offer a generous one. In fact, it's an ideal solution for all concerned!"

Bessie tapped her chest angrily.

"I'm the bairn's great-aunt. Am I not to have a say? I think it's criminal to let yon starchy, stuck-up wee besom steal a dead man's son!"

William Kennedy's eyes glinted dangerously, and his cheeks took on a choleric hue.

"Mind what you're saying, Bessie McCutcheon!" he warned ominously. "I'll not have my daughter-in-law's actions criticised by you! If you don't like what's been done, you're free to go!"

"Are you giving me the sack, Captain Kennedy?" Bessie demanded with icy dignity.

William glowered. She'd driven him into a corner he

couldn't wriggle out of without loss of face. He drew himself erect.

"If you put it that way, woman, I suppose I am."

"I see. Then I'll be out of your house once I've worked my week's notice. I'll no' stay where I'm not wanted." Bessie turned on her heel and marched out, banging the door.

She went to the kitchen, shocked and trembling. It was a matter of principle, and she vowed she'd never give way.

All the same, Bessie quailed at the thought of leaving this fine house that was her home. She looked around her spotless kitchen with misty eyes. Where could she go?

Not to her sister's. Poor Biddy had quite enough on her plate, what with grief over Danny and her bad legs. That left one other option. Bessie's heart was heavy as she contemplated the future.

William swore inwardly when Bessie stormed out of the study. Och, he'd done it now. Well, he wasn't going to be the one to retract! She'd apologise when she cooled down, and maybe he'd be lenient.

He couldn't imagine the house without Bessie. It was quiet enough already without his granddaughter, Georgina, who'd been with him for the past few months until Hughie ran away to sea on a jute ship.

Ina had given up her typewriting course at once and gone back to the farm to help her father and mother. William sighed. She was a grand lass, and he missed her. And now Bessie was threatening to go! Where would it end?

He went to the window and absently studied angry storm

clouds gathering to the west beyond the railway bridge. Last May Mr Asquith had brought in conscription for all men between the ages of eighteen and forty-one and Ernest had received his call-up papers.

William shivered. He'd be a worried and lonely old man, with nobody to care a jot for him. Not even Bessie!

* * * *

Ina went back to the farm with mixed feelings. She was excited at the prospect of seeing Tam again, but worried about Hughie being at sea.

The Germans had sunk the *Lusitania* early in the war with the loss of many lives, and Lord Kitchener himself had been drowned last June when *HMS Hampshire* struck a mine off Orkney. The sea was a dangerous place, with submarines everywhere!

Ina saw her own anxiety mirrored on her parents' faces as she hugged them. Jeannie and George Kennedy had aged appreciably. Her mother's bonnie, smiling face was thin and lined prematurely with anxiety.

"If only Hughie had told us how he felt!" Jeannie said worriedly. "I could have arranged for him to go to sea with my father on the trawler. At least his grandpa would have kept an eye on him!"

"Och, Jean, nowhere's safe." George sighed, drawing on his pipe. "You'll mind the Zeppelin that dropped five bombs at the mouth o' the Tay last April? And there were folk killed in Leith and Edinburgh. I don't know what the world's coming to!"

"It's getting smaller, that's for sure!" Jean smiled at Ina, for she'd a titbit of news for her.

"We've had a letter from the owner of the farm, the old man's nephew in Australia. He's enlisted and been posted to England. He hopes to come north to see us."

Ina wasn't particularly interested. She fidgeted, looking out the window towards the snowy hill.

"Where's Tam?" she asked.

Her mother and father exchanged a quick glance.

"He'll be at the sheep-pens. The ewes are all down from the hills now," George said.

Ina slipped away as soon as she could, on a pretext of walking the dog. Her feet flew along the track, muddied with the first snow of the winter. Oh, it was good to feel the clean air on your skin!

And there was Tam, just as she'd dreamed of him, standing in front of his cottage, the dogs at his feet. She paused, seized by an emotion so strong it brought tears to her eyes.

Putting her fingers to her mouth, she whistled. The dogs perked up their ears, and Tam looked up.

"Tam!" Ina waved and started running, the dog tearing after.

Once started, she couldn't stop. She ran straight into his arms, and they closed tightly around her.

She looked up into his face.

"Oh, Tam! How I've missed you!"

She couldn't pretend any more. She loved him too much.

Tam looked dazzled, pale beneath his tan. He held her

close and felt the attraction that had been between them, even when she was a young lass. Now she'd come back a lovely young woman, it was irresistible.

"Tam, what d'you think you're doing?"

A young woman had appeared in the cottage doorway. She stood glowering, fists planted on her hips.

Tam stepped back hastily. His head drooped, and he couldn't meet Georgina's eyes.

"Ina, that's Margaret, my wife. We got married three weeks ago."

"Oh, Tam. Why didn't you wait for me?" Ina whispered.

Tam shook his head blindly.

"I was so lonely. I didn't know. I never guessed how it was . . . until now . . ."

* * * *

The grocer was adamant. He wouldn't give Chrissie her job back. Her ill health had sorely tried his patience.

There was nothing else for it, Chrissie thought. She'd have to try the jute mill. She might be lucky; the mills were on overtime, keeping up with the demands for sackcloth.

The man on the gate knew her by sight, and was sympathetic.

"It's Massie, the foreman, you want to see, missus. Through that wee door there." He directed her, pointing.

The roar of the machinery made the ground tremble beneath her feet. A gust of hot, dusty air struck her when she opened the door.

Massie was in a wee cubicle of an office. He chewed his

moustache and frowned when Chrissie stated her business.

"And you've no experience?"

"I'm quick to learn," Chrissie said eagerly.

He frowned.

"Aye, well, Mrs Murphy, your man was favoured by the high heid yins, but you'll get no favours from me, mind."

"I'd expect none, Mr Massie!" Chrissie said coldly.

He scowled.

"And don't you be hoity-toity with me, my lady!"

And so Chrissie was taken on.

She was put under Bella Duncan's wing to learn the intricacies of keeping the yarn bobbins filled.

Bella was a big, cheery woman with a voice like a foghorn that carried even above the noise of the machinery. The factory was a bewildering scene of noise and movement, overhead shafts and pulleys, all contributing to the din. Chrissie put her hands over her ears, and Big Bella chortled.

"Och, you'll soon get used to that!" She caught sight of Massie glaring, and picked up the spinner's hook.

"Look, Chrissie, the rove bobbins are atop the spinning frame. That's thick thread loosely twisted for the warp, see? The weft's a looser twist, to fill in a' the wee windows in the cloth.

"The thread's fed through rollers and delivered wi' a twist to the yarn bobbins, spinning awa' on the frame. There's twenty ends to a frame, and your job's to keep the yarn bobbins filled from the rove. Like this."

Big Bella went into action, using the hook to join the ends

of the rove yarn to the fast-spinning bobbins. Her hands flew so fast Chrissie couldn't follow her movements.

"Oh, Bella! I'll never do that!" she shouted in dismay.

"Ach, there's nothin' to it! Here, you have a go. It's the only way to learn!" Big Bella bellowed.

She managed not too badly at first, but it was hard, relentless work. It was an endless process, the full bobbins being replaced with empty ones.

The machinery drove on and on tirelessly, spinning fast, requiring deep concentration to keep the ends of the yarn up. Chrissie's head began to spin dizzily. She got in a muddle, panicked and found Massie standing over her.

"What do you think you're doing? You're no' keeping your ends up!"

She wiped the sweat off her forehead.

"I'll let you off this time, but you'll have to do better or you're oot," he growled.

Big Bella sorted out the frame for her.

"Don't you mind Massie, lass. He's no' half the man your Danny was – an' he kens it!"

* * * *

Shortly before Christmas, Chrissie received a note from Lizzie. Would she like to bring the children to see Sammy?

Her spirits lifted. There had been changes that might end the stalemate of the war, and everyone was hopeful. Asquith, freeman of Dundee, had resigned, and the firebrand Lloyd George had taken over. People said the Welshman would get things done!

Chrissie patiently unpicked an old white shawl and knitted a tiny matinee jacket. Sandra and Mary Rose drew self-portraits for their brother to hang over his cot, so he wouldn't forget what they looked like.

The three of them were in a fever of excitement as they sat in the Downfield tram, marvelling at the fine houses and neat gardens. Arthur Kennedy's house, when they reached it, was the grandest of the lot.

The little girls were awed when a uniformed maid answered the bell, but Lizzie was right behind, arms outstretched.

"Come in, my dears!" she welcomed them.

Chrissie could hardly believe this was her stiff and starchy sister-in-law. Lizzie was plumper, and her eyes sparkled.

She squeezed Chrissie's arm as she drew into the house.

"You'll hardly recognise him, Chrissie! He's put on so much weight. Mind you, it was touch and go. He'd caught your cold and we thought we might lose him."

Arthur came up behind his wife, a portly, successful man now. He put an arm round Lizzie's shoulders proudly.

"This wonderful woman saved the bairn, Chrissie. She sat with him night and day, nourishing him until the fever broke. He's getting stronger every day, the wee lamb!"

He led the way into a room which made the children's eyes goggle. There was a Christmas tree in the window, hung with tinsel and coloured baubles, and a blazing fire reflecting its cosy light on shining brass and polished wood.

A cradle trimmed with white lace and blue ribbons stood

beneath the tree. Chrissie went towards it as if in a dream.

Sammy had grown, and put on weight. He was awake, but he looked up at her with a dark, unfocused stare.

She could see no resemblance to Danny or herself. His downy hair had a gingery tint, almost like Lizzie's . . . Chrissie backed away, a chill in her heart.

She handed the little matinee jacket to Lizzie.

"For the baby," she murmured, her vision blurring with tears. "It's not much, I'm afraid."

At least the children enjoyed the afternoon. Lizzie was wonderful with them, ever going down on her knees to help them open their presents.

The gifts had been chosen carefully. Mary Rose crooned happily over the baby doll with blue eyes that opened and closed in a smiling, china face. Sandra was overcome with joy at the elaborate wooden pencil case, and the five-year diary with its own private lock and key.

"Have you met Queen Alexandra, Auntie Lizzie?" She snuggled close to her aunt. "What's she like?"

Lizzie smiled.

"She's a very brave and gracious lady, pet. She's so easy to talk to, you'd never guess she's deaf. And she moves so gracefully you don't realise that her poor leg is badly affected with rheumatics."

Sandra hugged her knees and dreamily studied pictures in the fire. She wishes she didn't have to go home. She wanted to stay with Sammy, cocooned in warmth and luxury, for ever . . .

Chapter 16

IT was Harriet who broke the news to Chrissie that Ernest had been wounded in battle at the Somme.

I suppose it was no coincidence he should be brought to Etaples, where I'm based, Harriet wrote in the spring of 1918. *He was remarkably cheerful once the shrapnel was removed, congratulating himself on collecting "a Blighty one"!*

Indeed, he might even be back there by now. I pulled some strings, and arranged for him to recuperate at Glamis Castle so you can visit more easily. He is well, but his soldiering days are over. He'll limp for the rest of his life, but he should count himself lucky to be alive.

Oh, Chrissie, how I long for the awful war to end, and a return to sanity! I dream of peace, of settling down to a quiet, domestic life.

Have you seen Charles? Is he well? He sends me such amusing letters, but they do not tell me what I want to know.

Chrissie let the letter lie in her lap. Poor Ernest! How weary everyone was of war! Even the popular songs had lost their jauntiness, and had a sad, yearning note.

Chrissie herself felt tired all the time, although her hands flew as fast as Big Bella's now, and she could keep her end up in the mill. The noise and humid heat, the fibre dust, and most of all the small injustices of the work, sickened her.

Her girls were growing fast, and Mary Rose had started school. They had to be clothed and shod, so there was no escape from the mill.

She made up her mind to visit Ernest on her own, and set off for Glamis one Sunday morning. This time, she left the children with an obliging neighbour, for Biddy was far from well.

The bus left Dundee behind and climbed laboriously over the Sidlaw Hills towards the Strathmore valley. Chrissie looked back at the grey city with a sense of freedom and a lighter heart. For the first time since Danny's death, she was almost happy.

How delightful it must be to be able to go anywhere you wished, to control your own life as Harriet did! Chrissie suddenly longed to be free of care and responsibility. She sighed. A hopeless dream.

Glamis was like a fairy-tale castle, Chrissie thought, as she left the bus with a few other visitors and went through gates leading to a long driveway.

Sunlight lit the grey stone turrets ahead, and the green fields of the estate lay all around. A lark rose and Chrissie lifted her head to listen to its song. For a moment she felt young again, then she walked on with the others.

Wounded soldiers congregated in the gardens, all wearing light blue suits. They were all very cheerful, hailing the visitors with a hearty rendition of, "Hello, hello, who's your lady friend . . . ?"

Chrissie found she was laughing.

She finally located Ernest after a lot of backchat from his companions that did much to boost her morale.

Her cheeks were rosy and her blue eyes sparkling with laughter as she kissed his cheek. There was an immediate chorus of whistles and shouts of, "Ernest, you lucky devil!" and, "Hey, miss, what about me?"

"Chrissie, what a surprise! You look great!" Ernest smiled at his young sister fondly.

Chrissie sat down, examining her brother anxiously. Ernest looked remarkably fit. It was hard to tell he'd been wounded, apart from the tell-tale crutches resting by the seat.

A dark-haired, pretty young lady appeared beside them. She smiled at Ernest.

"How's the leg today, Ernest?"

"Not so bad. I'll be doing the eightsome reel any day now."

She laughed merrily.

"We'll see about that!" She turned to Chrissie. "Have they given you tea yet? No? I'll make sure you get a cup!"

Smiling, she hurried away. Chrissie stared after her, warmed by her concern.

"Who's that, Ernest?"

"That's the Earl of Strathmore's daughter, Lady Elizabeth Bowes-Lyon. She's an angel; goes round the wards every day."

Ernest paused for a few moments, then glanced sideways at his sister.

"Chris, I'm awfully glad you came. I've got something

important to tell you – at least it's important to me. I've met a terrific girl . . ."

"Oh, Ernest, I'm so happy for you!" Chrissie squeezed his arm.

"Her name's Geraldine Mason. She's American," Ernest went on eagerly. "I met her when I was on leave in London.

"She came over to England with her father after America entered the war. Mr Mason builds motorised vehicles, mostly tanks at the moment. He's offered me a job when I'm fit. I'd work with him in England at first, then go to America, to the engineering works in Detroit."

Ernest's eyes glowed with enthusiasm.

"I thought I'd be book-keeping for Papa for the rest of my days. Now I've got the chance to work in a new, exciting industry with so many prospects. And be with the woman I love! It's miraculous!"

He stopped abruptly, and the glad light in his eyes died.

"But it's no use, is it?" He sighed. "How can I leave Father?"

Chrissie put his hand urgently on his arm.

"You mustn't turn down a chance like this. You'd regret it for the rest of your life. Arthur can look after the business, and Bessie will care for Papa, surely?"

He looked at her strangely.

"You don't know, do you? Papa's a sailor – he had no head for business. He bungled the batching oil contract and Rankine cancelled it. Luckily, Arthur's affairs are separate. Last time he was here he told me the old man's ill and broken-hearted, and living all alone in that empty house. But he refuses to –"

"But Bessie's there!" Chrissie clutched her brother's arm.

"No. When Lizzie took your son, the old man and Bessie had a row and parted company. Nobody knows where she is . . . There's only one solution, Chris," Ernest said gloomily. "When I'm discharged, I'll go home and look after Papa."

"What about Geraldine?" Chrissie asked gently. "And Mr Mason's offer?"

Her brother shook his head.

"It's no use. I'll have to tell her to go home to America and forget about me."

"If she loves you, that won't put her off!"

"Maybe not." Her brother sighed. "But what have I got to offer her? A penniless cripple in Dundee?"

Chrissie was silent. Wounded soldiers were drifting towards a trestle table set up in the garden. The pretty young Lady Elizabeth Bowes-Lyon was helping to dispense tea to the convalescents, and Chrissie could hear laughter and the homely clink of teacups.

Some of the young men had three or more wound stripes on their sleeves. So much pain and anguish, Chrissie thought. At least, for them, it was over now. They could forget the past, get on with their lives, find happiness. Not like Ernest . . .

Why did it have to be him? Couldn't someone else look after Papa? Not Arthur – the old man could never live in the same house as Lizzie! And George and Jeannie lived so far away, and the farm was so lonely. That left her!

The thought chilled her. Could she give up her independence? The home where memories of Danny lingered so vividly?

But what independence had she? The mill six days a week! And the flat was no home with Danny gone. Besides, she was hardly there and her lassies were left to fend for themselves. And wee Sammy was being brought up by someone else . . .

She'd once loved her father so dearly . . . she still loved him. If he was sick and needed care, didn't she have a duty to care for him? And what about Bessie? Who'd looked after her, dried her tears, fought for Danny's son – and been dismissed for her pains? Yes, Bessie must be found!

She'd been staring at the crutches leaning near her brother's chair without really seeing them. What had Harriet written? That Ernest would limp for the rest of his life? Well, he had suffered enough!

"There's no problem, Ernest," Chrissie said firmly, before she could change her mind. "I'll look after Papa."

Ernest's eyes lit with hope.

"Would you?" He paused. "It won't be easy. Arthur says Papa's getting more and more difficult – but then you always were the apple of his eye!"

Tears rushed to Chrissie's eyes. Ernest reached over and squeezed her hand sympathetically.

"Are you really sure, Chrissie? The business is in a bad way. Poor Papa couldn't cope when I was called up. Och, how can I leave you with such a worry?"

Chrissie brushed the tears away and laughed.

"If I can keep my end up at the mill, I can cope with anything!"

"Aye, you've had more than your share of trouble." Ernest smiled and nodded admiringly. "On the bright side, Arthur and Lizzie will help. Arthur has a good head for business, and everything Mistress Lizzie touches seems to prosper!"

"Yes, I know!"

Chrissie hoped Ernest hadn't noticed her abrupt response. He obviously didn't know how much his innocent remark had hurt her.

Wee Sammy was thriving under Lizzie's care, and Chrissie and her daughters made frequent visits on Sunday afternoons to see her son. But the visits weren't a success.

Chrissie would hold Sammy in her arms and kiss the fluff of gingery down on his tiny head. Perhaps her longing disturbed him, because he would begin wailing fretfully within minutes. And he wouldn't be comforted until Lizzie took him and cuddled him . . .

A nurse was approaching, balancing cups of tea. Lady Elizabeth hadn't forgotten her promise. Ernest squeezed Chrissie's hand.

"I'll never forget this, Chris. You can't imagine how it feels to be free to live my own life!"

"Oh, yes, I can, Ernest, dear!" she replied, remembering a young girl who had willingly left comfort and ease to go her own way.

Chapter 17

CHRISSIE continued to work at the mill during the summer of 1918. Ernest had said William Kennedy was quite likely to refuse Chrissie's offer point-blank. The old man was stubbornly set against involving his daughter and her children in the disaster he'd created. It was a delicate situation, to be handled with diplomacy.

At least it gave Chrissie the chance to ask around to see if anyone knew what had happened to Bessie McCutcheon. But nobody could tell her anything, however carefully she searched.

Biddy said her sister had turned up with all her belongings in a carpet bag one morning towards the end of 1917.

"She made me swear I'd not tell ye she'd got the sack, Chris. She said ye'd enough to worry about. I tried to get her to bide wi' me, but she said she'd manage fine on her own, an' stomped oot the door. I havena seen hide nor hair o' her since!"

At least they needn't look for Bessie in the jute mills, Chrissie thought, remembering how the damp, stoury conditions made her old nurse ill. She must be in domestic service – but where?

The humid heat of that warm summer made the millworkers' jobs even harder. The long lines of spinning frames were manned carefully by tight-lipped women with sweat running down their faces. There was talk of wages being cut and women laid off because of bad trade, and everyone was on edge.

Even Big Bella grumbled.

"I'm sick o' this, Chris," she bellowed above the thunder of the machines. "The heat's fair murderin' my corns! The weavers have the best job, ye ken. The roof's higher in the factory than in the mill, and you can open a' they big windaes."

Chrissie was quite familiar with the various departments of the works by now. She knew that the yarn was prepared and spun in the mill, and woven into cloth in the factory. There was rivalry between spinners and weavers, who were inclined to think themselves the bees' knees.

But before she could reply, the foreman came stalking along the frames, scowling.

"No talking, you!"

"Can we no' have a breath o' fresh air in this place?" Bella glared at him.

"Fire risk. One spark wi' a wee puff o' wind behind it could start a mighty conflagration in the oily yarn. You ken the rules, Bella," Massie growled smugly.

Bella's hands were a blur of movement at the frame.

"Och, there's mair danger from the fags you puff on the sly behind the partition, you daft ass!" she muttered.

"What's that you said the now?" He advanced threateningly.

"I was thinkin' aboot the fluff ahent the partition, Mr

Massie. A fag-end dropped carelessly could set it aff. Somebody ought to tell the manager," Bella roared.

The foreman turned purple and Chrissie laughed. It was a while since she'd laughed. It refreshed her like cool water.

When she went home after work that Saturday afternoon, Chrissie studied her daughters' eager faces.

"Oh, all right!" Chrissie agreed recklessly.

The bairns cheered, Sandra insisted on wearing her best clothes and straw hat wreathed in roses, despite thundery showers. And, of course, Mary Rose had to follow suit.

While the little girls were getting ready, Chrissie raided the tea caddy. One pound twelve and sixpence.

She smiled as she recalled the foolish young bride who'd squandered Danny's cash. She'd learned good sense since then, but this was a special occasion. She slipped the precious savings into her handbag.

Sandra walked with her nose held so high she was in danger of tripping over her feet. She held Mary Rose's hand in a restraining grip and wouldn't let her skip. In her vivid imagination, the two of them were princesses . . .

Princesses wouldn't dream of skipping down the street. Or, she thought as she passed some friends, stottin' the ball . . .

"One, two, three, a leerie, Four, five, six, a leerie,

Seven, eight, nine, a leerie, Ten, a leerie, postman –"

Especially when you kicked one leg up high to let the ball stot under, and sometimes folk could see your knickers. Och, no, princesses would never do that!

And princesses wouldn't chalk on the pavement at the

head o' the closie for a game of peever, Sandra thought as she pointed her toes daintily, trying to avoid treading on the cracks in the pavement!

But, oh, the sight of the La Scala when they reached it! The gilded luxury of the cinema made Sandra's jaw drop as they joined the queue and began to shuffle across the marble floor. Her eyes goggled when they reached the scarlet-lipped woman, and her mother grandly asked for "A shilling and two halves – if you please."

Wait till she told them at school she'd been in the balcony! Sandra mounted the wide staircase as if in a dream. She really felt like a princess at that moment, walking on thick red carpets past white and gold plaster pillars.

There were stylish ladies with torches waiting to take your ticket and show you to your seat. One of them winked at Sandra.

"Better tak' aff your bonnet, hen. Folk behind'll no' see the picture for yon rose-gairden."

A man in a black suit came out and stood in front of the velvet curtains on the stage. The spotlights fixed admiringly on him as he flexed his muscles and bowed. Then he sat down in front of the piano, flicking out the tails of his jacket with a flourish. As the lights died, he began pounding away on the keys.

The film was about daft policemen chasing robbers acting so silly the young Murphys nearly choked themselves laughing. Sandra stole a glance at her mother. There were tears pouring down Chrissie's cheeks, and her mouth was wide open, laughing like the old days when Daddy said something funny.

Oh, Daddy, Daddy, I miss you sore!

It wasn't a bad place to cry for a lost daddy, amidst gales of laughter, with nobody to see . . .

Afterwards, they came out into the Murraygate, which was so crowded the trams couldn't get moving and kept grumpily clanging their bells.

It began to rain and the Murphys were carried along with the crush of folk right through the swing doors of Woolworths.

Glad of the shelter, everyone steamed happily in the heat.

Chrissie bought each of the girls a threepenny bangle. Sandra fitted hers on her wrist and her nose went higher in the air.

They slipped out of the packed store through the back pend and made their way, hand in hand, to the Mid Kirk Style. In the narrow wynd behind the Steeple Kirk, it seemed the crowds swarming round the wee Overgate shops had all grown hungry at the same moment. The air was rich with the smell of frying onions and sizzling chips.

Chrissie used her elbows and came out of the crush with her hat askew, clutching three pokes of chips and peas. They found a quiet corner beside the City Churches and ate hungrily with their fingers. Then they washed their hands genteel-like and drank from the drinking fountain, which spilled clear water from the lion's mouth.

Going home in the tram, nursing Wallace's meat pies for

their tea, Sandra had the future all mapped out.

She was going to marry a very rich man, and live in luxury for the rest of her life!

Shortly after the happy outing, Chrissie received a letter. It was from wee Hughie, the runaway, post-marked Bombay, India. It had taken weeks to come.

Dearest Auntie Chris,

I've written to Mum and Dad, saying I'm sorry for running away to sea. I can't be a farmer, I'm no good at it and, anyway, I'm scared of cows. I hope they will forgive me some day. I've told them everything's fine because I don't want them to worry, but I'm not fine, and I've hardly any money left.

It was awful hard work on the ship. I was seasick and scared most of the time in case a German submarine torpedoed us. When we reached Bombay I went down with a very bad fever. It was so bad the captain wouldn't have me aboard in case he and the rest of the crew got it. I was put in hospital ashore.

I'm better now, but the ship sailed without me and nobody else will take me on because I look so weedy. A friend told me I should go to the Samnuggur jute works in Calcutta. I might get work there and save money for my passage home because I come from Dundee. Auntie Chris. Tell Ina, if you like, about the misfortunes of . . .

Your loving nephew,

Hughie.

Chrissie didn't know what to think. She looked through

Danny's books and found a map of India. She was aghast to find the vast distance between Bombay to Calcutta. And Hughie was weak and nearly penniless.

After a lot of anxious deliberation, Chrissie wrote a cautious note to Georgina. Someone in the boy's family ought to be kept informed, though there was little anyone could do.

* * * *

Georgina Kennedy read Chrissie's letter seated on a rock on Craig Dubh. Her sheepdog was flopped at her feet and the sheep grazed peacefully on the hill.

She looked more like a slender, long-legged youth than a young woman, for she had taken to wearing a shirt and trousers. And her hair was tucked under a bunnet, much to her mother's disgust.

"You'll never get yoursel' a man dressed like that, Ina!" Jeannie had wailed.

Ina didn't care. Tam was married. What did it matter what she looked like? Besides, trousers were fine for scrambling up the hillside.

She kept her distance from Tam now, never speaking to him. It was safer. Margaret, Tam's wife, was expecting a bairn and flaunted her condition triumphantly when Ina was around. She frowned anxiously over the letter. Oh, poor wee Hughie! And nothing could be done while the miserable war dragged on!

"Hey, you there!"

Ina hadn't heard a sound, but she looked up to find a

soldier standing on the track, strangely out of place in this peaceful spot. She stood up, shading her eyes.

He came closer. For a big man, he walked softly.

"Well, I'll be – you're a sheila!" he exclaimed.

Ina stared at him, taking in the bush-hat turned up at one side and the sunburst badge on it. The light suddenly dawned. She smiled.

"Oh, you must be Bruce, Mr Cameron's Australian nephew. We've been expecting you. Have you come to view your inheritance?"

"If I can find it."

Ina laughed and waved an arm towards Craig Dubh.

"This is it. Nearly two hundred acres of hill and forest, fifty acres arable, a farmhouse where my mother and father live, and three cottages."

He had a trick of narrowing his eyes thoughtfully so that only a hint of grey showed.

"Hmm. That all? Hardly worth bothering about!"

She stared.

"How much land do you have in Australia?"

"Oh, around a hundred an' fifty thousand acres of grazing in the outback." He shrugged. "Australia's a big country. Not many men – or women, either. Women are scarce in the outback. Leastways, the right sort of women."

He looked at her appraisingly through narrowed eyes, and she felt herself go beetroot-red.

"If you will follow me, Mr Cameron, I'll take you to my father," Ina said coolly, leading the way down the track.

Chapter 18

THE Germans had launched another attack and driven the British and the French back ten miles. It seemed to the sorrowing and weary folk at home that the war would never be won.

But General Haig hung on and kept his nerve. This time he deployed armoured tanks, which Mr Churchill and Lloyd George favoured, and the fearsome things lumbered across the scarred and pitted battlefields to turn the tide of battle. Ludendorff's offensive crumbled. The end was in sight at last!

On September 18, Chrissie received a postcard from Ernest.

Dear Chrissie,

Papa has agreed at last, and will welcome you and your bairns when you arrive.

I have been discharged, and leave for London tomorrow (10th inst.) to join Mr Mason and Geraldine. I get around pretty well on one stick. I will write to you at greater length soon.

God bless you, my dear!

Ernest.

Chrissie drew in a breath and straightened her shoulders. There was so much to be done.

First, she had to give notice at the mill.

The workers were sad to see her go. They'd grown attached to her when they realised that she worked as hard as anyone to feed her bairns. Even Massie the foreman was put out.

"Just when you were some use to me in the spinning flat, woman!" he growled in disgust.

Chrissie smiled. That was high praise, coming from him.

They made her a wee presentation on the last day, gathering in the courtyard when the bells rang for the end of the shift. She was surrounded by beaming, kindly faces.

Bella draped a pretty blue shawl around Chrissie's shoulders. It was so light and finely knitted it would have passed through a wedding ring. The others cheered, and tears ran unashamedly down her cheeks.

"Oh, thank you!" Chrissie sobbed. "How can I ever thank you?"

Bella wiped her nose emotionally on her cuff.

"Oh, Chris, it's nothing, just a wee shawl knitted frae bits an' pieces. Here, fix it at your neck wi' your bonnie ship brooch."

Meanwhile, Sandra was saying her farewells. She headed for the back courts of the tenement after school. It was a bustling scene of activity, with hordes of bairns playing and yelling. There had once been grass on the greens, but it had long ago succumbed to the pounding of tackety-boots during the seven-weekies, the long summer holidays.

Sandra picked her way past a line of little girls with a skipping rope. One lass skipped, pig-tails flying.

"C'mon, Sandra, jump in an' keep the pot bilin'!" another yelled.

But Sandra moved on.

There was a screaming bunch playing high tig on the walls, and driving a wifie daft by jumping on her newly scrubbed steps. A more sedate group were bowling hoops down the closie and catching them with cleeks just before they rolled into the street and took the feet from unwary passers-by.

Stepping fastidiously round a tangle of laddies wrestling happily over a football in the mud, Sandra at last found what she was looking for – an intent little circle of boys in a quiet corner, playing bools.

"Hey, you, Norrie Gallacher!"

Nobody moved, but a red-headed boy deftly knuckled a marble into the centre of the ring and grunted, "Uh-huh?"

"I'm leaving tomorrow wi' my mum an' my wee sister. We're going to live with my grandpa in a great big hoose in Broughty Ferry," Sandra continued, not without a hint of pride.

"Oh, aye?" The boy swooped on three bools he'd knocked out of the ring. The others groaned.

"I'm to go to Grove Academy, Mum says. I'll not let on if I meet you when I'm oot wi' my new posh friends, Norrie Gallacher, but I'll give a wee wink, so's you'll ken it's still me," Sandra offered generously.

"Aye." He squinted and knuckled another bool.

"I'm to marry a rich man an' live in luxury noo," she

announced. "So I'm breakin' aff our engagement."

"Oh, aye?" His favourite marble with yellow and white swirls in it had scattered all the other bools in the ring.

"I just called to say bye-bye."

Norrie Gallacher collected his winnings and stuffed the bools into bulging pockets.

"Ta-ta," he said.

* * * *

A corner on Jimsie the carter's cart was all Chrissie needed. Harriet's little writing desk and one or two precious bits and pieces were all she took. The rest went to Maggie Glancey's for a few welcome shillings.

Jimsie generously offered the Murphy family transport on the cart. Chrissie accepted. She'd no intention of letting their possessions out of her sight.

When the carter had carried everything down and stowed it on the flat cart, Chrissie stood for a moment in the empty flat.

Danny wasn't here any more. The place felt dead and cold in the fitful sunlight.

She went out, closed the door behind her and descended the echoing stone stairs for the last time, fighting the tears that threatened to overcome her.

The two little girls were thrilled to be perched up with Jimsie behind the big brown horse.

"Has this horse been to the war?" Mary Rose asked.

"Naw, he wisnae called up. Mind you, he'd've gone if he'd got his papers. He's that willin', the big saftie," Jimsie answered, clucking at his old friend.

They moved off at an easy pace, heading down Lochee Road.

"I gave my Saturday penny to the teacher to help the wounded horses," Mary Rose said proudly.

"You're a kind wee lassie to spare a thought for the poor suffering beasties," Jimsie said with a sigh. "There's no' mony folk does."

It seemed to take ages to reach William Kennedy's house. Jimsie went by devious routes and stopped at least once to water his horse at a trough.

At last they came to a halt outside the gate, and Chrissie clambered down stiffly. Jimsie was lifting the little girls down after her, when the door opened, and William Kennedy came out.

Chrissie and her father looked at one another. Her heart missed a beat. How he'd aged! How gaunt and stooped he'd become!

And that sad, uncared-for look . . . He frowned at her slightly when he spoke.

"Must you come on a cart? Why didn't you get the removal van, and come in a cab like decent folk do?"

"That costs money, Papa!" She smiled as she went to him, feeling his proud aloofness as they embraced.

Mary Rose was staring, mouth open.

"Why are you greetin', Grandpa?" she asked curiously.

"I'm no' greetin'! I've got the cold." He hastily took out a handkerchief and blew his nose.

Sandra gave him a knowing look.

"It'll be the Spanish flu, Grandpa. It's terrible bad in Lochee. You'll need to get away to your bed wi' a hot toddy."

He looked down at the two concerned wee faces, and his stiff features relaxed into the glimmer of a smile.

"I see I'm to be well looked after. A toddy, you say?"

Mary Rose took his hand for comfort, and Sandra nodded wisely.

"Aye, Grandpa, A hot toddy wi' cinnamon, and go easy on the hot water. That's what Norrie Gallacher's granny takes when she's oot wi' the rag-and-bone cartie an' it comes on to rain."

Chrissie hid a smile as she turned away to pay Jimsie his due. The wee Murphys had broken the ice!

The house had been sadly neglected with Bessie gone, although Chrissie was touched to find her father had done his best to make them comfortable. There was clean linen on the beds and fires burning in her bedroom and the girls' room next door.

"I've had stone piggies in the bairns' beds all day, in case o' damp," William said gruffly.

"Oh, thank you, Papa!" Chrissie turned to him with misty eyes. She hugged him. Although he made no move to reciprocate and showed no emotion, she guessed he needed to be hugged – and frequently.

"I dinna ken where Bessie is," he said gruffly, turning his head away.

"Would you take her back?"

"Maybe." He looked sideways at Chrissie. "Will you take the baby away from Lizzie, now you're home?"

Chrissie had been thinking about that for days. She could care for Sammy herself now she'd stopped working at the mill.

"Yes, Papa. He's my son." She lifted her chin. "I want him!"

But why did she feel so badly about it? Surely she had a right to care for her own baby!

* * * *

Chrissie was kept so busy cleaning, cooking and seeing that her girls settled into their new schools that the ending of the war took her quite by surprise.

Perhaps it caught everyone by surprise. There was little joy in Dundee at the news, only a great upsurge of relief and mounting sorrow. There was scarcely a family that hadn't lost a father, son or brother. A generation of young Dundee lads, all gone.

Chrissie's brother, Arthur, arrived on the Sunday after the armistice was signed, ostensibly to rejoice with them over the good news. But he had a more personal matter on his mind, as Chrissie found out when their father went off to take a nap.

"Chrissie, do you intend taking Sammy away from us?" Arthur demanded bluntly.

She faltered and stopped at the look on her brother's face. He leaned towards her urgently.

"I know you've every right to take him – but please don't!"

"He's my baby – and Danny's!" Chrissie protested.

"It'll be the death of Lizzie," Arthur said quietly. "She says nothing, but I know she couldn't live without him.

"You have your two girls, Chrissie. Lizzie has nothing, no hope. And no future, if you take Sammy away."

Chrissie rose and went to the window. She couldn't sit still, for she trembled in every limb.

"But he's my son, Arthur!" she said brokenly, remembering how Lizzie cuddled the baby tenderly . . .

Arthur rose. He put a gentle hand on her shoulder.

"We love him so much. He's like our own son."

He sighed.

"Perhaps the loss would be easier to bear if Sammy was older and less dependent. I can't say. It must be your decision."

He picked up his hat and gloves and prepared to leave.

"Please consider it, Chrissie. I'm off to London tomorrow to a meeting to discuss trade with India now the war's over. When I return, I'll accept whatever decision you've reached."

Chapter 19

DR HARRIET BOWERS had returned to Dundee shortly before the Armistice. She was exhausted by the horrors she'd faced, and her superiors had persuaded her to leave the hospital at Etaples for a rest.

Mr and Mrs Bowers, justly proud of their daughter's achievements, would have immediately thrown an enormous dinner party, but Harriet wouldn't hear of it. Mrs Bowers settled instead for a small, intimate dinner, with Charles Rankine as the only guest.

Charles was still unmarried, though his reputation was somewhat tarnished because he hadn't gone off and got himself killed in the war. Even so, Mrs Bowers thought optimistically, he was still a good catch!

Diplomatically left alone after an excellent dinner, Harriet studied Charles with loving eyes.

He had changed. There were deep furrows in his brow and the gently humorous eyes looked tired and saddened. In his own way, Charles Rankine had had a cruel and punishing war.

He lit a cheroot, watching her through the blue scented smoke.

"Was it very bad – the war?" he asked quietly.

A spasm of pain crossed her face.

"Yes. Very."

Harriet stood up restlessly. She placed another log on the glowing fire and stared into the flames she had created.

How shocked she'd been the first time she had been called to a Casualty Clearing Station just behind the front line. The conditions were so primitive in the torn marquee. No running water, sugarboxes as medicine chests, sterilisers heated by meth burners in biscuit tins . . . And the wounded boys lying everywhere, covered in blood-soaked blankets. Harriet shivered.

"Harriet –" Charles gently broke into her thoughts.

She turned to face him, meeting his eyes honestly. Perhaps, at last, he would see how much she loved him. She was too tired to pretend,

"I asked you once if you'd ever be willing to give up your career, settle down and have a family. Has the time come, my dear?" Charles asked.

Harriet considered his words gravely. Were they a proposal? If so, she felt none of the joy she'd expected.

"Charles, did you know that when the Kitchener's volunteers were medically examined, a great many were undernourished? They were stunted, deformed by rickets and disease caused by poor diet, appalling slums and evil working conditions. The men were skilful and intelligent, but sadly ill-educated. Someone must do something!"

He rose and framed her vehement face with his hands.

"Does it have to be you, Harriet?"

"Perhaps." She looked up at him steadily. "Charles, what about Chrissie?"

She felt the shock of her words quivering through his fingers, but his voice was calm.

"Chrissie will never forgive me because I meddled in her life. Her man was safe in a reserved occupation until he discovered I'd put him there. The sad thing is, the lad had great ability. He didn't need me to speak for him.

"I'm no friend of Chrissie, Harriet. She told me so herself."

"Poor Chrissie!" Harriet sighed. "Yes, poor Chrissie."

With that Charles bent his head and gently kissed Harriet on the lips.

* * * *

William Kennedy wakened on Monday morning in no fit state to go to the office.

"Maybe I have caught this damned Spanish flu!" He groaned.

Chrissie shooed him back to bed and tucked him in.

"You've been overdoing it, Papa, that's all. You need a break."

"Och, how can I? There's only me to manage the place. The clerks were called up, and now Ernest's deserted, too!" He sneezed pathetically.

She looked at him thoughtfully.

"You've forgotten one thing, Papa. You have me now. Why shouldn't I look after the office until you're well again?"

"What?" His eyes opened wide. "You're a woman. An office is no place for you!"

Chrissie laughed.

"The world's changing, Papa. Women over thirty are getting the vote. I've worked long hours in a grocer's shop and in the mill. Why not work in an office?"

"It's no' seemly!" he spluttered weakly. "I dinna ken what the world's coming to!"

"You lie still and keep warm. I'll man the ship!" She bent and kissed his cheek.

"The customers'll no' like it! They'll be fair scandalised at having to deal with a woman, Chrissie!" her father warned.

She was almost out the door by then. She turned and blew a kiss.

"Then they'll have to get used to it, Papa. It'll do them good!"

Chrissie was glad to get out of the house. She'd grown used to going out to work, and sometimes found her father's house lonely and stifling.

She ran joyfully to catch the tram, enjoying the freedom of shorter skirts.

Reaching the Seagate, Chrissie unlocked the office door, and walked boldly in.

There were papers lying everywhere, some of them thick with dust. The office was dingy, dirty and smelled of stale whale oil. She wrinkled her nose in disgust.

As she hung her coat on the rack, she wondered where to start. There was a massive ledger lying open on the desk, and that seemed as good a place as any.

Chrissie's days in the grocer's shop had taught her some

elementary book-keeping, and she pored over the figures entered in the ledger. They were depressing.

She turned her attention to the chaos all around, and her spirits sank. Everything must be read and documented and filed away in its proper place. It was a monumental task.

"Well, sooner begun, sooner mended, my girl!" she said stoutly.

She pulled a pile of invoices towards her and started going through them. She was soon indignant. Some of her father's debtors had taken advantage of the old man and given themselves a handsome credit. Well, she'd soon put a stop to that!

By midday, she was dust covered and her head ached –and she'd only done a fraction of the work. Chrissie sat down before the ledger and sank her head in her hands.

The office door opened, and she looked up in surprise. She hadn't expected any customers on a Monday morning.

She was even more surprised to find that the caller was Charles Rankine. She had long ago lost most of her bitterness for his part in Danny's death. He had only been trying to help and so much had happened since . . .

So Chrissie's first sensation on seeing Charles was one of relief. Perhaps he could explain the mysteries of the batching oil trade!

She smiled broadly, and held out a hand.

"Oh, Charles, I'm so glad to see you. I need your help!"

Charles hadn't moved from the doorway. The shock of finding Chrissie here had left him speechless. She was as lovely as ever . . . and he wanted her just as much . . .

But she had hurt him badly and he had no intention of being hurt again! Charles turned and began to walk away . . .

"Charles!"

Chrissie's voice stopped Charles Rankine at the door.

He turned, obviously reluctantly, and she was dismayed at the lack of expression in his face. It was as if it had been wiped clean . . .

She could hardly blame him. Her family had brought him little joy. She had rejected his offer of marriage and her father had let him down badly over the oil contract!

But why stare at her in silence? Hadn't he anything to say? Chrissie had become accustomed to down-to-earth folk who left you in no doubt as to their feelings!

She sighed. Charles was a gentleman. Perhaps that was where the difference lay. And as an eligible bachelor he was still sought after by scheming Dundee mamas trying to coax him into matrimony. At least she could reassure him her interest was strictly businesslike!

She gave him a friendly smile.

"Charles, I'm trying to bring a semblance of order to Papa's affairs – but it's all so new to me. And there are some terms I simply don't understand. I'd be grateful for your help. I promise I won't detain you, and I shan't trouble you again. I'm not a helpless female, you know!"

"Very well, Chrissie." Charles relaxed a little. "What do you want to know?"

"To start with, why did you cancel your contract?"

He was shaken. This wasn't the sweet Chrissie he remembered. This young woman with shrewd blue eyes was actually challenging him!

"I was forced to. Your father couldn't deliver on time. I know whale oil's scarce these days, but he was unwilling to experiment with other sources. The batching department must have suitable oil to soften the jute fibres. Otherwise the fibres break on the carding machines and the whole procedure is held up, with the workers standing idle. They don't like it any more than I do."

He gave her an apologetic glance.

"Forgive me, Chrissie, I forgot you don't understand the manufacturing process."

"Oh, yes, I do." Her smile was grim. "You can't imagine how often I've cursed my father's trade! I could smell the whale oil all day long. The smell gets into your clothes in spite of a thick linen apron. And even after I'd boiled my linen in the steamie, the stink of stale fish used to cling until I thought I'd be sick."

"You worked in the mill?" He was staggered. "Oh, Chrissie, I didn't know!"

She shrugged.

"I had to after Danny died. It's difficult for a soldier's widow to live on the pittance they give you – especially with two bairns to feed and clothe."

Charles stared, seeing a new Chrissie. He had always seen her in a romantic light, never dreaming she had such strength.

"Oh, Chrissie, I could've helped!"

"How could you?" Her lip curled contemptuously. "Could you persuade the jute barons to pay another two bob a week instead of cutting wages? That's the only help I'd take from you and your kind. Decent wages for poor hard-working folk!"

He shook his head, as if to clear it.

Chrissie immediately felt sorry. How could she expect a rich man to know what it was like to be poor?

Studying him more closely, she saw that he had not escaped the war unscathed. He may not have fought in it – in fact, she'd even heard it whispered he'd been a conscientious objector, with folk shouting after him in the street, "Conshie! Conshie!"

How hard he must have driven himself to keep his factory going. Tiredness was etched on his features in deep lines and furrows, and his eyes looked haunted and melancholy. Chrissie had a sudden desire to make him smile, but didn't know how.

"I'm sorry. I don't mean to be bitter, Charles. The past is over and done – so let's forget it.

"Now, how can I restore your faith in the Kennedys? Tell me what I must do to regain the Kennedy contract, and I'll do it!" She laid a hand persuasively on his sleeve, smiling.

"Be dependable and keep your price competitive," he answered immediately, then paused.

"And you must have the hide of a rhinoceros, yet the soul of tact. That takes some doing in a man. As a woman you might find it well nigh impossible!" he finished bluntly.

Looking down at the hand resting on his arm, Charles wondered if she guessed how devastating her touch was. The slight pressure of her fingers had brought all his old feelings flooding back.

Charles was dismayed. He'd believed himself free from her spell at last. He'd even been on the point of asking Harriet to marry him . . .

Chrissie narrowed her eyes thoughtfully.

"Hmm . . . I see I've got a lot to learn – and male prejudice to overcome as well! But if I offer a high quality oil at a fair price and organise reliable delivery, you might reconsider?"

"Certainly!"

"Then I can't wait to get started!" She laughed gaily.

Charles was amused and touched by her high hopes. Didn't she realise the capital expenditure involved? He'd heard disturbing rumours in the city about old William Kennedy's difficulties. It was said that he was nearly bankrupt.

Indeed, he'd visited the office that morning to offer the old man some practical help. Instead he'd found Chrissie. What an ironic twist of fate!

Chrissie turned to the ledger. On it lay a pile of invoices she'd sorted out from the muddle.

"Look at this, Charles. I've checked the ledger, and these men haven't paid Papa a penny!"

He peered over her shoulder as she flicked through the invoices one by one. He whistled in amazement.

"But these should have been paid months ago!"

"Exactly. There's three or four hundred pounds due, possibly more. I'm going to get it out of the scoundrels. Even if I have to – to twist their arms!" she declared, lifting her chin.

Charles gave a smile of delight. He'd recognised the glorious tilt of the head, that joyous eagerness of eye. It was the look that had made him fall head over heels in love all those years ago.

"You'll be mighty unpopular with the high heid yins!" he warned.

"I don't give a hoot!" She laughed.

Charles eyed her with growing respect.

"Can I help in any way?"

She looked at him thoughtfully.

"Well, yes, there is something. I want a typewriter, but I don't know where to buy one. Can you advise me?"

"I can do better than that. We've a spare machine in the office. I could lend it to you – if you want." He glanced at her speculatively. "Can you type, Chrissie?"

"Not yet, but I'll learn. It's faster, more efficient, and bound to impress these rogues!" She tapped the invoices with a fingertip.

His heart was beating uncomfortably fast. He longed to sweep her into his arms and kiss her soundly, but common sense prevailed.

If he wanted Chrissie, he'd have to tread warily.

He stopped himself abruptly. He couldn't risk being hurt

again. It would finish him this time.

Harriet could make him content, even happy. Charles sighed. But Harriet couldn't bring joy vividly alive with just a touch . . .

He pressed a fist just underneath his quickened heart.

Presently the ache eased and allowed him to concentrate on other matters. Kennedy's papers to see what must be done to make the business solvent.

In the next few days, Chrissie struggled with the intricacies of the typewriter Charles had loaned her. Often, she thought longingly of her niece Georgina, who was an accomplished typist. She was tempted to write to ask for Ina's help, but knew that, as yet, she couldn't afford to pay her.

Chapter 20

INA, however, was otherwise engaged. The sudden appearance of Bruce Cameron, the Australian owner of the farm, had brought about a crisis in her life.

"He wants to sell the farm, Ina!" her mother whispered tragically when the Australian had been closeted all morning with George Kennedy.

"Oh, no!" Ina was aghast. Her father loved the farm, and rarely left it except to visit Forfar market. Where would he go if it was sold? And who would employ a man in his forties with a weak chest?

Her mother was sobbing quietly.

"It'll be the death of your father if he has to leave the farm, Ina. He's had enough worry as it is, with Hughie running off to India."

There was a scheme forming in Ina's head. It seemed shocking when it first occurred to her, but as she examined the idea more cautiously, she saw it had merits. She went in search of the tall Australian.

She found him leaning on a dry-stone dyke, reflectively chewing a stem of grass and studying his hilly inheritance.

"I want to talk to you," she said. He turned lazily and leaned back on his elbows against the wall. He looked amused.

"Fire away, I'm listening."

"Are you married?"

"No." His eyes narrowed. "The right sort of woman's not easy to find in the outback. It's a man's life – hard and lonely. Women can't stick it, unless they're the right sort."

She stood very straight and slim in her mannish clothes.

"Am I the right sort?"

"Well, I dunno. You might be." He fingered his chin doubtfully.

"Then I'll make a bargain with you, Mr Cameron. If you want a wife, I'll marry you! On one condition, though."

Ina came closer. She wanted to know what he was thinking. There was something akin to a gleam of amusement beneath the lowered lids. It encouraged her.

"Don't sell the farm. Leave my mum and dad in peace to manage it for you. If you do, I'll marry you whenever you like. If – if you want to, that is." She broke off, suddenly unsure.

Ina thought about Tam, and the blissful life they might have shared in the little sheiling on the brae. But that was just a dream now. Tam's wife was proudly carrying his unborn baby. Suddenly tears were bright in Ina's eyes.

Bruce Cameron noted them and wondered. This unusual girl didn't seem the weepy type. He couldn't make her out, but he admired her style. Maybe she was the woman he'd been looking for . . .

The tiny farm wasn't important. He'd more than enough land already, back home. If her folks wanted it that badly, it was OK by him. He studied Ina reflectively. She was a no-nonsense sheila and he liked that. There'd been no mention of love, but he guessed that would grow, given time. Bruce suddenly felt lighthearted, as if a weight had been lifted from his shoulder.

Wait till the boys back home found out he'd got himself a little Scots wife after fighting in the war! They'd be green with envy. Envy was just about the only thing that was green in sun-parched billabong, he thought, and grinned widely.

"OK, Georgie. Your pa and ma can keep the farm. I'll settle for marrying you, girl!"

Ina felt weak with relief. There would be time for regrets later. She held out a hand, and they shook hands on the deal.

* * * *

Luckily it was a mild variety of Spanish flu that had struck down William Kennedy. It was bad enough, though, to keep the old man indoors for weeks, giving Chrissie a free hand at the office.

Everything was tidy and orderly now, and she was negotiating with a local seedcrusher for linseed oil. When her father's debtors settled their bills, she would go ahead and order a batch.

The overdue statements had been sent out but, so far, no money had come in. Chrissie decided to send terse reminders to the worst offenders, and fitted paper into the machine. She could type quite well now.

The door crashed open, bringing with it a flurry of December sleet from the Seagate. A red-faced man strode in, icy droplets melting on his mackintosh. He flung an envelope on the desk.

"What's the meaning o' this?"

She picked it up. It was one of the bills she'd sent out.

"Your firm owes my father one hundred and twenty-five pounds, sir. Payment is well overdue. It's all set out quite clearly," she answered pleasantly.

"Oh, I can read, lassie!" He scowled. "Mr Kennedy and I had an agreement. I wasnae to pay until the beginning o' March."

Chrissie raised her brows.

"Oh? You'll have that in writing, I expect? With a calculation of the interest involved?"

"Och, no, of course not. I just had a friendly word wi' your pa, as usual!"

"I'm sorry, but if you want such long credit, I must add interest. Ten per cent is normal, I believe," she pointed out sweetly.

"What?" His voice rose to a roar. "You've already added a hefty charge to my bill, woman! This is extortion."

"No, sir." Chrissie smiled. "It's business."

She smiled to herself again after he'd gone, still blustering. He'd settled the account with bad grace and sworn he'd never darken her doorstep again. Well, she didn't need his sort. Surely there must be honest men in Dundee who'd deal with a woman without prejudice.

* * * *

Lloyd George, the Prime Minister, called for a general election within a month of the armistice. He assured the electorate his aim was to make Britain a country fit for the heroes to live in, and he wanted to get started right away.

"Well, I'm having nothin' to do with warmongers like yon!" Biddy Murphy had the vote for the first time in her life, and was proudly aware of a heavy responsibility.

"Who'll you vote for, Granny?" Mary asked curiously.

"Ah, that would be tellin', pet!" Biddy replied coyly. "Winston Churchill's a wise-looking chiel, but I'll maybe plump for Neddie Scrimgeour, seeing he's for Prohibition an' the bannin' o' strong drink."

She gave her husband a meaningful look. Patrick had been out with several of his cronies the night before, and looked sadly the worse for wear.

Sandra and Mary Rose visited their gran once a week to help put the washing through the mangle. That done, they pegged the clothes to the washing line that ran via a pulley from the kitchen window to the greenie pole. The little girls managed quite well, standing on the coal bunker in the kitchen.

Although Sandra grumbled on principle, she secretly enjoyed visiting her gran and granda. She could relax and be herself in the tenement flat, and needn't watch her ps and qs all the time. She'd let slip casually to her posh new academy friends that her granny lived in the West End. That was near enough the truth, and sounded swanky!

Sandra found life an awful strain these days, keeping up appearances. She was terrified her friends would find that she'd been born in a Lochee tenement. Take yesterday . . .

Sandra had been with her new best friend, Caroline. Caroline's father had a big house in Broughty Ferry and Caroline had a shiny black pony of her own.

Sandra was walking proudly arm-in-arm along Brook Street with Caroline, when who should come whistling round the corner but Norrie Gallacher, the boy who'd once fascinated her. She turned icy cold and tried to make herself small so he wouldn' t notice. A vain hope, for Norrie had eyes like gimlets.

"Oh, hello, there, Sandra! How're you doin' ?" He beamed.

Sandra hauled frantically at Caroline's arm, but her friend stopped dead, gaping curiously. No wonder – Norrie had flipped over into a handstand, and was teetering around on his hands, waving his legs in the air.

"Hey, you, Sandra! Notice anything? I've left the school and I'm into my first pair of long breeks. One an' six oot o' Maggie Glancey's, wi' a Kirkcaldy striped shirt thrown in for luck!"

He fell over in the gutter and picked himself up, much muddier but still cheerful.

"Me and my granny have two rag-an'-bone carties now, Sandra, and we're thinkin' o' buyin' a cuddy an' a flat cart come the spring. Has your ma any rags or jelly jars the day? I' m payin' a guid price, mind. You could hae a balloon an' a paper dolly free, if I get a wee kiss."

Sandra turned hot and cold with embarrassment, but maintained her dignity.

"I will inform Ma – er – Mother. Kindly step aside, boy!"

Dragging Caroline, Sandra pushed past and raced round the corner. Caroline kept looking back curiously.

"Sandra, who was that?"

"Och, just a poor boy my mother gives her cast-offs to," Sandra answered loftily.

"He's quite good-looking, isn't he?"

"Is he? I hadn't noticed." Sandra sniffed.

In the December election, Mr Churchill won a Dundee seat for the Liberals in spite of Biddy's vote for Edwin Scrimgeour.

There was peace in the land at last, but the standard of living of Dundee folk didn't improve any. Civil war in Russia did away with a lucrative market, and the Indian mills which had prospered during the war took vital work from the city.

Men came home from the Army full of hope, to find themselves standing aimlessly on street corners while their womenfolk worked.

The Spanish flu, mild though it was, had weakened William Kennedy. He was quite content to stay at home and let Chrissie take over the business. With her brother Arthur's help and a lot of hard work, she managed to scrape a fair living for her father and her children.

Charles Rankine's advice was invaluable, too. He was one of the few men who didn't condescend when speaking to her, and they'd had some interesting discussions about the jute trade and the way it was going. Chrissie had respect for his views. He was usually right.

She was writing up the ledger and attempting to ignore warm sunshine beckoning outside, when her sister-in-law, Lizzie, came into the office. Lizzie held little Sammy by the hand, which was unusual. She usually came alone – or with Arthur.

Chrissie's son was toddling now. He was pink-cheeked and sturdy, though still rather small for his age. He looked delightful in a white sailor suit with a navy-blue collar. Chrissie's heart gave a lurch, and she held out her arms. The boy immediately retreated behind Lizzie's skirts, peeping out at his mother with suspicious blue eyes.

The awful truth was that Sammy was afraid of the smiling woman. She seemed friendly and smelled nice, but she held him so close and looked so sad. It made him want to wriggle and cry.

When Chrissie was near, undercurrents of emotion from Lizzie and Arthur rocked his happy existence and frowns and whispers disturbed him.

Sometimes he would wake crying in the night, dreaming Chrissie had arrived and was carrying him away from those he loved. She was reaching for him now, and he was scared. He buried his small face in Lizzie's comforting skirts and clung on with all his might.

Lizzie patted Sammy's curly head.

"I'm sorry, Chrissie, he's shy. He won't let me out of his sight. It's just a phase he's going through, poor lamb."

She picked up the little boy and held him in her arms.

Sammy felt secure there. He sucked his thumb, watching Chrissie warily.

"Arthur's been offered a position in India, at the Titaghur mill," Lizzie announced. "It's a wonderful opportunity."

"Oh, Lizzie, I am pleased!"

"Yes, we're both delighted." Lizzie rocked the child, looking away. "I'll have to go to Calcutta with him."

There was a long silence. A bluebottle buzzed frantically, beating itself in vain against the impenetrable window-pane.

"And – Sammy?" Chrissie asked carefully at last. Her heart was pounding so hard she could hardly speak. Lizzie looked up.

"We've been assured the standard of life in India is excellent. Arthur has talked to people who have lived there. They're all agreed the risks to a young child in India are no greater than those in this chill climate."

There was a coldness in Chrissie's heart. A hopelessness.

"You want to take Sammy to India with you, don't you?"

Lizzie looked miserably uncertain, almost scared.

"Chrissie – he clings to me. He's devoted to Arthur. What would it do to him if you take him from us now?

"And how could you care for him and give him the attention he needs while running your father's business? It impossible. Disastrous for you – and for Sammy!"

Chrissie stood up. She slammed the ledger shut with a bang and threw down the pen with such force the nib spattered ink on the blotter.

"Am I never to get my son back?"

Lizzie was on the verge of tears.

"Chrissie – he loves us!" she pleaded frantically.

Chrissie held out her arms.

"Sammy, I love you so much! Come to me, my darling."

Sammy cringed away from his mother. He flung his arms around Lizzie's neck and screamed, a frantic, high-pitched screaming that went on and on. His nightmare was coming true! This woman wanted to take him away! He screamed in terror.

Chrissie covered her face with her hands.

"Lizzie! Lizzie, stop him! I can't bear it."

Lizzie rocked the hysterical child, whispering to him, soothing him. Gradually the dreadful crying stopped. Sammy lay spent against Lizzie's shoulder, with only an occasional sobbing hiccup to show how great his distress had been. Chrissie slowly uncovered her face, and the two women looked at one another over the boy's curly head.

"You see, Chrissie?" Lizzie whispered. "You do see?"

Chrissie nodded. The heart had gone out of her. She wanted to touch her son's soft, curling hair, but she didn't dare in case he started screaming again.

She turned away and watched the poor trapped bluebottle beating itself against the windowpane.

"You'll write to me, won't you?" she said huskily. "You'll tell me what he's doing?"

There was a feverish light of gratitude in Lizzie's eyes, and tears on her cheeks.

"Yes. Yes, of course I will. Oh, thank you, Chrissie!"

Chapter 21

THE woman and child must have stolen quietly away
because Chrissie roused herself with a start some time later
to find she was alone. She buried her face in her hands,
giving way at last to sorrow and despair.

Bessie had foreseen this, she thought. If only Papa had
listened and taken Sammy away from Lizzie, this would
never have happened. Bessie would have helped Chrissie to
care for him right from the start.

But Bessie had gone. Chrissie had searched and searched,
but her dear friend had completely disappeared. She wept
anew for Bessie.

A hand touched her shoulder, and she started up, ashamed
to be caught red-eyed and weeping. Especially by Charles
Rankine!

Charles was studying her with such a strange expression,
dark and shadowed. She pushed wildly at her disordered
hair. She must look a sight!

"What's wrong, Chrissie? What's happened?"

The whole story came tumbling out. She hadn't meant to
tell him, but she couldn't help herself. It was so long since
she'd had a sympathetic ear, so many weary years since
she'd had a shoulder to cry on.

"What else could I do, Charles? I love Sammy – I want
him! But if I take him it will cause so much unhappiness to

him – and to Lizzie and Arthur . . ."

Her lips trembled and she looked about to weep again. He took her hands and held them tight.

"Chrissie, your boy will come back to you one day. He'll come back of his own free will, whatever Lizzie says. Until then, you'll have to let him go, I'm afraid. The damage was done when you entrusted him to Lizzie as a baby."

"I blame myself, Charles!"

He smiled.

"Don't. It's not your fault, or Lizzie's. It's a twist of fate, difficult to understand until time has passed, and you see there was a purpose behind it after all."

He pulled her to her feet. Smiling, he looked suddenly younger, more carefree.

"You need the afternoon off, Mrs Murphy. A breath of fresh air and the sun on your face – never mind the freckles. I know just the place!"

Chrissie hung back. She felt a little breathless at the turn of events.

"But – but the ledger, Charles!"

"Blast the ledger!" he said cheerfully. He flipped over the printed card hanging on the glass door so that it read *Closed* to the outside world.

"Come along, Mrs Murphy, put on your bonnet!"

Was it instinct that drew him to the harbour, Charles wondered afterwards. They walked along Seagate, which once formed the heart of old Dundee and now held a different spirit, in the bonded whisky warehouse rebuilt after a disastrous fire. Then they turned south, down an old, narrow street realigned by the building of the new Caird Hall, towards Queen Victoria's Royal Arch that led to the bustling commerce of the riverfront.

Harriet Bowers, buying a newspaper in the shadow of the town house pillars, looked up just in time to see them disappear. It was like receiving a blow. Harriet actually put a hand on a stone pillar for support, she felt so shaky.

Charles had been attentive recently, so very kind and companionable that her confidence in their future together had grown.

He had even kissed her. Oh, not passionately or anything like that, just a gentle fleeting token. A love token? She had persuaded herself that it was.

He never mentioned Chrissie, and so Harriet had discounted her as a rival. Until now.

Charles was laughing, looking down at Chrissie. His bowler hat was tilted, and he looked as young and eager as a schoolboy with his first love.

Tears stung Harriet's eyes. She would have given all her medical skill, all the honours won in the war, to have Charles Rankine look at her like that.

He hadn't told her he was seeing Chrissie. That's what hurt most. She could have borne the shock if only he'd told her. It was like a betrayal.

Harriet walked away blindly.

"Hey, wifie, you forgot your change!" the news vendor shouted.

Harriet walked on unheeding. The man shrugged and grinned and cheerfully pocketed the unexpected bonanza.

* * * *

Chrissie hadn't visited the harbour since they'd sold her ship, the *Christina K*. Now, as she strolled along the wharves with Charles, she responded to the familiar atmosphere with delight. The smell of the sea and tar and fishing nets was just as she remembered.

There was a neglected old hull in the berth where the *Christina K* used to lie. Steamers loaded with wood from the Baltic occupied the quays where the whaling ships had once anchored.

Chrissie turned away abruptly. Was her ship lying deserted in some foreign harbour, rotting and forlorn?

Further along, men were unloading a jute ship newly arrived from India, dockers swarming round the bales. Chrissie paused to watch, thinking anxiously of her nephew, Hughie. There had been no word of him for months.

"Did you know my niece, Georgina, had married an Australian, Charles? It surprised us all, it was so sudden. George and Jeannie must be lonely, with Ina so far away and Hughie seeking his fortune in India," Chrissie remarked lightly, trying to hide her misgivings.

"There are plenty of great opportunities for young people in both countries." Charles smiled down at her.

She felt comforted by his words. Her niece and nephew would survive. They were Kennedys!

It was pleasant, walking in the sun. They left the docks,

laughingly dodging a pug engine chuffing along the rails, and strolled by the riverside. The marine parade, stretching before them to the railway bridge, was one of the finest in the country, a popular walk.

Charles stopped and leaned his elbows on the sea wall, watching the Fifie, the ferry linking Dundee with Fife, forge its busy path across the river. He was completely happy, acutely aware of Chrissie beside him. This afternoon had sealed his fate for good or ill. Charles had made up his mind.

"I want to kiss you, Chrissie. I want to take you in my arms and never let you go. I want to marry you, my dear," Charles told her quietly, his heart beating crazily, an uneven, palpitating beat.

Chrissie had been happy and content until that moment. The pleasure of warm sunshine on her face and soothing lap of water against the sea wall had been enough. Now Charles had spoiled it all.

Oh, she liked him! More than that, she felt warmth for him, tenderness and pity. But these emotions were pale shadows of the love she had for Danny.

And then there was Harriet. She'd loved Charles so long, so faithfully. And she was the perfect wife for him!

Chrissie turned to face him, and they looked at one another.

"Charles, I don't love you. Not – not in that way," she told him frankly.

He had known it was going to be difficult.

"I can accept that. To have you as my wife would be

enough for me."

"Would it? I don't believe it would be fair to marry you, without love."

She turned away.

"And what about Harriet? She loves you."

He smiled, grim and sad.

"I don't love Harriet, not in that way. I won't marry Harriet without love."

He cast her own words back at her, then touched her bare arm, caressing it.

"It's stalemate, Chrissie. But it doesn't change the fact. I love you and I want to marry you. On your own terms, if I have to!"

She drew her arm away, shivering, although the blood coursing through her veins felt hot. She didn't know what to do or say.

"Charles, I have to think. You must give me time to think!"

"Of course." He nodded gravely.

She turned to go. He would have followed but she stopped him.

"No, Charles. Please leave me. I want to be alone for a while."

He looked at her, and the yearning in his eyes made her heart beat faster.

"Just remember I love you, Chrissie. Enough for both of us, my darling."

Chrissie hurried away, almost running. She couldn't feel the pleasant warmth of the lovely afternoon any more because she was cold and dark inside.

One part of her wanted to marry Charles for the comfort and security it would give her father and children. Aye, and herself, too. But it wasn't a fair bargain for Charles, without love.

She was in terror in case she hurt him again. And yet, whatever she did, whatever she decided, she must hurt him. And Harriet, too. Her best friend, who'd loved her, supported her for as long as she could remember.

Chrissie let herself into the office. Automatically, she took off her hat and opened the ledger and sat staring unseeingly at the columns of neat figures.

Presently, a shadow darkened

the glass door, and she looked up.

Harriet came in qujckly almost jerkily. Quite composed, she looked at Chrissie.

"I've been waiting for you to come back. I must talk to you, Chrissie!"

Harriet sat in the chair reserved for visitors.

"I saw you with Charles just now, Chrissie!"

"Yes, it was such a beautiful day, Charles took me to the harbour. I hadn't been there since Papa sold the *Christina K.* and – and oh Harriet, I'm – I'm sorry!"

Chrissie felt guilty, but what had she done wrong? She'd never encouraged Charles Rankine. His proposal had taken her completely by surprise.

Harriet smiled. It took considerable effort but nobody would have guessed.

"Don't apologise. You've helped me out of a very awkward situation."

"Have I?"

Chrissie looked mystified, and Harriet laughed.

"Yes, dear! I'm very fond of Charles, and I've flirted with him shamefully since I came home. Mama and Papa haven't helped – they treat him as if we're already engaged. The poor dear must feel almost duty-bound to marry me – although I know he really doesn't want to!

"I've been dreading him proposing because I can't think how I can refuse without hurting his feelings. When I saw you two together I realised it was the perfect solution. You can take Charles off my hands, Chris!"

Chrissie stared at her friend in bewilderment.

"But l thought you were in love with him? Why would you refuse to marry him?"

Harriet shrugged.

"For a woman, marriage means total commitment to husband and home. That's just not possible for me. How could I abandon my medical career when there's so much still to be done?"

"But, Harriet –"

Chrissie would have argued, but Harriet pressed on hurriedly.

"l looked after women workers in a munitions factory before I went to France. It's shocking how many were suffering from chronic complaints which could have been cured easily if they'd been caught earlier.

"Call it false modesty and ignorance if you like, but they wouldn't dream of consulting a male doctor. I want to change all that!"

There was a zealous glow in Harriet's eyes which Chrissie found convincing. She had seen for herself how millworkers shrugged off "women's troubles" and went on working until they dropped, rather than visit a doctor or pay precious sixpences for a consultation.

"Well, there's certainly a great need for doctors who understand the trials and tribulations of womenfolk." She eyed her friend thoughtfully.

"I knew you'd understand, Chris," Harriet said, smiling her relief.

She'd succeeded. Chrissie was convinced she was dedicated to her career. Now she must remove herself from the scene and leave Charles free to marry the woman he loved.

Harriet leaned forward, eager to press home the advantage.

"Charles has always been fond of you. Look after him for me. I wouldn't want him to be lonely when I leave."

"Leave?" Chrissie was startled. "Where are you going? When?"

"I've been offered a job in Glasgow. A doctor there contacted me and suggested I might like to care for the women patients on his panel. Apparently my name had been suggested by one of my former colleagues who knew of my interest in the effects of living conditions on a patient's health. There should be plenty scope for research in the

Glasgow slums!"

Chrissie shuddered. She knew Harriet would work herself into the ground trying to solve insoluble problems. Why couldn't Charles have fallen in love with her? It might have been the saving of her . . .

"Oh, Harriet! Please take care!" she begged tearfully.

Harriet stood up. If she didn't get out of the cramped little office soon, she feared she would break down.

"I will, don't worry. Just make Charles happy, Chris. That's all I ask."

"Don't worry about Charles. He won't be lonely," Chrissie promised recklessly. "I'll see to that."

Harriet hugged her and walked out of the office. Outside, the rumble of wheels heralded the arrival of a string of horses and carts laden with jute bales. She stood patiently to let them pass, her eyes misted with bitter tears.

A tramcar clanged and clattered fretfully as it ground along the rails, hindered by the carts. Harriet paid no heed to the impatient sounds and earned a glare from the driver as she crossed the road in a daze.

The streets were thronged with shoppers out enjoying the sunshine, but Harriet scarcely noticed.

Charles had never loved her. Their love affair had just been a figment of her imagination . . . her hopes of married life with a husband and children only a wistful dream.

Harriet Bowers had faced up to reality. Now she turned away resolutely to begin a quite different future.

Chapter 22

CHRISTINA MURPHY married Charles Rankine in the autumn of 1919, when the leaves had turned rich gold and fallen in rustling carpets on the pavements. It was a quiet wedding, in an empty, echoing Broughty Ferry church.

Chrissie's two daughters were proud little bridesmaids and her brother, George, served as Charles's best man.

Her other two brothers were not present. Ernest had married his Geraldine in America, and was living in Detroit. Arthur had sailed for India a month before, accompanied by his wife, Lizzie, and foster son, Sammy.

William Kennedy found his eyes filled with tears of emotion as he watched Charles slip the ring on Chrissie's finger. He was delighted by the match, but not many of Charles's friends and relatives had turned up for the happy occasion.

He knew Broughty Ferry folk remembered Chrissie had once turned down Charles Rankine for a common juteworker. A taste of the hard life in the slums had turned her into a wee gold-digger, they said. Out to catch a rich husband this time!

And, as for Charles Rankine, he wanted his heid examined. Imagine marrying a poverty stricken widow with a puckle of bairns, when there were plenty young Dundee spinsters much more suitable!

Chrissie had heard the whisperings, too, but paid no

attention, although they were near enough the truth.

She didn't love Charles with the single-minded passion she'd felt for Danny, but she liked and respected him. And she needed a man to help with her father's struggling oil business. She'd been completely honest about her feelings, and Charles had been willing to settle for what she could give. On that understanding, Chrissie had agreed to marry him.

Chrissie dreaded telling Sandra and Mary Rose they would have a stepfather, but the two girls had taken the news well. A week or so before the wedding, they'd had a frank discussion with Charles, from which Chrissie had been excluded.

"What shall we call you?" Sandra asked Charles seriously. "We can't call you Daddy, because we already have a daddy in heaven. Papa's out of fashion, Father sounds a bit too swanky and Mr Rankine sounds awful like a school teacher."

Charles considered this very important question with due care.

"Don't you think Charles sounds nice and friendly?"

"Charlie is my darlin', my darlin' , my darlin'!" Mary Rose warbled cheerfully.

"Yes, indeed, Mary Rose. Charlie would also be acceptable between good friends such as ourselves," Charles agreed, endeavouring to keep a straight face.

Sandra studied the new man in her life critically. He was tall and thin, and so unlike her beloved daddy in heaven, it was impossible to make comparisons. Maybe that was a good thing, Sandra thought wisely.

"How big is your house, Charles?" Mary Rose asked.

"Quite big. It has four public rooms, eight bedrooms and two bathrooms. Oh, and a large conservatory."

Mary Rose's face fell.

"Och, isn't there a kitchen for Mummy? Where's she to do the cooking? Where's she to do the washing if there isn't a tub? Is there a steamie nearby?"

Charles smothered a grin.

"Your mummy won't work in the kitchen any more. Cook and the maids will see to the meals and housework, and the washerwoman will do the washing and the ironing for us all."

Sandra's eyes grew round as she viewed the dazzling possibilities.

"Charles, is there a paddock?"

"Well, there's a field behind the house. Would you like a pony, my dear?"

"No, thank you, Charles, not a pony, just riding togs. But only if you can afford it. I'm afraid they're awful expensive. Caroline's cost a whole pound." Sandra was scared stiff of horses, but she dreamed of cutting a dash in Broughty Ferry!

Mary Rose climbed hopefully on to his knee.

"I'd love a pony. Charles, but I'm no' fussy about the togs, if they're a bit pricey. Mind, if there's two bob to spare, a wee canary in a cage, like my granny's, would be awfy nice."

"I'll consider your good advice concerning my finances,

and let you know my conclusions in due course," Charles said gravely, a twinkle in his eye.

* * * *

Chrissie's daughters scattered rice with joyful abandon as she and Charles came out of church. It felt strange to be another man's wife.

Thinking of that other wedding years ago, sadness overwhelmed Chrissie. Although she laughed merrily and shook showers of rice from her hat, her eyes glistened with tears.

Charles's hands tightened on hers and Chrissie smiled at him gratefully. He seemed to sense her every mood and must have guessed she was thinking of Danny. It must hurt him, yet his eyes were kind and brimming over with love for her.

They were to spend their honeymoon at Beechyhill, Charles's family home near Broughty Ferry. His father and mother had died some years previously, and Charles had been living there on his own. He looked forward to the house coming alive again, the gloomy silence broken by children's voices and happy laughter.

William Kennedy had offered to look after his two granddaughters for a week to give Chrissie and her new husband a little time to themselves. Chrissie had found a housekeeper for her father, who had refused point blank to leave his home. She was a pleasant and kindly woman, though not a patch on Bessie.

Chrissie watched her father and the two children set off for home in a cab, the two girls waving frantically. She was suddenly terrified by what she'd done. Could she be happy marrying without love, and more importantly, could she make Charles happy?

For a few panicky moments she wished she could revoke the solemn vows she'd just made. Then she shook her head. It was too late now for regrets!

Charles helped Chrissie into the motor car and climbed into the driver's seat. Tooting the horn joyfully, he set off.

Chrissie waved to George and Jeannie and a few curious onlookers, then set her face resolutely towards her husband's house.

The servants were waiting by the front door, drawn up in a line according to rank. Chrissie counted a cook, parlourmaid, housemaid, a nervous wee tweeny who looked frightened out of her wits, and a string of elderly gardeners. They looked eager to cast a critical eye on their new mistress.

"I'm sorry, dearest." Charles was apologetic. "Most of the domestic staff left during the war."

"You mean there were more?"

He laughed as the car drew to a halt.

"'Fraid so! Come and charm your household, Mrs Rankine!"

Chrissie did her best exchanging a word with everyone and being careful to note the tweeny's name. She was encouraged to overhear a whispered exchange between the cook and the head gardener, as she and Charles passed into the hallway.

"Well, the new mistress seems a decent-like woman, Archie. No' the stuck-up bossy kind, and that's a God's blessing!"

"Aye, Cookie, she'll no' wear the breeks in this hoose. Maister Charles has a mind o' his ain!"

Having passed muster with the staff, Chrissie paused and looked in wonder at the carved staircase and the ornate ceilings.

"Come on, I'll show you round," Charles offered, watching her with a smile.

Holding her hand, he led her from room to room. Chrissie was staggered by the beautiful furnishings and the sheer size, but the ultimate luxury was the downstairs cloakroom and two sumptuous bathrooms upstairs.

She couldn't help comparing these with her tenement flat in Lochee, and the single tap, of which Danny had been so proud. They'd shared an outside toilet on the platty with five other families.

"And this is your room, Chrissie. I've had it redecorated for you," Charles was saying, opening a door at the head of the stairs. "Mine is at the end of the passageway."

Chrissie went slowly and thoughtfully into the rose-pink room with its delicate, feminine draperies and mirrored dressing-table. For a moment she stood looking round in silence. Then she wheeled round to face her husband, colour in her cheeks.

"Charles, I appreciate what you've done, but I won't be a wife in name only!"

He put his hands on her shoulders and looked down at her.

"But you don't love me! You told me so. I can accept that – and make no demands on you. It's enough to have you near."

Warmth flooded through Chrissie's heart. What a special man this new husband of hers was! But what he was suggesting was no marriage. It was a mockery of marriage – and she'd have nothing to do with anything so false and hollow. She put her arms around her husband's waist and looked up into his eyes.

"There are many different ways of loving, Charles. I want to be your wife and your friend. I want to be beside you always, good times and bad, not kept apart like a goddess in a rose-pink shrine!"

As his arms tightened round her, she reached up and kissed him gently on the lips. Charles's arms tightened round her and gave her a little shake.

"Oh, Chrissie! Chrissie, you're wonderful! I spent hours agonising over the blasted pink bedroom, and I needn't have bothered. Och, I could've saved the money and bought myself a new car!"

Laughing, Charles grabbed his wife by the hand and led her merrily along the passageway to his room . . .

* * * *

To her surprise, Chrissie found she enjoyed being waited on hand and foot by the staff. It left the newlyweds plenty of time to spend together and Charles drove her around the countryside, for the weather was clear and fine.

They visited Forfar, and the hilly little burgh of Kirriemuir. From the Northmuir, Chrissie viewed the foothills of the Grampians, lifting her head to let the keen wind blow through her hair.

Charles watched, enchanted. He was happy, even though he knew Chrissie had only married him for the security he could give. That thought was always there, at the back of his mind, even when she kissed him with warmth.

He was too happy. It couldn't last, he thought suddenly with a cold shiver that had nothing to do with the chilly wind.

"Come on. Let's go home, darling," he said, putting an arm protectively around her.

Chrissie went willingly. Tomorrow the holiday would end. Her two little daughters would arrive and Charles must return to work at the factory. Their married life would begin in earnest.

Sitting after dinner that night, Chrissie began making plans. Her hands were busy, embroidering roses on a dress for Mary Rose.

"The children can go to school with us in the morning, Charles. We'll all travel together in the car, but I shall come home from the office by tram as usual."

He glanced up from the paper he'd been studying.

"But, Chrissie, you don't have to work any more! I'm putting a clerk in your father's office to handle day-to-day transactions, and I'll keep an eye on the rest myself."

She stopped sewing, the needle poised mid-air.

"But the house runs like clockwork without me! I'll check accounts and order stores and see the linen's mended, of course, but there's nothing else for me to do! I can't lead an idle existence, Charles. It would drive me daft!"

"I gather ladies meet regularly for tea parties. Some of them play bridge in the afternoons, go shopping or do a little voluntary charity work. I'm sure you'll find some way of filling in your time, darling," Charles said.

His wife frowned furiously, then stamped her foot with frustration.

"I won't waste my time with gossip and cards! I've no intention of buying clothes I don't need and giving condescending help to poor folk! Put a clerk in Papa's office by all means, Charles, I could do with a help. But I'll work as usual, and you won't stop me!"

"Chrissie, it isn't done for the wife of a man in my position to work." Charles looked aghast. "What will people say?"

"I don't care what they say. I've never paid the slightest attention to malicious blethers, and neither should you."

He sat in silence for a moment.

"I'll tell you what they'll say. The men will blame me for not keeping my wife in order, and the women will condemn me for sending you to earn a living for yourself. Either way, I can't win. You and Harriet will start a revolution in Dundee between the pair of you!"

"Good! It's not before time!" She plumped down angrily into the chair and picked up her sewing, stabbing the needle into the delicate fabric.

Presently, she peeked across at her husband cautiously and met a humorous eye and raised eyebrows.

Chrissie's lips began to twitch. She couldn't stop herself, his expression was so comical. She was only just beginning to plumb the depths of her husband's humour, so different from Danny's boisterous wit. She burst out laughing.

"Oh, Charles! You were teasing me!"

"Well – just a wee bit. You're so beautiful when you're angry," Charles admitted.

* * * *

So Chrissie returned to her father's office, and found her task lightened by the clerk Charles had employed.

Joseph was a pleasant man in his late fifties. He worked quietly and efficiently and didn't mind taking orders from a woman. He and Chrissie got along famously.

Dundee had been badly hit by the post-war recession. The crowds of men standing on street corners grew steadily larger, and more and more women were out of work, too. There were many families cold and hungry that winter.

Charles Rankine struggled to keep his workers in full employment, but he had to work long hours to do it.

A slump in jute orders hit Kennedy's, too. Chrissie was at her wits' end looking for new outlets for oil when Charles inadvertently gave her an idea.

As usual, he arrived at the office to drive her home. He'd been having problems with the old car, and that day was no exception. He cranked the starting handle, cursing beneath his breath.

When he got the engine to turn over and splutter to life, he climbed in beside Chrissie.

"Charles, cars need oil, don't they?"

"Yes, to lubricate the engine. That's what's wrong with this one, it's burning too much. The engine needs rebored."

Charles glanced at Chrissie curiously.

"Why d'you ask?"

"Couldn't Kennedy's supply lubricating oil for engines as well as whale and linseed oil? Trams and buses must use a lot. And the market must be growing daily with so many vehicles on the road."

He changed gear thoughtfully.

"I'll look into it, Chrissie. We can cost it out and try our luck, if it's feasible."

Chapter 23

HARRIET'S little writing desk had gone with Chrissie to Beechyhill. She wrote regularly to Ernest in America, George on the farm and Arthur in India. She also wrote to her niece, Georgina, far away in Australia.

Chrissie's letters were a godsend to Ina, a precious link with home as she struggled to adapt to life in the outback.

One day, Chrissie sat down and wrote a simple letter to her Sammy, her little son, telling him how much she loved him.

Sammy was still too young to read, of course, but Chrissie hoped Lizzie would read the letter to him.

She illustrated the pages liberally with drawings. Mary Rose, riding her pony, and Sandra, decked in riding togs that had never seen a horse's back. She sketched the tabby cat purring by the fireside, and the canary trilling in its cage.

Chrissie discovered she had an aptitude for sketching, and smiled to herself as she read over what she'd written. It read like a storybook. She hoped the little boy would enjoy the stories about his big sisters and their pets, and think more kindly of his mother in consequence.

* * * *

Lizzie Kennedy frowned when the bearer brought a letter to Sammy in Chrissie's handwriting. Lizzie had just finished tiffin and was dining alone that afternoon, a punkah fanning the air gently above her head.

The ayah had removed Sammy for his nap, which was a blessing, because the little boy would be interested in the letter from Scotland, and Lizzie might have been forced to read it to him. She stared at the letter thoughtfully. Who was to know it had ever arrived? The bearer couldn't read.

Sammy had forgotten all about his mother, and seemed much more settled. He'd grown into a sturdy little boy who seldom cried and played happily all day long.

Was it fair to remind him of the threat to his security? Should she read Chrissie's letter to him, and risk upsetting him?

Surely not! Time enough for the problem to be faced when the boy was older and more able to cope with the complex situation.

The decision made, Lizzie couldn't bring herself to destroy the letter. She crossed to the bureau she'd had shipped out to India, and unlocked it.

One of the ornamental brackets inside was not what it seemed. It could be pulled out like a drawer to reveal a roomy secret compartment behind. Lizzie slipped the letter inside, and quickly closed the opening.

Just in time. She heard Arthur's step on the verandah outside and almost at once her husband came into the room. He had brought two strangers with him.

"Lizzie, dear, a most remarkable thing has happened!" Arthur exclaimed excitedly.

"You know I've been looking for my nephew Hughie – George's boy? Well, who should walk into my office this morning but Hughie himself. And here he is!"

Lizzie studied the young man. Hughie was very brown and dressed more like an Indian than a European. Clear, blue eyes reminded her strongly of Chrissie, as he came forward and dutifully pecked her cheek.

"Hello, Auntie Lizzie! I'm jolly glad to arrive at Titaghur at last! I've had some hair-raising adventures on the road from Bombay." Hughie grinned. "Remind me to tell you all about it some time."

Lizzie thought him a little too forward for a youth of eighteen. She enjoyed her new position as memsahib and had quickly become used to being treated with deference. Hughie's casual attitude rankled.

Hughie put his arm around the other visitor.

"Auntie Lizzie, this is my wife, Jani. I met her at the mission in Tundragore, and we fell in love at first sight! The missionary performed the ceremony just two months ago," Hughie announced happily.

Lizzie Kennedy gazed at the beautiful, dark-eyed Anglo-Indian girl in Hughie's arms and tightened her lips ominously. She could foresee many problems ahead!

* * * *

Charles continued his desperate battle to keep Rankine's factory going. Indian mills had captured the market for cheaper jute cloth, but Charles was one of the first in Dundee to adapt his looms to cater for a higher quality product.

The factory began producing carpet yarn and jute backing

for linoleum, which kept Rankine's workforce employed during hard times. Chrissie's firm was doing modestly well, supplying an increasing demand for engine oil.

The country had grown disenchanted. Lloyd George's promise of a better life for heroes had not materialised. The cost of food rose, and wages fell. Men who'd fought bravely for their country couldn't find work.

There were riots in Dundee when the Jute Trade Board announced another cut in basic wages. Men and women were bitterly angry, and the whole country was in a ferment of discontent. In October 1922, Lloyd George resigned as Prime Minister.

The prospect of a general election excited Chrissie. She remembered she'd carried a suffragette banner with Harriet before the war. Now she was over thirty, and had the vote for the very first time. It seemed a great triumph for women.

Dundee was in the grip of election fever. There were crowds of men at every street corner and outside every pub, arguing loudly. There were six candidates standing for two Dundee seats, but one candidate was seriously ill.

Winston Churchill had just had his appendix removed in London and was in no state to electioneer. His loyal wife, Clementine, took over. She arrived in Dundee with her infant daughter, Mary, and set grimly to work.

Clemmie was appalled by the misery she saw as she campaigned in the city. She wrote and told her husband so, commenting uneasily on the unrest abroad in the town, and how she couldn't blame the poor folk.

Clemmie experienced the bitter unrest at first hand. In the newly opened Caird Hall, her large audience barracked her speech repeatedly, and in Larch Street Hall the meeting she bravely attended ended in uproar.

Enough was enough. Winston got out of his sickbed and travelled north. An LNER engine in gleaming green and black livery brought him to Taybridge Station, but he fared no better than his Clemmie on the noisy hustings.

Sandra found the election procedure wildly exciting. All the schools closed on polling day, and gangs of children roamed the streets, shouting slogans.

Mary Rose was out riding on her pony, but Sandra put on her best coat and hat and walked into town to join in the fun. The scenes in front of the Pillars were enthralling. Crowds of people watched Mr and Mrs Churchill drive up Reform Street in a bright red car, smiling and waving.

Everyone was in high spirits on this fine November day. William Gallacher, one of the other candidates, was doing a tour of the polling booths in a gaily decorated horse-drawn landau. It was like Band Day at Magdalen Green, only better and noisier, Sandra thought happily.

There were crowds of rival supporters in the street, waving banners and shouting slogans, and as she'd expected, Norrie Gallacher was among them. He spotted her and came over, waving a placard. She was surprised by how tall he'd grown.

"Mind now, Sandra! Vote for my namesake, Willie Gallacher!" he urged.

"Och, save your blethers. I'm only fourteen," Sandra said.

"Oh, aye." He scrutinised her from head to toe. "I can see you're just a wee lassie yet. Never mind, I can wait!"

"You neednae bother, Norrie Gallacher. I've telt ye till I'm tired, I'm to marry a rich toff!"

Sandra put her nose in the air and marched off, leaving him grinning after her.

Chrissie and Biddy Murphy were excited and a little stunned when the man they'd voted for polled many more votes than Mr Churchill. The mill girls went shouting through the streets, wildly excited because their vote for a man of peace had changed the course of history.

"Neddie Scrymgeour's in!" was the shout all around the town.

Chrissie soon had another reason for rejoicing. She found she was expecting a baby after a long, fruitless wait. She had almost given up hope of having the child she and Charles wanted, but now the doctor had confirmed her suspicions.

"Oh, Chrissie, my dear!" Charles pressed his fist to his chest to stop the painful hammering of his heart. He was overjoyed, of course, but suddenly very frightened for the safety of his wife and child. Women died in childbirth, and babies were always a risk.

A little of Chrissie's joy faded at his expression. He had turned pale with shock. He'd been working too hard, as usual, and she knew what a strain that put on his weak heart.

She kneeled down beside his chair and took her hand.

"What is it, dear? Aren't you pleased?"

"I'm delighted – and absolutely terrified! Oh, darling, will you be all right?"

Holding his cold hand, she felt a protective warmth flow from her hand to his. It was a warmth that came straight from a heart touched deeply by his concern. She laughed at him gently, with emotional tears in her eyes.

"Oh, Charles, I'm as strong as a horse! Promise me you won't worry any more."

And so he promised. He hid his fears and worried in secret. Another worry, another weight of responsibility, another ache in his heart.

* * * *

Biddy Murphy died as she had lived, quietly, and with no fuss. Patrick found her sitting in her chair as if she slept, a gentle smile on her lips, her old hands folded across a framed photograph of Danny, the soldier son she'd loved so dearly.

Chrissie wept many sorrowful tears for her dear friend and mother-in-law. She insisted on attending the funeral, although she was heavy and awkward with the baby on the way.

Charles would have gone with her, but Chrissie asked to be alone, and he respected that. The girls were at school, and she let them bide there. They were sad enough as it was to lose their beloved granny.

What a turn-out there was for Biddy at the cemetery on the high hill! Patrick wiped his nose emotionally as he surveyed the crowds of folk, all blessed by Biddy's kindness at one time or another.

"Oh, she'd have been fair dumbfounded to see a' thae folk, Chrissie! She'd have been proud. Mind you, she'd have been worried sick in case she hadnae bought enough biled ham to go the rounds afterwards."

At the end of the service, Chrissie lifted her head and dabbed tears from her eyes. The crowds were dispersing quietly while Patrick was led away, comforted and supported by a group of Murphys.

A shadowy face turned towards Chrissie for a fleeting instant, staring at her from a group of dark-clad, shawled women on the path.

Chrissie felt the blood drain from her cheeks. Bessie! Was that Bessie? She started forward, pushing her way through the mourners.

"Oh, please – let me pass! Bessie!" she called frantically. "Bessie, where are you?"

She broke through, pushing the startled millworkers aside, but there was no sign of anyone resembling her old nurse. Chrissie looked round wildly. A movement caught her eye on the side of the hill beside a tombstone. It was the shawled figure of a woman, hurrying away.

Chrissie stared. It couldn't be Bessie! Why would Bessie run away? It made no sense – yet she was sure it had been Bessie's face in the crowd!

"Bessie, wait!" Chrissie called again, setting off in pursuit.

She was forced to rest so often she despaired of ever catching up with the figure hurrying ahead. Then she'd catch another glimpse of the woman in front, hobbling along, and the pursuit would start again.

Once, the woman paused and anced over her shoulder. She broke into a shuffling run as if terror-struck.

It couldn't be Bessie. This was an old, untidy woman!

Chrissie hesitated. What was the point of going on? Exhausting herself? Alarming the poor old soul?

But maybe she would know where Bessie was?

Chrissie hurried on. She dared not run. She was so heavy with the bairn, heavier than she'd been with any of the others.

"Wait! Please stop!" she called out desperately, but the old woman had reached the Hawkhill and was ducking in and out of the maze of wynds and pends.

Chrissie thought she'd lost her, then suddenly she appeared out of a close with a woman shaking her fist after her. Without looking round, she shuffled away down the street towards the slums they called the Blue Mountains.

Chrissie hurried behind, catching sight of a skirt disappearing into the darkness of a filthy close strewn with rubbish. Taking a deep breath, Chrissie plunged in after her.

Ahead, a broken door creaked on its hinges. Beyond it she could hear someone panting, gasping and coughing.

Chrissie pushed open the door cautiously and stepped into a miserable room. The woman she'd been chasing was huddled on the bed, her face hidden in her shawl, coughing.

Chrissie went over to the crouching figure and put a hand gently on her shoulder.

"I'm so sorry, chasing after you like this. I'm looking for a woman called Bessie McCutcheon. I'm sure I saw her at the funeral. Please, do you know where she is?"

The woman didn't answer. Clutching the shawl close to her chin, she turned slowly and stared up at Chrissie in silence . . .

Chapter 24

CHRISSIE gave a heartbroken cry. How could this poor old soul be Bessie? Yet, it was. The eyes were the same, and in the gaunt features a recognisable ghost of Bessie McCutcheon still lingered.

Chrissie flung her arms thankfully round her old nurse. "Oh, Bessie, dear. I've found you at last."

"I didna want you to!" Bessie sobbed. "Oh, Chrissie, I didna want you to see me brought so low! That's why I ran."

Chrissie glanced round the cellar with a shudder. She could smell the damp and decay. She knew Bessie was proud, but surely even she would have abandoned pride rather than live like this?

Why hadn't she asked for help? William Kennedy would have welcomed her back gladly.

A fit of coughing overcame poor Bessie. Chrissie held her close until the paroxym eased, then she helped her lie back in the bed.

Taking off her own coat. Chrissie covered the other woman in its thick folds. Bessie mumbled a weak protest.

"You bide here and keep warm, Bessie." Chrissie smiled. "I'm away to get a cab. I'm taking you home with me."

"Aw, Chris, no, dinna." Bessie shook her head frantically. "Away home and forget you saw me. It's too late. I'm finished and glad to join poor Biddy on the hill."

"Don't ever give up. Bessie McCutcheon! Heavens, how often have you said that to me? Well, just heed your own advice for once!"

Chrissie paused in the doorway.

"Don't you run away, mind!"

For the first time came the glimmer of Bessie's smile.

"Bless ye, Chrissie, I'll no' run. I couldn't take another step if Auld Nick himsel' was after me!"

Chrissie walked as fast as she could to the cab rank at the Nethergate. She could remember the horse-drawn hansoms of her girlhood, but today she approached a gleaming black motor car. Its proud driver had just put an extra shine on the bonnet with a duster.

When Chrissie told him where she wanted to go, the driver looked uneasy.

"If those Hawkhill bairns scratch my paintwork, missus, it'll be you that pays," he warned.

He drove the short distance, and Chrissie left him waiting apprehensively at the close-mouth. A crowd of barefoot youngsters had appeared as if by magic.

Bessie had sunk into a dull stupor, and stared at Chrissie vacantly as she supported her to the waiting cab.

The driver shot off his seat when they appeared, his face a picture of horror. The bairns cheered.

"You're not taking that dirty auld wife in my cab!"

"Oh, yes, I am!" Chrissie jumped on the running board and managed to load Bessie into the back seat. The driver was hopping with anxiety.

"I'll have to fumigate my motor after her! This cab is used by clean, decent folk!"

Chrissie calmly ordered him to drive to Beechyhill, and slammed the door in his face.

The good address effectively silenced the driver. There wasn't a cheep out of him until they pulled up outside the house.

He sheepishly helped Chrissie to lift Bessie out of the car, and beamed when she paid the fare and added a generous tip for his trouble.

Agnes, the parlourmaid, appeared in the hallway to see what the stir was about. She shrieked when she saw Bessie.

"Oh, Mrs Rankine! What are ye doing wi' that auld tinker?"

Chrissie gave her a stern glance.

"Don't judge folk too hastily, Agnes, my dear. She was a fine woman once – and will be again. Please help me take her upstairs."

Between them, they carried Bessie up. Chrissie ordered the maid to run a hot bath while she undressed Bessie. Then she sent the girl downstairs to burn the wretched rags and ask Cook to heat up some nourishing broth.

Agnes left with alacrity, the clothes well-distanced between finger and thumb.

Tenderly, Chrissie bathed Bessie and wrapped her in a warm dressing-gown. Then gently, spoonful by spoonful, she fed her the soup. All the while Bessie remained in a bewildered state, only reviving enough to groan, "Ah,

Chrissie, I'm so ashamed!"

Dismayed at how little Bessie had eaten, Chrissie put her to bed in the rose-pink guest-room with a hot-water bottle at her feet. She sat by the bed holding her hand as Bessie lay moaning and coughing. It was clear that she was very ill.

Presently, there was a tap at the door and Charles came in.

"What's going on, darling? Agnes is having hysterics about tinkers in the guest-room."

Chrissie explained quickly what had happened. Charles looked grim as he studied the sick woman, for he remembered Bessie well.

"I think we should call the doctor right away, Chris."

The doctor looked gloomy after he'd examined Bessie.

"Asthma and chronic bronchitis, aggravated by malnutrition!" He sighed heavily. "I've seen many poor souls like her recently. Her symptoms are like the bronchial fever millworkers call 'mill-hoast'. Has she worked in the mills, d'you know?"

"I shouldn't think so," Chrissie replied doubtfully. "She told me once that mill dust made her ill."

The doctor patted Chrissie's shoulder.

"Well, she's in the best place now, thanks to you. It's not so much the illness that worries me, more her lack of spirit. She seems to have no will to live. I'm afraid she could just fade quietly away."

All night Chrissie kept watch by Bessie's side, soothing her when she tossed restlessly, rejoicing when at last she drifted into a more natural sleep.

When dawn's grey light filtered into the bedroom, she studied Bessie hopefully. There was no change. Sadly, Chrissie went to the fireplace and added a lump of coal to the glowing embers. She put her hands to the small of her back, wearily easing her heavy body.

"Why, Chrissie, you're having a bairn!" Bessie cried out suddenly.

Startled, Chrissie looked up.

"Of course I'm having a bairn! Why else would I come seeking you, Bessie McCutcheon? You know fine I can't have a baby without you!"

A gleam appeared in Bessie's eye.

"My, I'll need to get my strength back quick by the look of ye!"

"The sooner the better." Chrissie laughed joyfully. "You'll take some broth today for a start. Cook's is nearly as good as yours!"

Bessie grinned weakly, then coughed.

Chrissie waited until the spasm passed.

"Bessie, I'll never understand why you didn't ask us for help months ago!"

Bessie was silent for a long time.

"Your pa never wrote me a reference, Chrissie. I thought at the time maybe he didn't want to 'cos I was impudent about Mistress Lizzie. Nobody'll take on a servant without references, ye ken, so there was nothing for it but the mills.

"I trekked eighteen miles to a jute factory in Kirriemuir, for I thought the country air would suit my chest, but it made no difference. I got very sick, then I got the sack an' trailed back to Dundee without a penny, and lived like a beggar. Oh, I was so ashamed to be seen!"

Chrissie hugged her, moved by her story.

"Bessie, dear, Papa would have given you an excellent reference, if only you'd asked! He didn't want you to leave, but you know how proud and stubborn he is. I suppose he forgot all about the reference. I'm so sorry!"

Bessie closed her eyes wearily. Presently, she stirred again.

"Chrissie, did you get your wee laddie back?"

"No, I didn't. Lizzie and Arthur took him to India."

Bessie tutted.

"I knew fine Mistress Lizzie wouldn't let Sammy go once she'd got her hooks into him!" She lay thoughtfully silent for a short while.

"I was glad when I heard you'd married Charles Rankine. He's a fine gentleman. When's the bairn due?"

"The middle of May. The doctor thinks it might be twins."

"Twins!" Bessie's eyes opened wide. "Heavens, Chris, I'll need to get oot o' this bed!"

* * * *

The twins were born a fortnight early, on April 28, 1923, two days after Lady Elizabeth Bowes-Lyon married her Prince Bertie and became Duchess of York.

News of the royal wedding had delighted Chrissie, who had fond memories of Lady Elizabeth as a young woman at Glamis. It seemed a happy omen when Chrissie's babies chose that week to arrive.

Charlotte was first to put in an appearance, followed by Ewan.

Presently, Bessie placed the two wee bundles in Charles Rankine's arms.

"There, Master Charles, a fine lad an' a bonnie lass. A gentleman's family, all in one go!"

"Oh, Bessie, this'll be enough for me." He hugged his children. "I couldn't go through all that again!"

He carried his babies tenderly to his wife, looking so proud and awkward Chrissie almost laughed outright. Watching Charles with his children flooded Chrissie with such a surge of love, the laughter died in her throat.

Danny had captured her youthful heart; this mature emotion she felt for Charles was quite different. There was absolutely no betrayal of her dear Danny at all.

She longed to tell Charles, but Bessie was hovering nearby and the doctor was buttoning his shirt sleeves, so the moment passed.

Charles placed the babies safely in Chrissie's arms, then kissed her.

"Thank you, my darling, for our two lovely bairns."

She looked at her man with tears in her eyes, and couldn't manage a word.

* * * *

The year 1923 was an eventful one. The new city hall, donated by one of the city's benefactors, was officially opened by the Prince of Wales.

Sandra went with Mary Rose to view the festivities on a

damp, showery day, and promptly fell in love with the handsome young prince. She hung over the barrier hopefully, trying to catch his eye.

Mary Rose knew all the signs by now.

"You haven't a chance, Sandra." She giggled. "He's to be King one day, so he has to marry a princess or a titled lady. Queen Mary wouldn't let you in the door of Buckingham Palace. You're not pan-loafie enough."

"I could be, if I set my mind to it." Sandra tossed her head.

At that moment, she caught sight of Norrie Gallacher. He was halfway up a lamppost to get a better view, and was yelling cheek down at her as usual.

Sandra stuck out her tongue defiantly at her tormentor, just as the Prince of Wales glanced in her direction.

Amid all the fuss surrounding the new Caird Hall, there were rumours the old Town House, designed by William Adam, was to be demolished. Nobody believed such nonsense. Why would anyone want to knock down the dear old Pillars? They'd stood at the very heart of the city for years, sheltering its citizens and housing the tramway offices and some good wee shops.

There were plans to raise a war memorial on top of the Law, the ancient volcanic pinnacle dominating the city. Charles told Chrissie that squads of navvies had already started laboriously digging a road through Dudhope estate, winding up the steep slopes to the top of the hill.

Chrissie was nursing the babies at the time, and Charles always headed straight for the nursery when he came home.

Bessie was helping to care for the twins, and this had proved a very happy arrangement. She grew stronger and more energetic day by day, and the twins were her pride and joy.

Today, while their parents chatted, Bessie lifted the babies one by one from Chrissie's lap and tucked them cosily in their cots.

"The memorial's to be built to the winning design in the competition they held recently, Chrissie." Charles knew the news must waken sad memories for his wife, so he hurried on.

"They say it's an impressive design, and the monument's to be built of Cornish granite, a stone that's particularly white and enduring. There's to be a beacon on the top, and it'll be seen for miles when it's finished. A constant reminder of the men Dundee lost in the war."

She was quiet for a while.

"Danny and l used to go courting on the Law. I remember he once said he'd be famous and they'd raise a statue for him on the top. And now they'll do it . . ."

Charles turned away, struggling with a wretched sense of inferiority. He'd not been able to be a soldier because of the fever that had damaged his heart in childhood. But that in itself had left wounds that would never heal.

"Danny was always the better man, Chrissie." He sighed.

She put her arms around him and kissed him.

"Not better, my dearest. Never better. You kept the factory going for men to come home to. That took courage, too."

Some weeks after the birth of Charlotte and Ewan, Chrissie received two letters from India by the same post. The first was from her sister-in-law. The tone of Lizzie Kennedy's letter was effusively joyful.

So you have a dear baby boy to call your own at last, my dearest Chrissie. And a lovely little girl, as well! I cannot find the words to tell how delighted we were to have your letter with news of the twins' birth. Arthur asks me to send his fondest love to you all.

You must be so busy and happy, my dear: I quite envy you the hard work of caring for your two little ones! Sam is such an independent six-year-old Ayah is not permitted to tie so much as a shoelace!

Sam attends an excellent European school, and can already read and write. The head of the school is a man after my own heart, Chrissie, and the standard of education is so good, we have decided not to send Sam to school in Britain. I have campaigned long and hard for good teachers to be sent out to expatriate children, and it seems I have succeeded.

We will keep Sammy in India to complete his education, knowing you have your own dear youngsters to care for now . . .

Chrissie crushed the letter angrily.

We will keep Sammy – as calm as you please! The cheek of the woman! Chrissie shook with futile anger.

And another thing, Sammy could read and write, but had made no attempt to answer Chrissie's loving letters. That's what hurt her the most.

Recovering somewhat, Chrissie ripped open the second letter with trembling fingers. It was from her nephew, Hughie.

The whole family had been relieved to hear that Hughie had thankfully survived his dramatic disappearance in India. George and Jeannie had been so overjoyed, in fact, they'd taken the news of their son's marriage to an Anglo-Indian girl quite calmly.

Hughie's letter was short, and Chrissie detected bitter overtones.

Jani and I have decided to leave India for good. We've suffered so many slights and inults from Jani's people and mine that we don't feel welcome in this country.

Uncle Arthur kindly gave me employment in the mill, but I'm no land-lubber. Auntie Chrissie. My heart's not in the job, and I long to be at sea again.

I've made friends with the captain of a jute ship, who suggests I should join his ship and take a Mate's ticket eventually.

Who knows, I may be ship's captain myself one day!

I'll work my passage and bring Jani to Dundee with me. Please, dear Aunt Chrissie, could you find a place for Jani to stay? I must sail with the ship when it leaves Dundee, and will have little time for house-hunting.

Chrissie took the problem of Hughie's wife to Charles. Lizzie's letter she kept prudently to herself, for she knew it would infuriate her husband.

"There's the lodge." Charles frowned thoughtfully. "It's been empty since old Henderson died last autumn. Jani could stay there."

Chrissie hugged him delightedly.

"Darling, that's perfect! I can make sure Jani's not lonely while Hughie's at sea. What a kind man you are, Charles. What would I do without you?"

Chapter 25

EWAN RANKINE was just a wee lad when he learned he
had an older brother. Chrissie told the twins about Samuel,
their half-brother, as soon as they were old enough to
understand. The news made no impression on Charlotte,
who was perfectly content to be petted and admired by her
half-sisters, but Ewan was thrilled.

Chrissie had tried hard, but she couldn't hide her feelings
as she spoke about Sammy. Ewan was an unusually bright
and perceptive child, and his mother's sad expression
worried him. He pretended to play with the motor car
Hughie had brought him from Hamburg. He pushed the car
along the patterned carpet.

"Brrm, brrm, brrm!" he went, so his mother would think
he didn't care about Sammy. Anything to stop her looking so
sad . . .

Chrissie watched her children play. Sammy was lost to
them, too, but they didn't seem to mind. She sighed. Who
could blame them?

But Ewan did care. His heart sang. He had a big brother
called Sammy who, for reasons Ewan couldn't grasp, lived
in India.

Oh, if only Sammy had lived in Dundee! They would have
such fun. They could climb into the high branches of the
monkey-puzzle tree. Ewan had tried yesterday, but he'd

fallen off and skinned his knees and Bessie'd had hysterics.

That night, when Bessie was hearing the twins' prayers, Ewan slipped in a special one which he kept to himself.

"Please, God, bless my brother Sammy and bring him home soon. Amen!" he whispered.

Then he lay contentedly while dear old Bessie tucked him in and kissed him. Ewan didn't feel lonely in this family of girls any more. He had a brother!

* * * *

The years seemed to fly. The Twenties was a frantic decade, in which life speeded up. Some whirled into a heedless round of pleasure, others into the very depths of despair.

Grimly, Charles kept Rankine's going through strikes and depression, patiently fostering links forged long ago between Dundee and America.

His brother-in-law, Ernest, was a great help. Ernest Kennedy was a successful man in the States now, with a happy, growing family, and a stake in the carpeting and upholstery of automobiles manufactured in Detroit.

Harriet's writing desk was in constant use, for Chrissie was a loyal correspondent.

From Harriet's hurried scrawls, Chrissie gathered she was running a clinic in one of the most deprived areas of Glasgow. Her friend was fighting against poverty, disease and prejudice with all her considerable skill and dogged determination.

Sometimes I'm even daft enough to think I'm winning!

Harriet wrote ruefully.

Chrissie also had news to pass on to her niece, Georgina, in Australia. Hughie and Jani had a little boy called Jamal, who was now three, but looking after her son was not enough to keep Jani occupied. She'd sought out Chrissie diffidently, holding the dark-eyed boy by the hand.

"Aunt Chrissie, there is a small shop opposite the school. I am thinking it could be a good business, with newspaper and sweets and groceries.

"Would it offend Uncle Charles if I leased the shop and worked in it? Would it be seemly for the wife of a First Mate, do you think?"

"Jani, I worked in a grocer's shop myself. I think it's a wonderful idea!" Chrissie had answered, smiling.

And you can guess what the Broughty Ferry folk call Jani's well-stocked little shop, can't you? Chrissie wrote to Georgina. *Yes, that's right, my dear. Jani a'thing!*

William Kennedy was a very old man, but still spry and lively. Secretly, he thought his eldest granddaughter Sandra Murphy was the loveliest lass in the whole of Dundee – though he'd never tell her so.

Sandra loved visiting her old granda. William had taken Biddy's place in her affections, Patrick having drunk himself to death years ago.

"Sandra, that skirt's scandalous short!" William complained when his stylish granddaughter appeared one day, showing shapely knees.

Sandra laughed merrily and admired her dashing silhouette

in the mirror above the mantelpiece.

"It's the latest fashion, Granda. Skirts are worn short, if you have the legs for it."

"Lassies didna have legs in my day," he grumbled. "And look at your hair – as short as a wee laddie's! Young ladies used to put their hair up when I was young, nowadays they let their hair doon once they leave the school!"

Sandra kissed him fondly on his bald patch.

"Poor Granda! I'm afraid you'll never get used to modern ideas. I'm a flapper – and proud of it!"

"Sounds mair like a daft wee fish." He heaved a sigh. "Aye, the Kennedys are long lived, but that's a mixed blessing, my lassie. Times change, your friends slip awa'. All the whaling skippers are gone, bar me.

"What I'd give to see the whaling fleet go sailing upriver just once more! The bonnie *Balaena*, the *Eclipse*, the *Active*, my ain *Christina K*!"

"That's the brooch Mum always wears, isn't it?" Sandra asked curiously.

He wiped his eyes with his hankie.

"Aye, your mother knows how it feels to love a ship. The *Christina K* was hers, too.

"A ship's only bits o' timber, sheets o' metal and canvas, Sandra, but somehow you grow to love her. Then when you lose her, it's like a part of you goes, too."

The visit to her granda sobered Sandra. She decided to walk home instead of taking the tram, to the detriment of her high-heeled shoes.

When she reached Beechyhill she had cheered up and was looking forward to the tennis dance that evening. Life was a whirl of parties, sport and pleasure, and pretty, popular Sandra was in the thick of it.

She was supposed to run the household with her mother, having completed a year's course at the domestic college, followed by six months typing and book-keeping. In reality, the household ran itself perfectly smoothly, leaving Sandra plenty of scope to enjoy herself.

She ran lightly upstairs to her room. Bessie had laid out her new dance dress on the bed. It was a short-skirted, daring gown of midnight blue satin, encrusted with dark-blue beads and finished with a deep, swinging fringe round the hemline. The whole creation was supported by thin shoulder-straps.

Sandra could well imagine the startling effect against bare, creamy-white shoulders and long silk-stocking clad legs. Belle o' the tennis ball, that's me! She giggled.

"Gosh!" Charles exclaimed when a vision of loveliness descended the stairs later in a waft of Evening In Paris. "Er – a bit daring, isn' t it, Sandra?"

"Oh, you sound just like Granda!" Sandra wrinkled her nose in disgust and wrapped herself in a dramatic black velvet evening cloak lined with white silk. "Ready, Charles?"

"Your carriage awaits, princess!" He crooked an arm.

Laughing, they swept out together.

After Charles had deposited Sandra at the dance hall, she cast an expert glance around and sighed. The same old crowd of youths gaping at her goggle-eyed, and a gaggle of green-eyed girlfriends eyeing the dress. Sometimes she wondered why she bothered!

And then she saw him.

Even without the fashionable Oxford bags he was wearing, he would have stood out from the common herd. He was tall, with an aristocratic air of boredom that made Sandra catch her breath.

As if he'd sensed her interest, the young man looked up and their glances met. His eyes widened and the bored look disappeared.

Sandra hardly dared to breathe. He crossed the room as she'd known he would, and was even more breathtaking at close quarters. He smiled, his eyes still studying her admiringly.

"Excuse me, but do you do the Charleston? The band is just striking up, and it's my favourite dance."

It so happened the popular Charleston was one of Sandra's accomplishments. She'd practised the steps night after night to the sound of the gramophone, much to the amusement of Chrissie and Charles.

With a smile, she took his hand and they were off, dancing so energetically that the other dancers cleared a space and clapped and cheered them on.

When the dance ended, they collapsed into one another's arms, laughing.

"You're jolly good." The young man looked down at her. "I didn't expect to find such a good dancer in a place like Dundee."

She could tell by his accent he was English, and looked at him archly.

"We are quite civilised in Scotland, you know!"

He laughed, taking her arm and guiding her towards the buffet table.

"Let's sit this one out, and you can tell me all about yourself."

They ended up sitting cosily on a turn of the main staircase, eating sausage rolls and drinking innocuous fruit punch, but they talked mostly about him.

"I'm called after my father, Sir Roderick Stirton. The eldest son is always called Roderick. It's sort of a family tradition, like inheriting the title and the family estate."

"You mean you'll be Sir Roderick one day?"

"Well, Sir Roddy, probably. I'm an informal sort of chap." He smiled.

Sandra played with the stem of her glass, her eyes cast down thoughtfully.

"You must be rich."

"I never thought about it, to be honest. My allowance never seems to go far enough."

He went on to tell her he'd taken a degree in economics at Oxford, and was now preparing to enter the family textile business.

"Cotton spinning mostly, but I'm in Dundee to get an

insight into the linen trade. My uncle, William Weatherall, is a shareholder in one of the mills here, and I'm staying with his family."

"I know the Weatheralls." Sandra was excited. "They live quite near us!"

He took her hands, and gazed into her eyes.

"Then I hope we shall see a great deal of one another, Sandra!"

"Oh, yes, Roddy, I hope so!" Sandra answered breathlessly. She'd met the rich young gentleman of her dreams, and fallen head over heels in love with him!

They arranged to meet next afternoon in Smith Brothers' tearoom. After that they met nearly every day, playing tennis at the club, or walking dreamily by the riverside.

For Sandra, it was an enchanted time during which the sun always seemed to shine. It must have rained in the weeks they spent together, but she didn't notice. She was in love for the first time, and she wanted to keep her loved one all to herself.

Chapter 26

CHRISSIE could hardly fail to notice what was going on. She came across the young couple now and again unexpectedly, but Sandra was so absorbed in her young man she didn't even notice her mother. It worried Chrissie and she determined to broach the subject tactfully.

"I saw you yesterday in Reform Street with your friend, my dear. He looks like a nice young man. Why don't you ask him to tea, so that we can all meet him?" she suggested.

Sandra's heart sank. She'd been trying to protect her tender love from the ridicule of her boisterous family. They could so easily spoil everything by teasing her, and break the enchantment.

The twins were a lively pair of scamps who led Bessie a merry dance. Charlotte was always up on her tippytoes, dancing around, and Ewan always seemed to be filthy, with skinned knees.

Mary Rose was less of a risk, being completely absorbed in her horses. But she was liable to turn up at the table cheerfully muddy.

Sandra met her mother's eye, which had a certain determined glint that she recognised. She sighed and gave in.

"Oh, very well, Mum. I'll bring Roddy to tea tomorrow!"

The next day, Roderick Stirton had no sooner been

introduced to Chrissie in the drawing-room than Charlotte appeared, dressed in a kilt outfit.

She laid down two crossed walking sticks and proceeded to do a wildly energetic sword-dance. Her twin brother watched, grimacing horribly.

"I thought you said the Scots were civilised!" Roddy whispered.

"That's enough, Charlotte," Chrissie said firmly. She frowned at her son. "If the wind changes, your face will stay that way, Ewan."

She turned to her guest, smiling.

"Don't pay any attention to these two. You'll stay for high tea, won't you, Roddy?"

"You mean dinner, of course, Mother!" Sandra looked agonised.

Sandra stood up. Her family were letting her down, and she was mortified. She smiled at Roddy.

"My stepfather keeps a small stable of horses. Would you like to see?"

Roddy agreed with alacrity. Sandra's mother had a way of looking at you as if she could see right inside your head, and it made him nervous.

He excused himself and went thankfully outside with Sandra. They linked arms. She was a dear girl, and he was madly in love with her. He pulled her into the shelter of the rhododendrons and kissed her soundly.

"I love you. You know that, don't you?"

"You keep telling me so, darling." Sandra nodded happily.

"But it makes it very special, telling me in my own home."

He let her go abruptly, suddenly remembering her mother's clear blue eyes. Sandra took his arm, and they walked on towards the stables.

Mary Rose had set up several jumps in the field, and was going round the course on Thrawn Jane, her favourite mare.

Sandra and Roddy leaned on the wall to watch, and Sandra swelled with pride as her young sister soared over the obstacles on the big black horse. Mary Rose on horseback was wonderful to see.

Roddy leaned his elbows on the wall and watched the slight figure with an expert eye.

"Your sister rides very well."

Sandra beamed with pleasure.

"Yes, doesn't she?" She could have hugged Mary Rose. Roddy had a better impression of her family now.

* * * *

Chrissie was annoyed. She'd specifically asked Charles to be home promptly at six to meet Sandra's young man. It was nearly seven-thirty now, and there was still no sign of him.

It was typical of him! When some problem arose at the mill, he forgot about everything else.

Chrissie fumed. If he really loved her he would be at home right now, helping to make conversation with Roderick Stirton. She was developing a pounding headache, and Cook would be grumbling furiously as the meat spoiled.

Sandra shot her mother another thunderous glance. What was going on? The conversation was becoming stilted; even

Roddy was running out of topics.

Mary Rose had changed into a blue dress that merely skimmed her slight figure. It was modest, yet somehow disturbing. Roddy found his eyes being drawn to her unwillingly.

She hardly said a word, yet he grew hot under the collar every time their eyes met. He shifted uncomfortably in his seat. He'd accepted the dinner invitation, otherwise he'd have politely taken his leave. When were they going to dine? His stomach growled its discomfort.

Chrissie heard the car arrive at last and gave a sigh of relief.

"Ah, here's Charles!"

She rose and went into the hall, still annoyed and ready to give her husband a piece of her mind.

She opened the front door, then stood frozen. It wasn't Charles. It was the family doctor.

He closed the car door and came towards her.

"Chrissie, my dear."

She saw his expression, the compassion in his eyes, and felt her heart lurch. She'd lived through this before, this terrible, numb, icy feeling . . .

"Is it – Charles?"

The doctor reached for her hand and held it in his warm, comforting grip.

"Yes, I'm afraid so."

"An – an accident?"

"No. He collapsed in the mill. I warned him some months

ago that he was working too hard.

"Fortunately, they contacted me quickly and I got him to the infirmary right away. He's very ill, Chrissie. I must warn you, I don't hold out much hope, my dear."

She felt her heart start to beat fiercely. Where there was life, there was hope! She felt strong, ready to fight.

"Would you take me to the infirmary, Doctor? I want to be with my man."

Chrissie ran back to the drawing-room and broke the news to her daughters. They were both very upset, but Roddy Stirton's presence helped. Chrissie left Sandra in floods of tears in his arms. Mary Rose just sat, numb and pale.

Rushing upstairs, Chrissie told Bessie what had happened, then dashed outside to join the doctor. He drove down the driveway in a spray of gravel and raced towards the infirmary.

The doctor's reckless speed told Chrissie the seriousness of Charles's condition. She hung on apprehensively as the car negotiated the final curve of the steep brae leading to the red brick building.

When they reached the ward, Charles was still alive and fighting. The doctor went into a corner for a hurried consultation with Sister.

Chrissie turned away from the inquisitive stares of the night nurses. She was embarrassed by her expensive dress and the beautiful Rankine rubies Charles had given her when they married. It must look like swank to these hard-working lassies! How could they know she'd just put them on to entertain Sandra's young man?

Then she shrugged. Who cared what they thought! Charles was all that mattered now . . .

The doctor appeared at her elbow.

"There's no change, Sister says. I think I ought to stay, Chrissie."

"It's good of you, doctor, but you're a busy man." She smiled at him. "I'll be all right. I'd like to sit with Charles a while, if I'm not in the way."

"Are you sure? How will you get home?"

"I've a guid Scots tongue in my head. I'll call a cab."

When the doctor had gone, Chrissie sat outside the ward feeling lost and scared. How could she live without Charles? Over sixteen years, she'd come to love him dearly, but she'd never managed to find the words to convince him. Now it might be too late. Angrily, she brushed away tears.

Sister appeared, stiff and starchy, but her eyes were kind.

"We gave Mr Rankine medication to ease the pain and make him sleep, Mrs Rankine. He's not wakened yet." She paused before going on.

"I'd be negligent if I didn't warn you that there's little we can do. But your husband's still fighting – and that's a good sign."

She led Chrissie to a bed screened off from the rest of the ward. Charles lay so pale and still that Chrissie gasped.

Sister pulled out a chair.

"You sit with your man as long as you like. I believe that it helps patients to have their dear ones near." She smiled conspiratorially. "But if you see Matron, slip out the side door. She's a stickler for discipline!"

Chrissie thanked her gratefully and sat down. The screens were pulled round and she was left alone.

She took Charles's limp hand and raised it to her lips. There was no response. She bent and kissed him on the mouth and whispered in his ear.

"Charles, please come back to me. How can I go on without you? I love you very much."

Still no response. She covered her face and wept silently.

A voice whispered her name. Lifting a tear-stained face, Chrissie found Charles watching her.

"Why are ye greetin', wifie? I'm no' deid yet!" he murmured in a broad Dundee accent, with the ghost of his usual grin.

"Thank God you've wakened, my darling!" she exclaimed. "I wanted to tell you how much I love you!"

The grin faded.

"No, you loved Danny. You were honest with me when we married, Chrissie. I respect you for it. Don't spoil everything with comforting lies now I'm dying."

Chrissie's sorrow exploded into wild anger.

"You're not dying, Charles Rankine! And I don't tell lies! Heavens, man, we've been married for years! Surely you know I say what I mean! So stop feeling sorry for yourself, Charles. I love you and need you. I'd be lost without you."

Chrissie stopped suddenly, horrified. Charles seemed to be having difficulty breathing.

"Oh, Charles, I'm sorry!"

She felt utterly helpless. Should she call for a nurse? Then she saw that her husband's eyes were wet with tears.

"Charles, you're crying!"

"I am not! I'm trying to laugh. Folk can die laughing, you know. I don't intend to." He became serious again, staring at her.

"All right, Chris, you've convinced me." He clasped her hand with surprising strength and gave her a long, pleading look.

"You'd never lie to me, would you, my love?"

Chrissie blinked back tears, smiling.

"I've only lied to you once in all the years we've been married. About this dress – it cost far more than I told you!"

"I don't give a damn about the price. It's beautiful . . ."

The effort of talking had exhausted Charles, but Chrissie imagined he looked better as he drifted off to sleep.

Throughout the night, Chrissie sat by her husband's side, watching and praying. He slept deeply, hardly moving. Surely that was a good sign?

At last, the ward began to waken. Lights were switched on, nurses washed patients and straightened beds. Night nurses left, and day nurses came streaming into the ward.

Behind the screens, Chrissie listened tiredly to all the bustle. Thankfully, Charles slept on undisturbed.

"Who's behind the screens?" a nurse's voice asked curiously.

"It's Charles Rankine, head man o' Rankine's Works. He

was brought in last night, half dead. It's his heart, Sister says. Wheesht, though. His wife's wi' him."

"Is that right? You mean her that used to work in the mills and married him for his money?"

"Keep your voice doon! Aye, that's her. Looks like she'll get his money soon!"

The voices faded as the nurses continued down the ward.

Tearfully, Chrissie kissed Charles and vowed she'd do everything in her power to make him happy. She vowed it, not because a trivial remark touched a tender spot, but because she loved him more than she'd ever known . . .

Chapter 27

FACED with two tearful young women, Roddy Stirton was out of his depth. He rose gallantly to the occasion, though, comforting Mary Rose as well as Sandra. He even managed to persuade them to eat some of the excellent meal Cook had prepared.

He tucked in so heartily himself that he gained the approval of Bessie McCutcheon, who'd appointed herself chaperone in Chrissie's absence.

"Aye, Sandra. That's a well-brocht-up young gent you've got!" Bessie whispered behind her hand. "He doesna pick at his meat like some posh folk. Just look at his plate, as clean as a whistle!"

Much later, Mary Rose stood in the darkness beside the front porch, watching Roddy kiss Sandra goodnight. The sight made her feel very odd.

Finally, she could stand it no longer and moved out of the shadows into the light of the porch lantern.

Roddy looked up with a start and met a challenging gaze. Something wordless and fleeting passed between himself and Mary Rose, and he abruptly released his hold on Sandra.

Mary Rose came forward and took her sister's hand.

"It's well past midnight, Sandra. Mum must be staying at the hospital with Charles. You can sleep with me tonight if you want."

Sandra wasn't too pleased at her young sister's interruption.

"Och, don't fuss, Mary Rose. I'm accustomed to keeping late hours, even if you're not!" She stifled a yawn just in time.

Roddy gave Mary Rose a conspiratorial wink over the top of Sandra's head.

"I'm just leaving anyway, Sandra. I think your mother would have got word to you by now, if the news was bad."

"Oh, Roddy, dear, you're such a comfort!" Sandra sighed soulfully.

Love shone unashamedly out of Sandra's brilliant blue eyes. She obviously believed every word he said. Roddy looked away uncomfortably. Secretly he didn't feel so confident about Charles Rankine's chances.

He looked up and met Mary Rose's eyes. Again something leaped between them with the swiftness of light. It was as if she'd read his thoughts accurately.

"Goodnight, Roddy. Thanks for being with us tonight," she said formally.

He nodded and walked away, wondering why he felt so confused.

* * * *

Charles made good progress and three weeks later was allowed home.

It was only then than Chrissie realised how weak he'd become. As the days passed she was forced to admit that his active life was almost certainly over.

His weakness made him despondent.

"How could I manage a full day's work in this state, Chrissie? Perhaps the time's come to sell Rankine's."

"Do you want to?" She handed him a cup of tea.

"No, but what option do I have? The other directors are past retiral age – they'd be fine pleased. But what about my workers? They're grand men and women and they were outstandingly loyal in difficult times. I'd hate to see them on the dole, and Rankine's reduced to a pile of rubble like the dear old Pillars."

Chrissie sipped the tea thoughtfully for a moment.

"There's a simple solution. You tell me what to do, and I'll go to the factory and do it."

"Won't that be too much for you, darling?" He frowned.

"Nonsense! It's a challenge, and I love challenges. Cook, Agnes and Sandra run the household very efficiently between them, Kennedy's needs little attention from me and dear old Bessie dotes on the twins. I was beginning to feel redundant anyway! Helping you to keep Rankine's going would give me a new purpose in life."

"More likely give you grey hairs!"

Charles stretched his long legs in front of the fire. It was chilly, with a cold haar lying grey on the river, and he was glad he didn't have to go out.

"Well, it's worth trying." Charles had decided Chrissie's suggestion had merits. "There's quite a hefty price rise due, and someone has to break the news to our American customers in Detroit. I'll draft a tactful letter, and you can get my secretary to type it. I'm afraid Benjamin Franklin Chester will not be overjoyed!"

"Who's he?"

"Head of Autofibres, Detroit. His firm has dealt with Rankine's for years. He's a very shrewd chap who firmly believes that if you keep a sharp eye on the cents, the dollars will look after themselves."

Chrissie was eager to embark on this challenge, but first she had something else in mind.

"Charles, I want to learn to drive. It would be a great help. McIntosh could teach me."

Charles looked apprehensive.

"McIntosh is an excellent coachman, Chris, but I'm not convinced he's mastered the complexities of the combustion engine yet. It always makes me nervous when he shouts 'Whoa!' when he applies the brakes!"

* * * *

Sandra was delighted to have her stepfather home, relieved that life was returning to normal.

Her mother's efforts to keep Rankine's going impressed her – and so did the speed with which Chrissie learned to drive. Sandra decided that she and Mary Rose must learn, too.

Sandra drew the line at being taught by old McIntosh, though. Roddy Stirton would instruct them in his own little black Morris!

He agreed equably enough, and lessons began around Beechyhill. As his pupil gained confidence, they ventured further afield.

Sandra was proud the first time she drove through the city centre. It looked rather strange. There was a gaping empty space where the old Town House had stood and the ancient buildings and narrow wynds that had formed the Vault had all gone.

The wanton destruction was enough to make a Dundonian weep, but Sandra paid little attention. Concentration was required to dodge buses, tramcars, horse-drawn carts and an impatient jam of motor vehicles.

Roddy was impressed – and relieved – by his pupil's driving. At the first opportunity, he instructed her to pull into the side, and hugged and kissed her more thoroughly than he'd intended.

"Jolly good show, Sandra!"

Sandra was pleased, but embarrassed. What would folk think? He was English, of course, and couldn't be expected to know well-brought-up Scots lassies didn't hug and kiss in public!

The day after the successful driving lesson, Sandra took advantage of a beautiful morning to walk to Broughty Ferry. She'd just reached Jani's thriving little shop when her path was suddenly blocked.

"Norrie! What are you doing here?" Sandra demanded of the tall, good-looking young man.

She hadn't seen Norrie Gallacher for months. In fact, she'd hardly given him a thought since she met Roddy.

There was a change in Norrie's demeanour, she noticed at

once. He looked grim and serious. She'd never seen him without a cheeky grin.

"I've been waiting for you, Sandra."

"For me?"

"Aye. They tell me you've met your rich man at last. An English toff wi' bools in his mooth."

"What's it to you if I have, Norrie Gallacher?" She tilted her chin and walked on.

He fell into step beside her.

"I saw you both yesterday, canoodling on the Perth Road. Are you going to marry him?"

Sandra considered the question breathlessly.

"Yes."

She glanced up apologetically.

"I'm awfully sorry, Norrie." She didn't know why she felt she had to apologise to Norrie Gallacher – she just knew she had to do it.

"Don't be sorry. It's me that's daft, waiting and hoping. You never gave me no reason!" he said bitterly.

"I told ye till I was tired, Norrie." Sandra felt like crying. "I was sick o' tellin' ye not to – "

"Love ye?" He wheeled round angrily, stopping her in her tracks. "Well, I do love ye, but I'll no' hang around to watch you marry your rich toff.

"I'm away to Canada. I've had it in mind for a while to go there an' try my luck now my granny's provided for. I've bought her a nice house in Broughty Ferry, big enough to take a' her bits an' bobs."

"You never!" Sandra gasped.

"There's brass in muck, so they say." He gave a ghost of a grin. "I've got six carts and a scrapyard, and a tidy wee removal business forbye. My gran'll never have to work again. There's servants looking after her now."

Sandra was stunned. There was nothing left to say.

Norrie held out a hand.

"You'll be happy wi' your rich toff, now, Sandra!" he growled fiercely.

She took his hand, on the verge of tears.

"Norrie, could you not write from Canada and tell me how you're getting on?"

"Better no'." He shook his head. "Your man wouldna like it."

He held her hand tightly for a moment, then let go abruptly and went striding off.

Norrie didn't look back, although Sandra watched hopefully until he was out of sight.

Tears blurred her last sight of him. She had a strange notion she'd lost something rare and precious.

* * * *

Mary Rose took to driving less readily than her sister. Roddy's presence played havoc with her concentration.

At first Sandra sat patiently in the back seat, but her sister crashed the gears so excruciatingly, she rebelled.

"Poor wee car – that's torture! I'm away to read my library book in peace."

After that, Mary Rose and Roddy were left alone together

to master gear changes and double-declutching.

At last, Roddy decided his pupil was fit for the open road. He persuaded Mary Rose to turn the Morris Bullnose cautiously towards the quiet country roads near Beechyhill.

Mary Rose soon began enjoying herself, bowling along the empty roads with fields of ripening grain waving in the breeze on either side, and herds of glossy black cattle grazing peacefully on higher ground. And Roddy by her side.

She wove a daring fantasy that he was madly in love with her, and they were driving off to . . . to . . . She didn't know where. She would go with him anywhere. He had just to say the word . . .

"Hey, there's a bend coming up," Roddy warned. "Better change down to third gear!"

Mary Rose came back to earth with a bump. Flustered, she tried to remember which pedals to press and which way to move the gear lever. She got it wrong. The car went faster.

Roddy bellowed with alarm and grabbed for the wheel.

"Watch out!"

There was no chance the little car would take the bend, but fortunately there was an open gate ahead. They trundled safely through the opening, the vehicle bumping and jolting over uneven ground. Finally it came to rest in a clump of whins.

Mary Rose was thrown forward, the breath knocked out of her. She revived outside the car with Roddy bending over her anxiously.

"Thank heavens! I thought I'd killed you."

"It's my fault. Oh, Roddy, is your car all right?" She began to sob.

"The car's fine. Oh, please don't cry!"

Roddy sat down beside her and put an arm round her, supporting her so that her head rested against his shoulder. Mary Rose felt suddenly warm and safe.

Her fine golden hair was delicately scented and tickled Roddy's cheek. He looked down at her. What on earth was happening to him? He'd imagined himself in love with Sandra, but he'd never felt like this before! The conflict of emotions scared him . . .

"Mary Rose!" he murmured dazedly. Her name sounded like music.

Mary Rose felt light headed, but her mind was crystal clear.

She knew Roddy wanted to kiss her, but if she let him, life would become complicated and difficult. She had only to get to her feet and make light of the incident and it wouldn't happen. The choice was hers. But, oh, how she longed for his embrace and kiss!

Mary Rose didn't move, couldn't move. She lay in his arms, staring at him breathlessly.

"Oh, my darling," he whispered. He kissed her. Her first kiss, yet she responded naturally and without awkwardness. Her arms went round his neck with an eagerness he shared, as if she'd waited all her life for their lips to meet.

They drew apart at last, laughing with a release of

spontaneous joy.

Roddy hugged her.

"I thought I just liked you because you're Sandra's sister – but there's more to it than that. There's something pulling us together. I felt it from the very first moment!"

"I know what you mean. I can tell what you're thinking, though you haven't said a word. It's as if I've become part of you now I've met you, and I'll never be completely Mary Rose Murphy again."

She shivered with a sudden premonition of disaster.

"Oh, Roddy, it frightens me terribly. I wish it hadn't happened. I wish we'd never met!"

"Don't say that! I love you." Roddy silenced her fiercely with a kiss.

"Roddy, what about Sandra?" There were tears in her eyes. His expression changed.

"We'll have to tell her."

Mary Rose broke down and wept in his arms.

"Don't! Please! Maybe she'll meet someone else. We have all the time in the world and I can't hurt her. I mustn't!"

He held her close, stroking her hair.

"Darling, don't cry. I'll be very nice to Sandra. I won't say a word about us, so long as we can be alone together sometimes. Oh, Mary Rose, please take ages to learn to drive!"

"Don't worry, I will." She laughed shakily. "I'd rather have horses any day."

Quietly preparing for matrimony, Sandra was living in a

dream world, and didn't notice what was going on in front of her eyes.

She had almost filled her bottom drawer, delighting in beautiful bed linen and other bits and pieces. But she drew the line at looking at wedding dresses. Time enough for that when Roddy popped the question.

She was confident he would. And very soon. He treated her so gently these days, restraining his feelings so admirably.

She could drive perfectly well now and had asked Roddy to concentrate on Mary Rose.

Whenever he had time off from the textile course he was attending, he and Mary Rose would set off in the Morris. Sandra didn't mind. In fact, she smiled affectionately as she watched them go.

Poor Roddy! Having to suffer her young sister's awful driving because she'd asked him to. What devotion!

Chapter 28

CHARLES was afraid he'd flung Chrissie in at the deep end. The jute trade was in a very bad state. Some works had been forced to close temporarily and others were on short time. Rankine's had kept going mainly because of American contracts.

Charles was nevertheless quite pleased to take a back seat. With his occasional assistance, Chrissie appeared to be coping very well.

She had learned to drive remarkably quickly and Charles had bought her an Austin 7. He had to smile, watching Chrissie speed off every morning in the little black car, the twins hanging out of the car window, waving as they set off to school.

Charles spent hours tinkering around with wireless sets, but always found time to help with homework. The twins were his greatest joy and he read to them at every opportunity.

Bessie didn't approve – and said so.

"Filling the bairns' heids wi' nonsense, Mister Charles!"

"It's not nonsense, Bessie, it's fairy tales!" Charlotte protested indignantly.

Bessie shook her head derisively.

"Och, that's one an' the same thing."

"Did Sinbad the Sailor go to Calcutta, Dad?" Ewan asked.

"He went pretty nearly everywhere, did old Sinbad."

Sitting on the rug, Ewan hugged his knees.

"I want to go to India, Dad. To see my brother, Sammy."

"Mistress Lizzie'll soon put a stop to that!" Bessie muttered.

Charles smiled and ruffled Ewan's hair fondly.

"Maybe you will go to India, Ewan. Charles Lindbergh has flown the Atlantic – and you saw seaplanes on the Tay the other day. The world is getting smaller and smaller. I'm sure you'll meet Sammy one day."

Ewan beamed delightedly, but Charles was left curiously saddened.

Chrissie was busy and happy. Her husband had accepted his limitations cheerfully, and her involvement with Rankine's had brought them very close. They were more than husband and wife – they were partners in every sense, she thought as she drove her little car through Dundee towards the office.

The city centre was a depressing scene of mud and chaos, but there was a grand new square promised. The gaping hole left by the demolition of the old Town House would be bridged by massive steel beams to support a real piazza like those in Italy.

Labourers were working to the east and west of the Caird Hall. New buildings were rising like stone wings to shelter the square.

Chrissie sighed nostalgically for the old city she'd grown up with, then scolded herself. Just look at the employment it offered to people who'd been out of work for months!

She drove on, heading for Rankine's Works.

"You're in Benjamin Franklin Chester's bad books, Mrs Rankine!" Maisie, Charles's secretary, smiled when Chrissie reached the office.

Taking the letter, Chrissie frowned. It was from Autofibres, Detroit, deploring in strong terms the recent price rise in jute weft yarn. It ended on a sour note.

Who is this Chris Rankine, anyway? The price has gone sky high since that guy took over. Send Charles back, will you? He's my buddy!

Yours etc.,

Benjamin F. Chester.

Chrissie laughed.

"Maisie – reply to Mr Chester's letter. Inform him the price of jute weft yarn has been somewhat reduced because of judicious buying. Send it with Mrs Christina Rankine's compliments, will you?"

"That'll gie him a red face!" Maisie grinned.

Chrissie put on the white linen coat she wore on her daily inspection. The workforce had stared the first time she made the tour, but now they welcomed it.

She collected the mill manager, and they set off. She was nothing if not thorough, starting with the stowers in the warehouse where jute bales rose in tiers, then moving on through batching and carding to what she knew best, the spinning frames in the mill.

Chrissie often lingered here. She'd watch the women at

work and remember how she'd toiled on the fast frames to keep her ends up.

Old habits die hard. On leaving the mill and entering the factory, Chrissie treated the weavers with due reference. The weavers heartily approved, smiling and nodding regally as she passed by the looms.

"She's no' a real toff, hen, only a half-toff wha used tae work in the mill hersel'. She kens fine whit it's like to feed bairns on little mair than ten bob a week. Guid luck tae her an' her puir, sick man!"

Returning to her office, Chrissie remembered the two letters she'd collected hastily from the postman before leaving home. She settled down to read her mail, noting with surprise that the letter from India was written in her brother Arthur's hand.

Lizzie has been ill, and has asked me to reply to your recent letter. The sickness struck very suddenly, and left her so weak and helpless the doctor are puzzled. I hope and pray it will pass.

We are troubled by strikes and unrest because of the demand for Home Rule. Mr Ghandi, their leader, was a perfectly respectable lawyer with a thriving legal practice in Bombay. Goodness knows where it will all end, Chrissie!

Sammy continues to be a comfort and a blessing to us both. He shows great promise as a budding engineer, the headmaster tell us. Sammy's father was also gifted in that direction, I believe . . .

There was more, but Chrissie skimmed over it. As always,

mention of her son upset her. She was sorry to hear about Lizzie's illness, but it didn't bring Sammy's return any nearer.

The boy never answered her letters, or even sent a message. It was as if she didn't exist for him. It was getting more and more difficult to write; often months would go by before she could pick a pen.

With a sigh, she turned to her niece Georgina's letter, from Australia. It contained happier news.

We have a baby girl! A bouncing 7 lb 6 oz little beaut. We have named her Jean Christine, after my dear mum and my favourite auntie. I hope you both feel honoured! I admit I never wanted children, but Jean Christine is adorable, the only beautiful thing in this hot, barren desert . . .

Chrissie studied the letter thoughtfully. Reading between the lines, she suspected Ina's marriage was not a happy one.

* * * *

Mary Rose could no longer ignore the situation. Something had happened which would force a decision — one way or the other.

"I'm going to have a baby, Roddy!"

They'd just reached their own special place on the moorland, a secluded grassy spot, surrounded by whins.

Roddy felt as if his heart had stopped.

"But – but – Mary Rose, are you sure?"

She blinked hard, trying to be brave.

"I've suspected for some time, and I was sick this morning again. Mum was sick in the mornings when she was expecting the twins. It's a sure sign, Roddy."

"Oh, my darling!" He held her close, petrified.

He was only twenty-two, and had never contemplated marriage – or babies! The awesome responsibility thrust upon him turned him to jelly.

Mary Rose was sobbing quietly.

"I don't mind about the baby. I want your baby. But they'll say I'm a bad girl, a disgrace to the family. I feel so ashamed, so wicked!"

"You're not!"

Suddenly he was angry. No-one was going to sneer at his lovely, generous Mary Rose. Not if he could help it! Somehow he would protect her – and his baby – from the cruel world.

His baby! A little living creature. His son . . . or his daughter . . .

"Listen, love, we'll say nothing about the baby to anyone. We'll just elope – to – Gretna Green. After we're married we'll go to my parents. Mother will look after you."

Mary Rose wiped her eyes. The speed of his planning left her breathless.

"But – but that'll cause a sensation!"

"Of course it will!" He laughed recklessly. "That's just the point! They'll think we've run off together because of Sandra. By the time the baby arrives you'll be a respectable married lady living in England."

She was quiet. It was a good idea – a wonderful idea – but . . .

"Poor Sandra," Mary Rose said softly.

"Sandra doesn't really love me," Roddy said cheerfully. "She'll get over it."

He hugged his intended wife.

"Leave everything to me, my sweetheart. I'll see to the details. You just pack your case and be ready to leave the moment I say the word!"

The days sped by once the decision was made. Mary Rose felt strangely helpless, borne along on the tide of events.

She had packed a small case and hidden it in the cupboard. When Roddy told her one morning that they must leave that night, the following hours were the strangest Mary Rose had ever spent.

Her mother and stepfather, her sister, dear old Bessie and the twins all went about, unaware that this was the last day they'd spend together as a happy family. When Mary Rose stole away their happiness would shatter. Sandra would be shamed and pitied and mocked . . .

And her horses! Mary Rose had shed many bitter tears before taking Caroline partially into her confidence.

Her friend had promised to exercise Thrawn Janet and Billy until they could be found good homes with kind people. Mary Rose knew she would never see them again. That was just another part of the heavy price she had to pay.

The sun was sinking, night drawing closer, the time of parting coming nearer. Tears running down her cheeks, Mary Rose sat at her dressing-table and wrote a letter. A last, simple letter to all her dear ones, asking their forgiveness.

Chrissie found Mary Rose's letter on her plate when she came down to breakfast with Charles next morning. He smiled as he reached for the toast and marmalade.

"A billet doux, love? I haven't missed our anniversary, have I?"

She smiled, but the white envelope addressed in her younger daughter's hand was vaguely unsettling. Her fingers trembled as she slit it open. When she read the few short sentences, her heart turned to ice.

"What is it?"

Chrissie had turned so pale, Charles had got to his feet.

Silently she handed him the letter. He read it through swiftly and sank back down in the chair.

They looked at one another, the full horror of the situation sinking slowly in.

"Oh, my God, Chrissie. What about Sandra?" Charles breathed.

"Who's taking my name in vain?" Sandra laughed from the doorway.

She'd wakened in a marvellous mood.

Yesterday she'd bought white satin pyjamas, very chic, very seductive, and laid them in her bottom drawer. It was filled with lovely things, all carefully folded and scented with lavender sachets.

When Roddy asked her to marry him, she would say yes. She was ready . . . impatient . . .

She paused halfway across the room. Why were her mother and stepfather looking so serious? Why were they staring at her so hard?

"What is it?" Sandra was alarmed now. "What's wrong?"

Chrissie's heart ached for her daughter – for both her daughters!

"Darling, you must be brave," she said gently.

Then she held out the letter in silence. It seemed the only thing to do.

Sandra took it as if in a dream, vaguely recognising Mary Rose's careful script. She read it through once, then read it through again numbly, although every word was etched in her mind.

She would never forget what it said. She'd never forget the humiliation and the shock. She'd never forget the crushing sorrow as all her plans and dreams crashed around her.

Most of all, she would never forget it was the sister she'd loved and trusted, who'd betrayed her and stolen her man.

Sandra's anguish tore from her in a shout.

"Forgive her! She asks me to forgive her! Well, I won't. I'll never speak to Mary Rose again as long as I live!"

Sandra flung the letter furiously into the heart of the fire. Then, turning blindly, she ran from the room.

Chapter 29

SANDRA didn't cry. She ached with hurt, but she stubbornly refused to shed a tear, even when she reached the sanctuary of her room.

She sat on the window seat and stared out. The first leaves of autumn had fallen and lay stirring in the breeze. Winter was coming, and she was glad. Everything would be bleak and cold as the ice in her heart . . .

There was a tap on the door and her mother came in.

Chrissie didn't know what to do for the best. Perhaps she had no right to intrude, but this was her daughter and she couldn't keep away.

She sat beside Sandra, who didn't even turn her head.

"Sandra, darling, I'm so sorry."

Chrissie's sorrow was sincere. She blamed herself for not noticing what was going on. If she hadn't been so preoccupied, she might have saved Sandra this humiliation. Now it was too late.

Sandra stirred.

"It's strange, Mum. When Queen Alexandra died I wept buckets, but I've been betrayed by the man I love and my own sister, and can't raise a single tear. I'll never speak to Mary Rose or Roderick Stirton again."

"Don't say that! In time you'll . . . forgive . . ."

"No, I won't, Mum!"

She stood up abruptly and began pacing the floor.

"Oh, I could forgive them for falling in love. What I can't forgive is that they kept it from me. Why didn't they tell me? I could have . . . could have . . ."

Sandra stopped abruptly, struggling not to weep. When she spoke it was in quiet, controlled tones.

"I'm going out. A walk will help me think. I have to decide what to do. I don't think I can stay in Dundee after this."

Sandra's unnatural calm unnerved Chrissie. She knew how stubborn her daughter could be.

Sandra walked out into the chilly autumn morning. Mary Rose and Roddy would be far away . . . perhaps already man and wife. The thought made her walk faster. She had no idea where she was going, but from habit she turned downhill towards the river.

A car tooted behind her, startling her. Sandra hastily jumped on to the pavement as a Ford saloon drew up beside her.

At first she couldn't place the woman driver. It was some time since they'd had a visit from Harriet Bowers, her mother's best friend. Sandra had always been fond of her.

"Hello, Auntie Harriet!" Sandra forced a smile.

Harriet leaned over and opened the passenger door.

"Can I give you a lift into Broughty Ferry? Come on, Sandra, hop in!"

As her passenger climbed in reluctantly, Harriet noted the signs of unhappiness on the young face. She was adept at diagnosing misery, because she'd had plenty of practice. Her clinic lay in the Clydebank area of Glasgow, where unemployment was rife.

"My, what a lovely young lady you are, Sandra! It's a good job your mother sent me a recent photo or I would have driven straight past."

"Were you on your way to see Mum and Dad?"

Harriet hesitated.

"No, I'm off to buy fish at Broughty harbour. My mother swears it's fresher."

She let in the clutch and the car moved off smoothly.

Since the twins had been born Chrissie's letters had been few and far between, and had given nothing away. Harriet had heard about the seriousness of Charles's illness from another source, and she was puzzled and a little hurt by her friend's reticence.

"How's everyone?" she asked carefully.

"Fine. At least . . . that is . . ."

Sandra hadn't meant to mention to a soul what had happened that morning, but she found herself telling Harriet everything. She poured out all the pain and disillusionment, and even told her sympathetic listener about her filled-to-overflowing bottom drawer.

"So you see, I can't go on living in Dundee. Folk will point me out as the girl who was jilted because her man fell for her young sister. I don't know what I shall do!"

Sandra stared through the windscreen, her eyes hot with unshed tears. She wouldn't cry, though. It was a matter of pride not to cry.

Harriet pitied poor Sandra. She could well imagine what the poor lass was going through. Hard work had dulled the ache of losing Charles, but the humiliation still lingered.

She drove to the harbour and parked on the front. There were fishing cobles drawn up on the shingly beach opposite the fishermen's cottages. It was high water, and a jute ship took advantage of the tide to reach its berth.

Harriet watched the vessel's progress abstractedly.

"Can you type, Sandra?"

Sandra was surprised.

"Type? Yes, I took a course in typing and book-keeping. I'm not particularly fast, though."

"That doesn't matter." Harriet turned in the driving seat and looked at her. "I need a receptionist at the clinic. Somebody I can trust to handle appointments and file patients' records. Would you like the job?

"I warn you, it's hard work. You'll see poverty that'll make you furious— but you'll also meet folk who are so brave you'll never forget them."

Thoughtfully, Sandra watched the river, the varnished fishing boats and painted ships, the Fifie on its monotonous course in the distance.

It would be a wrench to leave the ancient city she loved — but hadn't her grandfather sailed from Dundee so many times and always returned safely? And hadn't her father left home to give his life for the peace of the world?

Sandra made up her mind.

"All right, Auntie Harriet. I'll take the job. I just hope I'm up to it."

"You'll do fine, my dear." Harriet grinned. "But, please, let's drop the 'Auntie'. It makes me feel so old!"

The Rankine twins were sheltered from the disaster that had split their family, but the sudden departure of Mary Rose, followed very soon after by Sandra's trip to Glasgow, didn't escape their notice. Charlotte questioned Bessie, but all she got was a grim tightening of the lips.

"Mind an' pick a guid honest Dundee laddie when your time comes, my wee pet!" Bessie said.

The warning made no sense whatsoever to the bewildered little girl.

Ewan had more success.

He was a bookworm like his dad, and could be found in the living-room most evenings, his nose buried in a book. He gleaned a lot of useful information by keeping quiet as a mouse; grown-ups simply forgot he was there.

Chrissie had received a startling letter from Mary Rose six months after the elopement. She hurried into the room where Charles was twiddling the knobs on the wireless set. She was considerably agitated, and didn't see Ewan curled up in a corner of the sofa.

"Oh, Charles! Mary Rose had a baby a fortnight ago. A girl . . . Elizabeth . . . weighing eight pounds and four ounces!"

Charles looked up.

"Hardly a six-month baby at that weight! This explains everything, Chrissie."

"Yes. The possibility did cross my mind."

She sat down.

"Should we tell Sandra?"

He switched off the set, and the room fell silent.

"Yes, and right away. It was the secrecy that hurt her the most. Obviously the baby drove Mary Rose and Roddy to elope. If Sandra knows, it might help her to forgive."

"I do hope you're right." Chrissie sighed. "Oh, Charles! This is our first grandchild! Will we ever see her?"

A slight movement from the sofa caught Charles's attention. He raised a finger to his lips.

Chrissie caught a glimpse of her son's fair head and covered her mouth in dismay.

Ewan returned to his book. He'd heard all he wanted, and presently his mother and father were convinced he'd heard nothing.

Charles switched on the radio and the happy strains of "Alexander's Ragtime Band" floated jazzily through the air.

It was later that evening when a puzzled Ewan confronted Bessie as she was busy darning socks.

"Bessie, can wee babies drive cars?" Ewan asked.

"What are you bletherin' aboot noo?" She frowned at Ewan.

"Mum says Mary Rose has had a baby. She said that the baby drove Mary Rose and Roddy to get married. But how can babies drive cars, Bessie?"

Bessie didn't answer. She dropped the darning and began muttering to herself.

"Oh, michty me! The disgrace o' it! The shame! Poor Chrissie. Her heart must be sair!"

She fixed Ewan with a fierce glare that made him shake in his boots.

"Now listen, my lad. You've no' to let on to onybody aboot babies driving folk to get married. An' don't you go talkin' aboot Mary Rose's bairn till I give you the word. That goes for you, too, mind, Charlotte!"

The twins nodded hastily. When Bessie was in this mood, nobody argued.

Later, Ewan cleared up the mystery by referring to the large medical dictionary Charles kept on the library shelves.

Chapter 30

OLD William Kennedy slipped peacefully away in his sleep that summer. He was hale and hearty to the last, enjoying a good blether and a wee dram of whisky right to the end of his long, hard-working life.

Chrissie missed her father sorely, but she was glad for him. It was the way he would have wanted it.

Mrs Pearson, the housekeeper who'd looked after him for years, came to Chrissie diffidently. Might she be allowed to pay rent for the old house and keep a few respectable boarders?

"Just to keep the wolf from the door, now the dear captain's gone, Mrs Rankine?" she explained hopefully.

It was an excellent idea which neatly solved a problem. Chrissie had been reluctant to sell the family home. It still had too many memories. As a little girl she stood at this very window and watched her ship go sailing out to sea . . .

Chrissie sighed and turned her back on the river. All that remained of the beautiful *Christina K* was the brooch she wore pinned to her dress.

Sandra came home when she heard the news. She'd always been very fond of her grandfather.

Chrissie saw a great change in her daughter – though it was hard to put her finger on what it was.

Sandra was as pretty as ever. She'd always dressed

stylishly, but now her clothes, although well-cut, were on simple lines and in muted colours. They were go-anywhere clothes that wouldn't stand out in a crowd.

"Do you enjoy your job?" Charles asked as they sat in the garden, having afternoon tea in warm sunshine.

Sandra sipped, then replaced the cup carefully.

"No, I don't enjoy it, to be honest. I hate the ugliness, the poverty, and most of all, the smell." She lifted her head and looked at him defiantly. "It's because I hate it so much that I can't give up. Does that make any sense to you?"

He looked at her hard.

"Yes, my dear. I think it does."

She stood up with an embarrassed little laugh.

"Oh, dear, I'm beginning to sound like Harriet – and I'm not a patch on her! Did you know she hit a six-foot docker with the appointments ledger and knocked him out cold because he'd blacked his wife's eye? He's been a reformed character since then."

"I can imagine!"

So that was it, Chrissie thought. Her daughter had abandoned the imaginary world and come to grips with the stern realities of life at last.

The day before she returned to Glasgow, Sandra came face to face with Norrie Gallacher's granny, in Draffens of all places. Draffens held an unrivalled reputation as a posh shop, and one startled glance at Aggie Gallacher told Sandra the old woman was as posh as any high-brow lady.

Aggie's furs and elegant dress wouldn't have disgraced the

Duchess of York.

Sandra was delighted. She'd pleasant memories of
Norrie's granny in the days when she was six years old and
engaged to him. Despite a sharp tongue, the old lady's heart
was pure gold, and she'd given it wholeheartedly to Norrie,
the orphan laddie she'd brought up from babyhood.

"I'm so pleased to meet you, Mrs Gallacher!" Sandra held
out a hand, smiling.

Aggie ignored the hand and the friendly smile.

"Weel, I'm no awfy pleased to see you, Sandra Murphy.
Not after what you did to my Norrie. Sendin' him awa' frae
Dundee!"

"But I didn't do anything!"

"Aye, I ken. That's what I meant."

The conversation was taking a baffling turn. Sandra
changed direction.

"How's Norrie doing in Canada?"

"Fine."

"Is he married yet?"

"Naw, the daft gowk." Aggie snorted. "I keep tellin' him to
get himsel' a guid wife."

Something stirred in Sandra, a nostalgic longing for the
innocence of childhood. She remembered a wide, cheeky
grin and carroty hair, a persistent irritation she'd somehow
sadly missed.

"Mrs Gallacher, could you give me Norrie's address?" she
asked tentatively.

"Naw, I couldna." The old lady stiffened. "You had your

chance an' missed it!"

With a glare, Aggie swept out of the store, leaving Sandra staring after her.

* * * *

Although Dundee was feeling the full force of the Depression, life for a ten-year-old boy was full of interest.

Coming home from school in the centre of town, there were plenty of muddy puddles for Ewan and his pals to splash through as the extension from Dock Street to Ferry Road neared completion. And the setting in place of huge steel girders to bridge the cavern beneath the new city square was a sight which attracted large crowds, Ewan and friends included.

There was a silent battle going on in Dundee between buses and trams. The much-loved tramcars still numbered seventy-nine as opposed to a fleet of sixty-four buses.

Traffic congestion in the city centre worsened daily. The visit of the Prince of Wales in April 1933 caused chaos.

Ewan was in the thick of it, of course. An excited crowd descended upon the popular young prince, and Ewan felt small and frightened.

Prince Edward didn't seem to mind the crush. Smiling and joking, he disappeared inside the building to inspect what was being done in Dundee for the vast army of unemployed men and women.

"That laddie trails all over the place! Just look at the mud on his guid school shoes!" Bessie complained later in despair. "I'm no' so fleet as I was, or I'd meet him from school mysel' to keep him oot o' mischief."

The threat turned Ewan pale with apprehension.

Chrissie was also concerned by Ewan's wanderings, and told him so frankly. As usual, her son retaliated with a frustratingly reasonable compromise.

"If I had a wee dog, Mum, I'd come straight home from school to take it for walks."

"Yes, and I'd have to feed and look after it most of the time!"

Cunningly, Ewan played his trump card.

"The Duke and Duchess of York's wee girls have a dog, Mum, and they look after him themselves. It's a corgi, an' it's called Dookie, short for the Duke of York's puppy. Why can't I have a dog?"

Ewan knew his mother admired the Duchess of York. In September Chrissie had even made a special trip into the country to see the duchess open Belmont Castle, a home for old folk.

Chrissie eyed her son with fond exasperation. Once he'd got an idea into his head he never let go. This business of the dog had been going on for months. Perhaps . . .

"I'll have a word with Dad, Ewan," she promised weakly.

Ewan smiled to himself. He knew the battle was won.

Angus, a big, soft-hearted black Labrador pup, joined the family soon after. He quickly wagged his way happily into everyone's affections.

Although the Rankines shared the closeness most twins have, their interests differed. On Saturday mornings, while

Ewan roamed the countryside with Angus, Chrissie took Charlotte to dancing class.

She usually stayed to watch from the gallery. Charlotte was the star of the class. Tap-dancing, ballroom, hornpipe – her daughter's flying feet mastered them all. She was a natural dancer, her delighted teacher said.

Charlotte preferred Highland dancing, and she was one of those chosen to dance a reel before the Duke and Duchess of York when they visited the Royal Highland Show. It was being held in Dundee that year, for the first time since 1890, and the crowds were enormous.

Chrissie and Charles stood, hand in hand, watching their daughter, positively bursting with pride. Their visit to the show was a welcome break, for Charles had never recovered his full strength after his heart attack.

He visited the factory twice a week, despite Chrissie's protests, and was cautiously optimistic about the upturn in trade. Sandra had written cheerfully from Glasgow to say work had started once again on the huge liner in John Brown's yard, and things were looking up again in Clydebank.

By now, Chrissie was on good terms with Rankine's American customer, Ben Chester. They conversed in short postscripts, and Chrissie often giggled over his comments.

His latest postscript had made her uneasy, though.

Who is this guy Hitler? They tell me he's put Germany on her feet again, building roads like you never saw. Their factories are working full-time, making heaven knows what.

And what about the Duce, Mussolini? Sure, he drained the Pontine Marshes and made the desert bloom, but I think these guys are getting too big for their boots. They want watching, Chrissie!

Chrissie took the worry home to Charles.

"Do you think there'll be another war, darling?"

"They wouldn't be so daft! Europe's just recovering from the last fiasco." Charles knew his wife had good reason to loathe and fear war.

Chrissie seemed reassured by his comforting reply, but Charles was beginning to spend more time listening to the wireless and reading newspapers. All the news was disquieting. Charles watched his young son grow taller as he months went by, and began to feel afraid . . .

Worries about the future didn't trouble Ewan. When the weather wasn't suitable for walking the dog, there was always the pictures.

Bessie and Charlotte were also avid fans. Their favourite pastime on a wet Saturday was to take a tram into town and visit the Majestic or the Kinnaird, and watch a musical or a comedy or, preferably, a weepy.

After the show, their routine rarely varied. They went to Wallace's restaurant and sat in the cosy, onion-scented interior.

Bessie did the ordering in a pan-loafie voice, conscious of her best outfit and the fur Chrissie had given her.

"Two pies, a pot o' tea an' two sair heids."

"Oh, Bessie!" Charlotte had been mystified by this order

the first time, but now she collapsed in giggles.

The waitress returned with two steaming hot pies and two little iced cakes, each wrapped around with a strip of white paper. They looked for all the world like bandages on sore heads . . .

Ewan didn't go with Bessie and Charlotte. He preferred Laurel and Hardy, Mickey Mouse, and above all, westerns. Tom Mix was Ewan's hero.

He wished his father hadn't sold Mary Rose's horses. He would have loved to try riding like a cowboy. As it was, he had to make do with a long-legged, easy gait, hitching his breeks frequently, eyes narrowed keenly as his hands hovered over imaginary six-guns slung low on his hips.

Being a regular patron of the cinema, he was made aware of events elsewhere in the world. The Pathé Movietone news kept him up to date.

He watched King George and Queen Mary's Silver Jubilee procession take place in London in 1935. More ominously, news films began showing flag-waving soldiers, rank upon rank, goose-stepping in Germany.

The sight gave Ewan a curious feeling inside. Although he didn't really want to, he joined the school cadet force.

Chrissie always relaxed on Saturday afternoons. She enjoyed catching up with her correspondence, writing to widening circles of friends and relatives round the world.

She didn't write very often, though, to Harriet. She'd always felt embarrassed about putting down the trivia, the day-to-day news of her married life, when it could so easily be her friend who'd married Charles. And writing about her happiness was even worse – wouldn't that just make Harriet jealous?

And unhappiness – wouldn't Harriet just think that she could have done better? Where Charles's illness was concerned, it was very likely she could have . . . and could still do so. What if Harriet came back to Dundee and Charles found he needed her . . . ? Maybe she was being silly, but the thought still worried her.

So Chrissie wrote Sandra a chatty letter, then, more carefully, one to Mary Rose.

She hadn't known what to make of Mary Rose's short, noncommittal communications, nor of the information that she and little Elizabeth were moving to a small house in London. Apparently living with Roddy's parents had not been successful.

She picked up a pen to write the usual difficult letter to her sister-in-law Lizzie Kennedy in India. Lizzie's illness was a progressive one, and Arthur had written that she couldn't walk or use her hands very well now. Sammy's old ayah tended her devotedly, Chrissie's brother wrote, and Sammy himself, nearly nineteen, had left school and was working as an apprentice engineer in the Titaghur mill.

Chrissie stared at the blank page and sighed. Nearly nineteen! If she met Danny's son in the street, she wouldn't know him . . .

By the end of 1936, everyone realised they were witnessing historic events.

The popular prince, upon whom the country had pinned such bright hopes, abdicated rather than give up the woman he loved. Mrs Simpson had been recently divorced, and a consort for the new King with such a background was unthinkable.

The romantic story brought emotional tears to dear old Bessie's eyes, but it was a shattering blow to everyone concerned.

Chrissie and Charles were glued to the wireless set. The Duke of York, an unassuming, home-loving man, who'd never sought the limelight, would be their next King. The lovely, dark-haired girl Chrissie had met at Glamis Castle would be Queen!

Chrissie was absolutely delighted when it was announced that the coronation would go ahead as planned, on May 12, 1937.

Dundee was hit by coronation fever. The city took a personal pride in the new King and Queen and their two little daughters.

The youngest, Margaret Rose, had been born nearby, at Glamis Castle, and the family had been frequent visitors to the city over the years.

The City Square, declared open three years ago by the King's younger brother, the Duke of Kent, lent itself to decoration with bunting and flags. Chrissie, however, took the twins, who were newly turned fourteen, to a much more famous and traditional location.

Bernard Street, a narrow street of old stone tenements just

off Hawkhill, was famed for its ingenuity on such occasions. Chrissie and the twins left Hawkhill and rounded the corner, then stopped in their tracks to stare. A blaze of patriotic bunting and strings of small flags criss-crossed the street. Union Jacks fluttered from most windows, alongside red, white and blue balloons and banners.

"That's terrific, Mum! Even better than the City Square."

Ewan was clearly impressed, and Chrissie was glad. She wanted her children to remember this old street with brave flags flying.

Looking up at the brilliant colours transforming the smoke-grimed stone, she felt a fierce love for her city and its folk, but she was too choked with emotion to utter a word.

Chapter 31

I DON'T feel well, Mum," Charlotte announced suddenly. Chrissie studied her daughter anxiously. Charlotte had been tired and heavy-eyed at breakfast that morning, but she'd thought nothing of it. The girl looked really ill now, hot, feverish and shivering.

"My head hurts," Charlotte complained, bewildered. She didn't know what was happening to her. She was hardly ever ill, but now her legs had begun aching so badly they felt weak. She clung dizzily to her mother.

With Ewan's help, Chrissie got Charlotte back to the car. Then she drove as fast as she could to Beechyhill, and asked Charles to phone for the doctor.

The doctor washed his hands carefully after examining Charlotte.

"I'm arranging for Charlotte to be taken to hospital immediately. She should be kept in isolation," he said gravely to Chrissie.

"Isolation?" The word somehow struck terror in her heart. "What is it? What's wrong with her?"

"I believe it is poliomyelitis, my dear. Infantile paralysis. There have been a few cases in the town."

"Oh, no!" Chrissie felt the room sway. Charles was beside her in a moment.

Chrissie knew she should protect him from such worry and

stress, but he seemed stronger than she was at that awful moment. His arm was around her, strong and comforting. He looked grey and drawn with worry, but he smiled reassuringly.

The doctor was speaking, telling them all the things they must do. Ewan must be kept off school and in quarantine, in case he was infected by the disease, too.

It was a nightmare from which they couldn't seem to waken. Long days and longer nights dragged slowly by. They weren't even allowed to visit Charlotte in hospital, and they were only permitted a glimpse of her from steps outside the window.

At last the doctors told Charles and Chrissie that their daughter was going to be all right.

Charlotte would recover and lead quite a normal life. She would have to wear a strong metal calliper on her left leg, but she'd get around reasonably well once she got used to it. She'd been lucky, considering the severity of her illness.

Lucky! Chrissie rested her head against Charles's shoulder and closed her eyes in anguish. The doctors hadn't watched Charlotte dancing!

Chrissie allowed herself one last moment of weakness, then wiped her eyes and began to count her blessings.

Ewan had escaped the disease, and Charlotte was recovering. Charles had coped remarkably well and his heart condition was no worse. They had much to be thankful for!

But Charlotte couldn't accept what had happened to her. She just couldn't adjust to a leg that refused to do what she wanted it to, unless encased in heavy metal that dragged awkwardly when she tried to walk. So she didn't try very hard with the exercises she'd been given, and refused to go out. She hated the pitying stares she got.

Charlotte knew she was making her mother and father distracted with worry, and she was sorry, but she couldn't do anything about it. She couldn't even listen to music, because it made her want to dance— and she'd never dance again.

Ewan was sympathetic, but he had his own interests. That summer he went off with the school cadets to camp at Cortachy for a fortnight. He was a lance corporal, and extremely proud of the single white stripe on his uniform jacket.

Worn out with worry, Chrissie went down with a severe chill. Bessie struggled to cure her with all sorts of remedies, ranging from beef tea to Bile Beans. Charles had to go to the office each day and nobody had much time to spend on Charlotte any more.

She was lying moping in bed, wondering if it was worth the effort of getting up, when the bedclothes were tugged sideways and a cold draught hit the back of her neck. She sat up indignantly, then laughed.

"Och, Angus, it's you!"

The dog wagged his tail, then sat looking at her with mournful pleading. His ears dropped; nobody had any time to spare for Angus these days, either.

"Poor old boy. We're outcasts, you and me," Charlotte told him sadly.

He agreed, wagging his tail and whining. Then he leaped on Charlotte, nudging and prodding her energetically with his cold, wet nose.

She giggled and tried to fight him off.

"Hey, stop it, you daft dog! I can't take you for a walk!"

That was the wrong word to use. The dog's eyes brightened, and he uttered short, sharp barks of excitement.

He shoved and pushed at Charlotte and created such a rumpus she was forced to get up. How could you argue with such a determined Labrador that had his mind set on a walk?

Reluctantly, Charlotte dressed, buckling on the hated calliper. She sat and looked at the dog with tears in her eyes.

"Angus, I'd love to take you out, but I can't! I'm sorry!"

But, of course, the dog couldn't understand. He nudged Charlotte to her feet, then gently escorted her along the hall. There he bounded off and came back proudly, a happy gleam in his brown eyes, carrying his lead in his mouth.

She laughed.

"I hope you know what you're doing, Angus. I'm as slow as a snail!" But she bent down and clipped the lead on his collar.

To Charlotte's surprise, once outside, Angus padded slowly by her side. When they came to a slight rise, he pulled her up it. She began to gain confidence and decided to go on.

"Just to the park, mind, Angus. That's all I can manage."

Seated thankfully on a bench, Charlotte let Angus off the lead and allowed him to roam about busily on his own. She lifted her face to the sunshine. It felt good.

Maybe life wasn't so bad. Her legs were awfully tired and weak, but perhaps that was because she hadn't been using them much. If she walked more, as the doctors had told her to, they'd grow stronger.

A little group of youths came noisily along the path, enjoying the freedom of a public holiday. They whistled appreciatively and winked at her as they passed.

"What a smasher!" she heard one of them remark to his mates.

Charlotte smiled, colour in her cheeks. They hadn't even noticed her leg!

Filled with hope, she called Angus to her, and hugged the dog gratefully before setting off home.

Chrissie watched delightedly as her daughter grew stronger and more confident. Charlotte walked with a determined, limping gait, the devoted black dog padding along, patiently matching his pace to hers. Laughter came back to the house and music blared out from the wireless and gramophone. For a time Chrissie was happy, ignoring the threat that hung over the country.

Talk of war was on everyone's lips. Chrissie could hardly bear to watch Ewan as he left for school on Fridays, the day the cadets mustered. He looked so smart in his khaki jacket and Black Watch kilt that she was reminded of Danny.

At fifteen, Ewan was almost as tall as Charles, with his father's clean-cut, sensitive features and Chrissie's wavy fair hair, which he subdued sternly with hair oil. He was a full corporal now and confident he'd get his sergeant's stripes before leaving school.

He had no idea what he would do when he left school. Go into the family business, he supposed, though the prospect didn't thrill him. He felt restless, infected by the uncertainty and the scary rumours flying around.

And Bessie, placidly knitting socks, appeared unaffected by the jitters.

"Bessie, do you think there'll be a war?" Ewan asked.

"Wi' the Empire Exhibition on in Glasgow? No chance!"

"Dad says the factory's working flat out making sandbags," Ewan persisted.

"Aye. The flooding's been awfy aboot the River Earn."

"My pal's dad has joined the Civil Defence. He says they're to dig air-raid shelters in Dudhope Park, opposite the hospital."

Bessie sniffed and rattled the knitting needles.

"Och, I'm no' surprised, with all these flying boats clutterin' up the Tay. They'll be building shelters in case their daft inventions fa' oot the sky on decent folk's heids."

"They say Hitler will march into Czechoslovakia . . ."

"Mr Chamberlain'll no' let him. Dinna bother your heid aboot Hitler, lovie. The man's daft," Bessie said comfortably, and gave her full attention to turning the heel.

The glorious weather in the summer of 1939 belied the imminent threat of war. The sun shone from a blue sky hazy with heat.

Chrissie lifted her face to the hot sun as she pottered in the garden in one of her rare moments of leisure.

She was the only energetic one that Saturday. Charles lay snoozing in a deckchair on the terrace, and Ewan lazed in a hammock slung between two tall rowan trees, reading a book. Charlotte sunbathed, faithful Angus not far away, lying watchfully in the shade.

The birds sang and all round Chrissie lay a peace and tranquillity which she knew was false. Her nephew, Hughie, had recently been given command of a new merchant ship and only that morning his wife, Jani, had visited in tears.

"Oh, Auntie Chrissie, Hughie's ship is going to America. They are saying in my shop that the merchant ships will be torpedoed and sunk by submarines if this war comes! They are saying my Jamal and Ruby will be sent away from me to live with strangers in the country, and there will be no sweeties to sell in my shop! What will I do?"

Chrissie had smiled and hugged her.

"There's little we can do, I'm afraid. We must just wait and see."

Jani's tears had dried after a comforting chat and a cup of tea, but Chrissie couldn't dismiss her own anxiety so easily. She just couldn't settle to enjoy the perfect summer day.

She gave a small sigh of exasperation when she spotted a stranger walking up the drive. She was in no mood for visitors.

Chrissie shaded her eyes against the sun. Her visitor was a young handsome man of medium height. He was smartly dressed, but it was impossible to make out his features against the sun's glare.

She saw him hesitate uncertainly, then walk towards her. He stopped, the width of the rockery between them.

"Excuse me, are you Mrs Rankine?"

Chrissie felt suddenly apprehensive, almost panicky.

"Yes. What is it?" she answered sharply.

He studied her for a moment in silence, as if put off by her tone. Then he took off his smart hat politely and held it somewhat nervously by the brim.

"Well, you see, I'm Samuel Murphy. I'm Sammy," the young man announced.

Chapter 32

CHRISSIE had imagined her son's return often. Time after time, she'd rehearsed what she would say, before welcoming him into her arms. But now the moment had come and she couldn't think of anything!

"Why have you come?" Hardly a promising start!

"I wanted to visit Dundee before joining up."

"You mean – join the Army?" She was taken aback.

"Of course. That's why I left India."

She was aware of crushing disappointment and shaded her eyes against the sun's glare with a hand.

Her son's eyes were as blue and clear as Danny's. His hair not so black, but brown with coppery highlights. The discovery made her want to weep.

"So you didn't come back just to see your mother?" She kept her tone light and impersonal.

He didn't answer right away, but stood studying her.

"I was curious about you. I wanted to find out what sort of woman would give her son away. And then take no interest in him afterwards."

"What? How can you say that?" Chrissie protested. "I wrote to you – again and again!"

He looked politely sceptical.

"You wrote to Mother and Dad. That's not quite the same, is it?"

She stared at him in bewilderment. Obviously he hadn't got them . . . hadn't read those painfully composed letters in which she poured out all her love, all her longing for him. No wonder Lizzie and Arthur had always been "too busy" to come back to Dundee on furlough!

Sammy's expression had softened a little. He went on quietly, as if he had to talk to somebody.

"Mother died shortly before I left. It broke Dad's heart. I thought about staying in India to be with him, but I want to join a Scottish regiment if there's going to be a war. Dad understood. It's the only way."

His resemblance to Danny was remarkable as he talked about his plan. A shiver ran through Chrissie despite the hot sunshine. How could she let her son go off to war not knowing how much she loved him?

Chrissie was sure Lizzie had destroyed the letters she'd written to Sammy explaining the circumstances of his birth and fostering. No doubt she'd soothed her conscience by arguing that they would upset the boy. Typical Lizzie!

And now Lizzie was dead. She could never prove the letters had been written. And if she tried, she doubted if Sammy would believe her.

It would be just her word – a stranger's word – against that of the woman he thought of as his mother. She could well end up driving him away completely. Better to wait until he got to know her better.

"I'm very sorry," she said at last. "I didn't know Lizzie had died."

"It was very sad," Sammy replied briefly.

He didn't want to talk about it. The memories of his foster mother's last days were still sharp in his mind. She'd stared at him with such pleading eyes, as if begging for forgiveness. Forgiveness for what?

It had unnerved Sammy. He'd never forget it. In fact, just remembering made him shiver.

He put on his hat, pulling the brim well down to shield his eyes.

"Now I've paid my respects, I'll be going."

"No! Please don't go yet!" Chrissie pleaded.

"There's nothing more to say, is there?" He shrugged.

"Perhaps not. That – that's up to you, Sammy." There was so much she wanted to say to him, but he didn't seem to want to hear it. He was impatient to leave.

He hesitated for a moment, looking up at the old house at the top of the hilly garden.

"I'd like to meet my sisters," he admitted grudgingly.

"They're not here, I'm afraid. Mary Rose is in London and Sandra works in Glasgow."

"So you got rid of all the Murphys when you went up in the world." He gave a wry smile. "You must be delighted!"

Chrissie was suddenly furious with him. Whatever her faults, she didn't deserve this!

"It was no wish of mine to lose my bairns, Sammy. Fortunately, I have my twins and my dear husband for comfort," she said coldly.

Sammy felt bitter. She shouldn't have thrown that

information in his face.

"Ah, yes, your husband. You did very well for yourself the second time around. Better than with my poor father!"

As soon as he'd spoken, he was sorry. It was true, but he felt sorry all the same. He hadn't meant to hurt her, but he could see the pain in her expressive eyes.

She was a very beautiful woman, Sammy realised for the first time. She must be about fifty, so he'd expected her to look old, like his mother. But she was his mother . . .

No – Mother died in India, grey and haggard and exhausted. This woman's beauty would never fade, as it was there in the bone structure. He'd spent so many years resenting her and now he was calling her beautiful . . . Sammy was confused and disconcerted.

Chrissie had taken a threatening step towards her son.

"Nobody says that to my face! Not even you, Samuel Murphy! I think you'd better go – get out of my sight!"

She was too hurt and furious to think clearly. She just wanted him to leave so she could be alone with her misery and tears.

That was how Ewan found them as he came bounding down the rockery steps. As he approached he could sense tension in the air.

"Hey, Mum! Dad says there won't be any sandwiches left if you don't come now!"

She turned towards him. Ewan was shocked. He'd never seen his mother look like this before, strange, almost old.

"Ewan, this is your half-brother, Sammy," she said in a

282

chilly, strangled voice. "He's just leaving."

Ewan could hardly believe his ears. In his excitement, he almost shoved his mother aside, pumping Sammy's hand vigorously.

"I've been waiting to meet you for ages, Sammy! Have you come home for good?"

Sammy was shaken. The youngster's friendly enthusiasm was embarrassing under the circumstances.

"Well – er – not really. I'm volunteering – joining my father's regiment."

"Jolly good show!" Ewan breathed, eyes shining. "D'you think that the war'll last long enough for me to fight?"

"It hasn't even started yet! Maybe Hitler will accept Chamberlain's ultimatum and it'll all blow over."

Sammy smiled at Ewan, relaxing a bit. He liked the kid. And he liked the thought of having a brother, even a half-brother. It gave him a warm feeling of belonging somewhere.

He sneaked a curious glance at Chrissie. She looked so tragic, for a moment he pitied her. Perhaps he should say something comforting . . . ? But the words just wouldn't come.

He made a show of consulting his wristwatch.

"I'd better go. My train leaves soon."

Ewan felt a lump in his throat. His brother was just as strong and brave as Ewan had imagined. To think he'd come all this way to join up! If only he were older and they could go together! He caught Sammy's sleeve.

"You'll come back soon. Won't you, Sammy? Please?" he begged.

"We-ell –" Sammy glanced at Chrissie, then met his half-brother's pleading gaze again, and was forced to give in. He grinned and clapped the young lad on the shoulder.

"OK. I'll come back just to see you, wee brother."

Sammy wondered how Chrissie was taking the unexpected development, but he didn't dare look at her. He turned and went briskly down the drive.

In the quiet street he heaved a sigh of relief. It was over. He'd been dreading the meeting – and yet longing for it at the same time. And, as he'd half expected, it had been a disaster.

To be fair, though, he couldn't blame her – Chrissie – his mother – for losing her temper.

Ah, well, Samuel Murphy, your country needs you. Even if your mother doesn't!

Whistling cheerfully to keep his spirits up, Sammy stepped on jauntily towards the station.

The fine weather continued, making preparations for the war seem out of place. The river sparkled a serene silvery-blue, and the white war memorial on top of the Law glinted a warning nobody heeded. September 2, 1939, was to be the last sunny Saturday of peace.

Ewan went to the pictures with a pal to see John Wayne in "Stagecoach". Bessie and Charlotte queued patiently for over half an hour to watch James Stewart and Carole Lombard in "Made For Each Other".

Despite the issuing of gas masks, and the air-raid shelters springing up all over the place, the city appeared surprisingly normal. Home football supporters were cheery and boisterous that evening in the pub. Dundee were top of the second division.

"There's going to be a war, Chris. Warsaw's been bombed. Poland's gone," Charles said suddenly that evening from where he was listening to the wireless.

Chrissie put down the cups of Horlicks she'd brought for their supper.

"Maybe Hitler will accept the ultimatum and withdraw."

Chrissie cradled the hot drink in cold hands. She was glad the twins and Bessie were out enjoying themselves. Tomorrow everything would be different. For a moment she weakened and became tearful.

"Oh, Charles, Sammy will be in the thick of it. And, if it's a long war, Ewan will have to go, too."

She stopped, biting her lip to check her tears. Like many mothers that Saturday night, Chrissie found the future too awful to contemplate.

There was almost a sense of relief in Dundee on Sunday, after the Prime Minister had spoken. The ultimatum had been ignored. They were at war.

"Aye, weel, that's put the tin lid on it!" Bessie remarked grimly.

She was right. All over Dundee, members of the Civil Defence were donning tin hats and looking anxiously to the defence of the city.

Chrissie welcomed the hundred and one jobs that had to be done, because they gave her no time to think.

She'd already ordered yards of blackout material. She, Charlotte and Bessie spent hours lining curtains. Then they criss-crossed brown sticky tape over window-panes in case they shattered.

Charles had fitted out one of the underground cellars as an air-raid shelter. It was so large, he'd blithely issued invitations to the occupants of newly built houses round about to share its safety. The prospect of so many visitors appealed to his hospitable nature.

"When the siren goes, it'll be the biggest party we've ever had." He grinned happily. "Luckily we still have quite a good stock of wine in the cellar!"

Chrissie was sad when the child evacuees left Dundee. She'd volunteered to help the little ones on to trains at the East Station, and manfully wiped noses and dried tears – the mothers' as well as the bairns' – and located lost gas masks and mislaid teddy bears and dollies.

Jani's little girl, Ruby, went off happily with her best friend to a kindly farming couple in Fettercairn. Jamal dug his heels in and refused to go.

"Och, no, Auntie Chrissie, that's for bairns!" he said scornfully. "I'll soon be fourteen and leaving school. Then I'm going into the Caledon shipyard to learn to build ships, before I go to sea like my dad."

Jani gave a wee howl and mopped her eyes mournfully, but Chrissie smiled and gently ruffled Jamal's raven-black hair. Old William Kennedy would have been delighted to know the family's sea-faring tradition was safe in Hughie's son's hands.

There were changes in the Rankine household. The first to go was Agnes, the housemaid. She came to Chrissie, pink-cheeked and blushing.

"Mrs Rankine, ye ken the tubby wee air-raid warden wha comes to check on the blackout near every nicht? Well, I've clicked wi' him, and we're to get married. I'll hae to hand in my notice. I'm awfy sorry, 'cos you an' Mr Rankine have been so good to me!"

Poor Agnes dabbed her eyes with her apron, quite overcome. Chrissie had a job calming her down before she could offer her sincere congratulations.

Not long after Agnes left, Cook followed suit.

"My sister in Forfar's been landed wi' four evacuees, an' she's sair needin' a hand, Mrs Rankine. I dinna want to leave you in the lurch, mind.

"My niece, Emily McDade, is lookin' for a job. She's only nineteen, but a rare wee cook, an' light-handed wi' the pastry," Cook volunteered eagerly.

"I'd need to interview Emily first," Chrissie warned cautiously.

"She's down the stair." Cook grinned confidently. "I'll send her up, shall I?"

So Emily McDade took over in the kitchen. She was an attractive girl, with large, grey, lively eyes that sparkled with intelligence and fun.

Chrissie couldn't understand why she was content in domestic service. Housemaids, parlourmaids and cooks were flocking into the women's services, to munitions, or working as clippies on the buses. The war had liberated a great flood of domestics who vowed never to return to their old jobs again.

One day curiosity got the better of her, and she asked Emily outright why she'd chosen the job.

"Oh, Mrs Rankine!" The girl turned pale. "You'll put me out if I tell you!"

"Try me." Chrissie smiled. "I'm not so easily put off folk I like."

Emily collapsed on to a kitchen chair, looking tragic and close to tears.

"I've had TB. I was in the sanatorium for a year. The doctors say I'm cured, but folk are funny, Mrs Rankine. Even some of your best friends don't want to know you. You'll maybe no' want me in your house, now you know."

Chrissie went over and deliberately hugged the poor, unhappy girl.

"Of course I want you! More than ever now. You're cured, Emily. Put your illness behind you. Forget it."

Emily wiped her eyes.

"Bless you, Mrs Rankine. You mind me o' my own mum, before she died." She sobbed emotionally.

But Emily couldn't remain depressed for long. She was up again in a trice, cheerfully making a pot of tea while she chattered away.

"Mind you, Mrs Rankine, I was fair scunnered when I found out they wouldn't have me in the Wrens because of my chest. It's an awfy smart uniform!" she finished wistfully.

Chapter 33

AT the end of May 1940, the ominous calm of the first few months of war in Europe ended in the desperate evacuation from Dunkirk. Charles and Chrissie listened anxiously for news on the radio.

Ewan joined them as they tuned in. He clenched his fists uselessly.

"Sam'll be there, Dad! Oh, if only I could do something!"

"You can do something, son. Pass your exams and start training as an accountant. This country will need clever young men when the war is over," Charles pointed out.

But that wasn't what Ewan wanted to hear. Oh, he'd pass his exams all right, he thought confidently, and maybe even work in an office until he was eighteen. But then he was joining up and going to fight! And no-one was going to stop him!

Ewan's twin sister was restless, too.

Charlotte's schoolfriends talked importantly about doing their bit. Some were in the junior Red Cross before going on to train as nurses. Others planned to join the services when they were old enough, or go into munitions.

None of this was possible for Charlotte because of her leg, left weak after polio. The best she could do was offer to help at the forces canteen run by the local WVS. To her surprise, she thoroughly enjoyed the work. She welcomed the new fashion of comfortable slacks for women, because they hid the ugly metal calliper on her leg. Standing still, nobody could tell she was different.

Soldiers and sailors queueing for tea and buns and sixpenny cigarettes flirted lightly with the pretty young girl behind the counter. Charlotte laughed and joked with her many admirers and innocently began to have fun.

Sometimes one of the lads would play the out-of-tune piano in the corner of the hall. Charlotte's feet tapped to the new, catchy tunes of "Run, Rabbit, Run" and "Roll Out The Barrel", but she always firmly refused offers to dance.

Until Leon arrived.

He was one of a group of Polish soldiers billeted in the neighbourhood. They were popular with the ladies of the WVS, because of their exquisite manners. The day Leon arrived a dance was in full swing. He glanced around, caught sight of Charlotte standing beside the tea-urn, and came right over. He clicked his heels and gave a strange little foreign bow.

"You would like to dance, please, miss?" he asked politely.

"Oh, no, thank you." She blushed. "I can't dance."

He seemed surprised and gave her a straight, considering look.

"But everyone can dance a little, and this dance is very easy. Just trotting like a fox."

"No, really, I can't dance." She was hot with embarrassment.

He looked puzzled.

"Please tell me, why not? Is it because I am not speaking Scottish so good?"

Charlotte was distressed. She hadn't meant to offend him. He looked so nice. Not handsome, really, just nice.

"Oh, no, you speak very well. It – it's just –" Words failed her, and, to her horror, tears welled and ran slowly down her cheeks.

"I want to dance with you very much, but I can't. It's my leg. I had polio. I can't dance any more. I'm – I'm a cripple."

She had never used the word before, stubbornly refusing to admit to herself that it was true. But this nice Polish soldier demanded complete honesty.

"But with me, you can dance." He laughed gently. "Come, I show you how!"

He held out a hand, and she took it trustingly.

He drew her close, holding her so that they moved as one. He guided and lifted her, and set her feet down lightly with the precision of a ballet dancer.

Her natural sense of rhythm helped, and soon she was dancing again, light as a feather in the support of his arms.

He looked down at her, surprised.

"I do not even know your name!" he said with wonder.

She told him, laughing.

"Bessie, my old nurse, would give me a telling off if she knew. We should have been introduced first. I don't know who you are, either!"

"I am Leon." He smiled down at her with a twinkle in his

eye. "I would tell you my other name, but you will not pronounce it well. Scottish people never do."

But she pleaded, and he told her. As he predicted she stumbled over it.

He laughed, and declared it didn't matter. Nothing mattered, he said, except the music and the dancing, and being together.

Charlotte was ready to agree.

After that, if Leon Zielinska was there, she danced with him.

* * * *

It was Bessie who spotted the soldier coming wearily up the driveway on a damp, dreary day in early June.

She put on her specs and peered out the window for a better look, then gave a piercing shriek.

"Chrissie, it's him!"

Chrissie had been working on a dress of Charlotte's, trying to mend and make do. She looked up, startled.

"Who?"

"Your laddie. He's the spittin' image of his da. Look!" The old woman pointed with a trembling finger.

Chrissie looked, and started to tremble, too. She closed her eyes for a moment to compose herself, then went to the door.

"Hello, Sammy," she said as her son reached the door.

Sammy put down what was left of his pack. It flopped emptily on the ground, looking much like himself, flattened.

He couldn't feel anything very much any more. Only a mild surprise when their defeated Army was greeted by excited, cheering crowds on the quayside, as if he and his mates had achieved some sort of victory.

Maybe they had, in a way. He was too weary to care.

"They asked if I had somewhere to go until the regiment is reorganised. I'm sorry, but yours was the only place I could think of," he told her dully.

Chrissie's impulse was to fling her arms round him, to comfort him and wipe the terrible, hopeless, haunted look from his face. But she knew a wrong word, an impulsive touch, could send him flying away like a wounded bird. She stood aside.

"Come in."

He walked past her, trailing the half-empty pack. Inside, he stood passively studying the shabby hallway, until Chrissie guided him into the parlour.

Bessie was hopping from one foot to the other with excitement. She had no inhibitions. She grabbed Danny's son and planted a kiss on two days' growth of stubble.

"Sammy, my wee sojer laddie! Hame at last. I'm Bessie McCutcheon, your da's auld auntie. I was wi' your mammy when you were born."

Sammy's head was spinning gently. Another relative he hadn't known he possessed!

"Och, you're needing your tea, son. I'll away and stir up Emily in the kitchen. Maybe there's a wee bit bacon."

Bessie bustled away, leaving mother and son awkwardly together.

They sat on either side of the fire. Sammy unbuttoned the

pocket of his battledress and drew out a crumpled letter which he held out to Chrissie.

"I got this in France. Before communications broke down."

It was a letter from a Scottish lawyer in Calcutta, informing Sammy that his foster-father, Arthur Kennedy, had died suddenly.

Sammy was the sole beneficiary of Arthur's will. The estate consisted mostly of British stocks and shares and a quantity of personal effects and furniture, listed below, presently in storage.

Poor Arthur. Chrissie folded the letter and handed it to Sammy, struggling to hide her own grief for her brother.

"What will you do?" she asked carefully.

He shrugged.

"Not much I can do with a war on. I'll write and ask him to sell the furniture and give the proceeds to my old ayah. She deserves it."

Emily arrived with a loaded tray containing a heaped plate of bacon, scrambled eggs and sausage – one person's ration for a week.

She studied Sammy curiously, then smiled cheerfully.

"Eat it up while it's hot. It's dried egg, but it all goes down the same way when you're hungry. Bessie's airing a bed for you, 'cos she says you look dead beat. Oh, and take off your boots!"

"What?" Sammy showed more animation than he'd displayed so far.

"Your boots. Take them off. They look like you've been trampin' through a midden. I'll clean them for you," Emily offered.

"No. I've got holes in my socks," he objected.

"Oh, aye? Well, I'll have your socks an' a'."

She examined him closely as he reluctantly removed his boots and the offending socks and stretched his bare feet towards the fire.

"Your jacket an' breeks could do with a clean. Could ye no' –?" Emily began tentatively.

"No, I jolly well couldn't!" Sammy said hastily.

Emily gave a long-suffering sigh, collected his boots and socks and whisked them off to the kitchen.

Sammy sat staring after her, looking bemused.

"Who was that?"

"Emily McDade, our Jill-of-all-trades."

Sammy stayed with them for ten days, eating, sleeping and keeping out of the way. He spent more time with Ewan and Charlotte, or in the kitchen with Emily, than he did with Chrissie and Charles. He was scrupulously polite to his mother, but she wanted more from her son. Much more.

One day, Chrissie was at her desk, writing to her brother in America when Sammy came in. He seemed interested in Ernest and his family, and read his latest letter eagerly enough when Chrissie handed it to him.

Never one to miss an opportunity, Chrissie took a deep breath.

"I wrote to you, too, Sammy. Right from the start. When

you were too small to read, I used to draw you pictures. I never once got a reply, but I still kept writing because I loved you."

Her son didn't reply, but he got up and stood looking out of the window.

"I don't know what happened to my letters," Chrissie rushed on. "And I don't think I want to . . ."

Sammy's sigh interrupted her.

"No – I don't, either. I don't suppose we ever will, anyway."

An awkward silence followed for a few moments, before Sammy wandered out of the room. At least he believes I wrote to him, Chrissie thought delightedly. Perhaps there's hope for us yet . . .

When Sammy was recalled to his unit, he looked a new man, thanks to Emily's efforts. She was at the door to see him off, her eyes suspiciously moist.

"You take care o' yourself, mind!" Emily ordered fiercely.

"I will, don't worry!"

The lingering warmth of his smile was for Emily. There was only a cool, careful handshake and polite thanks for Chrissie. She could have wept.

War had come to Scotland with attacks on the Forth Bridge and Edinburgh. In September 1940, it was Dundee's turn for attention. A hit-and-run raider loosed a stick of bombs which straddled the city. One landed at the corner of Dalkeith Road and Nesbitt Street, uncomfortably close to Broughty Ferry.

The scare was enough to send Chrissie and the others to

the nearest air-raid shelter when the siren went off while she was queuing for potatoes.

"Well, fancy meeting you here!" Aggie Gallacher exclaimed as Chrissie sat down next to her.

Chrissie smiled at Norrie Gallacher's granny.

"How's Norrie, Mrs Gallacher? Sandra tells me he's gone to Canada to try his luck."

The old lady looked grim.

"He's high up in a company that recycles metal, he says. If you ask me that's just a fancy name for a scrapyard. You can tell Sandra he's thinkin' o' marrying a Canadian lassie." Aggie looked sad for a moment.

"I thought I'd be fine pleased to see him settled, Chrissie, but to tell the truth I'm no' happy at a'. He'll never come back tae Scotland noo."

A tear slid surreptitiously down Aggie's cheek. She took out a lace-edged hankie and blew her nose defiantly.

"Listen, there's a plane!" one of the other women in the shelter said.

"Is it a Jerry?" another nervous voice asked.

Aggie Gallacher put her head to one side, ear cocked towards the ceiling.

"No, it's one o' ours. I can tell by the steady sound. Jerries go 'wah-wah-wah'," she answered comfortably.

Sure enough, the all-clear went seconds later. At the end of November, yet more unexpected visitors arrived on the doorstep at Beechyhill. It was Charles who answered the door this time, and his yell could be heard outside in the garden, where Chrissie and old McIntosh were digging for victory in the vegetable patch.

"Chrissie, it's Mary Rose. And wee Elizabeth!"

Chapter 34

CHARLES hugged his stepdaughter and the seven-year-old girl. Everyone came crowding to the door, muddy McIntosh included.

Mary Rose and her daughter were borne inside to such a welcome, any misgivings she'd had about her reception were swept away for ever.

Chrissie was overjoyed to have her daughter and grandchild home at last. She couldn't take her eyes off the child. Black hair, eyes as blue as forget-me-nots.

Mary Rose was talking twenty to the dozen. The words spilled out as if they'd been held back a long time. She kept an arm round Elizabeth protectively as she talked.

"Roddy's joined the RAF. He's stationed with a fighter squadron – somewhere in England. His parents want me to leave London and go to them."

"It seems only wise, dear," Chrissie remarked.

"You don't understand, Mum," Mary Rose looked serious. "They don't want me, they want Elizabeth.

"They want to turn her into a proper little English miss. There's even talk of sending her to boarding school. A little girl of seven!

"I don't want that, Mum, but they're determined because Elizabeth will inherit the estate eventually. I can't fight them. So, true to form, I ran away," she finished, looking rather shamefaced.

There was an awkward lull. Mary Rose studied the floor.

"How's Sandra?" she asked quietly.

Chrissie answered because Charles seemed reluctant.

"She's still in Glasgow with Harriet, working very hard at the clinic. We see very little of her."

"Oh," Mary Rose said unhappily.

Presently she glanced up.

"Mum, would you take Elizabeth until the war's over? I'll miss her dreadfully, but I have to be near Roddy. I know she'll be safe and happy with you."

Bessie clasped her old hands joyfully, and answered for all of them.

"Oh, Mary Rose, my dearie, it'll be grand to have a wee bairn in the house again!"

Chrissie's smile was tinged with sadness. Her daughter would leave again soon, to live her own life. Still, there was Elizabeth! The thought brought a glow of joy.

The little girl was watching her.

"Excuse me, please, but are you my new granny?" she asked.

"Yes, dear. Will I do?"

Elizabeth examined her solemnly.

"You've got a nice face and I like your brooch. That's a funny-looking ship, though." When Chrissie smiled encouragingly, she added, "I think I'm going to like you."

Then she smiled a wide, beaming smile that was oddly familiar and tugged at Chrissie's heartstrings.

The year 1941 stood out afterwards in Chrissie's memory as the lowest ebb. The dreadful Clydeside blitz on the moonlight night of the thirteenth and fourteenth of March was followed by three days of agonised waiting before they had news of Sandra and Harriet.

The clinic had been totally destroyed. Harriet had broken a leg clambering over rubble to help victims of the raids, but Sandra was unscathed.

Chrissie and Charles breathed easily again, only to be driven to black despair when Ewan reached his eighteenth birthday in April. He was called up soon after.

There were pleasant memories, too, and laughter. Chrissie and Charles spent happy times round the wireless set with Charlotte and Elizabeth, listening to Wilfred Pickles, Cyril Fletcher's "Odd Odes" and, of course, dear old Tommy Handley's "ITMA".

Elizabeth, who'd quite a talent for mimicry, danced merrily around the house saying, "Can I do you now, sir?" like Mrs Mopp, Tommy Handley's charwoman. She also imitated, with gusto, the woeful tones of Mona Lott.

There was good news, though, from Chrissie's widespread family. She received a letter from her niece, Georgina, in Australia, the first for some considerable time.

I've had another baby, Auntie Chris! A beautiful little boy, Ina wrote. *We have called him Thomas, to lay a ghost from my past.*

Do you remember Tam, the shepherd? I had such a girlish crush on him. Thank goodness he married someone else, or I would never have had Jean-Christine and Thomas, or lived in Australia. Isn't love strange? You think you've lost it, then one day it pops up again, better than ever!

Rationing was a sore trial, although Emily worked wonders with potatoes, stale bread and dried eggs. Chrissie worried about Charles, but the spartan diet seemed to suit him and he looked better than he had for a long time.

Jani's little shop did surprisingly well. She searched diligently for the off-the-ration goodies such as cinnamon sticks and locust beans and always kept a wee treat or two under the counter for a bairn or an old body.

Her husband, Hughie, sailed with convoys, and had been remarkably fortunate so far. Sailors fell over themselves to sign on with him. He had gained the reputation as a "lucky" skipper.

The brightest spot in those dark days was the arrival of Benjamin Franklin Chester's food hamper. How the American had managed to send it, Chrissie couldn't imagine. There had certainly been no hint in his business letters.

A large, wooden box was delivered to the office. Chrissie, Charles and Maisie, the secretary, unpacked it with incredulous joy.

"Michty me! Tinned ham!" Maisie cried awed tones. "I canna mind when I last tasted tinned ham. Oh, my, and dates and sultanas, tinned pears and peaches! Chocolates, too!"

Charles and Chrissie did their best to send the staff home with a gift from the hamper, and doled out goodies to some of the weavers who were in hospital. There wasn't much left after that— a tin of Spam, a packet of dates and a tin of boiled sweets. The family ate these items slowly, savouring each unaccustomed bite.

Chrissie added a grateful postscript to her next letter to Autofibres in Detroit.

The hamper was heavenly. God bless you, my dear Benjamin Franklin. We all love you!

* * * *

It hadn't taken Ewan Rankine long to shed his romantic notions about soldiering. He then settled down grimly to endure the war and hopefully return to Dundee in one piece.

He was a good, dogged infantryman with no particular desire to become an officer, although by D-Day he'd risen to the rank of corporal. Ewan was content with that. He wasn't looking for any medals.

His unit crossed to Normandy on D-Day. By September it was part of Montgomery's spearhead up towards Holland. Ewan saw enough action on the way to convince him that war was a daft business.

He kept a sharp lookout for Sammy but, to his disappointment, he didn't meet up with his half-brother.

Ewan found something else, though. Something so incredible it fired his imagination as nothing else had done during this dangerous, miserable period of his life.

"What do we do in the infantry? We march, we march, we march . . . !" Ewan whistled cheerily, because he sat comfortably in a fifteen hundredweight truck while his mates marched up the road.

The 51st Highland Division had the job of winkling out the pockets of resistance left behind in the main advance into Holland, but Ewan couldn't imagine any problems in the little Dutch port. They'd been sent to pick up spare parts for the CO's staff car. A pleasant, cushy job.

Ewan consulted the scrawled directions he'd been given.

"Turn right, Taffy. Then go straight ahead until you reach the harbour."

They bumped over the debris and around shell craters, until Taffy halted the truck outside the warehouse where workshops platoon RASC were operating. Ewan grinned at the Welshman.

"You won't need me to carry a cylinder head and some spark plugs, will you, Taff? I feel like a breath of sea air."

"Help yourself, Jock," Taffy agreed obligingly.

It was good to be on his own for once, Ewan thought as he strolled along the quayside. There were Dutch fishermen busy around the little harbour, but they beamed at the lone Scottish soldier and courteously left him to his solitude.

Ewan watched the fishing boats for a while, then headed towards the entrance to the canal. The scene here was quite different, one of desolation and destruction. Lock gates stood wide open and were badly damaged, probably when the countryside was deliberately flooded in an attempt to stop the Allied advance.

Roofless warehouses and derelict quays added to the bleakness of the scene. Ewan hesitated, but curiosity drove him to explore.

He picked his way through the ruins and found himself in a deserted inner harbour which had become an eerie graveyard for several ships. The still water was dark, green and oily, and fringes of weed hung from mouldering mooring ropes.

Silence lay over the abandoned vessels, broken only by a chill breeze that made the dark water lap lazily against the quay. A lone gull screamed indignantly at Ewan's intrusion.

Ewan shivered. Some of the ships looked quite modern, others were aged hulks. One was tall-masted, with a rusting funnel and the tattered remains of sails.

On the point of turning back, Ewan paused, struck by an odd feeling of recognition. Slowly he paced the full length of the old ship. She was in a deplorable state, and he stared stupidly for some time at the name on her bow before it registered.

Christina K.

He'd found his mother's bonnie ship! Ewan couldn't believe it!

Chapter 35

SHE looked just like the old photographs and the brooch his mother always wore. But now her brasses were green and tarnished, and her paint was flaking. Poor old ship, once so loved, now . . . Ewan's eyes were gritty with emotion.

He came back to earth with a jolt. The keen breeze blew cold on his cheeks, and he scuffed his battledress sleeve across his eyes. He looked around wildly. Who owned the ship? What was she doing here?

Ewan scrambled over the rubble. An old fisherman was passing by.

"Please, do you speak English?"

"Yes, I sail many times to Aberdeen before the war." The face creased into a beaming smile. "Whisky is ver' good in Aberdeen."

Ewan explained about the ship.

"She was built in Dundee. A whaler . . . belonged to my mother's family. Do you know who owns her now?"

The fisherman nodded thoughtfully.

"Ah, yes, that one! I think she belong to a Norwegian who is trading in whale oil before the war. When Holland is invaded, the Germans don't let him take the ship to Norway in case he sail to Britain instead. So your Dundee ship lie here and rot."

Ewan heard Taffy calling in the distance. He must go, but

hated to leave the ship now he'd found her.

"What will happen to her when the war's over?" he asked.

"Maybe the Norwegians will return." The old man shrugged. "Maybe she break up and sink first. Who knows?"

"Jock! Jock, where are you?" Taffy sounded impatient.

Ewan searched desperately in his pockets and gave the old man a bar of chocolate he'd brought with him.

"Look, I must go, but when the war's over I'll be back. Please, keep an eye on her for me?"

The fisherman beamed.

"OK. I keep her afloat until you come. Maybe!"

* * * *

"Oh, I'm fed up with this!" Chrissie peered through the car windscreen into pitch blackness. The masked headlamps gave such a thin beam of light she could hardly make out the road. Driving in the blackout was positively dangerous. And all for a dozen eggs!

The mother of one of her granddaughter's friends had whispered to Chrissie that there were fresh duck eggs to spare at their farm.

"Emily could make a real sponge sandwich, Gran. She can have my jam ration to spread in the middle," Elizabeth offered graciously.

Chrissie's expression softened.

Maybe the nightmare journey was worth it after all to give the kids a treat.

"Yes, it could be your birthday cake, darling." She smiled.

"But it's not my birthday yet, Gran," Elizabeth protested.

"I'm still only eleven!"

"Och, who cares about a wee detail like that?"

"Oh, Gran, you are naughty!"

Elizabeth giggled. She settled back, hugging the eggs, utterly content.

Since Mary Rose had brought her little daughter to Beechyhill four years ago, Elizabeth had settled happily into the pattern of their lives. Charles doted on her and Charlotte regarded Elizabeth as a much-loved small sister.

Bessie McCutcheon, a spry seventy-eight, was rejuvenated now she had a youngster to care for. The nursery was a cheery place, filled with laughter even in the grimmest days of war.

Charlotte preferred to go to the pictures with Leon the Polish soldier now, occupying the chummy seats in Green's Playhouse, so Bessie accompanied Elizabeth to the Kinnaird or the La Scala and sometimes to the Queen's Theatre. There they joined heartily in community singing. They sang all the popular songs with a gusto that would have made Ewan squirm.

"Mairzy Doats And Dozy Doats, And Liddle Lambsy Divy" was Elizabeth's favourite because it was so daft it took your mind off upsetting things like the war and all its misery and shortages.

She started humming the tune as Chrissie negotiated Powrie Brae. Once, Chrissie told her, from this vantage point you could see the lights of Dundee shining like a necklace of bright jewels. That is, if the smoke from the factory chimneys wasn't too thick.

Elizabeth strained, but couldn't make out a glimmer of light anywhere. I must eat more carrots so I can see in the dark, she thought. After the war I'll come up here just to see all the lights . . .

She hugged the eggs. It was awfully cold in the car, and she was glad she had put on her thick coat and pixie hood.

Chrissie had noticed the small movement and glanced away from the road for an instant.

"Soon be home now, darling. It's lucky I had some petrol to spare, isn't it?"

Elizabeth agreed. She couldn't wait to show Emily the precious eggs, and was out of the car and darting towards the kitchen the moment Chrissie drew up outside the old coach-house they used as a garage. Charles came out as Chrissie was opening the doors, and something in his expression made her stop short suddenly.

"Where's Elizabeth?" he asked quietly.

"She ran into the house with the eggs. Why?"

"It's her father. Roddy was shot down on a bombing raid over Germany. There's no hope for him, I'm afraid. Mary Rose is just off the phone. She asked if we could break the news to Elizabeth."

"Oh, Charles, no!"

He held her close. She felt his lips brush her hair, and that, more than the loss of poor Roddy, released her tears.

Charles took out a hanky and offered it to her. She mopped her eyes.

"OK now, darling?" he asked gently.

She nodded. Hand in hand, they went into the house to find Elizabeth . . .

For years to come Elizabeth would never forget how she felt that night. She wished she could feel sad. All she felt was sort of numb.

She'd sobbed dutifully when Papa Charles told her about Daddy, but her tears had been for a handsome, rather awe-inspiring stranger in a smart RAF blue uniform, who'd come to visit her in Dundee once or twice.

There had been a funny awkwardness in the air when her father and mother visited Beechyhill. Granny and Papa Charles had seemed different and Bessie went around muttering. Auntie Sandra never seemed to be there . . .

Elizabeth remembered how she'd been secretly quite relieved when her mother and father left to go south. She cried for her father now, because she was sorry.

Despite the tragic news, Emily went ahead and made the unbirthday cake.

She and Charlotte gave up their sweetie ration to ice the cake with melted chocolate and sprinkle hundreds and thousands over the top. There was still one piece left when Mary Rose arrived unexpectedly.

Sandra was there from Glasgow. She was playing Pelmanism with Elizabeth when Mary Rose walked in. Sandra's face turned white and she stood up so abruptly the playing cards scattered all over the floor.

She pointedly ignored her sister, turning to Chrissie.

"I'm leaving, Mother. I have to get back to Glasgow."

Chrissie, who'd been making a dress for Elizabeth from old curtain material, stood up, too. But before she could appeal to her daughter, Sandra walked away.

Mary Rose glanced helplessly at Chrissie, then hurried after her sister. When she caught up with her she held out a hand.

"Sandra, Roddy's dead. Please, can't we be friends?" she pleaded.

Sandra's eyes were dark with emotion.

"I'm sorry, Mary Rose, but I can't forgive you. It's not so much that you took Roddy, as the sly, deceitful way you did it. And you have lost me the only other man I could have cared for. Because of you, I let Norrie Gallacher go to the other side of the world. You ruined my life. That's why I'll never forgive you!"

Mary Rose was devastated. It hurt her to be on bad terms with the sister she loved. The quarrel seemed futile now Roddy was dead, and Mary Rose had hoped to end it. Norrie Gallacher was a complication she hadn't suspected.

"Oh, Sandra, please don't hate me!"

Sandra stared wordlessly, then turned away.

"Sandra! Wait!" Chrissie called.

"Goodbye, Mother," Sandra said. The door slammed. Nobody moved until they heard Sandra's car start and go racing down the drive.

Chrissie sat down again, shaken. Mary Rose would have wept if she'd had tears left.

She went across and hugged her daughter, who looked white and shaken.

Then she glanced up at Chrissie.

"Mum – I have to take Elizabeth away. I'm sorry."

"Oh, no!" Chrissie whispered in anguish.

"Roddy's parents have begged me to let them take care of her while I go to college. I've decided to become a vet. I'll have to support us both." Mary Rose stared at her mother, silently imploring her not to make a fuss.

"She's all the Stirtons have now Roddy's gone. She'll inherit the estate one day. It seems only right she should get to know her other grandparents."

Chrissie was silent. How could she argue?

Mary Rose cupped her daughter's troubled face between her hands and looked at her searchingly.

"Darling, you heard what I said to Granny Chris. I know how happy you've been here, but Gran and Grandpa Stirton need you more.

"They're lonely and sad, and nobody can cheer them up like you can. I won't force you to go if you really hate the idea, Elizabeth, but please think very hard before you decide."

Elizabeth felt scared when she thought about leaving Beechyhill and going to live with strangers. It was on the tip of her tongue to refuse, then she paused and thought – how awful to be sad and lonely.

And it was rather wonderful to be needed so badly . . .

She stared at her mother, because she knew if she looked

at Granny Chris she'd weaken.

"I've thought about it, Mum. I'll go."

* * * *

"I miss the wee soul!" Emily said mournfully a few days later.

She and Charlotte were sitting in the kitchen doing each other's hair. Both heads bristled with metal curlers, and Emily was curling shorter locks with curling tongs.

Meg, the Labrador who'd replaced faithful old Angus, snoozed in her basket by the stove.

"I miss Elizabeth, too," Charlotte admitted. "I'm glad Leon's on leave just now." She brightened. "Why don't you come to the Palais with us tonight? It'd cheer you up to go dancing."

"I don't want to be a gooseberry."

"Nonsense. Leon wouldn't mind. Anyway, you'd soon click with a lad."

"I'm not sure I want to." Emily turned away. "Anyway, I've no stockings, and no coupons, either."

Charlotte frowned. The shortage of stockings didn't bother her. She'd made herself elegant satin trousers from an old nightie to hide the calliper on her leg.

"I've no coupons left, either. If you have some of that brown stain left in the bottle, why not paint your legs? Nobody would know."

"I suppose I could." Emily was tempted.

"I'll draw seams up the back of your legs with my eyebrow pencil if you like," Charlotte offered eagerly.

"Oh, thanks!" Emily hesitated, watching Charlotte. There was a glow about her. She radiated happiness.

"Will you and Leon get married?" she asked boldly.

Charlotte's happy glow faded.

"I don't know. He was studying to be a doctor when the Germans invaded Poland, and he wants to go back. He won't take me with him because he says it'll be too dangerous."

The two young women cheered up once the curlers were removed and their new hair-dos were revealed. With much giggling and squealing, Emily stained her legs a beautiful pale brown and Charlotte finished off the effect with dark brown seams drawn with a steady hand.

"There. Away and slip on your dress and shoes, and let's see how it looks," Charlotte ordered, proud of her handiwork.

Emily returned presently, dressed in a pretty shade of deep pink.

Charlotte gasped in envy.

"I thought you'd used up all your coupons. Where'd you get that dress?"

"It was an old sheet your mum said wasn't worth the mending." Emily blushed. "I dyed it pink with the beetroot McIntosh brought in from the garden, then made it into a wee frock for myself."

Before Charlotte had recovered from a fit of laughing, the doorbell rang.

"Charlotte, I can't answer it all dressed up like this!" Emily covered her mouth.

There was a commotion in the hallway at that point. Meg began barking and Emily eased the kitchen door open a crack. She turned as pink as the frock!

"Charlotte, it's Sammy!"

Sammy had been in two minds about coming back to Dundee. He'd been wounded in the arm, not badly, but enough to earn him some leave.

Should he go home? Home! That was a joke. Where was home?

Something had drawn him to Dundee. He wasn't sure what.

He'd liked Charles, his mother's husband. He'd been prepared to dislike him, but who could dislike such a kind, courteous man?

Standing in the hallway at Beechyhill, he shook hands awkwardly with Charles, and eyed his mother warily.

She kissed him lightly on the cheek just as the kitchen door burst open and a friendly black dog bounded out. The tail wagged harder as Sammy fondled Meg's ears.

Looking over the dog's head, Sammy saw a girl dressed in pink framed in the kitchen doorway. She was the loveliest sight he'd seen for many a day.

"Why, hello, Emily!"

She smiled, speechless for once. Sammy took in the pretty dress, the shining hair-do, the long legs clad in sheer nylon stockings, and felt suddenly anxious.

"Going dancing?" he asked casually. He was inexplicably annoyed.

"I see you have an American boyfriend."

"What are you blethering about?" Emily looked bewildered.

He pointed.

"The nylons. Yanks are the only ones who can get nylons for their girlfriends these days!"

Charlotte had appeared at Emily's shoulder. The two young women stared at Sammy, then at each other, and burst out into gales of laughter.

"They're painted on, you gowk!" Emily wiped her eyes. "I don't have a boyfriend, let alone a Yank that dishes out nylons."

"You don't?" There was a warmth in Sammy's heart. He suddenly understood why he'd come home.

Chapter 36

TUESDAY, May 8, 1945, was VE Day. Victory in Europe! For most people, the war was over. There were crowds in the City Square and street parties all around the city. A German submarine turned up in Dundee harbour to surrender, the young men in its crew just as relieved as everyone else to end the fighting.

Chrissie felt immensely grateful that, this time, her family had come through the ordeal safely. She mourned for poor Roddy, of course, and thought wistfully about little Elizabeth.

Her granddaughter had settled quite happily with the Stirtons. She was a day girl at a girls' school, and her letters were full of the good friends she'd made and the fun they had. Chrissie was glad for her.

Emily and Sammy were to be married after he was demobbed. There was still a gulf between Chrissie and her son, but cheerful Emily had gone some way towards bridging it.

Sammy had decided to take a degree in civil engineering at Dundee Technical College.

"There'll be roads and bridges to be built all over the country," Sammy declared firmly. "I want a say in it!"

Charles and Chrissie were concerned about Charlotte. Leon had gone, leaving her withdrawn and lonely. It had been a sad day when he left Dundee with the other Polish lads who had been made so welcome in the city.

When Japan capitulated in August that year, Chrissie felt she could relax at last. Ewan was demobbed some months later, and declared his intention of entering the family business.

With Chrissie safely occupied elsewhere in the house, Ewan told his father he'd found the *Christina K*.

"Dad, couldn't we buy and restore the ship?" he asked eagerly. "It would give Mum the greatest thrill of her life!"

Charles looked troubled.

"Nothing I'd like better – if we had the money, but we don't. In fact, the signs are that the jute trade's in serious decline. We've even lost our American connection now Ben Chester's retired. I don't know if you're altogether wise coming into this firm."

"It's a challenge. If we can't spin and weave jute, we'll have to find something else," Ewan declared stubbornly.

"There could be man-made fibre, certainly — but there's still so much to be done. It's not a viable proposition yet," Charles told him.

He didn't add that he was too exhausted and weary to try out new ways and methods. The years of war had exacted a heavy toll upon Charles Rankine.

* * * *

Leon returned to Dundee with little more than the clothes he stood up in and a haunted look in his eyes.

Charlotte saw him come hesitantly up the driveway, unsure

of his welcome. She gave a cry of joy and, forgetting her leg, ran forward swiftly, with Meg barking and bounding by her side. She flung herself into Leon's arms and they clung together, laughing, crying and kissing one another.

Watching from the window, Charles put his arm around Chrissie and smiled.

"Another wedding, if I'm not mistaken!"

He was serious for a moment.

"I'm glad the lad's come back. There'll be little joy for anyone in his country for years to come."

"I've been thinking, Charles. With Sammy and Emily occupying rooms upstairs, Ewan in the attic, Bessie in the nursery wing, and Charlotte and Leon maybe needing accommodation, why not convert the house into separate flats? It's much too large for us."

"Good idea!" Charles nodded in agreement. He returned slowly to his chair and lay back, closing his eyes wearily. "I won't have to climb those blasted stairs to get to bed!"

He didn't see the stricken look on his wife's face. He didn't know the frantic efforts she'd made to save his failing strength, or guess at the constant fear she hid from him.

* * * *

The time had come to sell old William Kennedy's house. His former housekeeper had decided to give up keeping boarders and retire to the country.

Chrissie let her family home go with many qualms, but her share of the proceeds did help to pay for the work at Beechyhill. She was sure her father would have approved.

Charlotte and Leon had decided on a quiet wedding, to spare Charles too much stress and excitement. Leon wanted to continue his studies to become a doctor in Scotland, and was more than grateful to have a roof over his head.

Shortly before the wedding, Chrissie inspected her wardrobe critically and made a face.

"Everything's shabby after the war. Even poor old Dundee looks rather down-at-heel these days. Everything could do with a fresh lick of paint."

"You look fine to me." Charles smiled. "But why not splash out for once? Take my clothing coupons and buy yourself a nice outfit. I don't need them. My old suit is far better than the utility rubbish they produce nowadays."

"You're a darling!" She kissed him gratefully.

Chrissie sallied forth the next morning, armed with two books of clothing coupons, more precious than gold. She browsed round the shop windows, then spotted a pretty blue dress and jacket in the Corner Shop, better known as G.L. Wilson's, or more affectionately, G.L.'s. She hurried inside.

"Weel, hello, Chrissie! Still as bonnie as ever!" a familiar voice boomed. There was big Bella, her friend from the old mill days, just as large and loud as Chrissie had remembered.

Chrissie hugged her with delight. "Bella, you haven't changed a bit!"

"Naw – still like something straight oot o' 'The Beano'!" Bella roared and laughed at her own joke, slapping Chrissie playfully on the back.

"I'm retired from the mill noo, though. Lady o' leisure, ye ken. Wullie's retired from the shipyard an' a'. He shook hands wi' the King and Queen when they visited the Caledon after the war and wouldna wash his hands for a month after.

"My dochter was workin' as a welder in the shipyard during the war, would ye believe? I dinna ken what lassies is comin' to these days!" Bella shook her head mournfully.

"My great-nephew Jamal Kennedy works in the Caledon, too." Chrissie laughed. "Though he's going to sea soon with Hughie, his dad.

"Oh, Bella, it's good to see you. Just like a tonic. Do you know I still have the bonnie blue shawl you gave me when I left the mill?"

Bella sighed and wiped her eyes.

"Aye, Chris, those were the days! We worked hard, but we had many a good laugh, didn't we? You an' me will never see the likes again!"

* * * *

"It must be a proper white wedding!" Chrissie insisted. Charlotte agreed dutifully. She was in such a state of bliss she'd have agreed to marry Leon dressed in a jute sack!

But a white wedding?

"You'll no' raise enough coupons for that, Chris!" Bessie put a damper on Chrissie's enthusiasm right away, then relented as she noted Charlotte's crestfallen expression. "There's always the ivory silk bedspread. Somebody – I'm no' sayin' who – spilled tea on the corner, but there's enough stuff left to make a bonnie dress."

Chrissie could have hugged Bessie.

"Of course! The very thing. We'll need to get a move on, though, if it's to be ready by January." She hurried off to track down the bedspread.

"And if you're needing a veil for the lassie, what aboot the bonnie net screens in the nursery?" Bessie shouted after her.

With a frenzied burst of activity, the wedding gown was finished by January 10.

Charlotte tried it on and it fitted perfectly. Chrissie arranged the filmy veil, setting a garland of white artificial flowers on Charlotte's fair hair. They stood back and admired their handiwork in silence. Charlotte looked beautiful.

"They always was awfy bonnie, those screens." Bessie wiped her eyes emotionally. "They set off the bedspread just perfect."

Charlotte was delighted with the finished effect. She twisted this way and that in front of the glass, admiring the beautiful gown.

"Oh, Mum! I always dreamed about a white wedding, but I never thought I'd have one!"

"I was determined at least one of my daughters would! There's nothing to beat a nice white wedding," Chrissie declared smugly.

It began snowing on January 12, 1947. It started with a light flurry, then got down to it in earnest.

Snow fell steadily from a slatey sky, with a strong northeasterly wind whipping it into drifts. In no time the city ground to a standstill. By Charlotte's wedding day the whole country was blanketed in deep snow and ice.

"Nobody'll get here," Chrissie wailed. "We've arranged drinks and meals for everybody at the hotel!"

"Leave it to me, darling," Charles said.

He got busy on the phone, then came back, beaming.

"That's OK, Chris. I've invited forty spinners and weavers from the factory. I was giving them a half day, anyway."

Ewan and Sammy had dug a path up the driveway for the taxi. They came in, their smart suits looking decidedly the worse for wear.

"That's the two taxis now —but one's stuck at the gate. We'll all have to put on wellie boots," they announced cheerfully.

"Oh, I do hope Leon got to the church all right!"

"Don't worry." Ewan grinned. "We made sure of him. We put him on the snowplough!"

They all put on wellingtons and heavy coats, except the bride and her father. Chrissie kissed her daughter fondly, and so did Emily, who was a picturesque bridesmaid with her macintosh covering her dress and boots beneath it.

Charles and Charlotte were left alone at last.

"You look really beautiful, love," Charles told his radiant daughter.

There were tears in her eyes as she hugged him.

"Thank you, Daddy. Thank you for everything – all the happy years."

The snowplough gallantly escorted the bridal car to church. Emily was waiting at the church door, dressed in pale blue with high heels and real silk stockings this time.

"You should see the crowd in the kirk," she hissed at Charles. "The whole factory's turned up!"

At that moment a packed bus drew up outside the gate. Harriet Bowers descended, followed by Sandra and all the other invited guests in wedding finery. Harriet beamed merrily at Charles.

"Just in the nick of time! We decided to hire a bus to be sure of getting here. Wasn't that a good idea?" she asked, still smiling.

Charles was speechless. He wondered what the hotel would say when they discovered the quiet wedding Chrissie had planned wasn't to be so quiet, after all!

When the spring came, Ewan returned to Holland. He had no hope of buying the *Christina K*, for business was too precarious in the aftermath of war. He just wanted to see the ship again to make sure she was afloat.

The scene was very different this time. Industrious people, the Dutch, Ewan thought admiringly. The little port was bustling, everything neat and tidy. The derelict warehouse had been reroofed and repaired.

But the *Christina K* was gone . . .

Ewan searched the wharves. He searched everywhere for the old fisherman, but he was nowhere to be seen. His questions were met with blank stares.

The ship had become doubly important to Ewan, because

it had become obvious that his father was very ill. Chrissie spent every moment she could at her husband's bedside, nursing him with a devotion that brought awkward tears to Ewan's eyes.

Watching his father sinking day by day, Ewan wished with all his heart he could have given his mother the ship. It would have been a comfort. Little enough, perhaps, but something to cling to in the dark days ahead.

Ewan managed to persuade his mother to go to the City Square to see the Lord Provost Garnet Wilson present the young Princess Elizabeth to the people of Dundee.

Chrissie was thrilled to see the daughter of the gracious lady she'd admired for years.

"She was lovely, Charles! Such a nice smile, as if she really enjoyed meeting everyone."

As she spoke, she studied Charles anxiously. Did he look a little better today? She imagined he did.

She took his hand, raised it to her lips and kissed it sorrowfully. He smiled without opening his eyes.

"I remember the moment I fell in love with you, Chris," he said. "It was at Lizzie Bowers's wedding, and you lifted your face to the sunshine and smiled. Such a small thing, but I fell in love with you there and then."

He paused, smiling.

"You didn't like me very much."

"Och, my head was filled with daft notions in those days." She leaned closer and kissed him on the lips. "I'll tell you one thing. I love you to distraction now, darling."

Afterwards, she was always glad she kissed him, and always glad she had told him she loved him.

Charles died quietly that night, while Chrissie lay beside him, holding his hand, her kind and gentle man.

Chapter 37

HARRIET came with Sandra to the funeral, but Mary Rose did not attend. Even the death of their beloved stepfather did not mend the sisters' bitter quarrel.

Chrissie herself felt strangely detached. Perhaps you do, when your life has lost all meaning and purpose, she thought dazedly. She almost took a delight in wearing the deepest mourning, because she knew it drained all the colour and spirit out of her.

Harriet embraced her friend, then studied her with observant eyes.

She forgot her own grief in concern for Chrissie. Harriet recognised the danger in numb detachment, that terrible calm. If only Chrissie would weep! But her gaze was dry and fixed like a sleepwalker.

With Harriet and her children all around her, Chrissie got through the funeral in a numb, icy state. She doubted she would feel emotion of any kind ever again.

Dear, faithful Bessie clutched at her elbow.

"Come away, pet. You'll feel stronger when you've had a wee bite o' biled ham. There's a wheen o' folk comin' back to the hoose this cauld day. The word's got roond."

So Chrissie played hostess with dignity and grace. Awkward in their sincerity, the guests gradually drifted away, until there were only Harriet and the family left.

Sad and subdued, Chrissie's children departed to their respective flats and left Chrissie and Harriet alone together. The two women who had loved Charles Rankine. It seemed fitting.

They sat in silence. Harriet searched desperately for some way of breaking through the barrier Chrissie had set around herself.

"Oh, Chrissie, don't you like me any more?" she burst out. It wasn't what she'd meant to say. It was a cry from the heart.

"What?"

Chrissie was startled out of her depression and saw Harriet clearly for the first time that day. She saw the tears, the inconsolable grief which her friend must bear all alone. Harriet had no children, no happy memories, nobody to comfort her. In fact, nothing at all, not even her best friend's friendship.

Chrissie wanted to comfort Harriet, but to do that she must explain why their warm friendship had turned cold. She began talking agitatedly, the words spilling out.

"I was so jealous of you, Harriet. I grew to love Charles so much, and the more I loved him, the more terrified I was that you'd take him from me. You're so witty and clever – all the things I'm not. I should have known you'd never do anything like that. Can you ever forgive me?"

Chrissie was weeping brokenly by the end, the healing tears pouring down her cheeks.

Blindly, she held out her arms. Harriet hugged her

thankfully. There was no need for words. They both knew their friendship was as strong and firm as it had ever been—and that was the way Charles Rankine would have wanted it.

* * * *

"Don't you think you should stop wearing black, Mum?" Charlotte ventured. "It's months now since Dad died."

"It seems like only yesterday."

Chrissie picked up a magazine and laid it down again listlessly. She didn't seem to be interested in anything these days.

"They're going to build a road bridge across the Tay because the Fifie can't cope with the traffic. Isn't that exciting? We'll be able to drive to St Andrews in no time. Leon is very keen on golf these days," Charlotte added hopefully.

"That's nice, dear." Chrissie closed her eyes wearily. She dozed a lot since Charles died. What else was there to do?

Charlotte stood looking at her mother, frustrated. They'd all agreed they must be patient with her, but if only she'd snap out of this lethargy and take an interest in life again. She was only in her early sixties, after all.

Maybe it would be different when the baby arrived, Charlotte thought. But that wasn't for five months yet!

After Charlotte had gone, Chrissie picked up the unread magazine and laid it down again when the doorbell rang. Frowning, she glanced at the clock. She wasn't expecting anyone.

The man standing in the porch was big, broad-shouldered

and powerful. He took off his hat respectfully when Chrissie answered the door. His hair was thick, and shone pure silver in the sunlight.

"I came whenever I heard," he said.

"I beg your pardon?"

"I've been to the bull sales in Perth, and I heard about Charles there. I came right away."

Chrissie was none the wiser.

"Well, I'm sure that's very thoughtful of you, Mr – er –"

He stared at her, then laughed.

"Forgive me. I feel I know you so well, Chris. I forgot we never met."

"I'm sorry, but I don't –" Chrissie was mystified.

He held out a large hand, grinning.

"I'm Ben Chester, Mrs Rankine. Benjamin Franklin Chester, that's me!"

* * * *

Once her mind was made up, Chrissie lost no time making arrangements for the journey to London. She and Ben decided to travel by train. His hired car was no bigger than a roller-skate, he declared, and he wouldn't subject his worst enemy, let alone his dear Chrissie, to a long journey in it!

Chrissie also decided to buy some new outfits. She'd never forget her love for Charles, and still mourned him, but she bundled up all her black clothes and handed them to the Salvation Army.

Carrying her shopping home, she tried on everything nervously in front of the mirror. It was years since she had bought new clothes, what with rationing and make-do-and-mend. To her relief her good taste hadn't deserted her.

She arranged her new hat at its most becoming angle and admired her reflection. She could imagine what Bessie, her old nurse, would have said.

"Oh, my. Twenty-one bob for a wee bit bonnet? You're jokin'!"

Chrissie smiled defiantly. Extravagant or not, she must keep her end up with those posh London folk!

When Chrissie's family were told of her intentions, they were flabbergasted. A few days before her departure the twins, Ewan and Charlotte, turned up one Saturday afternoon with baby Natasha.

Chrissie was delighted to see them.

"I must have second sight! I've just been baking!"

Chrissie bustled about the kitchen while her children watched solemnly. She filled a plate with currant slices and handed it to her son.

"Bessie used to call these fly cemeteries. D'you fancy one?"

"Er – no, thanks, Mum." Ewan exchanged a significant glance with his sister as they followed their mother to the drawing-room.

Comfortably settled on the sofa, Chrissie reached for the baby.

"She gets bonnier every day, Charlotte!" she said, admiring the little girl.

"Yes. I hope you don't intend staying away too long,

Mum. She's growing up quickly," Charlotte said pointedly.

"We all agree you deserve a holiday," Ewan chipped in. "But is it wise going off with a strange man?"

Chrissie laughed heartily.

"I've known Ben Chester for years. He's a nice, kind man and very respectable. Remember those lovely food parcels he sent us during the war?"

"Yes – he seems a decent bloke, but – well –" Ewan lapsed into awkward silence.

"What will folk think, when they hear you've gone off to London with him?" Charlotte ventured.

Chrissie lifted the sleepy baby against her shoulder.

"They'll think the worst – and say a great deal, all of it nonsense. It's never bothered me what people think, love, so long as my own conscience is clear."

The twins studied their mother in baffled silence. Chrissie tactfully refrained from laughing.

"Do help yourselves to a fly cemetery, my dears!" she urged them with a smile.

Sandra, in Glasgow, had begged her half-sister to keep her informed about their mother's expedition. Charlotte lost no time passing on the news that Chrissie was determined to go ahead.

At the end of their telephone conversation, Sandra replaced the receiver and sat frowning.

"Well, really! I don't know what's got into my mother!"

Harriet, working nearby, looked up with interest, so Sandra explained.

"I think it's an excellent idea," Harriet declared staunchly. "Chrissie could do with a holiday. And obviously it's safer travelling with a male companion."

Sandra didn't say anything. Trust the two old ladies to stick together!

"By the by," Harriet went on with studied nonchalance. "I'm thinking of retiring."

"Retiring?" Sandra sat up with a jolt. "But, Harriet, you'll be bored."

"No, I won't. I'll go back to Dundee and look for a worthy cause. I've slowed down a lot, you know, and tire too easily these days. Time to hang up my stethoscope."

"The clinic won't be the same without you," Sandra muttered unhappily.

"Nonsense!" Harriet grinned. "It might even be better!"

Later that day, Sandra found herself closeted with Dr O'Reilly in the private cubby-hole where old medical records were stored.

"Darren – did you know Harriet was thinking of retiring?"

"She did mention it." He gave Sandra a quick glance. "Don't talk her out of it. It's time she took things easier. If she doesn't, then I'm afraid . . ." He paused eloquently.

Sandra stared unhappily at the neat stacks of folders.

"I'll miss her. She's been like a second mother to me since long before the war. I'd go back to Dundee myself if – if it wasn't for – problems."

"There's a man in the picture somewhere, isn't there?" Darren asked quietly. "Care to talk about it?"

She hesitated, then found herself telling the sympathetic young doctor all about Norrie and his yearly visits.

"I see. That explains a lot. I wondered why an attractive woman like you had never married."

"Harriet advised me to wait for Norrie and take what scraps of happiness I could find." Sandra sighed. "But I'm not convinced she's right."

"Harriet's wrong for once!" Darren declared firmly. "I think this man of yours wants to have his cake and eat it! He's just being selfish!"

He moved closer, and she could read the anger and indignation in his eyes. Then his expression softened.

"If – if I loved you, Sandra, I wouldn't have married anyone else, not ever. Norrie Gallacher has no right to ask you to waste your life waiting for him. I'd make a clean break if I were you."

"Would you, Darren?"

"Yes, I would. Oh, Sandra, how I wish –" He paused and lowered his gaze unhappily to the loaded shelves.

Sandra studied his downcast expression with sudden understanding, and laid a kindly hand on his arm.

"I'm a middle-aged woman. I'll never marry now. Perhaps I'm the faithful type, like you."

He looked up quickly.

"So you'll wait for Norrie to come back?"

"No." Sandra sighed. "I'll take your advice. When Norrie comes to Glasgow next year, I won't be here to meet him."

"I'm glad," he said with quiet sincerity. He looked at her

wistfully, knowing she would never accept anything from him, not even admiration.

"Oh, if only I were older, Sandra!" he whispered longingly.

She laughed and gently patted his cheek.

"And if only I were a young lass again!"

* * * *

Ben Chester was well aware of opposition from Chrissie's children. Before he and Chrissie were due to leave, he made a point of dropping into Rankine's for a word with her two sons.

The younger men ranged themselves behind Ewan's desk to receive him, Sammy standing with his back to the wall. They positively bristled with polite hostility. Ben judged this to be a time for speaking out.

"Before your mother and I go off to London together, I guess I should tell you that I hope to marry her – when she feels the time is right. Meanwhile, I'd welcome your thoughts on the matter."

The direct approach startled them both. Sammy, the older brother, spoke first.

"It's no use asking us to put in a good word for you, Mr Chester. Mum has a mind of her own. To be honest, we wish she wouldn't go with you. We don't want her to be hurt."

Ben's square chin set grimly.

"Let's get one thing straight. I'd never hurt your mother. Surely you don't grudge her a pleasant vacation with a caring, undemanding companion? Because that's how it's gonna be, so help me! I would do anything, anything at all, to make your mother happy, I swear."

The two young men looked at one another, and there was a thoughtful pause. Ben was growing worried he'd gone too far with the straight talk when Ewan spoke up.

"OK, Mr Chester, we believe you. There is a favour I'd like to ask you in return." He paused, looking at his half-brother again.

"Would you keep an eye open for the *Christina K* when you get back to the States?"

This took Ben by surprise.

"You mean the ship Chrissie told me about? The brooch she always wears? Is it – is she still afloat?"

"We believe so. Sammy found she was taken to Bergen in Norway after the war, then sold to an Alaskan shipping line."

Sammy took up the story, grinning enthusiastically.

"We want to do something special for Mum to thank her for everything she's done for the family over the years. If we can find the *Christina K* and buy her . . ."

A vision formed in Ben's mind. A tall-masted ship sailing up the calm waters of the Tay estuary . . . and Chrissie standing watching, her face filled with wonder and amazement . . .

"Yeah, that surely would please her," he breathed softly.

He stood up, leaned across the desk and held out a hand.

"Count me in. I'll see what I can do," Ben promised.

Chapter 38

CHRISSIE very nearly changed her mind at the last
minute. The day of departure dawned cold and grey, but all
the family turned up to see her off. They were early, so they
stood shivering in the shadow of the imposing West Station,
where Danny Murphy had once seen Queen Alexandra, and
gained a name for his baby daughter.

So many memories! Chrissie felt a sudden rush of emotion
and was furtively dabbing her eyes when she was dealt a
resounding slap between the shoulder blades. Big Bella's
delighted shout froze everyone in the street for a startled
second.

"Oh, my, Chrissie! Fancy meetin' you!"

Chrissie was genuinely delighted to see her old friend
from the Lochee mill. She hugged Bella's stout figure, and
smiled at wee Eck, Bella's husband, who lurked in the
background.

"We're just awa' across on the Fifie tae Newport. My sister
on the Boat Brae's been awfy no' weel wi' shingles," Bella
volunteered.

"Me an' Eck are livin' in a prefab, but we're to get a
council flat when they get round to buildin' it. My lassie's
working as a weaver in yon newbuilt Taybank Works.

"Talk about swank! You should see the place, it's like a
cinema frae the ootside, but it's Buckingham Palace in the

weaving flat. There's no stour floats in the tea there, I'm telling ye! Changed days, Chrissie!" Bella stopped for a breath at last and sighed.

"Aye, changed days!" Remembering, Chrissie could almost smell the peculiar fishy odour of jute yarns on the frames. She found herself brushing her hand automatically down her spotless skirt, expecting to find it dusty.

Bella dug her slyly in the ribs and lowered her voice to what was, for her, a whisper.

"They tell me you've clicked wi' another man, Chrissie. One o' the wifies at the kirk was washin' her windaes when the two of you passed, airm in airm, an' awfy pally."

So the news was getting round, Chrissie thought ruefully. Bella stole a curious glance at Ben, who was engrossed in conversation with Ewan and Sammy.

"That'll be him, the big yin in the soft hat? Aye, weel, Chris, guid luck to ye. One man's enough for me!"

When Chrissie bade Bella and her man goodbye, it was time to catch the London train. She was glad of Ben's steadying hand, because she was suddenly terrified by what she was undertaking.

Then came a flurry of goodbyes, hugs and hasty kisses before they climbed aboard. Emily hugged her last of all, whispering, "Chris, have a lovely time. But, please, please, come back soon!"

As the train moved off, Chrissie waved and waved to the little group standing on the platform.

The station and the city suddenly blurred with tears. Don't

be daft, she told herself. You're only away for a short holiday . . . you'll be back before you know it . . .

But she still stared intently from the carriage window as they reached the long bridge spanning the river. The whole city spread before her, gathered on the river's south-facing shore, and behind lay the green slopes of the sheltering peak. Danny's monument upon its summit looked starkly white against grey rainclouds. The sight brought more tears to her eyes.

Ben leaned forward and squeezed her hand.

"Happy, Chrissie?"

What could she say? That her heart was aching? Then she looked into his kindly, concerned face, and was comforted.

"Yes, thanks, Ben." Chrissie smiled. "Very happy, my dear."

* * * *

Harriet Bowers returned to Dundee shortly after Chrissie left. Sandra came with her, moving into Chrissie's flat while training to be a social worker.

Harriet's situation was more complicated. She'd sold the family home, so had nowhere to live. She moved into a dirty, run-down tenement in a shamefully neglected area of the city. From that moment on, the other startled residents knew no peace.

"Hey, you! It's no' your mornin' for the stair, it's mine!" Connie McPhee yelled indignantly when she came upon Harriet scrubbing.

Harriet studied her wristwatch.

"It's nearly three o'clock, Connie. Rather a late morning, wouldn't you agree?"

"I was gettin' roond tae it, after." Connie glowered and went over and sniffed suspiciously at Harriet's bucket.

"What's that awfy funny smell?"

"The strongest disinfectant I could buy," Harriet retorted.

Harriet had scrubbed her way doggedly to the mouth of the close when Sandra arrived.

Sandra grinned.

"My, this makes me feel like a bairn again. Fancy you washing the stairs!"

Harriet pushed at her flyaway grey hair.

"Come on upstairs. I'm dying for a cup of tea."

The tiny flat had been thoroughly scrubbed and painted, its walls distempered white. There was new lino on the floor, a scattering of cosy rugs and a few pieces of practical furniture. Harriet put the kettle on the gas and flopped in a chair.

"Any news of your mother, dear?" Harriet asked.

"Plenty!' Sandra answered grimly. "Just wait till you hear this!"

She produced a letter written in Chrissie's beautiful, distinctive hand and began to read.

Dear Sandra,

Ben was quite right about poor old London. How wartorn and weary it looks, though rebuilding has started here and there.

We walked along the Embankment, and I was delighted to

find the old Discovery, *Captain Scott's ship! She was built in Dundee, and I saw her once when I was a little girl. It fairly took me back over the years! She did look sad and neglected. I couldn't help wondering if the* Christina K *is in a similar state somewhere.*

It's hard to believe I've been away almost six weeks. We spent a pleasant week with Mary Rose and her nice new husband, and, of course, there has been so much of interest to see in London. I waved to the King and Queen, quite close! I don't think she remembered meeting me once at Glamis!

I have something so exciting to tell you!

Ben had to phone America (isn't it wonderful what they can do these days?) and it was so easy, he suggested I call your uncle Ernest. I needed a little persuading, but I did it eventually.

It was so wonderful to hear his voice after all these years. We talked non-stop for what seemed like ages. I'd almost forgotten how well we got on in our young days.

Ernest had always planned to come back to Scotland to see us all when he retired, but he has such bad arthritis in his leg now, travelling is quite impossible. Remember, he was wounded in the Great War? He begged me to visit him in Texas instead – and I found myself agreeing!

It seems the ideal opportunity finally to meet my brother's wife and family, with Ben as an escort. He makes everything so simple and has already helped to organise the documents I need. They are fussy about visitors to the States just now,

342

but fortunately I was never a "Red", so the authorities might let me in, Ben says. (I suspect he teases me!)

So when you receive this letter, I shall have flown the Atlantic. Fancy that, an old lady of sixty!

I miss you all so very much, darling. Please give Natasha a big kiss from her loving gran, will you?

Sandra folded the letter and looked up.

"What do you think of that?" Harriet looked thoughtful. "I would say, offhand, that our Chrissie was thoroughly enjoying herself!"

"Yes." Sandra frowned. "Will she marry him, do you think?"

The kettle began whistling, and Harriet got to her feet.

"I wouldn't like to bet on it, love. She has a mind of her own, your mother."

* * * *

America! Chrissie could hardly believe she was actually there.

She had a dazed impression of towering skyscrapers – so different from the streets of Dundee – then endured another internal flight which brought home to her the vastness of the country.

Ernest and his wife, Geraldine, had retired to the outskirts of Houston. The Texas climate suited Ernest's arthritis better than that of Detroit, apparently. Their house was only a few hundred miles from Ben's ranch which, by American standards, was nothing, he assured her.

Ernest and his sister were close to tears when they

embraced at the airport. He turned emotionally to Ben.

"Thanks for bringing her, Ben. I thought I'd never see her again!"

He was very lame and walked painfully with sticks, Chrissie noticed with sorrow. There were those who still paid a price for that terrible war!

Ernest's beautiful house was an eye-opener to her.

"Oh, my, it's like a film star's place. You've even got your own swimming pool!"

"Swimming's good for Ernest's leg." Geraldine smiled. "I guess it's kind of medicinal, Chris."

"D'you mind how we used to watch those hardy souls taking a New Year swim in Broughty Ferry harbour, Chrissie?" Ernest grinned. "They sometimes had to break the ice with their bare feet!"

"Ye Amphibious Ancients Bathing Association? They still take a New Year dook."

He shivered.

"Better them than me! To think I used to swim in the Tay myself when I was a young lad, and never noticed the icy water! I must be getting old, Chris."

Tactfully, Ben and Geraldine left the brother and sister alone on the porch that evening after dinner.

Ernest lit a cigar. The aromatic smoke scented the warm evening.

"Y'know, Chris, I miss Scotland terribly." He sighed softly. "I still think of Dundee as home. I often dream about the river – the other night I was a wee lad again, playing chuckie stones on the Grassy Beach."

She understood at once, for she felt the same.

"I know. I doubt if I could live happily for long anywhere else," she said.

"Ben's very fond of you." He gave her a keen glance. "What if you marry him?"

She became very still.

"I don't know. I try not to think about it. I keep stalling, and he's very patient. He just keeps on waiting."

The light was fading fast. All she could make out was the outline of her brother's head and the glowing tip of the cigar, but she knew he was watching her.

"Seeing you has been like a breath of home to me, Chris. I know I'll never see my ain folk again – or walk by the banks of the Tay, but – well, I don't mind telling you I'd be delighted if you married Ben and stayed over here."

"Oh, Ernest!" Tears sprang to her eyes, and she reached out and took his hand.

He squeezed her hand, and his voice lost its American twang.

"Och, I'm a sentimental auld fool! Maybe Ben just wants help with his charity work? Maybe that's all he has in mind for you, my lassie!"

"What charity work?" Chrissie was intrigued.

"Ah! He can tell you about that himself." Ernest smiled mysteriously.

When Chrissie challenged Ben about his "charity work", he just grinned sheepishly and refused to tell her anything.

"I guess you'll find out soon enough – but you'll have to come with me to the Good Hope Ranch!" he told her.

That was all she could get out of him for the rest of the visit. It wasn't until they'd finally waved goodbye meantime to her brother and his wife, and Ben's hired automobile was eating up the miles to the ranch, that he raised the subject.

He'd been silent for some miles, frowning thoughtfully.

"I hope you won't be too shocked. Maybe I should have told you. Prepared you for it –"

"Oh, I know all about ranches, Ben," she answered him airily. "Ewan was a Wild West fanatic for years so I know all about cowboys, stampeding cattle and rustlers. I'm prepared for anything!"

But she wasn't prepared for the dozens of boys all ages, sizes and colours who came racing down the dusty track towards them. Ben slowed and stopped, grinning as a tide of yelling youngsters engulfed the automobile, clambering all over it.

Leaning on the steering wheel, he turned to Chrissie.

"My boys, Chris," Ben said simply. "Outcasts and orphans mostly, little criminals and thieves, kids from slums who never had a chance. Little devils past redemption, some of 'em – decent kids, most of 'em. There were about fifty at the last count.

"Chrissie – meet my boys."

He put the heel of his hand on the horn and kept it there in a blast of warning sound. Then, very slowly, they inched their way forward. Excited children rode on the roof and bonnet, others jogged alongside, and, at last, they reached the sprawling complex of buildings that made up the Good Hope Ranch.

Ben got out. He cleared a path through the milling youngsters to open Chrissie's door and helped her out. Holding her hand, he turned to the curious boys.

"I promised you kids I'd bring back something real good. Well, I have. Chrissie's a lovely Scottish grandma. How long she'll stay is up to you an' me, I guess. So let's be good to her!"

He looked down at Chrissie, and she caught her breath at the love and admiration shining in his eyes. The boys whistled and cheered and made a fiendish din until Ben held up a hand and silenced them. He seemed to exercise complete control.

"OK, off to the cookhouse, boys. Then it's baseball practice, I guess, being Friday."

When Ben had shown her into the comfortable ranch house, Chrissie turned to him with glowing eyes.

"Ben – it's wonderful what you're doing for these bairns!"

He shook his head modestly.

"I'd no time for my own kids, Chrissie. I was too busy making money. Now I have more money than I need and plenty time on my hands. It seems only right I should spend some of both on these unfortunate youngsters. There's a trained staff to look after them, of course, but the kids know they can speak to me any time."

He grinned down at her.

347

"Only thing missing is a beautiful Scottish grandma. I'm offering you the job if you want it, Chris!"

The grin faded, and he became quietly serious.

"No strings attached — if that's the way you want it, Chrissie. I promise."

Chapter 39

SAMMY MURPHY and his wife Emily were having a blazing row – the worst they'd ever had all their married life.

The awful thing was that it was happening when all their fondest dreams had come true at last. Their own longed-for baby, a boy, was lying in a cot between them, while they shouted furiously at one another over his head.

They were forced to shout as Daniel Murphy was screaming at the top of his remarkably powerful lungs.

It seemed to his weary parents that their perfect, healthy baby had cried steadily from the moment he was born until now, only stopping when he was picked up and cuddled, or fed. Night after night, without ceasing, he'd roared.

"What's the matter with him, for heaven's sake? There must be something wrong. You're his mother, Emily, you should know! I'm going to pick him up and give us some peace!" Sammy shouted desperately, the piercing howls going through his head like drills.

"Don't you dare pick him up! There's nothing wrong with him – just a touch of colic, the doctor says." Angrily, Emily tapped the book on babycare she held in one hand.

"The book says you mustn't keep picking him up, Sammy Murphy! You'll spoil him. The book says to let him cry. It's good for him, the book says. Crying develops his lungs."

Sammy ruffled his hair.

"For heaven's sake, woman! His lungs are perfectly well developed already. You shouldn't go by that blasted book, it's just a load of nonsense!"

"It isn't! It isn't!"

As she screamed at him, something gave way inside Emily. She lifted an arm and threw the book at Sammy. It caught him on the forehead, then dropped to the floor in a sudden deathly hush. Even the yelling baby seemed stunned into silence.

Emily stared at the red mark and burst into tears.

"Oh, Sam, I'm sorry!" she wailed. "What's happening to us? I thought we'd be so happy when the baby came. I thought we'd be closer than ever, but now all we do is quarrel over him!"

Sammy took his weeping wife in his arms. He knew she was tired out and as bewildered and depressed by the baby's crying as he was. It was all so new, so strange, so wonderful to have a son of their own!

Daniel lay quiet as a mouse. It was as if he knew fine he'd overstepped the mark, young though he was. Sammy felt a little gurgle of laughter begin to rise, the first chuckle he'd had for weeks.

"I'm glad you threw that awful book away, Emmy. Pity I happened to be in the way at the time!"

Emily stopped crying. He heard a weak answering giggle and breathed a sigh of relief. They could still laugh, which gave hope for the future.

She threw her arms round his neck.

"Oh, Sam, if only your mum would come home! If she was here, I could cope with everything – I know I could.

"I was sure she'd come for the Queen's Coronation – you know how she admires the Royal Family. But that was ages ago, and there's still no word. She didn't even offer to be with me when Daniel was born. What's she doing out there all this time?"

Emily's tone was aggrieved, and Sammy kissed her tenderly.

"Mum's been looking after Ben's Lost Boys. Maybe they need her more than we do.

"I'll tell you what – if it'll cheer you up, I'll write and ask when she intends coming home to meet her new grandson. In the meantime, why not put that blasted book in the bin and pick up our son and cuddle him? He deserves it. He's been quiet for almost five minutes!"

* * * *

Chrissie laid Sammy's letter thoughtfully beside the other one she'd received that morning. The little boy sitting on her knee patted her face to get her attention.

"Gra'ma Chrissie – sing 'Bonnie Dundee' for Elmer!" he ordered.

"For the umpteenth time!" She made a comical face at the little African American Down's syndrome boy.

He held up a hand, fingers spread.

"Five time, Gra'ma Chrissie!"

"Elmer, you're smart!" She hugged him delightedly.

So he was. He'd come on leaps and bounds since he arrived, blank-faced and unresponsive, at the Good Hope Ranch. Since then Ben had found kindly adoptive parents for Elmer, who were prepared to love and accept him as he was. He would be leaving soon – another success story.

Chrissie was proud to have been one of the team that had helped Elmer – and so many other boys. She'd always loved children, but now she'd discovered she also had a capacity for sympathy and understanding that drew the youngsters to her. For months she'd been enthralled, dedicated, calling again and again on what Ben called her "guid Scottish common sense . . ."

As if he knew she was thinking of him, Ben chose that moment to come into the big, airy room. Chrissie glanced at his expression and lifted the little boy off her knee.

"Mama Dakota's baking cookies. You go ask her for one, lovie."

As the little boy ran off obediently, Chrissie saw that Ben was accompanied by a young woman. Behind her was a plump little boy who was about nine years old.

Ben looked at Chrissie. He seemed decidedly ill at ease. .

"Look who turned up out of the blue, Chris! This is my daughter, Miranda Steele – and my grandson, Rufus!"

He laid a hand tentatively on the boy's shoulder. Rufus moved away.

Miranda nodded vaguely towards Chrissie, then turned towards her father.

Chrissie studied Ben's daughter with interest. Miranda

might have been pretty if she hadn't looked so worried and washed-out. Her clothes looked expensive but, oh, that style of suit!

"The divorce went through without a hitch," Miranda was saying. "I got custody of Rufus."

"What am I supposed to do, honey, congratulate you?" Ben smiled sadly.

She shrugged, her mouth twisted.

"Please yourself!"

"Mommy, I'm hungry." The boy tugged at her skirt. "I wanna hot dog with mustard pickle."

She turned on him.

"Will you stop going on about hot dogs? Where d'you think I'm gonna get a hot dog in the middle of Texas?"

"I wanna hot dog!" His fat little face set in stubborn lines.

Miranda glanced at her father hopelessly.

"Look at him! Your grandson's a mess. All he does is eat. His school says he's downright lazy and unco-operative and his grades are an absolute disgrace."

There were tears in her eyes as she stared at her plump, dour-faced son.

"I can't do anything with him, so I've brought him here for the summer vacation." She stared at her father with thinly veiled bitterness. "You never did anything for me. See if you can do something for him. You're keen enough to help other kids!"

Chrissie pitied Ben as the sulky little boy scowled at his grandfather.

"I wanna hot dog. With mustard pickle, right now!"

"Come with me." Ben held out a hand. "I'll show you the cookhouse."

Rufus eyed the hand suspiciously, then studied the angle of Ben's jaw. He clasped his hands firmly behind his back and followed his grandfather reluctantly.

The two women heard Rufus still protesting loudly as he disappeared.

"It's gotta be mustard pickle, OK?"

Miranda flopped into a chair wearily and lit a cigarette. Eyes narrowed against the smoke, she smiled at Chrissie. She was attractive when she smiled.

"I'm glad I've met you at last. I don't mind telling you I've been worried sick since a friend told me Dad had brought a Scottish woman to live with him. I guess he's at an awkward, lonely age. Mostly it's his own fault, though part of the blame's mine, too, I guess."

Chrissie smiled. She liked this frank American, but Miranda had her and Ben's relationship all wrong.

"You needn't worry about me, Miranda. Or your father. He keeps very busy and happy."

Miranda drew on the cigarette thoughtfully.

"What I can't figure is what you get from working in a Godforsaken place like this, with a bunch of problem kids even worse than Rufus."

"I like it, believe it or not. Some problems we can't solve, but most we can do something about. That makes helping your father with the boys very worthwhile."

Miranda was silent, studying the glowing tip of the cigarette with a frown.

"Sure, that sounds very noble, but you know what I think? I think you want to marry my father and get your hands on his dollars. You're a widow, aren't you? I don't blame you, but I have Rufus's future to think of. Dad's a very wealthy man."

"Miranda, you're insulting! The question of marriage hasn't arisen," Chrissie retorted.

Ben strode into the room. He looked angrier than Chrissie had ever seen him.

"Chrissie's right, Miranda. You're insulting. You owe us both an apology!"

For an instant, Miranda resembled her sulky son, and Chrissie was sorry for her. Then the young woman stubbed out the cigarette and stood up.

"OK. I'm sorry, Dad. I'm sorry I visited you. I'll be going as soon as I've said goodbye to Rufus. Where is he, by the way?"

Ben's quick anger had faded. He looked miserable.

"He's in the cookhouse eating sausages and baked beans with the other kids. You don't have to go, Miranda . . . I'd like it if you stayed."

She glanced wryly in Chrissie's direction.

"Thanks, but three's a crowd. Anyway, I've a plane to catch."

She gathered her things together and kissed her father on the cheek, then gave Chrissie a quick, nervous smile.

355

"I'm sorry if I offended you, Chrissie. I only meant to speak the truth."

"You made me think, my dear," Chrissie said. "Perhaps that's a good thing."

Rufus didn't fit in at the Good Hope Ranch. He lay around listening to the radio all day and refused point-blank to participate in games or expeditions.

The other boys teased him unmercifully at first about his weight, then ignored his sulky silence. And, when he wasn't sulking, Rufus moaned about the plain, wholesome diet, until Ben began to lose patience.

"To think my own grandson should be one of the worst pains in the neck we've ever had to deal with, Chris! What's up with the kid?"

"Give him time. He's a very intelligent little boy. And a very unhappy one."

Ben blinked in amazement.

"Intelligent? How d'you make that out? He's not interested in anything but that awful rock 'n' roll."

"Mmm – I'll admit he listens to the radio a lot. But it's not just rock and roll. Haven't you noticed he's always around when there's a financial programme on? You know – what's doing with stocks and shares on Wall Street and that sort of thing."

She hesitated before going on.

"I like to sit quietly after lunch and knit or sew. Rufus usually comes and reads the papers then. Rather an unusual interest for a wee boy, don't you think? It's the financial pages that fascinate him. He doesn't seem to mind me," she finished softly.

"Wall Street, did you say?" Ben said thoughtfully. "You think there's hope, then?"

"Yes, I'm sure there is – if we can get through to him."

"Sounds as if you're well on the way already. Thank goodness you're here, Chris!"

Chrissie hesitated. She'd been doing a great deal of thinking recently. Perhaps this was the time to tell Ben about her conclusions. He'd be upset, she knew, but there was nothing she could do about that.

"Ben – I had a letter from my niece, Georgina, in Australia. Remember I told you my brother, George, died recently and his widow left the farm and went to Montrose? Ina's husband owns their farm and now wants to sell it.

"Well, I've decided to buy it and start a Scottish version of the Good Hope Ranch. I've been so impressed with what you've done here, I want some Scottish folk to have the same chance."

"But, Chris – that means you'll go back to Scotland."

He looked so distressed it alarmed her. She went to him and took his hand.

"Yes, dear, I want to be there to organise everything."

"If you go, you'll never come back," he said heavily. The healthy colour left his tanned cheeks, and he looked suddenly old.

"Ben, I've been thinking about this for a long time. It's something I want to do. I daren't put it off any longer. I'm not getting any younger! Besides, I long to see my family again. If you need me, I'll come back. I promise!"

He lifted her hand sadly to his lips.

"You know I always need you, but don't make promises you don't intend to keep, Chris. I couldn't bear it."

"Oh, Ben!" She wanted to weep. What could she say to ease the pain? Nothing – her mind was made up. She wouldn't change it.

Ben's mind worked fast in his desperation. He clasped both her hands in his.

"Chrissie, why not take Rufus with you? The kid's miserable here, and he'll probably be more miserable when you go. Besides, with him along, there's more chance you'll come back!"

Chrissie was startled. She'd never expected this!

Then she began to think about it. Rufus didn't seem to resent her as much as other adults. In a strange country would he turn to her? Would she make the breakthrough he so desperately needed?

He was patently unhappy, a poor, mixed-up wee boy who needed help, and he was Ben's grandson...

"Very well, my dear." Chrissie smiled. "If Miranda agrees, I'll take Rufus. If you can persuade him to go with me, that is!"

Chapter 40

RUFUS hated the Good Hope Ranch. The food was awful and the other boys made his life a misery because he was, well – kind of plump. Scotland couldn't be much worse, the boy declared ungraciously. He'd go with Granny Chris . . .

Ben had been very silent since Chrissie had told him she was leaving.

Her brother, Ernest, was upset, too, and she found herself wondering often, during the days before her departure, if she was doing the right thing. Then she'd throw herself into checking her travel arrangements and packing, and try not to think about what she was doing to the two men she loved.

She'd return to Texas – wouldn't she? It was her second home – wasn't it?

But lying restlessly awake at night, listening to the grasses in the meadow stir and sigh in the soft night breeze, Chrissie wondered if she would ever come back. There was Rufus, of course, but the boy's return could easily be arranged . . .

Miranda, his mother, was the only one who wholeheartedly approved.

"You mean you really want to take Rufus to Scotland?" Miranda had gasped incredulously when Chrissie phoned. "What does he say?"

"He seems keen. There's only one snag, Miranda. I'm not sure when I'll get back, and I wouldn't want him to miss any time at school."

"Don't worry about it. Rufus has been missing school since day one. He's just not interested in anything but food."

There was a pause, then Miranda went on hesitantly.

"Chrissie – don't get me wrong. I love him dearly. He's all I have now.

"His father remarried when the divorce went through, and moved with a new wife and stepson to Australia. He didn't even say goodbye to Rufus. I guess that hurt him badly. Maybe that's why . . . well, maybe what Rufus needs is a kind of grandma like you."

"I'll do my best for him, my dear." Chrissie paused. "But it's your father I worry about. Could you keep an eye on him when I'm gone, Miranda?" She was fully expecting to be told to mind her own business.

"It's funny you should say that," Miranda replied thoughtfully. "I have a good job in a store, but I don't seem to be enjoying it any more. I keep remembering what you said about Dad's work being so rewarding. If I give up my job I could spend time with Dad on the ranch. We might even get to know each other."

The night before she left, Chrissie walked along the deserted track overlooking the prairie. It was very beautiful. There was so much space all around she felt she could walk on for ever.

In the distance she could hear the boys singing cheerfully round a camp fire. A drift of woodsmoke mingled with the aroma of scorched hamburger came to her nostrils, making her smile. Oh, how she would miss them!

There were tears in her eyes when she reached a copse of sweet-scented shrubs, where it was safe to weep.

There were still tear stains on her cheeks when Ben tracked her down some time later. He took her hand, resisting an overwhelming desire to kiss her.

"Chris, I wish you wouldn't go. I may never see you again."

"Oh, Ben, when I've bought Ina's farm I'll be back." She laughed shakily. "I told you so."

"And what if your niece won't sell?"

"Don't worry, she will." As she smiled, she pulled him from the dangerous seclusion of the copse into full view.

"Come on, walk with me! Did you ever see such a glorious moon?"

He wanted to tell her how his heart was aching. He longed to ask her to marry him and stay with him, but he hadn't the courage. She might refuse him . . . and how would he cope with that?

So Ben Chester enthused about the full, silver moon rising above the prairie, and remembered the glorious scene as one of the saddest moments of his entire life.

Next day, Chrissie was glad she had a wee boy to see to, or she might have broken down in Ben's arms and abandoned the trip.

Not that Rufus was a demanding charge. He spent his money on a large supply of candy, and ate it on the plane taking them to New York. The steady munching set

Chrissie's nerves on edge, but she kept silent.

On landing they checked into a hotel near the airport to be ready for their morning transatlantic flight. Chrissie allowed Rufus to choose what he wanted for dinner.

Obviously the best way to Rufus's heart was via his plump little stomach. He gave Chrissie an embarrassed little kiss on the cheek when she tucked him in for the night. Progress, indeed!

Chrissie spent a long time selecting reading material from the airport kiosk the next morning. Apart from choosing a comic, Rufus was disinterested. He'd enjoyed an enormous breakfast and was feeling far from energetic.

His mother would have nagged about the breakfast, but this Scottish grandma hadn't said anything. He glanced at Chrissie doubtfully. When somebody didn't care how much you ate, it took all the pleasure out of eating . . .

Rufus sat staring straight ahead as the plane droned on and on. There was nothing to see out of the windows but sky and clouds, and nothing to do.

He'd read the comic from cover to cover and worked out all the puzzles in no time at all. He was so bored he wished himself back at the ranch.

He stole a cautious peep at Chrissie. She was engrossed in a book, but didn't seem to be enjoying it much. Catching sight of his eyes on her, she stopped her puzzled frowning and smiled at him.

"Oh, Rufus, I can't make head nor tail of this!" She angled the book to let him read the cover, "A Simple Guide To

Stocks And Shares".

"What d'you want to know?" Rufus sat up with a jerk.

"Well, just about everything! I'd like to invest some spare cash in reliable stocks and shares."

Rufus began talking excitedly. Chrissie listened in amazed silence. She had not been strictly honest with Rufus. She had a very shrewd grasp of the stock market herself. At least, enough to realise that the child knew what he was talking about!

"That's very interesting, my dear," Chrissie said when they'd gone over the options and Rufus had handed out some sound advice. "You're quite a mathematician." She gave him a level look. "So why don't you do well at school?"

"School's just boring." He hung his head. "When the teacher writes sums on the board, the correct answer just pops into my head. It's so easy I can't be bothered writing it out in my book, so I just sit an' think about interesting things while the other kids do their work."

"Rufus, you know what your problem is?"

He swivelled in his chair and stared at her.

"You're very smart. Much smarter than the average boy your age," Chrissie told him. "You should be four or five grades above the one you're in, then you wouldn't be bored. You need a challenge. You need to be stretched!"

Rufus looked extremely startled. He pondered Chrissie's words for some time in frowning concentration, then gave her an endearing grin.

"Yeah. Maybe if I was stretched some, then I wouldn't be fat!"

Chrissie laughed with him. Rufus was learning to laugh at himself, and that couldn't be bad . . .

* * * *

Sammy Murphy was waiting at Prestwick airport with his wife and young son when his mother's plane arrived.

Chrissie hugged and kissed her son and daughter-in-law, then turned at last to her small grandson. This was a very special moment. They all felt it, even Daniel, who put his thumb in his mouth and stared back at her, shyly and solemnly.

"Daniel Murphy. My wee Danny." Chrissie could see no trace of Danny – or herself – in this wee lad, Danny's grandson. He resembled Emily, his mother, very strongly. And that's how it should be, Chrissie thought.

Rufus took in every detail of the emotional little scene. He didn't belong to this united family. He didn't belong anywhere . . .

Emily picked Daniel up, laughing softly.

"He's not usually so quiet, Chrissie. He's a wee chatterbox. C'mon, son, give your gran a kiss!"

Watching, Rufus felt suddenly frightened and forlorn. He tugged at Chrissie's sleeve.

"I'm starving. Don't they have hamburgers in this crummy place?" he whined grumpily.

The other two grown-ups studied the fat little boy with the tight-lipped disapproval he'd come to expect. But Chrissie's expression was filled with love and compassion, just as if she understood his misery. She smoothed his hair with a gentle hand.

"It' OK, Rufus, dear. Don't worry."

He didn't get his hamburger, but Rufus felt satisfied. He trailed along behind the little family, and never once took his eyes off Gran'ma Chrissie's back.

Chrissie's children had laid on a grand dinner to welcome the travellers. They all congregated in the flat Chrissie would share with her daughter, Sandra.

Chrissie looked round the family gathering proudly. How delighted Charles would have been by it, she thought, with a lump in her throat. There was only one face missing, though.

"If only Mary Rose were here!" Chrissie said wistfully.

There was a sudden hush. Sandra turned beetroot-red, then everybody started talking with enforced jollity.

Ewan proudly presented Linda, once his secretary and now his wife.

They had a ready-made family, Ewan explained laughingly, ruffling the dark hair of Linda's little daughter, Kate, who was Natasha's age.

The two wee girls were obviously great pals, and danced around Chrissie merrily.

Chrissie's gaze kept returning to her little granddaughter, Natasha. She'd rarely seen such a bonnie wee girl, small and very fair, with a natural grace that reminded Chrissie strongly of Charlotte before she contracted polio.

She turned to smile at her daughter Charlotte.

"So we have another little dancer in the family. I'm so glad!"

Charlotte smiled, patting the latest black Labrador which never strayed from her side.

"They've produced a vaccine against polio, Mum. Tashie will never suffer as I did, thank goodness!"

Rufus couldn't describe his feelings adequately when he met Natasha.

She was so nimble and quick and perfect – everything he was not. He felt as clumsy as an elephant, just watching her dance by.

A rush of muddled emotion quivered through the boy, a compound of resentment, jealousy, and something else so deep and hidden it made him want to disgrace himself and howl. But he never, ever cried, not even when boys teased him cruelly. It was a point of pride with Rufus not to cry.

He caught Tashie's eye as she went past, and scowled ferociously. Tashie took a stealthy glance around the adults, found them absorbed in chat, and rudely stuck out a small, pink tongue.

At that point, the door was flung open, and a beaming woman in a spotless white apron appeared in the doorway.

"Your denner's on the table. Come an' sup yer broth while it's hot!" she shouted above the din of the conversation.

"That's Connie McPhee, Mum," Sandra whispered in Chrissie's ear. "One of our success stories. Connie was nearly down and out when Harriet discovered what a marvellous cook she is. She's been with me ever since."

"There's no' enough chairs tae go round sic a gang," Connie announced. "The bairns can have a piece in the kitchen wi' me."

The two little girls looked at one another, giggling.

"A piece of what, Connie?" they shouted.

"None o' your lip, or it'll be a piece o' my mind!" But Connie was grinning.

Chrissie pushed Rufus forward.

"You go with Tashie, Rufus. Take her hand. You'll have fun with her in the kitchen, I bet."

Obediently, Rufus held Tashie's hand as Connie marched the children out. Tashie's hand felt cool and light as a feather in his hot, sweaty, embarrassed palm.

Chrissie took Harriet, Rufus and Natasha with her to inspect Ina's farm a few days later.

The last time Chrissie had driven through sunny Strathmore had been with Ben Chester, and she thought wistfully about him now. Despite the excitement of meeting her children and grandchildren, she missed Ben's company.

Harriet had been thoughtfully silent for a mile or so.

"Chris, would you let me look after things on the farm? It's the sort of job I've been hunting for. My old tenement will be demolished soon, and I shan't have a home to go to then."

"Oh, Harriet, that would be perfect!" Chrissie was delighted.

"As you know; I'd like to run the place as a refuge for women and bairns who need a holiday or a friendly ear.

Then there are the youngsters who need time to sort themselves out in peace and quiet. As a social worker, Sandra will be able to refer needy cases to us. Don't you think Charles would have approved of Rankine's funding this project, Harriet?"

"I'm certain he would. He was the most caring and generous man I've ever met," Harriet agreed quietly.

The farmhouse George and Jeannie Kennedy had lived in for so many years seemed to extend a welcome to Chrissie as she walked in. It was just the right sort of house – homely and comfy. She could understand why her sick brother had loved this place.

Her eyes smarted with tears, which she brushed away impatiently. The two children had explored the house by now and were casting longing glances at the farmyard. She smiled at Rufus.

"Take Tashie outside. Look after her, mind!"

It was muddy in the yard, so Chrissie warned them to wear the wellies they'd brought. The ungainly black boots made Rufus feel even clumsier than ever.

Tashie's wellies were bright red. They twinkled in the sunlight as she darted around exploring.

A horrid sensation came over Rufus, a nasty, jealous resentment. He was so big and ugly and fat, just like an elephant. He wanted to tease her, as he had been teased so cruelly and so often . . .

When she came dancing past, Rufus stuck out an arm and stopped her in her tracks.

"You have a funny name," he said accusingly. "Foreign."

The little girl pulled in her chin and straightened her back proudly.

"Natasha Zielinska. It's a very good Polish name, my daddy says."

"You're a Polack!" Rufus sneered.

Natasha stamped a boot angrily in the mud.

"I am not a polecat, you horrid boy! Anyway, you're a fatty. You're a great big fatty, Rufus!"

Rufus stared at her. He couldn't deny the taunt, because it was true.

He should hate her, like he hated all the other kids who took delight in baiting him – but he couldn't. He couldn't hate this lovely, bright little creature. Instead, he hated himself.

His lip quivered. The quivering ran right through him, spreading out from somewhere deep inside. He was going to cry, Rufus thought with amazement. He'd never cried before, but now tears poured out of his eyes.

"I don't wanna be fat! I hate it. They say I'm fat an' stupid, but I'm not stupid, Tashie. I'm not!"

Tashie was alarmed by the storm of tears. Her own tender little heart ached for this big boy who was sobbing as if his heart was breaking.

She stretched her arms round Rufus and hugged him as sympathetic tears ran down her cheeks.

"I know you're not stupid, Rufus. And you're only fat 'cos you eat a lot. Connie says she'd rather keep you for a week than a fortnight."

Rufus put his arms gingerly round the slight figure and rested his chin on top of her head. The sobs gradually stopped and he was at peace again. He'd expected to feel ashamed, but he didn't. Instead, the tears left him clean and refreshed.

"Gran'ma Chrissie says I'll be OK if I'm stretched, Tashie."

"Oh, Rufus!" She thought that was very funny. "Like elastic?"

He started laughing, too. He couldn't ever remember laughing so freely. He didn't care so much about being fat any more. He could fix that.

Tashie and Gran'ma Chrissie believed he was smart, and for the first time in his life, Rufus began to believe in himself.

Chapter 41

STOP here a moment," Harriet ordered on the way home.

Wondering, Chrissie pulled into the side of the road and they all got out of the car.

They were at the top of Powrie Brae, with the city spread out before them. A young policeman had brought Chrissie's granddaughter, Elizabeth, here one romantic, starry night three years ago. Now the young couple were happily married and living in England.

Chrissie shaded her eyes against the westering sun. She saw how the city was changing, spreading into the countryside. There weren't so many tall factory chimneys belching smoke these days.

"Look, Chris!" Harriet tugged at her arm.

Chrissie followed the pointing finger with a deep sense of shock. The bronze statue of the Black Watch soldier looked so like her Danny. He stood quietly, watching over the city of his birth, as braw and handsome as in life.

Chrissie wept silently, covering her face. She was getting old. Tears came so easily these days, and the memories were so sweet and sair . . .

Harriet's comforting arm was round her shoulders and two concerned little faces looked up at her.

"I thought you'd want to see the Black Watch memorial, Chris," Harriet said softly. "Isn't it impressive? The Queen

Mother unveiled it in 1959."

Chrissie dried her eyes and smiled at her friend.

"Thank you, Harriet. I can't tell you what this means to me. Danny never had a resting place, but now I think he does. Here. Guarding his town."

* * * *

"Gran'ma Chrissie, I want to go home to America," Rufus said a few weeks after their trip to the farm.

"Aren't you happy here, dear?" Chrissie asked anxiously. Rufus had changed quite a bit recently – for the better.

He squirmed uncomfortably.

"Sure, I'm very happy. This is the best place I've ever been, but I – I want to go back to school. The new semester starts in about a month and I don't want to miss any of it."

"You want to be stretched. Is that it?"

"I sure do." He grinned.

"Rufus, I can't go with you just now. The negotiations to buy the farm are at a difficult stage. You'll have to travel alone. Can you do that?"

"I'm not scared." He looked at her gravely. "You can trust me."

"I know that." She hugged him.

She'd grown to love Ben's grandson and would miss him when he went. Then there was Natasha. The two had become inseparable. The little girl would be very upset.

* * * *

Ben Chester felt as if his worst fears had been realised when Rufus came back to Texas without Chrissie.

He was so despondent that his daughter became more and more worried as time passed. She tried desperately to think of some way of distracting her father from his brooding depression.

"Dad, remember that wonderful trip we had to Hawaii before the war? Why don't you go back – you need a holiday.

"You could take Rufus. He's just the age I was, and he deserves a treat for working so hard. School's out in couple of weeks – and I could keep an eye on things while you're gone."

Ben remembered that holiday. He'd been on the lower rungs of the ladder to success and climbing steadily. It was the first exotic holiday he'd been able to afford for his wife and kids and, oh, gosh, how they'd all enjoyed it! Maybe a holiday with his grandson would recapture some of the magic.

He smiled at his daughter. Miranda had been wonderful. He couldn't have gone on without her, and now they were as close as they'd ever been. He knew his depression worried her and made an effort to be enthusiastic.

"Well, honey, that's a great idea! What d'you say, Rufus?"

Rufus looked up from a recent copy of the "Wall Street Journal" which he'd been studying.

"Sounds OK to me, Gran'pop!"

Miranda gave her son a thoughtful glance. There had been quite an improvement in him since he'd returned from Scotland, but he still didn't have much to say for himself.

But Hawaii was a bit of a disappointment, as Ben had suspected it might be. He couldn't recapture the joy of that first holiday, when the whole world had lain at his feet. Returning would have been a ghastly mistake, if it hadn't been for Rufus's delight in everything.

They'd been to Pearl Harbor, an emotional experience, as Ben explained about the sudden Japanese air attack on the Naval base in December 1941. From there they visited some of the smaller Hawaiian islands.

"Gran'pop, I'm real hot an' thirsty," Rufus said on Mauna Kea one hot afternoon. "Could we go some place for a drink of water?"

Ben looked around. They were in the harbour area, the air tangy with sea salt, and the tarry, hempen smell from fishing nets drying in the sun. An unlikely area to find drinkable water, he thought, but there was a cafe sign nearby. Some enterprising individual had set out a few tables with inviting, shady parasols on the deck of a nearby ship.

Ben and Rufus headed for this oasis. It was pleasantly cool aboard the *Aloha*. Ben relaxed and sipped a cool beer, while Rufus tackled a lemon soda.

He and Rufus got on remarkably well now, Ben thought. Had Chrissie waved a magic wand?

He studied the boy more carefully. You couldn't call his grandson a fatty now. He'd lost weight, and the leaner look suited him.

"Rufus, you've grown," Ben observed thoughtfully. He didn't mean in height alone. There was more to it than stature, a sort of expansion of spirit.

Rufus made a suitably exuberant noise with a drinking straw in the empty glass, then grinned.

"I guess I'm stretching. Gran'ma Chrissie says I ought to be stretched, Gran'pop!"

"Ah, she does, does she?" Ben said thoughtfully.

His drink finished, Rufus leaned back in the seat and looked around with interest. It was an old ship, but the brass fittings gleamed like gold in the sunshine. There was a ship's bell you could see your face in hanging not far away. Rufus leaned over curiously to read an inscription on the bell.

"Well, what d'you know, Gran'pop? This ship was built in Dundee!"

"What?" The glass raised to his lips, Ben almost spilled the beer. "How can you tell?"

"It says so on the bell." Rufus read out the inscription. "This bell respectfully presented to Captain William Kennedy, master on the occasion of the vessel's maiden voyage, June 1, 1895, by management and staff of Lilybank Foundry, Dundee, as a token of esteem."

Ben stood up slowly. He stared slowly upwards at the mizzenmast soaring above him into the blue sky, bleached with heat, trying to take in what Rufus was saying.

Chrissie's ship – here in Hawaii? Well, that made some sense. Whales were hunted in these waters, too. But could it really be the *Christina K*? This ship was called the *Aloha*.

"Come with me!" Ben ordered Rufus. He strode to the companionway and confronted a startled waiter.

"I want to see the manager, if you please."

The manager proved to be a young man, on the defensive because he expected some complaint. He relaxed when he discovered all Ben had in mind was information, and invited the pair into his office below decks.

"Yes, you're quite right, she was originally the *Christina K*." He nodded. "I bought her in Alaska for a song, from a whaling company which had gone bust.

"I'd been looking for a whaler for some time. I wanted to start a small business in Hawaii, something that would reflect the history of the islands and be a tourist attraction as well. I think you'd agree this is an ideal solution!" He grinned.

"It could be I have a better use for her," Ben said quietly. He leaned forward, his eyes on the younger man.

"You said you got the ship cheap – but that won't enter into our negotiations. Name your price. If it's a fair one I'll pay it!"

The young man looked taken aback for a moment, then his expression set stubbornly.

"Sorry, but she's not for sale. Price doesn't come into it. This has been my dream ever since I left high school, and I'm not likely to change my mind now I've made it come true!"

Ben had a lifetime of experience in business negotiations, and he knew this wasn't a bluff. This was a young man with a vision and, as he'd said, money didn't come into it.

Ben sighed. He took out his business card and jotted down

the ranch phone number before handing it over.

"If you ever change your mind, contact me. Promise?"

The younger man studied Ben and decided he would be a good man to do business with. He smiled and held out his hand.

"OK, Mr Chester, I promise to let you know if I ever think of selling my ship. But I hope that won't be for many years!"

When Ben and Rufus were once more on the quayside, they paused for a long time, just looking at the ship in silence. Ben put a hand on Rufus's shoulder and the boy looked up.

"Rufus – when the time comes to buy this ship, I may not be around any more. Will you promise me something? Will you use some of the money I leave you to buy Gran'ma Chrissie's ship and see she goes home to Dundee? Will you do that for me, son?"

Rufus felt the weighty responsibility of the promise fall around him like a heavy cloak. To be entrusted with such a task made him feel scared, but very proud. It was the most wonderful thing that had ever happened to him in his whole life. He met his grandfather's eyes bravely.

"I promise," Rufus declared staunchly. "You can count on me, Gran'pop."

* * * *

It took time to get the farming venture in Scotland up and running. The project was greeted with suspicion, both from those they were trying to help, and from others who should have known better.

Some neighbouring farmers were up in arms, declaring that Teddy Boys and other undesirables would take over the district, given half a chance.

Chrissie and Harriet battled on: Based on Ben Chester's Good Hope Ranch, the old farm steading was converted into private cubicles, a spacious living and recreation area and a spotless kitchen.

Tam, the shepherd, was retired, but he and his brisk little wife agreed to stay on in the cottage. They formed the nucleus of the staff Chrissie hoped eventually to employ.

Then there were a few sheep, dogs, cats and kittens, Donald the donkey, a small herd of goats and a flock of hens. All these would have therapeutic value, Harriet maintained.

But it all took time. As the months passed, Chrissie became more and more involved in the lives of her family, and more engrossed in the life of the city.

Great changes were taking place. New housing estates were being built where the jute barons' country houses once stood, and old tenements were being demolished for new buildings in the city.

As Connie McPhee remarked grimly to Chrissie, "You'd best keep a close eye on your hoose, in case the bulldozers come along when your back's turned!"

Work was starting on a road bridge across the Tay. The obdurate thudding of the piledrivers could be heard for months as the structure edged out across the river.

It was an exciting time for a Dundonian and Chrissie became absorbed in it. America and her life there seemed far away.

She was on the point of writing her regular weekly letter to Ben when she was disturbed by a frantic knocking. It was Emily, white-faced and wild-eyed with fear.

"Oh, Chrissie, come quick! There's something wrong with the bairn!"

Chrissie felt her heart lurch. Wee Daniel had seemed fine yesterday, apart from a cold.

She hurried after her daughter-in-law.

"Have you called the doctor?"

"Sammy's been trying to get him. But he could be too late. The bairn can't breathe!" Emily wailed frantically.

Chrissie took one look at the gasping toddler in Sammy's arms, then turned to Emily.

"Is the water hot? Really hot?"

"What?" Emily gaped at her. "Yes, the immersion's been on, but what would – "

"Then run a bath," Chrissie ordered briskly. "Scalding hot."

Emily stared unhappily, then ran to do her bidding.

Chrissie took the wheezing bairn gently from his father's arms and carried Daniel into the bathroom, which was rapidly filling with billowing clouds of steam. Chrissie sat on the bathroom stool, Daniel on her knee, smiling at Emily and Sammy.

"It's a bad attack of croup. Many's the time I've let the

kettle boil merrily to ease my bairns' wheezing. This steam will do the trick just as well. See, he's breathing easier already."

It was true. Daniel's rasping breathing had quietened dramatically.

"Oh, Chrissie, what would we do without you?" Emily collapsed with relief.

"You'd manage fine. You'd have to!"

Chrissie kissed the top of Daniel's head and handed him over to Sammy. His breathing was normal again.

The doctor arrived soon after, and confirmed Chrissie's diagnosis, but the incident had left her uneasy and restless. Suddenly the future seemed unclear.

Her family needed her, depended upon her. So did all the folk at the farm. Should she return to America, as she'd promised Ben – or stay here for her children's sake? Chrissie dithered unhappily for days.

* * * *

When the phone rang, Chrissie was surprised to hear Miranda's voice. It was an excellent connection. Miranda sounded so close. She also sounded desperately worried.

"Chrissie – I wondered, are you planning to return to the States soon?"

Chrissie put a hand up nervously to the brooch she always wore. The little carved ship never failed to calm her.

"I – er – haven't made any plans yet, dear," Chrissie replied noncommittally.

"It's Dad, Chrissie." Miranda sounded on the verge of

tears. "I'm in a callbox near Rufus's school because Dad wouldn't let me phone you from the ranch. He's changed so much since you went away.

"He's lost interest in everything, even the ranch and the boys. I – I'm terrified he'll lose interest in life itself! It's just heartbreaking to stand by and watch him fade away and know you can't do a darned thing!

"Oh, Chris, there's only one person who can help him and – and that's you!" Miranda was sobbing now, a heart-rending, desolate sound that reached out to Chrissie across the miles.

"Don't cry, my dear." Chrissie was deeply distressed. "I'd no idea Ben was in such a state. His letters are always so cheerful. To be honest, I thought that – well – he didn't care about me being with him any more."

"Care about you!" Miranda gave a gulping sob. "If only you knew what those letters cost him! He's such a proud man. He won't plead, Chris, he says you must come of your own free will. But I'm afraid that could be too late."

"I'll be there as soon as I can!"

With the decision made, Chrissie felt better. She was in command of her life once more.

Her affections had been torn two ways, between her family and dear, lonely Ben Chester. In the end, it was only a question of who needed her most. And Miranda had just supplied the answer.

Chapter 42

MIRANDA and Rufus met Chrissie when the plane touched down on Texan soil. Ben was too ill to make the journey, Miranda explained. Chrissie's heart sank and suddenly she felt frightened.

"Hi, Gran'ma Chris. See how I stretched!" Rufus's greeting was accompanied by a wide grin.

And so he had. He was a full head taller and had lost weight, looking healthily fit and bronzed

More importantly, he walked with his head held high, displaying a new confidence. No trace was left of the fat, unhappy little boy she'd met last time.

Miranda drove Ben's big Cadillac, chattering non-stop.

"Rufus is top in everything, Chrissie. Would you believe it? The boys and girls in his class are all three or four years older than him.

"Apparently he has this fantastic IQ. Nobody ever suspected it before. He's streets ahead of other kids his age. Can you imagine my little Rufus – a genius?" his mother declared proudly.

Rufus met Chrissie's eye with a wink and the endearing grin she remembered so fondly.

So he could still laugh at himself. She was sure he'd never forget how cruelly he'd been teased. Perhaps that would give him a unique insight into the problems of other people.

Chrissie had high hopes for Rufus!

There were no lively boys waiting at the Good Hope Ranch this time. There was only a solitary figure standing on the porch, watching them arrive in a cloud of December dust.

"Oh, Dad!" Miranda groaned, and glanced at Chrissie. "He shouldn't really be up!"

When they drew alongside, Chrissie was saddened by the change in the big, energetic man she'd known. His clothes hung on him, and he leaned weakly on a stick. Had she done this to him?

But Ben Chester felt on top of the world today. His eyes were suspiciously moist as Chrissie climbed from the car. He held out his arms as she hurried to him.

"Chrissie! So you came back, after all!"

She hugged him.

"I told you I'd be back – and I always keep my word!" She looked up at him. "Mind you, your letters were so cheery I thought you were managing fine without me. I wondered whether to come back to you at all!"

"Oh, Chrissie – if only you knew!"

Miranda paused as her father spoke, holding one of Chrissie's cases.

"He was told to take life easy, Chrissie. Of course, he didn't. He'd worry about you, then drive himself ever harder to try to forget. Finally his stomach ulcer flared up again – and he's been real ill.

"Oh, boy, Chrissie, he's a difficult patient! I hope you have more success making him eat properly. I can't get him to touch a salad!"

Ben laughed for the first time in months.

"Gee, Miranda, greens are for jack-rabbits. You've never tasted a Scottish high tea, girl. Chrissie must show you some time."

He winked at her.

"When I visited in Dundee she fed me on pie and peas, scones, butter and jam, and iced cake, all washed down with two cups of strong tea."

"Dad! You never ate that, did you?" Health-conscious Miranda looked horrified.

"Sure I did. Every crumb – and without a stomach ache, too!"

He put an arm around Chrissie, and painfully slowly they made their way into the cool ranch-house. Miranda and Rufus followed with the baggage.

Chrissie looked round and sighed with pleasure. She'd forgotten how welcoming the ranch-house was. Another homecoming – but very different from the one in Dundee with her children and grandchildren gathered round! But she was needed here in Texas, and as always, that was a powerful incentive.

She smiled radiantly, and Ben began to hope . . .

* * * *

"I'll walk to those oleander one of these days – even if it kills me!" Ben declared on his daily walk accompanied by Rufus.

"What's so important about it, Gran' pop?" Rufus was curious.

"Never you mind!" Ben grunted. He was leaning on the boy's shoulder as he struggled back to the house.

"Any word about the *Christina K* from the man in Hawaii?" Rufus demanded.

Ben look crestfallen.

"No. I don't wish the poor guy any misfortune, but I expected his cafe to go bust long ago."

He gave his grandson a stern glance.

"Not a word to Chrissie about it, though. I don't want her thinking she'll maybe get her ship back – and then nothing comes of it. Remember we're dealing with someone with a vision. There's no knowing what a guy like that will do!"

* * * *

With a sigh, Chrissie folded the letter that had just come from home and tucked it into the envelope. It was from Emily, and contained joyful news – or not, depending on which way you looked at it.

Her daughter-in-law wrote that she was expecting another baby in the spring. She and Sammy were thrilled, of course, but – well, Emily wondered how on earth she'd cope.

Chrissie would remember what a livewire wee Daniel was, and he was ten times worse now he was older. He'd nailed a whole pound of sausages to the kitchen floor in an orderly line of links, and nearly driven Bertha, the daily, crazy, trying to pick them up.

Emily wished Chrissie would come home. She missed her

so much, and felt really lost without her . . .

Poor Emily, Chrissie thought indulgently. She would cope, though. She had Charlotte to help her, and Sandra's sound common sense. She'd have to cope.

The letter was unsettling, though, particularly as Ben had been so oddly preoccupied since Chrissie's arrival six weeks ago.

Had he changed his mind about wanting her to stay?

Restlessly, Chrissie went outside. It was funny sort of weather, the air breathlessly still, although high thunderhead clouds towered ominously on the horizon.

There had been no sign of Ben since lunch and she assumed he was having a siesta. She was too restless to doze, so she walked slowly down the track.

Of course, the torrential downpour started when she got too far from the house to turn back. She darted into the shelter of the nearby copse.

Someone else had had the same idea, apparently.

Chrissie cannoned into Ben standing beneath the trees. He grinned as he steadied her.

"Well, what d'you know? I guessed my persistence would pay off some time.

"There's no peace for us to speak privately up at the house, what with the boys and Rufus, and Miranda yakking on. I've been coming back here often since I got my strength back. I knew you'd turn up one day, and I'd have you all to myself!"

"Ben, what are you blethering about?" She laughed,

suddenly breathless.

Rain was spilling down the leaves on to her hair. He pulled her closer into the shelter of the branches.

"I'm not blethering. I've been practising, and I'm word perfect."

He took a deep breath, looking down into her blue eyes.

"Christina, I love you very much. Would you do me the honour of becoming my lawful, wedded wife?"

He broke off, grinning widely.

"There was more, Chris, romantic poetry and all that, but I guess I'd better skip it. And don't expect me to go down on one knee, 'cos I doubt if I'd get back up again. Anyway, I got the important part OK. Say you'll marry me, Chrissie?" he begged.

So many ways of loving, she thought. A new love for Ben and herself in their old age. Ah, well, true love grows neither old nor cold!

A surge of happiness washed through Chrissie as she kissed her tall American.

"Aye, I'll marry you, Ben Chester. I thought you'd never ask!"

There was a flurry out on the track, and a golfing umbrella sprouting muddy jeans suddenly appeared. Rufus lifted a corner of the brolly and took in the two people embracing in the shelter of the bushes. Being smarter than average, he immediately reached the correct conclusion.

"Wowee, Gran'pop! When are you two gettin' married?"

"Just as soon as Miranda can bake a wedding cake, son!"

"Where are you goin' for a honeymoon?" Rufus asked curiously.

"Oh, I dunno, Rufus. I guess Paris, France, would be nice."

"Gran'pop, could I come to Paris with you? School will be on vacation soon, and I wouldn't be any bother, honest! I'd just love to work out on the spot how Gustave Eiffel built the Eiffel Tower, Gran'pop!"

"Not on your life!" Ben looked shocked.

Chrissie burst out laughing.

"Oh, go on, Ben, let him! Let's go on honeymoon with our grandson! That must be a record of some sort!"

Chrissie had never been to an American wedding. Theirs was to be a quiet affair with just the family and a few neighbours, Ben assured her.

That suited Chrissie, who wanted no fuss. Then she happened to glance at the guest list Miranda was preparing.

"But there must be over two hundred names!"

"Yeah, two hundred and thirty. Just a nice, quiet, little wedding." Miranda nodded, adding another four names that had just occurred to her.

"That's quiet?"

"Oh, sure. There were over a thousand at mine. And look what a mess that marriage turned out to be – apart from Rufus!"

Chrissie said no more. She'd been married twice before, but was obviously still a novice at the game.

Miranda, who'd once worked in a big store, organised

everything down to the colour of stockings Chrissie would wear with the lovely biscuit-coloured suit and hat they'd chosen together.

Chris had thoroughly enjoyed going shopping with Miranda. The American shops were wonderful, with so much to choose from, and her future daughter-in-law enthusiastic and tireless in her search for what was "just right". It almost compensated for not having her daughters there.

She'd extended a warm, open invitation to all her family, of course, but the wedding was at such short notice and so far away, none of them could make it. Chrissie was sad, but tried to put her disappointment out of her mind.

Ben's Lost Boys were in a ferment of excitement, because most of them had never attended a real country wedding. Ben solemnly gave each one a task to see to. Chrissie smothered a grin as he did so. With so much scope for error, the day promised to be lively!

Chapter 43

BEN and Chrissie were married in the little white church Ben attended in the nearest small town. It seemed to Chrissie, when she arrived with Miranda, her maid-of-honour, that everyone in town was packed in there.

Her eyes met Ben's as he stood before the altar. She smiled radiantly, happy for her own sake, and for this modest man who'd done so much good for the community.

The locals certainly appreciated him. The ceremony over, they clapped and cheered and sang as Ben and Chrissie left the church to join the cavalcade of automobiles waiting outside.

It was as lively a reception as Chrissie had predicted. What with the younger generation competing to see who could wear the shortest mini-skirt, and the older generation expressing shock and disapproval, nobody noticed when one of the boys dropped a barbecued chicken in the fruit punch.

It sure was a pity the barbecue caught fire and and fused the fairy lights strung around the garden.

"But what the heck," Ben said. "Who needs fairy lights with a moon like that?"

And the firemen were friendly guys who stayed on well after midnight to join in the fun.

Rufus was in his element, being in charge of the music. It had to be the Beatles, of course, played loud.

"She loves you, yeah, yeah, yeah . . . !" greeted Ben and Chrissie wherever they turned.

It was also Rufus who gave Chrissie the only moment of sadness she experienced all that magical day.

She'd been delighted when Ben's son, Alexander, turned up. Miranda had invited her brother without much hope, but he had made an effort to come and meet his stepmother for the first time. Chrissie really appreciated it.

He looked very smart in his Marine dress uniform.

"I'm on leave from Vietnam at the moment, Chrissie," Alexander explained. "I'm stationed in Saigon."

Rufus was listening wide-eyed to his uncle.

"You mean you're fighting Reds? Oh, I wish I were old enough to go!"

Alexander glanced at the growing boy with a curiously sad expression.

"Don't wish for it, boy. You will be old enough, one day."

He looked up and met Chrissie's frightened stare. She saw in his eyes the same look she'd seen once in Danny's long ago – hopeless, sickened, the look of a man who must fight whether he wants to or not.

Impulsively, she laid a hand on Alexander's arm and, stricken, looked at Rufus.

So much promise and talent . . . would it be lost, just as Danny's had been?

"Have a drink, Chrissie. A little more champagne?" Alexander urged gently, watching her with sympathy.

So she drank another glass of champagne and laughed

again. But the shadow of Vietnam remained at the back of her mind until she and Ben climbed into the Cadillac later that evening.

Rufus clambered proudly into the rear seat, regally ignoring the gale of good-natured laughter. Ben blew the horn jauntily and they were off, a string of old shoes and tin cans clattering behind.

Chrissie snuggled down beside her new husband with a contented sigh. They were exhausted by the festivities but, oh, so happy!

"Now for the start of a new life together, Ben!"

Rufus stuck his head between his grandparents.

"An' me, Gran! Don't forget about me!"

"Don't worry, Rufus. I've got a feeling we won't be allowed to forget about you!" Ben replied.

Then he burst out laughing. It proved infectious, and laughing uproariously, the unlikely trio set out for a blissful honeymoon together in Paris, France.

* * * *

Sandra Murphy's love for Daniel, her nephew, probably had much to do with her being a childless old maid, she thought. Although those fighting for women's lib would have been up in arms at the thought!

Sandra had listened patiently to all the arguments. Women were free now to live their own lives, without having men and bairns to care for. But as far as she could see, most of these women had made an awful mess of their lives. It didn't seem to register with them that marriage, in most cases, was a partnership.

Sandra sighed. Chrissie's Farm, as it had come to be known over the last few years, had done a lot of good work with Harriet in charge. They'd helped hundreds – no thousands – of scared and despairing youngsters, victims of the permissive society.

But that didn't solve the problem of Daniel Murphy. Even Sandra's love for the lad didn't blind her to the fact that, at seventeen, he was a tearaway.

She loved his brother, Patrick, devotedly, too, but in a more chummy, conspiratorial fashion. Patrick and Sandra often sat together over large mugs of cocoa and had a right good moan about Daniel's exploits. That's what they were doing this evening, in front of a roaring fire.

"Of course, I'm very fond of your mum, Patrick, but Emily as a disciplinarian is absolutely useless.

"If she'd skelped Daniel when she had the chance, he might have turned out differently!" Sandra observed grimly.

"Yes, I know." Fourteen-year-old Patrick cradled the cocoa mug in his hands. "Fancy letting him have a motorbike! I mean, Daniel, on a motorbike! Can you imagine anything more lethal?"

"No, quite frankly, I can't!" Sandra was desperately worried about her nephew's increased mobility.

"He did swear to Mum and Dad, hand on heart and hope to die, that he'd be a careful, responsible rider. There was quite a stushie before they finally gave in and bought him that second-hand bike. He's been quite sedate ever since, actually," Patrick said loyally.

He had hopes of a motorbike himself when the time came, and didn't want too much drama attached to his brother's latest acquisition.

"He hasn't even passed his test yet!" Sandra said gloomily.

"Yes, that might mean putting the brakes on." Patrick took a long, thoughtful swig of cocoa. "I thought maybe he was a reformed character because of his new girlfriend."

"Another one?" Sandra sat up. Daniel was very popular with the girls, being wickedly handsome.

Patrick shrugged.

"She's a bit of a mystery woman. Mum's having kittens because Daniel hasn't brought her home to be inspected. Come to think about it, he doesn't say much. Maybe there's a dark, shameful secret somewhere!

"I haven't met her myself, but the bits I have seen on the back of Dan's bike look first class, I must say," Patrick remarked appreciatively.

Sandra had an opportunity to view her nephew's mysterious new girlfriend a few days later. She heard an approaching roar as she took her walk along the Broughty Esplanade, and recognised Daniel's distinctive blue machine.

There was a girl perched on the pillion. Sandra was glad to see they were both dressed sensibly in leather gear, and wore spaceman-like safety helmets.

Daniel was taken aback when he saw his aunt. His inclination was obviously to keep on going, but he and

Sandra had always got on well together. Reluctantly, he stopped the bike and put his black boots down firmly, balancing the roaring monster, which grumbled away noisily.

"Hi, Auntie Sandra. Going in for a swim?"

"That'll be the day!"

Sandra pointedly eyed the girl in the helmet and waited. Daniel smiled foolishly, but no introduction was forthcoming.

"Aren't you going to introduce me to your friend, Daniel?" Sandra prompted frostily.

"What?" He looked round vaguely, as if noticing the young woman perched behind him for the first time.

"Oh, yes! Well – this is – er, um – Tiger Lil, Auntie Sandra."

"Tiger Lil?" Sandra's voice rose to a squeak.

Daniel nodded solemnly. The girl clutched Daniel and said something that was drowned out by the grumbling motorbike. Sandra stared at her, but all she could see beyond the helmet's visor was a pair of laughing dark eyes and smiling lips outlined boldly in red.

Tiger Lil! Oh, help, Sandra thought.

The motorbike roared impatiently and Sandra stepped back.

"Don't let me hinder you!" she remarked caustically.

"Well, we are in rather a hurry, and I promised Dad I wouldn't go over sixty on the Kingsway, so – " Daniel shot away thankfully with a deafening roar. Tiger Lil, hanging on with one hand, gave Sandra a cheeky wave.

"Well, really!" Sandra glared after the feckless pair.

What would poor Emily do when Daniel produced his latest girlfriend for inspection? Faint clean away, probably! Really, it was too bad of Daniel, taking up with a girl like that!

The next day, Sandra was still wondering what to do about Daniel and the company he was keeping when the doorbell rang.

She found a neatly dressed young woman standing on the doormat. Sandra didn't recognise her, yet she had a feeling she'd seen her before.

The young woman looked extremely ill at ease, though she smiled and held out a friendly hand.

"Hi! I'm Tiger Lil, remember?" Her accent sounded slightly American.

"Won't you come in?" Sandra held the door open grimly.

The girl smothered a laugh as she accepted Sandra's invitation.

"Oh, that Daniel Murphy!" she said. "Fancy calling me Tiger Lil! The first thing that came into his head, he says. My real name's Lilian, Miss Murphy."

When Sandra had settled Lilian in a chair, her young visitor stared at her worriedly.

"Miss Murphy, I – I don't know how you're going to take this. I'd hoped Daniel could keep it quiet about me and my family. Then, when we met yesterday, I knew I'd have to tell you all about myself."

"You can say anything you like to me – in complete confidence, my dear. I won't be shocked."

The girl studied her doubtfully.

"I think you will be. Very shocked." She paused before going on. "I didn't tell you my full name. It's Lilian Gallacher. I'm Norrie Gallacher's daughter."

Sandra was glad she was sitting down. The room reeled and she felt herself turn pale.

She stared mistily at the girl. She was pretty, dark-eyed with a pale, sensitive face. Now she knew, Sandra could discern a haunting resemblance to Lilian's father . . .

Norrie's daughter! She might have been mine if Fate hadn't played cruel tricks! Tears stung her eyes.

Lilian flung herself down on her knees and chafed Sandra's cold hands.

"Oh, I've upset you – and that's the last thing I wanted!"

Sandra made an effort to recover her composure.

"What – what are you doing in Dundee?" she asked shakily.

"Studying design at the art college. I always loved Dad's stories about the city and made up my mind to come and see it for myself. Before I left, he told me how he'd loved you – and tried to persuade you to meet him every year . . ."

"He told you about that?" Sandra closed her eyes in pain. "Oh, Lilian, I couldn't do it. I wanted to, because I loved him so, but I couldn't."

Lilian squeezed her hand.

"I know. When he came back to Glasgow and found you'd

gone, it broke his heart. But he says now he thinks it was the saving of him. He decided to stop hankering over what might have been, and pay attention to his own marriage."

Lilian smiled.

"I guess you could say I'm the result of his good intentions. So I've got you to thank for being here.

"They're very happy now, my mom and dad. It's a good marriage.

"Dad thought you might like to know how it turned out – if I met you. When Daniel told me you were his aunt, I swore him to secrecy. I was terrified of meeting you and telling you."

"So – so Daniel knows, too?"

"Yes, he does, I'm afraid. I had to tell him. He's very fond of you, and he was scared stiff you'd be upset." Lilian met Sandra's gaze honestly.

"Daniel's nice. The nicest boy I ever met. We got together when I started at art college; he was first year Architecture. I could hardly believe it when he told me his name was Murphy."

"Daniel's a wild rascal, Lilian!" Sandra warned.

The girl's expression softened.

"No, he isn't. He's funny and imaginative and creative, and he'll be a wonderful architect one day. He just needs a little help and encouragement, and – and a little love, perhaps. "

Chapter 44

RUFUS at twenty-six was a very different person from the
happy little boy who'd gone off on honeymoon with his
grandparents fifteen years ago.

Rufus had been stretched. Stretched almost beyond
endurance, he thought bitterly as he lay on a lumpy bed in a
shabby rooming house in Boston. It was about as far away
as he could get from the after-effects of the Vietnam War.

As forecast by school and university, he'd turned out
brilliantly. His mathematical ability soon attracted the
attention of the government, and he'd been destined for
great things in the design of armaments and guided missiles
when he'd received his enlistment papers.

They hadn't wanted him to go. They'd done everything in
their power to stop him, short of putting him in jail. But he'd
gone anyway, as an enlisted man, in a blaze of patriotic
fervour.

He still had nightmares about Vietnam. That's why he'd
never design weapons again and why he was working as a
clerk in a shabby office overlooking the harbour, where all
he had to do all day was watch the peaceful ebb and flow of
tides. Never again would he use his impressive brainpower
to destroy innocent people.

He just wished he could be happy.

Rufus got up. Somebody had pushed his mail under the

door – a bill or two, and a letter from his grandfather.

Rufus opened it with the guilty feeling that he'd failed someone very dear to him. He would have liked to be a success, for dear old Gran'pop's sake . . .

His attention soon quickened, and he sat up straighter as he read Ben's letter.

This is between us two, Rufus. I just had the results of some medical tests, and things don't look good. I'm not complaining. The past fifteen years have been the happiest of my life, and I've been fit and active until recently.

I'll be sorry to leave Chrissie and make her sad. I haven't told her the tuth, but being Chrissie, I think she knows. We're both doing an excellent job, kidding one another that everything's fine!

I guess it's up to you to take care of the Chester empire now, Rufus. Alexander is pretty high up in the Army and he told me he doesn't want to leave.

One thing would give me real pleasure, though – if you could buy the Christina K *for Chrissie. I heard from the guy in Hawaii yesterday, just a cryptic note scribbled on the back of the business card I gave him all those years ago.*

It sounds hopeful. I want you to go to Scotland and put Chrissie's sons in the picture first. Suggest they form the syndicate they once proposed to buy the ship and carry out any repair work that's needed.

After that, you're free to negotiate however you like. The funds will be made available to you.

I know I can leave things safely in your hands, Rufus. That makes your ever-loving gran'pop happy and content. God bless you.

Tears ran down Rufus's cheeks, sorrowful, unashamed tears.

He cried for a long time, then washed and shaved and reached for a clean shirt.

After he'd packed a case, he looked around the dingy little room for the last time, then he closed the door quietly upon another chapter of his life.

* * * *

"And a one, and a two, and a three, and a four. That's good! That's splendid, Mr Simpson!" Natasha Zielinska beamed at the octogenarian performing wonders in her Dundee pensioners' keep-fit class.

Natasha had forty senior citizens in various stages of fitness under her care. Maggie Carmichael, a large lady, fanned herself weakly.

"Och, lassie, I'm fair melted. Could we no' hae a wee break?"

"I'm puffin' an' a'," the redoubtable Mr Simpson admitted.

Natasha, trim in a purple leotard with a white belt clasped around her narrow waist, smiled and relented.

"Oh, all right. Ten minutes for a tea break, then back to work!"

She smiled to herself. She knew the old folk enjoyed the blethering during the tea break as much as they enjoyed the simple dance movements and the catchy old tunes.

When the room emptied, Tashie twirled up on her toes and performed two grand jetes to the last few bars of recorded music. Every movement was a pleasure to watch, from the poise of her head to her slender arms and expressive hands.

Natasha could have had a career in ballet if she'd wanted to. Instead, she'd chosen to help the large and the clumsy, the unskilled and unco-ordinated to experience the joy of movement.

She still couldn't explain why she'd turned down the chance of fame when it was offered. Perhaps there was a reason hidden somewhere in the past. It would come to her one day, she thought.

She did love helping people, she thought, sinking to the floor in a deep curtsy as the music played its final dying chords.

Natasha thought she was alone, and a sudden burst of clapping startled her. A young man stood in the doorway, applauding enthusiastically. Tashie scrambled up, her face hot. He moved towards her, smiling.

"That was great!"

"Oh – er – thanks!" She squinted up at him curiously. He was tall and lean and very handsome, a complete stranger.

"Were you looking for someone?" she asked.

"Yes." He grinned. "You, Tashie. I wanted to renew our acquaintance."

She frowned, bewildered.

"But we've never met, have we?" Tashie studied him. If they'd met she would certainly have remembered him!

"We met years ago." He laughed. "I cried on your shoulder, and you were kind to me. It's me – Rufus!"

Tashie's jaw dropped.

"Rufus? The fat boy?"

A confused memory came rushing back. A muddy farmyard, and a big, clumsy, ugly boy crying in her arms as if his heart would break. She looked speechlessly at the tall, amused man.

Rufus nodded.

"I know. It takes some getting used to. I stretched. Like elastic, I guess."

They laughed and Tashie felt herself relax.

"Talk about the frog and the prince, Rufus! What a transformation!" She laughed.

"Yeah – and you only held me in your arms. Who knows what a kiss might do?"

He moved closer. The big, empty gym suddenly seemed small and intimate. Tashie hastily skipped backwards.

"Rufus – I'd better tell you. I'm engaged to be married." She held out a hand to display the sparkling ring her fiance had placed on her finger not so long ago.

Rufus didn't seem unduly perturbed.

"Yeah. I figured there might be someone. Only natural."

He looked at her and Tashie felt her head spin. He had such unusual, compelling eyes, so warm and sympathetic. They made her feel weak.

"Don't marry him, Tashie!"

She felt like crying, she was so angry and confused.

"You've got a nerve!" she cried. "I hardly know you! Mark and I have known one another for years. It's always been understood we'd marry one day. Our parents are delighted!"

He just kept looking at her. Tashie wished he wouldn't. She couldn't look away.

He put a hand on the graceful curve of her neck, a touch that was electric, thrilling her.

"Rufus, don't – " she whispered with tears in her eyes, pleading with him to stop the confusion.

"Don't marry him, Tashie!" Rufus repeated. "Look, I have no time. I'm leaving Dundee tomorrow and I don't know how long I'll be away. But you can be sure I'll be back, Tashie. I swear I'll come back."

His hand moved gently down the long line of her neck and rested on her shoulder.

"Tashie – please don't marry him."

"So that's why we got our tea break early!" Mr Simpson's jocular tones cut across Natasha's thoughts. "Just so's you two could canoodle?"

The pensioners came crowding back, ready for more effort. They stood around grinning and nudging one another delightedly. There was nothing her elderly friends liked better than a hint of romance!

But, oh, if only they knew the muddle she was in!

* * * *

She was a widow again. Chrissie could hardly bear the sorrow, although it had been six weeks since Ben had died.

She was an old lady now. Her fair hair had faded to the beautiful soft sheen of old silver, but at eighty-five Chrissie still walked erect. She inspected the bunkhouse and cookhouse every day and listened sympathetically to any problems the boys and staff might have. Just as Ben had done to the end of his long life.

Chrissie moved to the ranch-house window, which looked out across the porch towards the pool.

It was so hot today that all the lads were there. Hank, Miranda's second husband, had organised a swimming gala, and the youngsters were making a joyful, unholy din. It was a scene of youth and boundless energy. She was old now, and had no part in it . . .

If only Rufus would come, Chrissie thought longingly. But she had lost Rufus years ago.

He'd gone to Vietnam, and for three years she prayed desperately for his life. Well, he'd been spared – yet she'd still lost him. Rufus never came to see her now. He hadn't even attended the funeral of his beloved gran'pop.

She'd had a letter from him, though – a lovely, loving letter, postmarked Hawaii. Still, it had hurt that he obviously hadn't thought it worthwhile breaking his holiday to see her.

He'd just written that he was taking control of all Ben's complex business affairs. She wasn't to worry about a thing – he was a mathematical genius, remember?

She turned away from the window. All very well to tell her not to worry – but she did. She worried about all of her dear, scattered family.

Miranda had been sitting so quietly watching her that Chrissie had almost forgotten her stepdaughter's presence. They smiled at one another, a smile of complete trust and understanding. They'd grown very close over the past years, like a real mother and daughter.

"You're not happy, are you?" Miranda asked abruptly.

"How could I be, with Ben gone?"

Miranda frowned.

"No – apart from missing Dad. I miss him terribly, too, but that just makes me all the more determined to carry on his work. But with you it's different. I don't think you want to stay on the ranch any more."

Chrissie stared at her.

"But the ranch is my home, Miranda!"

"Is it?"

Miranda rose and walked towards her stepmother. She stood studying Chrissie sadly. Even in old age, she still had such a lovely face, full of character and humour, the mouth firm and determined.

"I've watched you. You look so far away sometimes – as if – as if you've gone away from us, away back to Scotland. Oh, Chrissie – I wish I could help you be happy!" Miranda didn't often weep, but tears threatened now.

Chrissie hugged her and forced a laugh.

"My dear, I'm an old wifie – well, over eighty. How can I go flying home to Dundee at my age?"

Home! It had just slipped out, but they both realised the significance.

Miranda sighed and dabbed her eyes.

"What has age to do with it – if you feel like that?"

Chrissie gripped Miranda's arms.

"Tell me what I ought to do?" she begged.

The younger woman stared at her for some time in silence, then shook her head wearily.

"I can't tell you what to do, Chrissie. You'll make up your own mind. You always have!"

Miranda was right. After a lot of heart-searching, Chrissie did make up her own mind. Old woman or not, she had to go home to Dundee.

Once the decision was made, she wondered why it had taken her so long. The two men who had given purpose to her life in Texas had gone. First, her brother, Ernest, and now her dear husband, Ben.

Miranda bowed bravely to the inevitable, and she and her husband, Hank, Ben's foreman, did everything they could to help. Ben's Boys were dismayed when they heard the news, and protested loudly at the loss of their adopted grandma.

"Don't worry, lads!" Miranda told them. "There's a replacement right here! See the grey hairs I got from looking after you lot? Don't I qualify for the job?"

There and then, Miranda was voted unanimously into the vacant position.

While her stepdaughter was arranging her departure, Chrissie was giving anxious thought to her arrival on the other side of the ocean. She knew her decision to return would be causing concern.

She couldn't blame her children for feeling worried, suddenly faced with the care of an ageing mother, but Sandra had said she was welcome to live with her.

Chrissie had accepted the offer, but could see trouble ahead. Two strong-willed women occupying the same kitchen? It was a recipe for disaster!

After some deliberation, Chrissie sat down and wrote two letters.

Miranda, watching her, wondered what Chrissie was up to. As she wrote, she wore the harmless old lady smile usually reserved for tough little boys. Miranda knew that deceptively innocent look well. Chrissie was up to something!

The days flew by, and soon it was time to leave. Chrissie had hoped that Rufus would turn up to see her off at the airport, but as they called her flight, there was still no sign of him. She had lost her brilliant boy . . .

Chrissie blinked back tears. There were enough of those already, pouring down Miranda's cheeks.

"Oh, Chrissie! Will I ever see you again?"

Chrissie wasn't having any of that depressing talk.

"Don't be daft – of course you will!" She hugged Miranda fondly. "I won't be far away. The world gets smaller every day."

Hank, the big, quiet Texan on whom Ben had depended to run the ranch smoothly, put his arm around his wife as they watched the spry little figure trot away. Turning, Chrissie smiled and waved gaily.

"Oh, Hank! How can I bear it?" Miranda whispered.

He grinned.

"You heard what the little lady said, honey. Somehow I don't think we've seen the last of Gran'ma Chrissie!"

Chapter 45

SANDRA was a bag of nerves, waiting for her mother's plane to arrive. What state would she be in after the marathon journey? Would she need a wheelchair, a doctor, a swig of brandy – or all three?

Would the flat be warm enough in this chilly weather, after the heat of Texas? Would her mother be all right in the car to Dundee? Would she manage the steps outside the flat?

Sandra sat in a corner of the airport and pretended to be interested in a magazine. Chrissie's unexpected decision had taken the whole family by surprise – but they were all abolutely delighted and were looking forward eagerly to her arrival. It was OK for them, Sandra thought. I'm the one who will have to look after her!

But she knew there was no choice. She was the only one without a family of her own. If only her mother wasn't so strong-willed . . . like me, Sandra thought with an inward sigh.

The plane had landed and passengers were disembarking and crowding into the concourse. Sandra hastily bundled the magazine into her bag and hurried forward, nervously scanning faces.

There she was! For a moment Sandra forgot all her apprehension in the joy of seeing her mother again.

She was an old lady now, of course, yet somehow not old.

There was something everlastingly youthful about the interested poise of Chrissie's head with its crown of pure white hair. Love and happiness washed away Sandra's misgivings. Mum was home!

"Mum! Mum, here I am!" she shouted and waved.

But as she began to push her way through the crowd, another figure darted forward and reached Chrissie first, hugging her delightedly.

"Oh, how lovely to see you! How absolutely wonderful!"

Sandra's jaw dropped.

"Mary Rose!" Her voice was shrill and indignant.

Her sister whirled and went white with shock.

"What are you doing here?"

"Meeting Mum, of course!"

"But so am I! Mum wrote and said you couldn't meet her, so she asked if I could do it!"

"My letter said I must be sure to meet her – because nobody else could come! Oh, Mary Rose, I don't understand this!"

The two sisters looked at one another with a dawning suspicion. Then they turned and stared hard at their mother.

Chrissie smiled sweetly,

"Dearie me, what a mix-up! Fancy me making a silly mistake like that. I'm getting quite forgetful in my old age.

"Mind you, it's nice to see you two speaking again. High time all that nonsense was finished and done with!"

The two sisters gaped at her, then Sandra began to laugh. Presently Mary Rose joined in. Neither of them had laughed so much for years.

Weakly, Mary Rose flung her arms around her sister and they clung together, laughing and crying at the same time. Chrissie looked on with a smug smile.

Sandra wiped her eyes.

"Oh, Mum, it's good to see you again!"

Mary Rose touched her sister's arm hesitantly.

"Sandra, I'm sorry for what happened. I really am. Can you forgive me now?"

Sandra was silent. She was thinking about all the work she'd done, all those people she'd helped and comforted. She remembered the Glasgow folk during the blitz, and those despairing youngsters in Dundee . . .

And Sandra thought about Norrie Gallacher, living happily with his wife. And of young Lilian Gallacher and Daniel Murphy . . .

She'd never been a wife and mother, but her life had been rich indeed. And all because Mary Rose and poor, brave Roderick Stirton had fallen in love.

Sandra kissed her sister's cheek.

"There's nothing to forgive, dear. In fact, I've just realised how much I owe you. I should be thanking you!"

Returning to the city she loved after fifteen years was a delight – and a shock – to Chrissie.

"They've done away with the Overgate, Mum!" Sandra said as they drove into Dundee.

"Never!" Chrissie couldn't imagine Dundee city centre without the ancient, narrow thoroughfare, dirty and tumbledown though it had been.

"That's not all!" Sandra went on. "The Wellgate steps have gone, and the lovely old gas lamp we used to call 'bobby's helmet'. They're building a shopping centre there. All the shops will be under cover, with a fountain playing all day long."

"That'll be to remind folk of the rain pouring outside," Chrissie remarked dryly. Then her voice rose. "Just look at those skyscrapers!"

"Those are multi-storey flats, Mum. Big Bella and wee Eck live in that one, on the tenth floor. She says the view's grand, but you can't throw a jammy piece down to your grandchildren when they're playing in the court, like you could in the old tenements. She tried, and the seagulls got it halfway."

Chrissie liked the road bridge across the Tay. It opened up great possibilities; the Kingdom of Fife lay waiting to be explored.

"The Queen Mother opened the bridge in 1966," Sandra informed her. "Pity you weren't here. You would have enjoyed it."

By this time they had reached the gates of Beechyhill and Chrissie breathed a sigh. She was home – but she didn't know whether to laugh or cry.

"Why the lodge is empty!" she noted with disappointment as they drove past. She'd been looking forward to seeing her nephew, Hughie Kennedy, and his Indian wife.

"Yes, Jani sold the shop ages ago to her cousin from

Pakistan. She and Hughie have retired across the water to Tayport. Jamal is chief engineer on an oil tanker and his young lad, William, is going to sea, too."

Chrissie fingered the little brooch pinned to her blouse.

"Another William Kennedy – and a sailor, too. How proud your grandfather would have been!"

* * * *

A lesser man than Rufus might have given up many times during the past month in Hawaii. But Rufus had more than his fair share of determination, so he was still there, waiting.

The *Christina K* was still berthed in Mauna Kea, older and grubbier, a little more paint flaking and wood crumbling. She was still named *Aloha*, and supplied food and drink to passing tourists.

Miki, the Hawaiian chef in charge of the restaurant, said sure, she was for sale. But how do you buy a ship when there is no sign of the owner?

Rufus knew his name by now – Michael Faraday. And he'd systematically combed the islands looking for him. Everyone he asked beamed and said sure, they knew Michael Faraday well. But nobody had any idea where he was.

Sitting aimlessly on the beach watching the waves, Rufus was acutely aware of the relentless passage of time. Gran'ma Chrissie had just had another birthday – her eighty-sixth. What if he couldn't buy the ship in time? What if she never saw the *Christina K* come sailing up the Tay?

Grown man though he was, Rufus felt tears threaten. Not

only because his grandmother was growing old, but because he might fail to keep his promise to his grandfather. And would Natasha wait? Why should she? Because a complete stranger had begged her to? Months had passed since he'd seen her dance and fallen in love. He could see her dancing now, if he closed his eyes . . .

"Ahem – you got a minute?"

Rufus looked up, startled. Miki, the fat little chef from the *Christina K*, squatted beside him on the sand.

"I remember something about Michael Faraday. Quite suddenly it come to me. I think he go whaling!"

"Whaling!" Rufus's brows shot up. "No. He's not the type, Miki."

"He's not killing whales – he's saving them!

"I think I remember he tell me about whales one day, how intelligent they are and cry for their families and how they are cruelly hunted and someone must stop it.

"He said he would go fight for whales if this rich man would buy his ship, but he got no reply. So he said I could lease the ship, and he would maybe go anyway."

"You think he's gone to save the whales?"

"It is possible." Miki nodded solemnly. "He's a good man, fine man, but a little – you know?" He tapped his head significantly.

* * * *

"Now your grandmother has settled in, how about fixing a date for your wedding, Tashie?" her mother asked hopefully.

Tashie's heart lurched sickeningly. She didn't understand

415

why, but it did.

"Maybe in a year or two?" she suggested tentatively.

Frowning, Charlotte sat down and studied her daughter. Tashie was quiet and preoccupied these days. It wasn't like her.

"Darling, why wait so long? Don't you want to get married?"

"Yes, of course! But -" Tashie turned away, biting her lip.

Why must she remember Rufus? Not even the handsome man, but the fat, ugly, weeping boy she'd held in her arms? Rufus had been transformed, but he still needed her, and had begged her to wait. But he was taking so long! Oh, why didn't Rufus come?

Charlotte levered herself up and limped across to kiss her daughter.

"Tashie, it's just an attack of nerves, darling. I'm sure you'll feel more confident if you and Mark name the day, and soon."

Tashie smiled vaguely, but didn't answer her mother. Nobody understood. How could they? There was only one person who knew Rufus and loved him. One person who might tell her what to do. Her grandmother!

* * * *

"Mum, what were you up to at that unearthly hour this morning?"

"It was half-past six! I was only making myself a cup of tea in the kitchen," Chrissie replied mildly.

"But you can make tea in your own room and have it in

bed." Sandra sighed.

"I want to be up and doing!" Chrissie replied with a flash of spirit.

With difficulty, Sandra choked down an angry retort. She loved having her mother home – but if only Chrissie would let her look after her! She was so determined to be independent, she was almost as bad as Harriet, who was refusing to hand over the running of Chrissie's Farm to a younger person. Sometimes Sandra felt at the end of her tether.

"I wish Harriet would come back to Dundee, too. I'm terrified she falls again. Her hip's not right – she needs looking after," Sandra complained worriedly.

Chrissie took a sip of tea.

"I've been thinking about that, too. Why don't Harriet and I move into the lodge? We could look after one another. And you could keep an eye on us both!" Chrissie's eyes sparkled. "It would be rather fun!"

"Fun!" Sandra stared. "It's cold and damp, and hasn't been painted in years!"

"It's amazing what a lick of paint will do. And we could put in central heating. It's a dear wee house. Harriet would love it."

Sandra bit thoughtfully into a slice of toast. It was a solution. In fact, the more she thought about it, the more attractive the idea became.

Natasha found Chrissie on her own when she called later that day.

Chrissie was delighted to see her granddaughter.

"Come into the kitchen, Tashie. I'm baking scones. I don't get a chance when Sandra's around. She treats me like an invalid."

Tashie perched on a kitchen stool, watching her work.

"Gran – you know Rufus well, don't you?" she ventured.

Chrissie's happy expression faded.

"Yes, I suppose I know Rufus better than anyone, dear."

Tashie took a deep breath and told her grandmother all about her last meeting with Rufus.

"You see, I felt there was a strong bond between us. I couldn't possibly ignore it. I wanted to wait for him, to help him, to know him. But – but he hasn't come back.

"Should I marry Mark, or should I wait? Can I trust Rufus, Gran?"

Slowly, Chrissie dusted flour off her fingers. It would be so wonderful to watch Rufus and Natasha fall in love, to see them marry! But could Rufus be trusted with Tashie's happiness? Recently he'd hurt so many people he said he loved . . .

"No, Natasha – you mustn't trust Rufus!" Chrissie warned. "He's brilliant and I love him very dearly, but somewhere along the line he went wrong. It was Vietnam – it changed him. He can't be trusted any more."

She took the sad young woman's hands gently in her own floury ones.

"If you want my advice, forget about Rufus, my love. Set a date for your wedding. Marry Mark."

Chapter 46

CHARLOTTE was delighted by her daughter's decision to
marry Mark in December. It didn't give much time to
organise a big wedding, so Charlotte decided to make the
dress herself.

Tashie was amenable to all her mother's excited plans. She
had become oddly docile, almost listless, once the decision
had been made. Pre-wedding nerves probably! Charlotte
smiled tenderly, and began to work on the gown.

By the end of August it was almost finished. Charlotte had
Tashie stand on the dining-room table for the final
adjustment of the hem.

How beautiful her daughter looked, Charlotte thought
emotionally, like a little lost ballerina, wistful and sad . . .

Charlotte paused abruptly in her pinning and studied her
daughter intently for the first time. What was wrong?

Before she could ask, Connie McPhee burst in.

"There's a man at the door, a king for Tashie," she
announced. "A Yank by the sound o' him. Wi' a funny name.
Rufus!"

Natasha felt her whole being light up with joy. Her body
seemed to lift from the table without effort, fly through the
air and land lightly, poised on her toes. Then she was
running as he'd never run before.

Rufus saw her come to him like a vision straight out of his

dreams. He opened his arms, and she flew straight into them.

"Oh, Rufus! What took you so long? You were very nearly too late!" She looked up into his face, her eyes shadowed with sadness.

"Gran said you weren't to be trusted. I didn't know what to do, so-"

He laughed and kissed her for the first time.

"I guess Gran'ma Chrissie doesn't know the whole story, darling. And I can't tell her yet. But I promise you can trust me, Tashie. With your life . . ."

He held her close, his eyes so honest and sincere that all Tashie's doubts melted away.

"I know that, Rufus," she said.

"Tashie. I have to find someone. He could be in Japan, Norway – anywhere. But, first, 1 had to come back to you before it was too late. I love you and want to marry you. Say you will, my darling. Marry me – and come with me?"

Tashie didn't hesitate. She knew she'd had a lucky escape. She'd tried to please her parents and nearly married a friend instead of her own true love. Now she must please herself and follow her heart. She slipped Mark's engagement ring off her finger and laid it gently on the hall stand. She felt free then to make another promise.

"Yes, Rufus. I'll go with you – anywhere."

* * * *

Once the upheaval caused by Natasha's change of heart had died down, she and Rufus were married quietly with only the close family present. After they set off on a travelling honeymoon, Chrissie and her old friend, Harriet, settled down to life in the lodge.

"This works fine, Chrissie!" Harriet enthused after a cautious start. "I hate cooking, and you love it, so you're welcome to rule in the kitchen. We both like pottering around the house and garden, so that's OK. We agree to differ on some things, but, otherwise, we're a perfect old pair!"

The old ladies grinned at each other.

In the course of a year or two, Harriet collected one abandoned dog and three stray cats. They were all as happy as Larry.

Chrissie's family found the lodge a haven of peace and comfort and the two old ladies a constant source of amusement and wisdom.

Chrissie's sons, Ewan and Sammy, were now the respected elder statesmen in the trade. Rankine's had long since amalgamated with a larger consortium.

"It was the only way forward once the jute trade declined, Mum," Ewan explained. "We're spinning polypropylene now. It's a strong, man-made fibre, used to make bulk containers for chemicals and suchlike and foundations for roads and seawalls."

"What would your father have thought?" Chrissie wondered. "So many changes. Even the money's different. They did away with the old tanner and threepenny bit while I was in Texas. And I do miss the dear old half-crown piece and ten-bob note!"

Ewan laughed and reached for another piece of her delicious shortbread.

"Well, it's an ill wind, as they say. Decimalisation meant new cash registers and that took Dundee into the field of new technology and the micro-chip.

"Linda and I are delighted young Charles has decided to join the firm when he leaves school. One day there'll be another Charles Rankine to head a new technological age in the city!"

* * * *

In the summer of 1986, Rufus received a cryptic cable from Miki in Hawaii. It consisted of two words.

He's back!

"What on earth does that mean?" Natasha asked as she nursed three-month-old Leonora. Four-year-old Benjamin was playing on the floor of the Good Hope ranch-house.

"If it means what I think it does, we've found the man we've been hunting for, my love!" Rufus was jubilant and bent to kiss his wife.

"Tashie, I'm sorry to break our holiday, but I'll have to leave for Hawaii at once. You know how crucial time is, don't you?"

"Yes, darling. I know." She met his eyes gravely.

Rufus was anxious as he finally strode along the dockside at Mauria Kea. He had no idea what he would find when he reached the *Christina K*. He hadn't seen her for over ten years. A long time in the lifetime of an old ship – and a very old lady.

He saw her three masts first, towering along the quay. At least she was still afloat!

He walked on – and found himself staring at a scene of dereliction.

There was a lanky old man with a grey beard leaning over a rail, staring soulfully at the sea. Rufus went up the gangplank and approached him.

"What happened to Miki?" he asked.

The man turned and leaned his back on the rail, surveying Rufus.

"Miki went bust." He looked ruefully along the deck littered with rubbish, and at the blistered, peeling paint. "Poor old lady. She's a mess, isn't she?"

"She could be fixed."

The greybeard gave a bark of incredulous laughter.

"Who are you? Santa Claus?"

"I might be."

"You're serious." The man narrowed his keen, blue eyes. "I believe you're really serious!"

"Did you save the whales, Mr Faraday?" Rufus asked quietly.

Michael Faraday threw back his head and laughed.

"You're the guy who's been hunting for me, aren't you? And to think I've been dodging you!

"Sure, we saved the whales. There was legislation passed in 1982, protecting them. But am I too late to save the ship?"

"What has to be done to make her seaworthy?"

Michael Faraday started along the deck, Rufus by his side.

"Her hull's sound – so far as I can tell. It should be – it's very strong, built to withstand crushing by the ice. But part of the stern, the counter and the lower mizzen mast would have to be renewed. Her auxiliary engine needs completely overhauled and the rigging and the sails will have to be replaced. It would take time – and cost a small fortune."

"The money's available, but time – well, that's something else," Rufus said sadly, going on to explain about Gran'ma Chrissie, still hale and hearty, but at ninety-five . . .

"Let me get this straight." Michael frowned. "You intend to refit the *Christina K*, then get her back to the east coast of Scotland? All to please an old lady?"

He paused for a long moment and stared at Rufus.

"You must love your Gran'ma Chrissie as much as I love this ship!"

"We do," Rufus said simply, gripping the older man's arm. "Michael, if I give you the cash – and the authority – will you see to it that the *Christina K* is completely refitted? Then sail her to the Tay when you think she's ready?"

"I'd need a good crew," the grey-bearded man pointed out cannily. "I know a few good men, but not enough."

"Don't worry." Rufus grinned. "You'll have your crew. As many willing young lads to train as you can handle!" he promised.

* * * *

"A wonderful old lady, the Queen Mother. Just fancy, ninety years old!" Sammy Murphy remarked as the car drew to a halt, patiently negotiating a snarl-up in Dundee's traffic.

Chrissie, although in total agreement, couldn't resist a little friendly rivalry.

"Oh, she's just a young thing. I can give her ten years."

Emily, seated beside her husband, twisted round to look at the old lady in the back.

"You'll have to give some thought to your hundredth birthday. It'll cause quite a stir, especially with the plans for Dundee's eight-hundredth celebrations."

"The Hogmanay street party was grand, with merry-go-rounds and buster stalls in the streets again," Chrissie recalled with relish. "It was just like the good old days in the Greenmarket. Sandra would only let me have one poke of chips, though, and wouldn't let me go on anything." She sounded disappointed.

"Sometimes I'm glad Harriet was spared all the fuss of living to be a hundred." Chrissie missed her friend, though Sandra had moved into the lodge. Mother and daughter got along very well, now they were both elderly.

"Well, I'll have my hair done – and maybe get a new outfit. That and a wee glass of whisky and lemonade will be enough celebration for me." Chrissie laughed.

Sammy and Emily exchanged a look.

Chrissie's eyesight was still keen, and their secretive glance upset her. She knew her loved ones were keeping something from her.

The car was on the move again. Passing the dock gates, Chrissie caught a glimpse of the masts and rigging of Captain Scott's *Discovery*. As always, the sight gave her a queer feeling of sadness and regret.

In 1986 she'd gone with Sandra to watch the *Discovery* come home to Dundee from the Thames. It had been so emotional, Chrissie had cried. It was wonderful to watch the historic vessel take its place near the ancient man-o-war, the Unicorn, in the dock, but it had made her think about her own *Christina K* and wonder where her poor old bones lay rotting.

The great day arrived at last. Chrissie thoroughly enjoyed playing hostess to her distinguished guests who crowded into her cosy living-room to celebrate her hundredth birthday. Of course, they asked her what the secret of long life was.

She thought about it seriously.

"Well, I could say it's porridge every morning – or maybe because I had the good fortune to be happily married three times," Chrissie answered with a grin.

Then she looked at her three daughters and her two fine sons, all elderly now and so very dear to her. Her eyes misted.

"But I think it's the love my family gives me that keeps me going. Their love has been as steadfast as the river flowing out there.

"They grew from wee bairns to men and women with lives and bairns of their own, but their love seemed to grow stronger as I grew weak and old. It carried me along until I reached a great age – just as that bonnie river gathers strength until it joins the sea."

Her head nodded drowsily and the guests tactfully took their leave, allowing Chrissie to catnap. Ewan gently woke her some time later.

Chrissie grinned at him.

"My, Ewan, what a grand party that was. The best birthday I ever had!

"And to think we have Dundee's eight-hundredth birthday still to come yet, on the first of June. There's to be a grand parade and sideshows in the streets, and a fireworks display at night. Oh, I do love fireworks!" she declared with relish.

"Your own birthday party's not over yet, Mum. Put on your coat. It's a wee bit chilly out."

Sandra piled so many woollies and scarves on Chrissie she protested she could hardly waddle. Outside she was glad of the extra warmth when she felt the chill air of the April afternoon.

Ewan tucked his mother tenderly in the front seat of his car. Everyone seemed to have turned a little deaf, for nobody answered when Chrissie plaintively demanded to know where they were going.

Ewan headed for the Grassy Beach past the spot where the Kennedys' house once stood. There was a row of neat, small houses there now.

Chrissie smiled mistily, remembering an excited little girl on a birthday many years ago, tugging at her father's sleeve.

"Oh, Papa! There's my ship!"

When she closed her eyes, she could almost hear her own excited, childish voice . . . and there was Papa's deep,

delighted laughter, and Ernest's awed whisper as the
Christina K came sailing majestically past the window.

"Papa, she's beautiful!"

"Mum, we're here!"

Chrissie opened her eyes with a start. Ewan had driven the
car close to the shoreline, and she stared in surprise.

"My, Ewan, what a crowd of folk! What's going on?"

Ewan laughed.

"Come and see!"

He helped her from the car, and then tucked her arm firmly
through his and guided her down the rough path on to the
beach. She smiled as she recalled how she'd played at
chuckie-stones here – and met a poor, despairing mill-lassie.

The crowd standing on the shore turned and cheered as
Chrissie approached. She hung back, confused and startled
by the unexpected noise and laughter.

Ewan smiled and urged her on. When her eyes became
accustomed to the brighter light, Chrissie realised, with a
sudden lift of her heart, that she knew everyone. This was
her beloved family, come from near and far to be with her on
her special day. From the oldest to the youngest wee babe in
arms, they had come just to see her.

What a magnificent gesture. What a wonderful surprise!

Rufus and Tashie came forward to kiss her. Hank and
Miranda were close behind.

Chrissie stood and looked at her large family. Gradually a
hush fell as they waited for her to speak.

She wondered why they'd chosen the Grassy Beach to

hold the reunion. She felt suddenly full of high spirits, and her eyes twinkled.

"Aye, well, if you're expecting me to go swimming at my age, you're in for a disappointment – all of you!"

A gale of laughter greeted the remark. Her family's love wrapped round and warmed her like a shawl. She felt herself borne along to the edge of the silvery water which rose high on a spring tide, lapping at her feet.

Rufus's arm was around her shoulders.

"Look, Gran'ma Chrissie. Look – here she comes!" he shouted, pointing towards the estuary, his voice full of excitement.

Wondering, Chrissie looked where he pointed, shading her eyes with a hand. She looked past the Fairway and Lady and Newcomer buoys, the markers that had safely guided whalers to harbour long ago, past Broughty Castle on its rocky promontory.

Then Chrissie saw her. A graceful yet sturdy ship with three tall masts, creamy furled sails rigged and flag flying bravely in the breeze. A drift of smoke from the tall funnel was dark against the pale April sky . . .

Chrissie stared, and thought her old eyes were playing tricks. Then she saw the young lads lining the rails and waving furiously. A drift of cheering came to her across the water, like remembered echoes of voices singing round a campfire. Ben's Boys!

"It's the *Christina K*," she whispered.

She looked up at Rufus, afraid to trust her eyes.

"It really is the *Christina K*, isn't it, Rufus?"

He nodded. Emotion choked him and he couldn't speak.

A wonderful, joyous glow lit his grandmother's face so that she seemed like a bonnie wee girl again. All the work and worry of the past few years – and the dangers faced by Michael Faraday and his young crew as they'd sailed the old ship home – had all been worthwhile.

There were tears in Chrissie's eyes as she watched the last Dundee whaler sail past. She rejoiced, not only for herself, but for her father and all the other brave men who'd faced hardship and danger in Dundee-built ships.

The *Active* and the *Balaena*, the *Windward* and the *Diana* and the *Polar Star*, and so many more grand ships, were all gone now. But Chrissie's ship – the *Christina K* – sailed on towards the harbour.

It made her feel very proud and very humble.

She understood now why her loved ones had guarded their secret so well.

Chrissie turned to Rufus and her family, who had crowded round to watch her delight.

"How can I ever thank you? Oh, why did you do all this for an old Dundee body like me?" she cried with deep humility.

Rufus bent and kissed her cheek, spokesman for them all.

"Because we love you, Chrissie. And we love Scotland – and Dundee – and that bonnie ship. We want the *Christina K* to go on sailing for years, with young lads who want to learn all the skills the old Dundee sailors knew. Can you think of a better reason?"

She couldn't. She just stood smiling at them all, her eyes bright with happy tears.

Presently, they brought a tiny baby to her, easing the shawl away from the baby's face to let Chrissie see the bonnie wee girl better.

"Look, Gran'ma Chrissie. She's another Christina Kennedy – another *Christina K*!"

Chrissie looked down at the sleeping baby and memories flashed through her mind. Some happy, some sad – all mingling to make a rich, rewarding picture.

Fumbling a little, Chrissie unfastened the silver brooch with its carving of the *Christina K* from her blouse. Carefully, she pinned it to the baby's shawl.

"There, wee Christina Kennedy. This is yours now. I don't need it any more. My own bonnie ship is safely home."